# PRO

# THE PROMISED LAND

Caroline Gray

PAN BOOKS

This edition published 1999 by Pan Books
an imprint of Macmillan Publishers Ltd
25 Eccleston Place, London SW1W 9NF
Basingstoke and Oxford
Associated companies throughout the world
www.macmillan.co.uk



British Library Cataloguing in Publication Data

Gray, Caroline, 1930-

The promised land
I. Title
823.9'14 [F]

ISBN 0 330 39652 8

This is a novel. All situations in this publication are fictitious and the characters are invented and are not intended to portray real people, living or dead. The events have not yet happened.

Typeset by Palimpsest Book Production Limited,
Polmont, Stirlingshire, Scotland.
Printed and bound in Great Britain by
Mackays of Chatham plc, Chatham, Kent

# Prologue

"Oh!" Miriam Grain gasped, as the ship seemed to fall away from beneath her. "Oh, my God!" she screamed, as the bunk came back up and slammed into her body. "We should have flown. Oh, we should have flown."

"Now, Mums," Matilda said severely. "You know we couldn't afford to fly."

Miriam groaned as the ship hit another wave with a shuddering jar. "If we were on a bigger ship . . ." William ventured.

"We'd be in second class," Matilda reminded her brother, brutally. "Gosh, that was a big one."

Once again the ship came to a shuddering stop, and spray splattered across the cabin windows. Joanna rolled out of bed, reached for her robe, and staggered to the door. She didn't think she was going to be sick; she just didn't want to hear them wailing and complaining any more.

She dragged the door open, lost her footing as the ship rolled, and landed on her hands and knees. Gathering her nightdress almost to her thighs she pushed herself back up. The cabins on board the *Caribee Queen* opened directly in to the saloon, and there were lights on in here, although thankfully at two in the morning it was empty of people; Joanna staggered across the heaving deck and reached an armchair, into which she collapsed, gasping. It was bolted to the deck.

It was remarkable, she thought, how small the ship suddenly felt. The *Caribee Queen* was eight thousand tons, one of a line of freighters that traded between England and the Caribbean, which took twelve passengers; she had seemed quite large enough when they had boarded her in Georgetown, five days before. Now she seemed just a plaything, her engines racing as her propellers cavitated, more spray rattling across her windows.

Joanna wondered if she was going to die, was surprised at being less afraid than curious, and somewhat disappointed. She was sixteen, but big for her age, both in height and body; William, two years younger but a keen student of the female anatomy, used to annoy his older sister Matilda by telling her that Jo's boobs were as big as hers. Matilda, at eighteen very much the grown-up, had no sense of humour where figures were concerned; hers was the best.

The door to the deck opened, and Joanna hastily sat up, scooping her long yellow hair back from her face, dragging the robe over her shoulders. The man who came in didn't notice her for a moment as he took off his oilskins, draping them across the bar. Then he turned towards her, and grinned. "Good morning."

Joanna nodded, unable to frame an adequate reply. He came across the deck towards her, apparently able to maintain his balance with perfect ease. "Not scared, are you?"

Joanna pulled the robe tighter around her shoulders. He sat in a chair beside her.

"You're Joanna Grain," he remarked. Well, he would know who she was, as all the passengers ate together at the big table at the far end of the saloon. He had not taken any notice of her before, though, apart from smiling at her when they had been introduced the previous day; he had joined the ship in Barbados.

It had been an impressive occasion, the officers standing to attention and several of the crew, too, as he had come up the companion ladder from the launch. He was not a big man, hardly taller than herself, with slim build and strong features to go with his black hair. But he was the owner of the Shipping Line. His name was Howard Edge. Now he was frowning at her. "There really is no need to be afraid," he said. "This ship could drive through a hurricane."

"Isn't this a hurricane?" she asked, faintly.

"Good lord, no. This is a gale. We'll be out the other side in a couple of hours. You go back to bed and sleep sound; when you awake, it'll all be done."

"I'd rather stay here," Joanna muttered.

"Bit crowded in there, eh? I'm sorry about the accommodation. Especially having your brother in there with you."

"Oh, we want him there," Joanna protested.

"I know," he said sympathetically. "You need to be together." She glanced at him, suspiciously; how much did he know?

"You're going home to relatives?" he asked.

She nodded, and he held her hand. Her instinct was to withdraw it, then she let it lie. How old was he? There were little touches of grey at his temples, but his hands and eyes were young. Forty, perhaps. Old enough to be her father. "What's it like, to own a shipping company?" she asked, desperate to make conversation.

He grinned. "In the middle of a gale, concerned."

"You said there was nothing to be afraid of."

"There isn't. But there's always the possibility of damage to the ship, and that costs money."

"Do you sail on every voyage?"

"Chance would be a fine thing. I love the sea. But I can only sail when I can spare the time. Would you like to sail all the time?"

"Oh, yes," she said without thinking.

"Who knows, maybe one day, you will." And to her consternation he kissed her.

# Part One

# The Man

'England – a happy land we know,
Where follies naturally grow.'
Charles Churchill

# Chapter One

# Coming Home

"There!" Mother pointed. Like most of the passengers, the Grains had been on deck since dawn. It was a fine summer's day, with little wind and calm seas through which the freighter was ploughing at full speed, her wash creaming away from her bows to meld with the wake that drifted astern and out of sight; the mid-Atlantic storm was, as Mr Edge had promised, nothing more than a bad memory. Because of the calm weather there was mist.

But the sun was up, and the mist was burning off. And in front of them, suddenly, were low green hills. "Could be Barbados," William said.

Matilda squeezed Joanna's hand. "The Promised Land," she whispered.

The three siblings were remarkably alike, given the difference in their ages. Matilda was tall and willowy, small-breasted and slim-hipped. Her face was too aquiline to be pretty, but was certainly handsome. Her hair was a pale gold; unrestrained this morning by her habitual Alice band, it floated in yellow profusion about her head in the wind created by the ship's speed. Joanna was an improved model, as if the Creator, having considered Matilda, had determined that He could make some advantageous improvements. Joanna had the same blonde hair, but hers was a deeper yellow and more thickly stranded; it moved together instead of scattering. Her features were more rounded than her sister's, and promised genuine beauty. She was somewhat shorter than Matilda, but was still growing, as was her figure, equally more rounded and promising – but she had the same long legs.

In her more intense moods, which were common enough, Matilda was jealous of her baby sister. But recently, since the tragedy, they had grown closer together. Mother was sometimes a most practical, capable person, but she needed protecting, in their opinion. And they both adored William. He was already as tall as Joanna. He had the sharp features of Matilda, but the thick yellow hair of the younger sister. His body was muscular – until recently he had attended a school in which he had been one of only twelve white boys in six hundred blacks, Indians and Chinese, he had needed early to cultivate a self-assurance, an assumption of inherent superiority, which was all the white races had really possessed for so long, in their dominance of the dark.

But those days were surely behind him, now.

"Good morning, ladies." Howard Edge came down the ladder from the bridge. "At last, eh?"

"Good morning, Mr Edge," Mother said, effusively.

He smiled at Joanna, and passed on.

"He fancies you," Matilda whispered, enviously.

"Rubbish," Joanna said, remembering that kiss. But it had been a quick, chaste kiss, and nobody else knew of it. And since then he had treated her like any of the other passengers. Except that when he looked at her . . . "He's old enough to be my father."

"They're the worst," Matilda said. "Middle-aged men with ants in their pants for young girls. He should be locked up."

Joanna stuck out her tongue at her. Wouldn't it be marvellous, she thought, if he were to ask for my address in England. That would drive Tilly out of her mind.

"Aunt Ethel said she'd drive down to meet us," Mother said. This was important. Miriam Grain had no idea what her children were going to make of this country they had all been brought up to regard as 'home', but which none of them had ever visited before.

Even she had not been home – and it *was* her home – for twenty-two years. When, in the summer of 1938, she had accompanied her husband back to British Guiana, where he had been a police inspector, she had been assured that there would be 'long leave' every four years; his terms of contract were in four year tours, renewed, except in exceptional circumstances, after each tour. The war had put an end to that. Together with her pregnancies. They had enjoyed a long honeymoon for the first four years, preferring to consider a family as a distant prospect. But when it had become obvious that the War was there to stay, and thus long leave gone for the foreseeable future, the condoms had been thrown away, and Matilda had duly appeared in the spring of 1942. Joanna had come a year and a half later, and William two years after that.

By then the War had been over, but long leave remained a distant prospect. England had not seemed very attractive in those grimly austere days, money had been tight, and there had been a lot to do in the colonies, with talk of independence filling the air, and civil unrest filling the streets. Leave had been postponed again and again, and she had been resigned to watching her children grow up as total colonials, to whom England was a myth, perhaps to become reality in adulthood. That had been before a vengeful Indian, arrested and charged with murder by Superintendent Grain, but acquitted by the courts, had crept up to the window beyond which the police officer had sat at his desk, and blown away his head with a single shotgun blast. This time the assassin *had* been convicted of murder, and had been hanged. But that had meant an abrupt change of status for the policeman's widow and family.

There was a widow's pension, but it was not very great. There had been nothing else; police officers lived in houses owned by the Government, as they were regularly moved from one post to another in the huge colony, itself the size of England. England had beckoned, in circumstances Miriam Grain had never envisaged. At least, in England, William would be able to complete his schooling, free from racial tensions, and with perhaps more congenial companions. And the girls should be able to find jobs which would not entail possibly having to work beneath bosses of different races and creeds. Miriam Grain would have angrily rejected the suggestion that she was a racist; she had merely been re-educated, during her years in Guiana, to the belief that the white man, or to be more accurate, the British white man, was the superior of any other living creature. This belief was an absolute necessity where an officer like Gordon Grain, with the assistance of perhaps one other junior white inspector, had to rule a district the size of Yorkshire, containing to be sure another score of white men, perhaps, overseers on the sugar plantations, but which also contained more than fifty thousand blacks and East Indians – even his policemen were nearly all black men. It was an assumption that had ultimately cost Gordon Grain his life.

England also meant that she would be back with her family, in the person of her sister Ethel. Ethel, some years older, was also a widow, but a relatively wealthy one, and, herself childless, she had written suggesting that she would welcome a ready-made family – Ethel had never really cared for Gordon, and even less for the concept that her baby sister should be swept away into the wilds of South America. Most important of all, removing the children to England meant that she would be relieved from the greatest fear that any English mother in the colonies could have – that one of her children might marry 'colour'. Miriam had seen this happen to other families, and had thus watched over hers with especial care, but she could not be with them twenty-four hours a day. They were naturally gregarious. They went to school with black boys and girls, and Indian boys and girls. They made friends. Gordon had never allowed them to bring their dark friends home, but they had been to their friends' houses. And they appeared to be totally unaware of the colour question; if they paid lip service to it when at home, Mirian knew it was with the mental reservation that 'Mummy and Dad were always going on about these things'. That too was a problem now behind her.

"Plymouth Hoe," William said, as the ship nosed her way up the

Sound to her berth. "Where Drake played bowls before beating the Armada." William prided himself on his knowledge of history, as was to be expected in the son of a man who had been so history-minded that he had named his three children after medieval kings and queens.

The women were less interested in Drake's feats than in the land on which they would be setting foot after ten days at sea. And in the people who would be there. Miriam shaded her eyes and looked for Ethel in the crowd on the dock. Matilda studied the various women, considering fashions, and was amazed, but excited, at the shortness of the skirts.

Joanna just stared. Never before had she seen such a sea of white faces. Suddenly she felt concerned for the other passengers on the ship, most of whom were black. They were immigrants, seeking a new home, and perhaps prosperity as well. She was coming home! Then she saw three people standing apart, a woman, and two small children. The woman was short, slim and *svelte*; she wore a genuine fur coat and dark glasses. It was difficult to tell if she was good-looking or not, but she stood with an aura of permanent superiority. Suddenly Joanna knew who she was. She felt quite sick.

Getting through Customs and Immigration took a very long time, and it was nearly noon before the Grains were finally allowed into the huge exit hall, where, happily, Aunt Ethel was indeed waiting for them. Ethel was an older edition of Miriam, and had somewhat severe features, but these softened as she embraced her nieces and nephew. "What lovely children," she remarked, which didn't go down very well with Matilda. But they were all still trying to stop staggering about as their feet insisted on allowing for movement that was no longer there.

"We'll eat on the way," Ethel said. "It's a long drive. In fact, we won't make it today. But I know a neat little hotel where we can spend the night. I've booked us in."

Joanna hardly heard her. Howard Edge had said goodbye to them, as he had said goodbye to all the passengers, formally, before joining his wife and children for a huge hug and a kiss; he had then got into a waiting Rolls-Royce and driven off. He had kissed her that night on the ship. Matilda was right, after all; he was just a dirty old man.

Now she stared out of the window of the little car – they were very tightly packed in the back – as they left the city behind and drove into the Devon countryside. This was unlike anything she had ever seen before in her life. In Guiana, if one travelled several hundred miles inland, either by aircraft or river – there were no roads in the interior – one came to very high mountains; she had made two such trips. But the coastal strip, a couple of hundred miles wide and some four hundred deep, was flat alluvial plain. Once it had all been forest, but on the coast itself the trees had been felled to make way for the sugar estates and rice plantations. Outside of the capital city of Georgetown, one could go either east or west; there was only one road in either direction. And the road itself was composed mainly of burnt earth, liable to wash away or pothole in the wet season – which continued for most of the year. In places there were eighteen-inch-wide concrete strips, laid an average car width apart, which provided a smoother passage – providing one could keep the tyres on the strips. One drove endlessly past waving cane or flooded paddies, with the courida swamps which kept out the sea filling the other side, through scattered villages crowded with naked children, while the journey in each direction was punctuated by river crossings which involved driving across two planks laid over the rushing water, much narrower than the concrete strips, onto the deck of a ferry – and driving off again on the other side.

Joanna had looked forward to getting her licence in the coming year, before Daddy had been murdered. She had no doubt it would be easier to obtain over here, because driving was so much easier. The road was wide, and metalled, and smooth, and it was only one of a hundred roads which wound in every direction, intersecting and writhing to and fro. There were no animals. Occasionally there was a sign to beware of leaping deer, which she found entrancing, never having seen a deer before, whether leaping or still. In Guiana one was fortunate to drive ten miles without killing a chicken, or being halted by a herd of pigs or a flock of sheep, or a straying cow.

"It's so grand having you here," Aunt Ethel said. "Now we must talk about what you're going to do. I've spoken with the headmaster of our local school, and he is sure a place can be found for William. What form were you in in BG, William?"

"I was in the Fifth," William said, importantly.

"Oh, splendid. You'll have to take an entrance exam, of course, but there shouldn't be any trouble about that."

"I shouldn't think so," William agreed.

"Now, Joanna . . . you don't have to go back to school if you don't want to."

"I'd rather get a job," Joanna said.

"Are you trained in anything?"

"Well, I was doing secretarial . . ."

"That's the ticket. We'll get you into a secretarial college for a year, then you'll be ready to take on the world."

"Won't secretarial college be very expensive?" Miriam asked.

"We'll sort something out," Ethel said. "And what about you, Matilda. What is your special talent?"

"Dancing," Matilda said.

"Dancing?" Aunt Ethel took her eye off the road for a moment to look at her sister.

"Matilda's brilliant," Miriam said. "She won a competition, last year."

"In British Guiana," Ethel said, doubtfully. "You mean, ballet?"

"Oh, no," Matilda said. "Well, I've done ballet, of course. But my speciality is tap."

"Tap." Aunt Ethel was more doubtful yet. "I'm not sure there's much demand for tap dancing in England, at the moment. But we'll see," she added optimistically.

* * *

The small country hotel Aunt Ethel had chosen was a place of hushed voices and soft carpets. By the time they arrived they had already sampled English food, at the pub where they had stopped for lunch, and where Joanna and William had been forbidden to drink the beer. But they had enjoyed the pickled onions and hard-boiled eggs, again quite unlike anything they had encountered before. The food for dinner was thinly sliced and utterly tasteless beef, with carrots, beans and sautéd potatoes. None of them had much taste either. But Aunt Ethel pushed out the boat and ordered a carafe of house wine, and this time Joanna and William were allowed to join in. "When you say tap," Aunt Ethel returned to the subject, "what sort of music do you tap to?"

"Tilly can tap to anything," Joanna said enthusiastically. "Even Bill Haley."

"Bill who?"

Joanna looked at Matilda, desperately trying to stop bursting into giggles. But Matilda's eyes were drifting from the dining-room to the bar beyond, where a group of young men had just gathered. They were all dressed alike, with velvet collars to their jackets, ties which looked very like strings, sideburns, and very narrow trousers. "Teddy boys," Aunt Ethel remarked, disparagingly.

"What?" Mirian asked.

"That's what they're called. Teddy boys. They're a symptom of the degeneration of the country. Shocking. And now this business of Princess Margaret going to marry a commoner! Really. The country is going to the dogs."

"I thought he was rather good-looking," Matilda ventured, to be silenced by a glare from her aunt.

Aunt Ethel had only been able to secure three rooms, two doubles and a single. William had the single, and the two pairs of sisters shared. The bed was a double with a feather mattress, and Joanna and Matilda found themselves virtually in each others' arms, which meant a sleepless night so far as Joanna was concerned – Matilda was very restless. "Do you think you will find a dancing job?" Joanna asked.

"I'm going to try. Are you really going to secretarial college?"

"I'd like to do what you do," Joanna said. She knew she would never be as good a dancer as Matilda – she wasn't sufficiently light on her feet – but she wanted them to be together.

"Did you see that louse Edge and his wife?" Matilda asked. "And the Rolls."

"I never noticed," Joanna lied. She was trying desperately never to think of Howard Edge again. But what had she expected, even if he hadn't been married and a father? That he would sweep her off her feet and carry her off to his castle, or whatever?

She felt such a fool. Even if only she knew she had been a fool.

"What did you think of the teddy boys?" Matilda asked.

"I thought they were rather cute." The sisters giggled. There had been nothing like that in BG.

Aunt Ethel lived in a northern suburb of London, but deliberately, she took the Great West Road into the West End before swinging up the Tottenham Court Road. The delay was only brief, and she wanted her nieces and nephew to see something of the city. They were predictably astonished, and not merely by Trafalgar Square and the traffic and the crowds of people. Georgetown, British Guiana's capital, had few houses or indeed shops and offices, taller than two stories, simply because the city was built on mud and any excess weight would cause the buildings to subside. Now they looked up and up and up.

"Wait till you go to New York," Aunt Ethel remarked.

Matilda and Joanna hugged each other.

After all the difference and excitement of the journey up from Plymouth, Aunt Ethel's house was disappointingly ordinary. It could indeed have been a Guianese house, except that it was situated in what was called a close, a cul-de-sac of identical buildings. The rooms were smaller, and of course it was not built on stilts, as were all Guianese houses to keep out the flood waters. But it had the same two floors, the same matching rooms up and down, the same staircase, and an almost identical bathroom, except that there was no shower.

Like the hotel, she had only three bedrooms, or to be exact, two bedrooms and a boxroom which she had converted into a bedroom for William. "I know it's a bit cramped," she acknowledged, "but it'll only be until you can get a place of your own." And she smiled brightly as if to suggest, either together, or singly.

Mummy did not look very happy about that, but Joanna was content; the room she was to share with Matilda had twin beds.

Settling in to living in England, and being English, was in the first instance a matter of shopping. This alarmed Miriam because of the expense, but it was very necessary. They had arrived at the end of September, and while the days were on the whole fairly warm, there were sudden dips in temperature, a portent of what lay ahead. And they had only tropical clothing. They needed warm underwear and at least one coat each, and they also needed to buy a school uniform – blazer and grey long trousers – for William, who duly passed his entrance exam, but not for a place in the Fifth at his new school. "Fourth Form!" he announced in disgust. "I can't be a fourth former."

"It's to do with your age," Aunt Ethel explained, not wishing to suggest what she knew for a fact, that educational standards in the colonies were at least one form lower than those in England. "You can't really be a fifth former at fourteen." William refused to be mollified, and went into a mope.

Joanna fared very little better on her introduction to secretarial college. "Mmmm," remarked Mrs Hill, the teacher who had just given her some shorthand to take. "Mmm. We've a lot to do, my dear."

Matilda, predictably, refused all offers of help, and went out on her own, looking for work. "What you need to do," Aunt Ethel suggested, "is sign on at the Labour Exchange. They'll know if there are any vacancies for tap dancers."

She was, as usual, disparaging, confident that Matilda would find out soon enough that her chosen profession was simply not on, and would then have to come down to earth. But Matilda, who went out every day with her golden hair swinging in time to the rest of her, and wearing her shortest skirts, remained equally confident, and they had not been in England a fortnight when she announced that she had found a job. "That's splendid, darling," Miriam said. "As a tap dancer?"

"No." Matilda grinned at Aunt Ethel. "Those aren't thick on the ground. I'm to be a receptionist."

"At an hotel?" Ethel was intrigued; surely one needed some training to work in an hotel.

"At a club," Matilda said.

Now everyone was intrigued. "What kind of club?" Ethel asked.

"Well, actually, it's a dance club," Matilda explained. "They wouldn't give me a job as a dancer, but they said I could work as a receptionist."

"A dance club?" Aunt Ethel was doubtful.

"A very popular place," Matilda assured her. "I work from eight until four."

"Those seem very reasonable hours," Miriam commented.

"You'll have to get up a bit earlier than usual," Joanna said, slyly.

"At night," Matilda said.

There was a sudden silence. Aunt Ethel was first to recover. "You mean you go to work at eight in the evening, and don't come in till four the next morning?"

Matilda nodded. "That's when the club is open."

Ethel looked at Miriam. "I don't think—" Miriam began.

"Now, Mums," Matilda said, "please don't be difficult. The pay is very good. Because of the unsocial hours, you see."

"Yes, but . . . a young girl, coming home alone at four in the morning—"

"Oh, I'll always get a lift with one of the other girls," Miriam said, and suddenly flushed, as if she might have said something she shouldn't.

"I still don't think it's right," Miriam said. "Do you, Ethel?"

"Definitely not," Ethel agreed,

"I've taken the job," Matilda said. "The pay is very good." She knew this was important, because Mummy was starting to worry about all the money she had had to spend on their clothes. Thus she had a trump she was quite prepared to play. "If you don't approve, I – I'll move out. I can afford to."

Everyone stared at her in consternation. Even Joanna, who had always known that Matilda had a very strong will, was taken by surprise. "Well!" Aunt Ethel commented.

"Well," Miriam said. "If you're sure . . ."

Ethel glared at her, and Matilda smiled.

"Poor old Mums was really upset," Joanna said in bed that night.

"I know. I did hate worrying her. But she really can't go on running my life. As for Aunt Ethel . . ." Matilda giggled. "I thought she was going to blow a gasket."

Joanna had a practical mind. "I don't see how you're going to keep awake until four in the morning. Is it every night?"

"Except Sundays. I'll sleep during the day, silly." She switched the light on again. "Anyway . . . can you keep a secret?"

Joanna was suddenly excited. "Yes."

"I'm not really going to be a receptionist. I'm going to dance."

"Tap dance?" Joanna was incredulous.

"No. As I said, there doesn't seem to be much of that over here. No, just dance. I'm in a chorus, with a lot of other girls."

"Just like that?"

"I had to audition. Oh, they said I wasn't very good, but I could learn. I think they liked my legs. And, well . . . anyway, I got the job."

"A chorus girl!" Joanna wasn't quite sure whether or not she was being over-critical. Presumably all dancers started in the chorus line.

"I wear a fabulous costume. Would you like to see it? See the show?"

Joanna sat up. "Oh, could I?"

"Let me get settled in first. Then one evening you could say you're going to the pictures, and come along to the club. I'll get you in."

"That would be super." Joanna lay down again.

"But remember," Matilda said, "you mustn't say a word to a soul."

"Because you're to be a chorus girl? What's wrong with that?"

"Mums just wouldn't understand," Matilda said. "Neither would Aunt Ethel. You promised, now." She switched off her light.

Joanna had no intention of breaking her word; she would never let Matilda down. But she was highly excited, and jealous, as she sat at her desk mis-hitting typewriter keys, as Mrs Hill had blindfolded her. "You're supposed to be reading from your dictation, not looking at the keyboard," she insisted. "And using all your fingers."

Matilda had the knack of living an exciting life, while she . . . presumably she was just too timid. Matilda had started going to grown-up parties in Georgetown before Father's death, and on one occasion had taken Joanna along. Joanna had been shocked. The eldest guest had been about twenty, and they had come in all complexions; there had been a good deal of alcohol, mainly rum, the wine of the country, and a good deal of necking, too. Joanna had done her share of necking with boys from Queen's College, Georgetown, at various parties, but she had always checked roaming hands; Mother had instilled in both of them that the preservation of one's body until one's wedding night was an absolute must if one was a lady, and she was not only talking about virginity.

But the necking at Matilda's party was of a variety she had never encountered before, with hands going everywhere, on both sexes, even sliding under skirts. Joanna had had an urgent desire to be home in bed, alone, but had had to stick it out until Matilda had been ready to leave. By then Matilda, with several drinks inside her, had been flushed and excited, while Joanna felt as if she had been at the bottom of a rugby scrum. And when they had reached the safety of their bedroom, she discovered that Matilda no longer had a bra. "Oooh," she had giggled. "That Sandy wanted it. Oh, so badly." Joanna had been left wondering whether the bra had really been 'it'.

Matilda's new lifestyle was very upsetting for the rest of the family. She had to have her evening meal at seven, where Aunt Ethel normally served at eight. Then she was gone all night. For the first few nights Miriam tried sitting up to see her in, but she was invariably fast asleep in an uncomfortable chair when her daughter did return. Following which Matilda had a quick breakfast and retired to bed, just about the time Joanna was getting up. She normally surfaced again for lunch before going back to bed for the rest of the day. She was certainly exhausted, and this was an additional concern for her mother. But she said, "I'll grow into it."

Joanna found it upsetting the way Matilda's hair smelt of cigarette smoke, and the absence of their little chats. But she remained intrigued. "Don't forget you were going to let me come to the club one evening," she reminded her.

"Ah," Matilda said. "Yes. Are you sure you want to?"

"Shouldn't I be?"

"You must promise never to tell Mums about it."

"I have already promised that, and kept it," Joanna pointed out.

"Actually going there will be different," Matilda said.

But she was obviously equally anxious to show her sister what she was doing, and a week later she was awake when Joanna got in from another unsatisfactory day at the secretarial college. "Tonight," she said.

"What about tonight?"

"I've arranged for you to come to the club. Now listen very carefully."

Joanna was so excited she wasn't sure she had listened to everything Matilda told her. But it really was a perfectly simple matter. "Some of the girls from the college are going to the pictures this evening," she told her mother. "They asked me to go along."

"How nice," Miriam said. "I'm so glad you're starting to make friends," and she gave a speculative look at William, seated in the corner doing his homework. There was no evidence of his making any friends, as yet. As if she had, either, Joanna thought. She had little in common with any of the other girls at the college, whose interest in life centred around Skiffle and Lonnie Donnegan, and whose dream was to go shopping in Carnaby Street. But what Mummy didn't know couldn't hurt her, and she put on a smart frock and her new coat and had an early supper with Matilda.

"I'll walk you to the cinema," Matilda volunteered. Once round the corner they caught a bus. Joanna had never known Matilda to be so nervous. "You'll remember your promise," she said, when they got down at Piccadilly Circus.

"Of course I do," Joanna said. "You're making me think this is some kind of crooks' gathering."

"It's a nightclub," Matilda explained, leading her down a side street. "Where people go to have a drink and dance after dinner. It doesn't really hot up until nearly midnight."

"Oh." Joanna was disappointed. "I have to be home by about eleven. That's when the cinemas come out."

"That'll do," Matilda said. "The first show is at nine."

"How many shows do you have to do a night?" Joanna asked.

"Just the two. One at nine, and the other at midnight. That's the big one."

"Then what keeps you here until four?"

"Well . . . it's nice to stay and chat with the customers, don't you think?" She winked. "Makes them come back again."

They had reached a very plain door set in a windowless stone wall. Matilda pressed the bell, and a moment later a panel slid back. The face blinked at Matilda, then the door was unbolted and opened. "Can't be too careful," Matilda explained to her sister.

The man wore a sweater and a flat cap and looked like a boxing second. He looked Joanna up and down. "This the kid sister?"

"Yes," Matilda said, suddenly breathless. "So watch it."

He grinned, and smacked Joanna's bottom. Joanna decided not to make an issue of it, but nearly ran down the corridor behind her sister. "Who is he?" she whispered.

"Just the bouncer." Matilda was descending a flight of steps into a brightly lit lobby, in strong contrast to the passage above them. "Home from home."

The lighting, if bright, was mostly concealed. The room was quite large, but low-ceilinged, and although at the moment empty save for a couple of barmen polishing glasses, still stank of cigarette smoke from the previous night. The bar ran the full length of one side, while in the centre there was a dance floor. The tables and chair surrounded the open space. Matilda walked across the floor, Joanna at her heels. "Boss in yet?"

One of the barmen nodded, and they both ceased work to look at Joanna. She felt that she was on the menu for dinner. "My sister," Matilda said.

"We can see that," the other barman said.

Matilda parted a curtain on the far side of the room and led Joanna into another corridor, off which there opened several doors. The first on the right led into an office. "Here she is," Matilda said.

Joanna was mystified. Matilda had said something about smuggling her in, but she was being announced like a visiting celebrity. But she liked the look of the man behind the desk, who was surprisingly young, with sleek black hair and a handsome face. He wore no jacket, but his shirt and tie were both silk, and his cufflinks gold. He got up, and came round the desk. "Sixteen?"

"Nearly seventeen," Matilda said. But she was again breathless.

The man walked round behind Joanna, but when she made to turn to face him, Matilda shook her head. "This is my boss," she explained. "Anthony."

"And you're Joanna," Anthony said, returning to Joanna's front. "Tilly has told me a lot about you."

Joanna gazed at her sister in amazement, and Matilda winked. "I told Jo she could see the show," she said. "First." She and Anthony were talking some language of their own, Joanna understood.

"Sure," Anthony said. "Keep her sober. Sixteen." He chucked Joanna under the chin. "Nice meeting you, kid."

Matilda escorted Joanna outside, and down the corridor to the second door on the right. "Does he own all this?" Joanna said. "He's so young."

"I shouldn't think he owns it. He runs it," Matilda said. "He's great fun. You'll like him."

Am I going to know him? Joanna wondered, and checked as Matilda opened the door, which gave access to a large, very brightly lit room, filled with a row of dressing tables and full-length mirrors. There were three other girls here already, and to Joanna's consternation two of them were naked, while the third wore only a pair of panties – and one of them was carefully lipsticking another's nipples. "Sammy, and Corinne, and Lou," Matilda said carelessly. "This is my kid sister, Joanna."

All three girls stopped what they were doing to cluster round. Once again Joanna had the feeling she was a particularly succulent dish for supper. Had Matilda not been standing beside her she would have turned and run. "Nice going," Lou said.

"She's come to watch the show," Matilda said, with considerable emphasis. "Over here, Jo." She led the way to a dressing table in the corner. "I'm the new girl," she explained, "so I get this one." Joanna watched in increasing consternation as her sister stripped until she was naked. "What do you think?"

She held up an enormous feathered headdress, sparkling with sequins. "Eye-catching," Joanna said.

Peering at herself in the mirror, Matilda carefully placed the headdress over her hair, pulling it down firmly, then using pins to keep it in place. "Is the rest of it as dramatic?" Joanna asked.

Matilda turned round and gave a little shimmy. "Don't you think so?"

Joanna's jaw dropped in consternation. "You have got to be joking."

"It's what the men come here to see," Matilda pointed out.

Joanna turned to look at the other girls; there were seven of them now, each naked except for her headdress. "Now you can help me make up," Matilda said, and handed Joanna a lipstick tube. "Navel as well."

"You're going to dance naked?" Joanna asked, unable to believe what she was saying.

"That's what I'm paid to do. I lied when I said I was a receptionist. Anthony took one look at me, and said, 'You're for the line'."

"And you went for it? Have you any idea what Mums will do if she finds out?" She didn't dare consider Aunt Ethel's reaction.

"She isn't going to find out, unless you tell her," Matilda said.

"Yes, but—" Joanna felt she should say something about the morality of it, but Matilda was her big sister, to whom she had looked up all her life.

"Twenty pounds a night," Matilda said. "And that's only starters, Anthony says."

The door opened. "Five minutes," a man shouted. With the door open, Joanna could hear a rumble of sound coming from up the stairs.

The girls filed out, chatting to each other as if they were getting on a bus. "You can watch from behind the curtain," Matilda said.

Joanna had a strong urge to run all the way home. But she was supposed to be at the pictures. In any event, she knew she had to see this. Twenty pounds a night! One hundred and twenty pounds a week. Why, that was six thousand pounds a year! But to waltz around naked in front of a lot of slobbering men . . .

She hurried along the corridor. All she could immediately see were legs, as the girls climbed the stairs. She followed them, panting. "That's far enough," the man said, grasping her arm. "You're over-dressed."

She glared at him, and he grinned; he was quite pleasant-looking, but he hadn't shaved for at least twenty-four hours, and had had garlic for lunch. "I'm Ted. You're Tilly's sister, ain't you?"

"Yes," Joanna said, peering through the slight opening in the curtain at a three-piece band playing soft music that was mainly drums, and at the eager faces beyond, as the eight girls stamped around the dance floor, shaking their breasts and bottoms.

"Not much of a crowd, yet," Ted said. "It doesn't really fill up until after ten. But these are the hard-core guys. They come to watch the girls, and maybe have a drink. The ones who come later are here to have a drink, and maybe watch the girls. Some difference. Some of them even bring their women."

Joanna licked her lips and stepped back; she'd seen enough. But she was curious. "Doesn't it . . . well . . . I mean . . ." she could feel the heat in her cheeks.

Ted grinned. "Doesn't it turn me on, having all these bums and tits around all night? You get used to it. Bunch of cows, really."

"You are speaking of my sister," Joanna said, coldly.

"Well, she's a cut above the rest, sure. But not as much as you. You really going to join?"

"To—" Joanna opened her mouth to tell him he was mad, and was checked by a drumroll.

"Queen Bee," Ted said. "Lily."

Joanna peered through the curtain. The woman who had just come on – she was definitely not a girl – was tall and voluptuous, and moved with aggressive thrusts. It couldn't be called dancing. None of it could. But it was certainly posturing. The audience clapped excitedly. "I didn't see her downstairs," Joanna said.

"Lily is the Queen Bee, like I said. She's got her own dressing room. You could be up there, one day."

"Not my style," Joanna said, and turned to find her way out. She'd rather walk the streets for an hour, until it was time for her to go hone, than watch any more.

But Anthony was standing beside her. "Nothing to it," he said. "Matilda tells me you want to join."

# Chapter Two

# On The Make

"Matilda . . . ?" Joanna was incredulous. "I'm sure she didn't mean it."

"Why else did she bring you here tonight?"

"Well . . ." Joanna glanced at Ted, who was grinning.

"Don't tell me you're afraid to take your clothes off?" Anthony asked. "Next thing you'll be telling me you're a virgin."

"I am a virgin," Joanna protested. "And so is Matilda," she added.

"I think the correct word is 'was'," Anthony said.

"You mean – you bastard!"

"Keep your voice down. Look, I haven't laid a finger on your sister. In this business, you don't mess about with the girls, or you find you're doing nothing else. But our customers like to date the chorus after the show, and that's big money. Matilda isn't one to pass up big money." He had just described her sister as a prostitute. Joanna felt she should slap his face. But she had an uneasy feeling that if she did that he might break his own rule and hit her back. More importantly, she couldn't get it out of her head that he might be telling the truth. "So how about it?" he asked. "Come down to the office and let me have a look at you. Not that I think there's going to be any doubt about it."

"I'm sure you mean that as a compliment," Joanna said, as coldly as she could, "but quite frankly, I wouldn't be found dead working in this dump, with or without clothes." She stalked along the corridor, paused at the door to look back at them, half expecting them to be coming after her. But they were both just grinning. She pushed the door open, stepped into the nightclub lobby, where the actual receptionist was just relieving two men of their coats and hats – very expensive coats and hats. Joanna hesitated, and they both turned to look at her. One of them was Howard Edge.

"Well, hello," he said. "Joanna Grain! Don't tell me I've missed you. I'll complain to the management."

Joanna's knees felt so weak she nearly fell down. But he was a dirty old man. Save that now she was looking at him again she realised that he really wasn't that old. "I don't work here," Joanna said, surprised she could speak at all.

"But you must work somewhere," Edge said. "Just name it."

"I work in an office," Joanna said, stretching a point. But she was going to work in an office when she qualified as a secretary.

"Then you should change jobs." He fumbled in his inside breast pocket, produced a piece of cardboard. "Telephone my secretary tomorrow morning, and we'll find you a place."

Joanna goggled at him, and he chucked her under the chin. "Don't forget. Just coming," he said to his companion, who was looking impatient. Parked in the street outside the club was the Rolls.

"You really are a noodle," Matilda remarked, falling into bed and stretching. "God, I'm exhausted. I set everything up for you . . . do you have any idea how many girls apply for a job at the club every week? Anthony only takes the best. And you turn him down flat. You need your head examined."

"I'm sorry," Joanna said; she hadn't actually been asleep; the night had been – she supposed exciting would have to be the word. The most exciting night of her life. But the overwhelming thought was that Howard Edge had spent an evening looking at Matilda, naked. In fact, as he had appeared perfectly familiar wih his surroundings, he was probably a regular. Matilda obviously didn't know that, as the customers sat in semi-darkness – and she wasn't going to tell her. "I am not parading naked in front of a lot of dirty old men."

"You'd rather be a secretary and be felt up by one dirty old man, is that it? Do you know what you'll earn as secretary? I doubt it'll be twenty pounds a week. Anthony pays twenty pounds a *night*!"

"You told me," Joanna rolled over and closed her eyes.

"As it happens," Matilda said, "and luckily for you, you really turned Anthony on. He's prepared to give you another chance."

Joanna pretended she was asleep. But she kept seeing Howard Edge's face. He had not looked lecherous or depraved or even particularly amorous, although he had definitely had a lot to drink. But as regards her, he had simply been admiring. Of course he wanted to get his hands on her . . . she wondered what *he* would pay to accomplish that? And he was a husband and father!

When she got up, as Matilda was fast asleep, she was able to study the card at her leisure. Caribee Shipping Line. Howard Edge, Chairman & Managing Director. Who wanted her to work for him. With what else in mind? In any event, it was all only a pipe dream: she wasn't even yet qualified as a secretary.

Yet the knowledge that she was pretty enough to have turned-on, as Matilda would put it, two such different men as Anthony and Howard Edge could not help but be exciting. Inspiring. She found herself glancing at herself in shop windows as she went to the college next morning, admiring herself. Was narcissism such a terrible crime? The important thing was that it seemed such a waste to possess so much, for only a few years, really, and not put it to its best effect. Which was . . . certainly not showing her all to a bunch of perverts.

Equally it was not something to be conceded to any Tom, Dick or Harry. As it happened his name was Dick. He was also studying shorthand and typing, and was definitely interested. He was quite an attractive boy, although he had acne. But he seemed so *young*. "How about a drink?" he asked one evening in early December when they left the college together. "There's a cute little pub just round the corner."

"I'm sorry. I'm not eighteen."

"Aren't you? Who's to know? You *look* eighteen."

"Do I really?" She was complimented; she had had her seventeenth birthday only the previous week.

"Come on, I'll vouch for you."

She had never been in a pub before, was astounded at the crowd of people, all drinking and talking at the tops of their voices. They had to fight their way through the throng to reach the bar, while Dick bought the drinks. "What is it?" she whispered, eyeing the glass of brown liquid; he was drinking beer from a tankard.

"Port and lemon," he whispered back. "It's what women drink."

"Do they?" Mummy and Aunt Ethel usually drank gin. But she rather liked the taste, and was happy to accept another. Then they found themselves in the lounge bar, where a group of young men were strumming washboards and blowing through combs.

"Skiffle," Dick explained. "It's the in thing."

Time passed so quickly it was half-past seven and Joanna was on her third port and lemon before she looked at her watch. "Crumbs! I must get home."

"Hang about," Dick suggested. "We can get a bite at the fish and chip bar."

"No, I really must go."

"Well . . . it's been fun. How about the pictures?"

"Lovely," she agreed.

Joanna had the sense to stop at a late night chemist on the way home and buy some peppermints to disguise her breath but that did not save her from a wigging for being late for supper. But the family interest was concentrated on William, who had a black eye and a cut lip. "Had a fight at school," he explained, proudly. "Chap called me a colonial."

"You are a colonial," Joanna pointed out. "Have you been to the hospital?"

"Don't you start. Aunt Ethel wanted to take me in, but really, for a black eye?"

"What did your master say?"

William grinned. "That's tomorrow. Happened after school."

Joanna was rather proud of her kid brother too, and even more so when he told her the following day that he had been whacked. "Six of the best," he said. "So did Tommo."

"But he started it," Joanna protested.

"The beak said I shouldn't have responded so violently. We're the best of friends now. Tommo and me, I mean."

Joanna had to rush, to meet Dick at the pictures. It was something with James Mason, but she didn't have an opportunity to see too much of it, for Dick had got them tickets in the very back row, and the feature had only just started when he had one arm round her, one hand on her breasts, and was kissing her cheek. "Come on," he whispered, feeling her stiffness.

"Dick! We're in public!" she protested, making the mistake of turning her head, so that he could kiss her mouth.

"Everyone's doing it," he said, when they got their breath back. Which was perfectly true, and not only in the back row.

Actually, what he was doing was rather nice; no one had ever fondled her breasts before, and he was very gentle. She even let him slide his hand beneath her skirt, although she kept her thighs firmly clamped together; with her eyes shut she could imagine it was Howard Edge. "You could try touching me," he whispered.

But she couldn't bring herself to do that, although he became more insistent over their following dates, while making it plain that he wanted to go the distance. That Joanna would not have. She thoroughly enjoyed the pub and the skiffle groups and the necking in the back row, but when she gave herself completely she wanted it to be with someone memorable, possibly even with marriage in mind. "You are becoming the most utter prig," Matilda remarked, when she attempted to discuss the situation with her sister, who had spent most of New Year's Eve fighting Dick off.

"Just because you've . . . well . . ." Joanna flushed. She had never revealed to Matilda what Anthony had told her on that night at the club.

Matilda knew to what she was referring. "Do you know," she said, "I have four hundred pounds in my bank account? How much have you?"

"I don't have a bank account," Joanna confessed. "As you well know."

"Of course, because you have nothing to put in it. I am going to buy a car next month."

"Whatever for?"

"Everyone who is anyone has a car," Matilda pointed out, crushingly.

Joanna thought of the Rolls, and remembered that she had made no progress towards getting a driving licence. "What sort of a car are you going to buy?"

"A Mini. They're all the rage. Don't worry, I'll take you out in it. Sometimes."

Matilda's obvious success was bewildering. Joanna had never been quite sure of the difference between amoral and immoral, but it did seem that her big sister was both. While she was stuck with the prospects of an extremely low-paid and futureless job – and boys like Dick. And dreams.

Then came the day she awoke to find the other bed empty and unslept in. She sat up in alarm, driving her fingers into her hair. If Mummy and Aunt Ethel were to find out what Matilda really did for a living, or even if they found out she had spent the entire night out . . . She hadn't finished dressing when the phone rang. Aunt Ethel answered it, her voice rising. When she hung up, to face both Miriam and Joanna, waiting on the stairs half-dressed, with William hovering behind them, she wore an expression of mixed triumph and tragedy. "That was Matilda," she announced

"Matilda?" Miriam was incredulous, and instinctively looked at Joanna.

"I . . . I was about to tell you," Joanna confessed. "Matilda didn't come in last night."

"Didn't come in?" Miriam's voice rose to match her sister's.

"She didn't come in because she is in prison," Ethel announced.

"Prison?" The three Grains spoke together. Now all their voices were high.

"Well," Ethel said, "under arrest, anyway. She needs bail money. Twenty-five pounds, would you believe it."

"But why has she been arrested?" Miriam asked, clearly disbelieving the whole thing.

"It appears the club at which she works was raided in the small hours of last night, and everyone there has been arrested. Even the receptionist." Joanna gave a sigh of relief. "That means it was a very shady club," Ethel continued. "I always thought there must be something odd about it, the way they took Matilda on so quickly, and gave her such a good salary."

Miriam sat on the stairs. "My God," she said. "My daughter, arrested? Didn't she tell them her father had been a policeman?"

"I shouldn't think that would have made the slightest difference," Ethel commented. "It might have made things worse."

Joanna sat beside her mother. "We have to get her out. Have you got twenty-five pounds?"

"Well . . ." Miriam looked at her sister.

"I suppose I'll have to lend it to you. But it's a loan. Matilda must pay it back."

"She will," Miriam promised. "Now, I suppose—"

"I'll do it," Joanna volunteered. She didn't want Mummy getting mixed up with Anthony and his people. Or even finding out about them.

"Are you sure? You'll be late for the college."

Bugger the college, Joanna thought. "They'll understand," she said.

William came with her as far as his school. "What am I to say?" he asked, very embarrassed.

"Say nothing. She's not likely to be in the papers," Joanna pointed out.

The police station was more crowded than she had expected, and there were several reporters there. She had to fight her way to the desk. "Matilda Grain," she panted.

The sergeant checked his list. "You're inside," he remarked, puzzled.

"I'm her sister," Joanna explained. "I've brought her bail money."

"Oh, right. Let's be having it, then."

Joanna hesitated. She had never had any dealings with the English police, before. "And she'll be let out?"

"Surely."

Joanna handed over the money, and someone at her shoulder said, "Well, hallelujah." She turned, and gazed at Howard Edge. He was unshaven, and his tie was slipped down to allow the top two buttons on his shirt to be opened. He was also surrounded by people, two of them obviously minders and a third his companion at the nightclub, but the rest from the media, snapping away. As she was in the direct line of fire it suddenly occurred to Joanna that she was also being photographed. Hastily she turned back to the desk.

"Hey," he said. "I'm not actually a criminal. Just in the wrong place at the wrong time."

"I don't want to be in the papers," she muttered.

"Don't blame you. You're here for Tilly, right?"

"Let's be going, Howie," said the friend, wrapping a topcoat round Edge's shoulders.

"Hold on," Howard said. "We'll wait for Miss Grain." He looked past her at the door to the cells, through which Matilda was at that moment emerging, accompanied by a woman policeman. Matilda had obviously been arrested while working, for she wore only a man's coat which barely came down to her thighs, leaving her legs exposed. "My God!" she gasped as she saw Howard. "Mr Edge? You were at the show?"

"Let's get out of here," Howard said. "My car is waiting."

Matilda looked at Joanna. "He'll take us away from here," Joanna said. Her heart was pounding so hard she was sure everyone could hear it.

They allowed themselves to be bustled outside, still surrounded by shouted questions and snapping cameras. Although it was April it was very cold, and Matilda shuddered as the wind got at her. "You drive, Billy," Howard told his friend. "I'll get in the back." He held the door for the sisters. Matilda got in first, and Joanna was in the middle. The two minders got into the front beside Billy. "And put the heating up," Howard commanded.

"You own this?" Matilda asked.

"My company does," Howard explained, and grinned. "But I own the company."

"You are a little devil," Matilda told her sister. "Criticising me . . ."

"It's not what you think," Joanna protested.

"Joanna is absolutely right," Howard said. "We met again at your club one evening, oh, some time ago, before Christmas. She was just leaving, and resisted my every advance. Do you know, I was prepared to fire Billy for taking so long to turn up and get me out of that hellhole. Now I think I'll give him a rise. If he hadn't been so tardy, we would never have met again."

"Yes," Joanna agreed, and looked out of the window. "Where are we going? Home is the other way."

"Is it? You didn't say. I thought you might like a good breakfast."

"I'd love a good breakfast," Matilda said. "But . . . like this?"

"It's a very private place," Howard assured her.

"College! I have to get to college," Joanna protested.

"College? I thought you said you were a secretary?"

"I . . ." she bit her lip. "I'm studying to be a secretary."

"Well, we'll phone in sick." The car turned through an arched gateway into an inner courtyard, pulled up outside a very ordinary-looking door. "My London *pied-à-terre*," Howard explained. "Chaps."

The two heavies got out and formed a sort of guard-of-honour, between whom Matilda was able to dash into the doorway, which had been opened by Billy. Howard escorted Joanna behind her. The heavies remained outside, while the two men showed the girls up a narrow flight of stairs into quite the most sumptuously furnished flat Joanna had ever seen. It was small, lounge, bedroom, and kitchen, but the furniture all came from places like Fortnum and Mason's, and through the opened doorway she could see a magnificent tester bed, with red and gold drapes. This was a *pied-à-terre*?

Billy was in the kitchenette, breaking eggs. Matilda prowled around the flat, examining the various ornaments, pausing before the pictures; Joanna supposed they were prints, because one or two were very familiar. Howard was checking his ansaphone, and listening to a woman's voice, with a quizzical expression. "My wife," he explained, when the machine stopped.

"Your—" Joanna swallowed. "Listen, Mr Edge, I really must get to college."

"I said we'd call in sick. Do you have the number?"

"No, I don't. I—"

"Do you think I could have a bath?" Matilda asked.

"Surely. Help yourself. But don't be too long. I need one myself."

She disappeared into the bathroom, closed the door. "If your wife finds us here . . ." Joanna said.

"My wife is at home. Which happens to be in Berkshire."

"Does she know you spent the night in a police cell?"

"I didn't spend the night in a police cell. It was six hours between the raid and Billy appearing. And that was long enough. No, Alicia doesn't know that. I'm going to have to work out a story. But it won't be difficult. Sit down and have something to eat."

Billy was laying the table. "I've had breakfast," Joanna protested.

"Then have a cup of coffee. We need to talk." He sat down himself, by the phone, dialled. “Darling! Yes, I know. Sorry I didn’t let you know, but Billy and I had a few too many and I thought it best to sleep here at his place rather than drive home and risk a d/d charge. Of course I’m all right. No, I don’t think I’ll go in this morning; I need some sleep. Maybe this afternoon. Kiss kiss.” He hung up.

Joanna sipped her coffee. “Do all men lie to their wives?”

“At some time or other.” He sat opposite her. “We have to do something about your beautiful sister,” he said. “Billy, go and size up Miss Grain, and then go out and buy her some clothes which fit.” Billy obeyed with alacrity. There was a faint shriek from the bathroom, then silence.

“He’s good at sizing up women,” Howard said. “Amazing. I thought Matilda was the prettiest girl in the show, but I knew you’d be prettier.” He had to be referring to her body, as he knew what her face looked like. “I’ve been going there regularly, but you never turned up again. And Matilda wouldn’t give me your address.”

“You’ve spoken to Matilda?”

“Of course.” And what else, Joanna wondered, feeling utterly jealous of her sister. “But you refused to work there, so Tony told me. Why? It’s good money, while it lasts.”

“Dancing naked?”

He studied her for several seconds. “I’m glad you feel that way,” he said at last. “But what are we going to do with Matilda? Now she’s going to have to start all over again. The club will be closed down. They always are, after a raid.”

“Oh lord.” Absently she ate some toast.

“Now let’s talk about you. How much longer have you got at secretarial college?”

“God knows. I’m not very brilliant.”

“I regard that as the understatement of the year.” He looked up as Billy emerged from the bathroom, looking somewhat hot and bothered but also very pleased with himself. “Got everything?”

“Oh, yes,” Billy said.

“Off you go, then. You’ll catch them just opening. Don’t be too long. But I want a complete outfit." Billy nodded, and ran down the stairs.

"Are you really going to buy Matilda a complete set of clothes?"

"I can't very well send her home in a short jacket, now can I? She'd catch cold. And she'd be arrested all over again, and on the same charge – indecent exposure. Where is home, by the way?"

Joanna gave him the address without thinking.

"Your mum's place? I know about your dad. Captain Heggie told me. I'm very sorry."

"Thank you." But Joanna couldn't resist a slight giggle; she was feeling fairly hysterical. "He was a police inspector."

"In British Guiana. I remember. Do you remember that night, in the storm?"

"You said you owned the company."

"Well, I have a majority shareholding, and I am both chairman and MD. But I'd rather talk about you."

The bathroom door opened, and Matilda appeared, wrapped in a man's dressing gown. "That man—"

"My man. He's gone out to get you some clothes."

"Oh." She sat down on the settee, knees pressed together. She had washed her hair, and it lay as a golden mat on her shoulders.

"Jo has been telling me something about you. May I be very rude and say that yours doesn't sound the sort of family background for a go-go dancer?"

"Well . . ." Matilda licked her lips. "We're not very well off since Daddy died."

"And Anthony paid well. I can imagine. You do realise that's gone? He'll lose his licence. He may even be charged with operating a brothel." Matilda clutched the dressing gown more tightly. "I'm not criticising," Howard told her. "I'm explaining. Will you find another dancing job?"

"Well . . . do I have an alternative?"

They gazed at each other, and Joanna realised that she was watching a very subtle negotiation. Matilda was hoping to become

mistress to a very wealthy man, who was also young and handsome.
"Do you have any skills?" Howard asked. "I mean, out of bed?"

Joanna gasped. She had never heard it put quite so bluntly.

"Only dancing."

"Ballet?"

"Tap."

He stroked his chin. "I might be able to find you a job. Would you like me to do that?"

"I'd be ever so grateful." Matilda's eyes were liquid. Joanna just could not believe what she was seeing. And hearing. Her adored big sister, offering to sleep with a man in return for some help . . . but hadn't Matilda already been sleeping all over London?

"Then we'll see what we can do. Now I'm for a shave and a bath. Billy'll be back soon with some clothes for you." He grinned at Joanna. "Look up the number, call your college and tell them you have whatever it is women have. We still haven't had our chat."

The door closed behind him. "Talk about falling on our feet," Matilda remarked. "Jesus!" She hurried to the table and began wolfing food.

"Tilly, listen," Joanna said urgently. "Howard may be very handsome and dashing and rich, but he's on the make. He lies to his wife, he—"

"All men lie to their wives," Matilda said.

"And you'd go to bed with him, just like that." Joanna snapped her fingers.

"I should think that would be rather fun," Matilda said. "But it's not me he wants to get between the sheets, goose. It's you."

"Me?"

"No accounting for tastes. Or maybe he likes virgins."

"I think we'd better get out of here." Joanna got up, put on her coat.

"Don't be silly. Firstly, we can't get out of here until I have something to wear. And secondly, if we pass this up we need our collective heads examined. And don't start that crap about morality. He's going to find me a job," Matilda said. "I need a job. But if you walk out on him he probably won't help me. Men are like that, darling. Believe me. You've just told me that he's a cad. So—" Matilda looked up as the outside door opened, and Billy came in, accompanied by his two henchmen; each carried a stack of boxes.

"Quick, eh?" he enquired. "I was there when the doors opened."

Matilda was on her feet, peering at the labels. "Harrods? They're all from Harrods!"

"It's the nearest," Billy said, somewhat apologetically.

Matilda was on her knees, allowing the dressing gown to fall apart as it chose, tearing paper apart, cutting ribbons with scissors Billy had helpfully produced, pulling open the boxes beneath. "Oh!" she cried. "Oh!" as she took out the black lace underwear, the beige twinset, the green skirt. "Oh, my."

"Those must have cost a fortune," Joanna gasped.

"Not a cheap store, Harrods," Billy agreed.

"I think you should try them on," Howard suggested, from the doorway. Like Matilda, he was wrapped in a dressing gown.

"Oh, yes," Matilda said. "Help me, Jo!"

Joanna scooped up the various garments and hurried behind her sister into the bedroom, closing the door as she did so. "You can't accept these," she said.

"Why not? How am I supposed to get home?" Matilda asked, smoothing the black lace panties around her midriff and bottom, and turning in front of the mirror.

"I'll go home and get some of your things," Joanna said.

"You have got to be nuts." Matilda was adjusting the bra straps.

"Tilly, that man is a complete stranger."

Matilda giggled as she pulled the jumper over her head. "Of course he isn't. We've sailed on his ship, had dinner with him every night for a week. Anyway, he's quite a regular at the show. He knows what I look like."

"You don't mean he's one of those—"

"I do not mean that," Matilda snapped, pulling on the skirt. "But he's looked often enough, hasn't he?"

"And you don't think that if you accept all these gifts he'll want to do more than look?"

Matilda had put on the cardigan, and was again turning in front of the mirror. "That would be rather nice. But as I said, I think it's you he wants to get his hands on. I'm not complaining. I think you're on to a winner. How does that look?" She had used one of Howard's brushes on her somewhat tangled hair.

"You look like a million dollars," Howard said, having opened the door, unheard. Joanna turned, flushing scarlet. "Now," Howard said. "Give me your phone number."

"Don't you dare," Joanna said.

"She's very young," Matilda explained, sitting at the desk to write out the required information.

Howard folded the piece of paper in two. "Give me a day or two, and I should be able to call you about a job. Meanwhile, I'm going to a party on Sunday. I'd be flattered if you two young ladies would accompany me." He smiled at Matilda. "Billy's going as well."

"We'd love to," Matilda said.

"Will your wife be there?" Joanna asked.

"Ah, no. On Sunday Alicia is taking the children to see her mother."

Joanna sat down on the chair beside the bed. "Then I really don't think we can accept."

"She'll be there," Matilda assured him. "Even if wearing handcuffs."

"Dress casual," Howard said. "But bring swimsuits."

"Have you any idea what Mummy is going to say?" Joanna asked, huddling in a corner of the back seat of the Rolls. She was trying not to think about Aunt Ethel at all.

"We won't tell her." Matilda sat upright, smiling through the window at those who would gawk.

"I'm talking about the clothes."

"Ah, well . . . let's worry about that later."

Which was all of ten minutes away, after the car had stopped outside Aunt Ethel's house. Both the ladies had apparently been watching from behind half-drawn curtain – as was everyone else in the street – and they waited for the front door to close before emerging. "Where have you *been*?" Miriam cried when they were safely indoors. "I called the police station, and they said you'd left hours ago."

"Well," Matilda said. "We needed to have breakfast, and a chat."

The two older women had finally taken in her clothes. "Where did you get those?" Miriam demanded.

"Someone gave them to me," Matilda said.

"You . . . that's over a hundred pounds worth!"

"At the very least," Matilda agreed. "I think they're super. Do you mind if I go upstairs and lie down? I've had a very harrowing night."

The two older women stared at her with their mouths open.

"Why aren't you in school?" Miraim inquired of Joanna.

"I felt I should stay with Tilly," Joanna explained.

Once again Miriam and her sister were speechless.

The situation was irretrievable, although perhaps no one recognised it at that moment. It took time to sink in. The fact that the two girls had come home in a Rolls was overlooked in all the other trauma, but it surfaced again on Sunday when the Rolls reappeared. "Whose car is that?" Miriam demanded.

"Just a friend's," Matilda said carelessly. She had spent some of her hard-earned money on a new sporty outfit, and even bought a new jumper for Joanna as well, and new bathing costumes for each of them; black one-pieces which made them look extraordinarily sexy. Joanna had wanted to protest, but had been carried along with the idea. It was certainly exciting; her life seemed to have entered a new dimension, even if she knew in her heart it was going to be disastrous from a family point of view. As did Matilda. "I really don't think I can go on living there anymore," she said as they drove away. They were alone save for the chauffeur. "I feel as if I'm being stifled. Don't you feel that, Jo?"

Actually, Joanna did, but she wasn't going to admit it. Her family was all she had in the world, and she didn't feel up to cutting off those links. Besides, she couldn't legally. But then, neither could Matilda. Or could she? Tilly was nineteen. "I bet Howard could find us a flat somewhere," Matilda said, half to herself. "Where we could do our own thing."

"And who'd pay for it?"

"Well . . ." Matilda winked. "If you played your cards right . . ."

"You are just impossible," Joanna snapped. "I have told you before—"

"Sssh," Matilda said, for the Rolls was stopping at a pub to pick up Howard and Billy, and two more young women. They had all already had a good deal to drink, and were in a very happy mood.

"Oooh, pretty," one of the girls said, and kissed Matilda. "He said you were pretty."

The other girl was seated next to Joanna, regarding her somewhat disparagingly. "Which cradle did they get you from, darling?"

"If they annoy you, say so," Howard said, "and I'll tan their asses. Or better yet, you can tan their asses."

"Chance would be a fine thing," the first girl said.

"Annie and Lou," Howard introduced. "Joanna and Matilda. Two very special friends of mine."

He and Billy occupied the jump seats opposite, and Joanna could feel his eyes boring into her all the way out to the friend's house, which was well out of London, and set in a walled park. The house was large, and there were at least fifty people there – not counting the waitresses – cavorting in and out of the swimming pool. Joanna had never actually seen a bikini before, in the flesh as it were, and was at once embarrassed and astounded. "I must get one of those," Matilda muttered, as they changed, together with

Annie and Lou, both of whom wanted to kiss and cuddle and hug as they did so.

"I thought we were here to entertain the men," Joanna muttered, wondering if she was about to be raped.

"Men!" Annie said, disparagingly. "All they're good for is paying the bills."

Joanna freed herself, adjusted her strap, and hurried outside, to be greeted by a chorus of wolf-whistles. She took refuge by diving into the deep end of the pool, forgetting that she had not intended to wet her hair. She went a good way under water – brought up in Guiana's rivers, she swam like a fish – and surfaced at the shallow edge. "That was quite something," said an admiring male. "Champagne?"

At eleven in the morning? But she took the glass anyway.

The other girls had joined them by now, and there was a good deal of horseplay going on. Joanna moved back into deeper water, where she felt safer, carrying her glass in one hand. There she was joined by the man who had given her the drink. "I'm Andy Gosling."

"Joanna Grain."

"You don't really look as if you belong in this crowd."

Like her, he had one arm on the coronation, where they had both put their glasses, now being topped up by an attentive waitress, all black-stockinged leg. Now he allowed his own legs to drift against Joanna's. "Don't I?" she asked; he was being dismissive of her own sister. But really, Matilda, at that moment being fondled by two of the men to the accompaniment of squeals of laughter, deserved to be dismissed. "Too elegant," Andy said. "I gather you're Howie's discovery." Joanna raised her eyebrows, and drank some more champagne. "Quite a lad, our Howie," Andy said. "But you want to be careful. He's a love 'em and leave 'em lad. On the other hand, I'm a great snapper-up of unconsidered or cast-off trifles. Do remember that."

"I am not a trifle, Mr Gosling," she pointed out, finished her champagne, and took another dive under the water. When she surfaced, at the deep end, she found herself facing another young man. But this was like no one she had ever seen before. He was dazzlingly handsome, his good looks and superb body enhanced by his dark complexion.

"The sun," he said, "has risen." Joanna goggled at him, and wondered if she should submerge again. But he too was offering her champagne. "Dare I say that you are the most beautiful woman at this party? Perhaps in London."

Joanna had got her breath back, following a sip. "You can say it."

"And do nothing more. Because your name is Joanna Grain, and you are Howie's ladylove."

"Has he told everyone? But you're wrong. I am not his ladylove. I am not anyone's ladylove."

"Then there is hope for me yet. Dearest, beautiful lady, allow me to take you away from here. We will mount a magic carpet together, and travel forever towards the moon."

Once again she was breathless. She was quite relieved to discover Howie standing behind her charmer. "She's bespoke, Hasim," Howie said.

"I feared that," the man called Hasim said. "May I at least help you from the pool, Miss Grain?"

He took her hand and lifted her from the water with the greatest of ease. "I hope, no, I know, that we shall meet again, Joanna Grain," he said. "Perhaps when Howie is occupied." And to her consternation he kissed her hand.

"Who on earth was that?" she whispered, as she got her breathing back under control.

"His name is Prince Hasim ben Raisul abd Abdullah."

"Did you say 'prince'?"

"He is the son and heir of the Emir of Qadir. That's in the Gulf. His family is one of the richest in the world. That allows him to be an international playboy, who gobbles up sweet young things like you."

"You're jealous!"

"Of course. Both of his money and his looks. But he's a good friend." Wearing trunks, he was splendidly built himself. And he had told everyone she was his! She really should be annoyed about that. "You swim to the manner born," he said.

"I'm a West Indian."

"I thought you came from the mainland?"

"I do. But British Guiana is always considered part of the British West Indies. I should have thought you'd know that, trading with them."

He grinned. "I did. Are you planning on going back?"

"Not immediately."

"Because if you do, you must certainly travel by Caribee Lines."

"How many ships do you have?"

"Four eight-thousand tonners. So you see that I am not in Hasim's class. But I'm hoping you'll be faithful." Chatter and laughter flowed around then, and he secured two more glasses of champagne from a passing tray.

"If I have much more of this stuff I'm going to pass out," she told him. "What time is lunch?"

"Another half hour, maybe. But I think you should get dressed. You're looking chilled." He wrapped her in a large towel. No one took any notice; Joanna had an idea that they had been told to ignore them. He led her into the house, and to her alarm, came with her into the girls' changing room, closing the door behind them.

"Do you mind?" she asked.

"Have a hot shower," he recommended, sitting down and crossing his knees.

"While you watch?"

"You can draw the curtain." She hesitated, but he obviously had no intention of leaving. She stepped into the shower stall, draped the towel over the rail, took off her swimsuit, and turned her face up to the deliciously warm jet. There was shampoo, and she washed her hair, rinsed, then wrapped herself in the towel.

"That must feel better. Do you know, every time I look at you I am more and more sure I am falling in love with you."

"I don't suppose you'd have a hairdryer?" she asked, because she had to say something noncommittal.

"No. But if you look in that cupboard you'll find another towel." She did, and wrapped her hair in it. "How're things at home?" he asked. "Was there any problem with Matilda's night out?"

"I think she means to move out. If you can find her a job to pay the rent."

"Suppose I said I'd take care of the rent?"

"For Tilly?"

"For both of you."

"I can't leave home. Mummy wouldn't go for that. I'm only seventeen, you know. Anyway, your wife—"

"Please don't bring Alicia into this. She's my wife. Period. But I have fallen in love with you."

"You're crazy. You've never touched me. Or—" she bit her lip, thinking of that kiss.

"I know. Love is a crazy thing." He got up, and came towards her. "I want you more than I have ever wanted anything in my life." He stood against her. "And I want you to want me. Do you think you could do that?"

Joanna stared at him. It would be so easy to do. "It's not possible," she whispered.

"Everything is possible." He kissed her on the mouth. Again.

# Chapter Three

# Surrender

It seemed the most natural thing in the world for Joanna to allow her lips to be parted, for Howard to delve as deeply as he wished. Nor did she make any attempt to resist him as he gently freed the towel and let it fall to the floor around her ankles. Yet her brain was whirring, telling her that she had to stop this while reminding herself that she was entirely in this man's power at this moment. That she wanted to be in his power. His hands stroked her thighs and came up to her breasts. "Where have you been all of my life?" he whispered into her ear.

He stepped back to look at her. His arousal was easy to see in his bathing trunks, but he had as yet made no move to take them off. Joanna concentrated on getting her breathing under control. "We have three ways of playing this," he said. "I will buy Matilda a flat. Tomorrow. Your choices are, one, to run away from home. Unless either you or your sister tell her, your mother will not know where the flat is." He studied her expression. "But that's not your scene. Your second choice is to let me come and have a talk with your mother. I will make it worth her while to allow me to take responsibility for you."

Amazingly, he had still not yet made any move to touch her again. But she had to protest. "You mean you think you can buy me, like some slave? Mummy would probably call the police."

"There is nothing criminal in asking for a woman's company. All she has to do is say no."

"You said there was a third alternative." She was having trouble with her breathing again.

"That we play it secretly. You continue as you are now, but we arrange to meet at Matilda's flat whenever possible."

This is incredible, she thought, that I should be standing here, naked, with a man who has barely touched me, talking about . . . him touching her a whole lot more, and having the right to do so. She licked her lips. "There is a fourth alternative," she said. "If you truly love me as much as you say."

They gazed at each other. "I did not say I loved you," Howard said. "I said I wanted you, very, very badly. I will pay a lot of money, grant a lot of privileges, for the right to have you. But I cannot break up my marriage, and perhaps lose my children, for the sake of a fuck." He grinned. "We might not take to each other."

"So your idea would be that we give it a trial spin."

"Is that such a heinous concept?"

"In a man's world, I suppose it is quite natural. But what happens to me if, as you say, we do not take to each other?"

"I would make it worth your while."

"You would make me a whore."

He was beginning to get angry. Joanna supposed he had never before encountered such opposition, when he chose to put his money on the line. "So you tell me how you want to play it," he said.

"I would like to be taken home, now," she said.

"You mean you have accepted my hospitality, displayed your all, and think you can just walk out when you're ready?"

"It's a free country. If you attempt to stop me, Mr Edge, I will see you in court." She turned her back on him, dressed herself. She expected him to grab her, touch her . . . she wasn't at all sure she wouldn't carry out her threat. But instead she heard the door close, gently. She turned, totally confounded. He was gone.

She finished dressing, opened the door again, and found his chauffeur waiting there. "You wanted to be taken home," he said.

Joanna was again utterly surprised. "Yes, please. But I should tell my sister."

"Matilda seems to be occupied," he said.

Joanna went on to the pool surround. There were still several people in the water, but Matilda was not one of them. And the most delicious smells were coming from the dining-room. "Is she eating?"

"Lunch has not yet been served. *Do* you wish to go home?"

Joanna chewed her lip. But she did wish to leave, and she had no desire to come face to face with Howard or any of his friends again. While Matilda could certainly take care of herself; she was probably earning hundreds of pounds right that minute. "Yes, I do want to go home," she said.

Having announced that she would be out for lunch, there was not a lot at home; Mummy and Aunt Ethel and William had also gone out. But Joanna was just happy to be alone, had some bread and jam, and went to bed, to stare at the ceiling. I should be in bed now, she thought. With a man on top of me. Or would it be underneath her? She had no idea. And she did so want to find out. But not as someone's mistress, to be discarded the moment he got bored with her.

The real catastrophe was that she had almost certainly cost Matilda the flat she dreamed of. She decided against telling her; what the eye can't see the heart doesn't grieve over. Matilda naturally treated her behaviour as a joke. "Too hot for you?" she enquired when she finally came home, about six.

"I suppose it was. Too . . . jet-setty."

"That's the way to live. But I thought you and Howie had something going?"

"We don't," Joanna said, definitely.

Matilda did not pursue the matter, and Joanna returned to her world of typing and stenography, and Dick, who was angling for the same result as Howard Edge, but was far less sophisticated and confident. Have I burned my bridges? she wondered. Is my world going to be entirely that of Dicks rather than Howards?

She started reading the newspapers, looking for little bits of information. But Aunt Ethel took the *Daily Mail*, which didn't go in for ship movements or business news other than the sensational; the sensation that summer was the Americans putting a man into space; that did not seem likely to affect her future. So Joanna started spending a few hours a week at the local library, where she had access to *The Times*. Caribee Shipping was really a very small company, with rather small ships, but every so often she would come across a mention. Trading with the West Indies! With British Guiana! She wondered if she would ever have the money to return to her birthplace? Travelling once again by Caribee Shipping. Suppose Howard was travelling? Would he know she was? As Chairman of the line he would obviously have access to all passenger lists. If he was still interested.

But would she ever wish to go back, really? British Guiana seemed to be slipping into virtual civil war as the ethnic clashes between blacks and East Indians became ever more violent.

"I hope you won't mind, Mums," Matilda said at breakfast, one chilly morning in the new year. "But I'm moving out."

There was total silence for a minute, then William dropped his spoon. "Moving out?" Aunt Ethel was first to recover.

"I've found a flat," Matilda explained, ears pink.

"But . . . you're only nineteen," Miriam protested.

"I'm an adult. And I shall be twenty this year."

"How can you afford a flat?" Aunt Ethel enquired.

"My new job pays very well," Matilda told her.

As before, no one knew what her new job was, not even Joanna. But Joanna suspected the worst, because, again as before, she kept some very odd hours. She could hardly wait to get her sister alone. "You louse."

"I'd have thought you'd be pleased. Now you can have this room all to yourself."

"You could've told me you were flat-hunting."

"Actually, I wasn't. I did, but as Aunt Ethel says, they really are very pricy. Most girls my age share. I'd just about made up my mind to do that when Howard came along."

"Howard?"

"And the beauty of it is, if you want to meet him there, you can, with no questions asked."

"Howard?" Joanna said again.

"Your boyfriend, remember?"

"He's not . . ." Joanna frowned. "Has he ever made a pass at you?"

"Well, he actually makes passes at almost everyone in a skirt. But I told you, it's you he's really after. Don't tell me he hasn't had you?"

"I have not laid eyes on Howard Edge since that party last summer."

"And what happened there? I saw him follow you into the changing room."

"Nothing happened. I turned him down."

Matilda gazed at her for some seconds. "You have got to be nuts. He's loaded. Didn't you know that?"

"He's also married, with two children. Who he has no intention of abandoning."

"What did you expect? He's one of *them*, and we're two of *us*. We may have been aristocrats in BG, merely because our father was a police officer and we have white skins, but over here we're sweet Fanny Adams. Don't you realise that? But . . . if you didn't give him a fuck, why's he bought me this flat? And he has bought it for me; I've the papers."

"You'll have to ask him," Joanna said. The bastard! He was still on the hunt. And buying a flat for Matilda would be like her putting a shilling in the poorbox at church.

"You are going to come and look at it?" Matilda asked. Joanna couldn't resist that, whatever the risk. They took the bus into the heart of Westminster; the flat was in Maddox Street. "Isn't it super?" Matilda stood in the centre of the lounge, hands on hips.

"Bit garish," Joanna suggested, feeling enveloped by the deep pink wallpaper.

"Oh, I mean to change all that. And in here." She opened the bedroom door. Here the decor was in deep red.

"Just who had this place before you?" Joanna enquired.

"God knows. I'd say he was a bachelor with an inflamed libido. But it's mine. All mine."

"Presented to you by Howard. With not a single string attached?"

"Well, he found me this job as well. Dancing."

"With nothing on?"

"Well, yes. But I'm the main attraction. And it's a cut above Tony's because it's a private club. To which Howard belongs. He's deep. The string is obviously you."

"What do you think he would say, or do, if I up and married someone, right now?"

Matilda, inspecting the plumbing in the bathroom, turned in consternation. "You're not doing that?"

"Who knows," Joanna said. "I might."

It was her turn to gasp in consternation as the front door opened.

"I have keys," Howard explained.

"And you knew we'd be here?"

"Well, it's Saturday, so when I called at your house and was told you were both out, I reckoned you weren't at school."

"You called at the house?" Joanna went to the window to look down at the street, and . . . but it wasn't the Rolls. It was something sleek, and stream-lined, and obviously very fast.

"It's a Jaguar. Called an E-type," Howard explained. "The very latest thing,"

"You've sold the Rolls?"

"Good lord, no. The Rolls is the company car. This is my runabout. Would you like a run about in it?"

She wondered what Mummy and Aunt Ethel would make of her being driven home in that!

"It's super." Matilda hurried in from the bathroom.

"Bit garish, I'm afraid."

"That's just what we were thinking. I'll redecorate." Now she looked out of the window as well. "Oooh! Is that yours?"

"A Christmas present I gave to myself."

Joanna was peering at him, frowning. He had changed. He had lost weight, and allowed his hair to grow too long, and he hadn't shaved that morning, and . . . "You're drunk," she accused.

"I am not," he protested. "I may have a hangover. In fact, I do have a hangover. You wouldn't happen to have anything, would you, Tilly?"

"I haven't actually moved in yet," Matilda said.

"Ah. Right." He felt in his pocket and produced a wad of notes. "Be a doll and go down to the off-licence and buy two bottles of champagne. Is that fridge on?" He knelt before it, turned various switches. "Try to get one of them cold, will you."

Matilda looked at Joanna, uncertainly. "Oh, I'm coming with you," Joanna said.

"No." Howard pulled himself to his feet. "You and I need to have a chat."

"Alone?"

"That's the idea."

"I don't think it's a good idea."

"Listen," he said. "I am not going to touch you. Unless you ask me to. You have my word. Before a witness."

"I'll get the champagne," Matilda said, and ran from the flat.

"Sit," Howard invited. Joanna sat on the settee; her knees were in any event feeling weak. She expected him to sit next to her, but he chose a straight chair on the far side of the room. "Alicia has left me."

"What did you say?"

"She's packed up, taken the children, and gone home to mother."

Now Joanna was feeling weak from the waist down. "But why?"

He shrugged. "We had a fight. We often do. She's hot-headed.

And it seems one of the people at that party last year told a friend of hers how I'd been seen sneaking into the ladies' changing room. God-damed cheek, spying like that. So this friend told Alicia. She didn't say anything about it at the time, but she was clearly simmering. And then the little bitch started having me followed."

"But we haven't seen each other since then."

"She found out I'd bought this flat, in the name of Matilda Grain. She only knows that the mistress I'm supposed to have acquired is named Grain."

"Shit, shit shit!" Joanna muttered.

"Anyway, once again she just simmered, until we quarrelled the night before last. Then she came out and said, why don't you get off with your little West Indian whore. I lost my wool, told her you were a far more moral person than she could ever be – well, she was my mistress for a year before we married."

"So she went off in a huff. She'll be back."

"I'm not sure I want her back."

Joanna stared at him. "You mean you're going to divorce her? What about the children?"

"We'll have to sort something out. But if she's spying on me, and generally poisoning the air, I'm not sure the best thing for them *is* for us to be together. As for divorce, well, in time. She's left me. I have a case for desertion. It's in the hands of my solicitor."

"But if you take up with me—"

"She can sue me for adultery. That's the idea. Desertion is a long term prospect. Adultery is immediate. You have any objection to being named?"

"Well, of course I do. Especially as it wouldn't be true."

"That could be adjusted."

"Oh, no," she said. "Oh, no, no, no. That would be conspiracy."

"I am asking you to become my wife," he said.

Her turn to stare. "Are you?" she asked at last.

"That's what I said."

"And I'll accept, once you're free."

He made a gesture of irritation. "You realise that means I'll have to commit adultery, somewhat publicly, with someone else?"

"I'm sure you'll find someone, Howie."

"You are really the most absurd girl I have ever met. I love you. I want to marry you. All I am asking—"

"Is that I stick my neck out, and say, chop it off."

"You are saying that you don't trust me, that I belong to the fuck 'em and flee 'em brigade. After, well . . ." he made another gesture. "I've played fair with Tilly."

"You have the wealth to play fair with whoever you choose, Howard, so long as you choose to do so. I should hate to think that you will now throw Tilly out. But I possess only one asset. Would you, a businessman, expect me to throw that on the floor and say, take it or leave it?"

He held her hands. "I thought we were talking about love. I love you, Jo."

"That's not what you said at the party."

"Well, you didn't expect *me* to put all my cards on the table first time around. The fact is, I have loved you from the minute I first saw you. Do you know, I have never heard you say that you love me."

He was drawing her forward, and she allowed him to kiss her. "I could love you, Howard," she said. "Very easily, and with all my heart. But there's a big difference in how we stand. You have to raise me to equality, if we're going to love each other. I won't be purchased off the peg."

She released him as the door opened. "Champagne!" Matilda announced.

"I was just leaving," Joanna said.

What have I done? she asked herself when she got home. That man, a millionaire, handsome, eager, has asked you to marry him. And you have turned him down flat! He had claimed to love you. The first man ever to do that. And you have turned him down flat. Who are you keeping yourself for, Dick?

She had, in fact, been supposed to meet Dick at the local palais de danse that night, but she didn't go. Thankfully, Matilda had not returned by then either. "I wish I knew what was going on," William complained, coming into her room after tea. "Mummy and Aunt Ethel keep muttering at each other, and then clamming up whenever I appear."

"I don't think they're happy about Tilly moving out," Joanna suggested.

"Golly, I wish I could move out," William said. "I will, you know, just as soon as I can afford a place of my own."

"Me too," Joanna agreed.

But of course Mummy and Aunt Ethel had more on their minds than just Matilda moving out. "Someone came here for you this morning," Aunt Ethel said at dinner. Matilda still hadn't come home. "A Mr Edge. In one of those new fast cars. A Jaguar. We didn't know you knew anyone who drove a Jaguar."

"He's a friend of Tilly's." Joanna had already determined the story in her mind.

"But he asked after you, dear," Miriam said.

"Yes, well . . . he probably thought I knew where Tilly might be," Joanna said, desperately.

"And just who is this man?" Aunt Ethel inquired.

"He's that shipping magnate," Joanna said, enjoying their consternation. "You remember, Mums? We met him on board the *Caribee Queen*, two years ago. Mr Edge. He owns the line."

"Such a nice man," Miriam said. "But . . . whatever can he want to see Matilda for?"

"I'm sure I have no idea," Joanna said,

When she awoke next morning, Matilda was in the other bed, also awake. "You really are a noodle," Matilda said. "You don't deserve him."

"Well, I'm obviously not going to get him," Joanna said. "His ideas and mine are poles apart. I'm sorry if I cost you the apartment."

"The apartment has nothing to do with you," Matilda said. "I'm moving the rest of my things today. You going to give me a hand?"

"If you can promise me Howard won't turn up again."

They took a taxi with Matilda's various boxes. Mummy and Aunt Ethel sniffed and disapproved as much as was possible but William, equally excited, accompanied them. "Wow," he said. "This is swell. And all your own! However did you afford it?"

Matilda and Joanna gazed at each other. "I've put something by," Matilda said. "Not as much as your sister, of course."

Joanna opened the fridge, and spotted immediately that the two champagne bottles were absent. "I see he's a careful man with his money," she remarked.

"Who?" William asked.

"Willie, I'd be ever so grateful if you'd take the garbage down," Matilda said. "There are bins in the front forecourt."

"Oh. Right." William dragged the paper sack out of the holder, and a champagne bottle fell out, struck the carpet with a dull clunk, and rolled across the room.

"Ooops," William said. "Sorry."

"You are a clumsy oaf," Matilda remarked, reaching forward. But Joanna reached the bottle first, picked it up, and opened the sack to thrust it in. The other one nestled, waiting for its partner. William disappeared through the door.

"I'm very happy for you," Joanna said.

"Don't be even more of a noodle than you already are," Matilda said. "The bottles were there, so we drank them. He means to marry you, Jo. I have never known a man with such single-mindedness."

"He'll get over it," Joanna said, taking clothes out of the suitcase and spreading them on the bed preparatory to finding hangers. "He'll get over ideas about the divorce. Do you have any idea what it would cost him? Adultery?!"

"He has that all sorted out," Matilda said. "Companies within companies within companies that his wife can't touch. She can bankrupt him, but she can't bankrupt *him*, if you follow me."

"I always knew he was an utter thug."

"Your future husband."

"No way."

Matilda held her shoulders and shook her. "Listen to me, idiot. He loves you. He's rich. He's going to make you rich."

"With companies inside companies inside companies?"

"It's up to us to sort that out. Before you say yes. But it's up to you to say yes, when we have it right."

"Us?"

Matilda kissed her. "We're partners, right?"

Joanna felt that she was caught up in a gigantic whirlpool, carrying her . . . where? For another fortnight she heard nothing from either Matilda or Howard, was left entirely to herself. Yet she found herself putting off Dick time and again, to his obvious annoyance. So much so that she at last accepted a Saturday night dance date. Dick was wildly passionate, rubbing himself against her on the dance floor, and when a rock number came on, grabbing her all over the place, ostensibly to throw her about, but leaving her feeling as if she had been in a wrestling match. "Whew!" she said when the music finally stopped. "I think I've had enough for one night, Dicky. Let's go home."

As usual, they caught a bus on the corner, sitting on the upper deck, which at this time of night held only one other couple, who were very obviously courting. They paid no attention to the pair behind them, and no sooner had they sat down than Dick had his arm round Joanna's shoulders, while his other hand was caressing her breast. "Dicky," she protested. "We're in public!"

"Who cares? There's nobody looking at us." He kissed her, with the same urgency he had shown on the dance floor, and she realised with some alarm that he had come to a decision about them. Didn't she have a say in that?

But she submitted to his kisses, because she didn't want a scene on the bus. Then suddenly he stood up, pulled the cord, and led her to the stairs. "This isn't our stop," she protested again.

"It's three away. Let's walk a bit."

"Oh . . ." but the conductor was grinning at them, and she allowed Dick to help her off the bus on to the pavement.

"Super night," he remarked.

Joanna looked up at the nearly full moon, and wondered if it was having some effect on his libido. They held hands as they strolled along the pavement. "I think we're at least a mile away from home," she grumbled.

"So what have you got against taking a walk? Good for you. Listen. I've been thinking about us. It'd be great if we could set up, someplace. Together."

"You have to be nuts. What would we live on?"

"I'm graduating next month. I have a job all lined up."

"As a male secretary? What are they paying you?"

"Not a lot. But you'll be out in the autumn. With our joint incomes we could afford a flat. I'd marry you, if you wanted that." What a throwaway line, she thought.

"Does that turn you on?" he asked, squeezing her fingers.

"I'll have to think about it."

"I'll take that as yes. Hey, a friend of mine lives over there."

Joanna looked across the street. Although it was nearly eleven, there were lights on in the house, behind the drawn curtains. "Oh?" she asked, without interest.

"He's still up. Let's drop in for a nightcap."

"I don't really think we should."

"Listen, you have to be home by midnight, right? That gives us more than an hour. Let's live a little."

"Calling on a friend, who's probably in bed?" But she allowed herself to be led across the street, waited while Dick pressed the bell.

"Who's that?" asked a voice from the other side of the panel.

"Dick. And lady."

"Well, hi." The door swung in to reveal a young man in his shirt sleeves; the shirt was half out of his pants. Behind him the corridor was conventional enough, but there was a peculiar smell in the air.

"I always keep my word," Dick said. Joanna glanced at him, frowning, wondering what he meant.

"Then doubly welcome. I'm Ron."

"Joanna." Joanna stepped into the hall, and to her consternation was seized and both hugged and kissed by her host. She looked at Dick, but he merely winked.

"Come on in," Ron said, and opened a door on the right of the hall. Here the lights were low, and there were about eight people present, Joanna estimated from a quick glance. They were all smoking, and the strange scent was much stronger in here; in fact, the air was heavy with it. The sexes were equally divided; the four girls had kicked off their shoes, and were sitting or lying on the floor, being fondled by the men, while passing their cigarettes from hand to hand.

She didn't like the scenario at all. "I really think we should be going," she said. "We only dropped in for a nightcap . . ."

"But as you're here, you have to have a drag," Ron said.

None of the other people in the room had taken the least notice of their entrance. "I'm sorry," Joanna said. "I don't smoke."

"This ain't tobacco," Ron explained. "It can't do you no harm."

Joanna found herself sitting in a chair, and the cigarette, as she had supposed it was, was taken into Ron's mouth for a long suck, before he gave it to Dick. It's unhygienic, she thought. But as it came to her from Dick's mouth it didn't seem very important. She only wanted to humour them and then be away. The rasp of the marijuana took her breath away, but she had sucked twice before she realised she had done so. Then the roll was taken away to be passed around, while Ron busied himself making another one, carefully pouring the grains in the paper before rolling it over. "You okay?" Dick asked.

"It was ghastly. God, I'm thirsty."

He got up and went to the bar, poured a glass of some liquid. She took it with suspicion, but to her relief it was water. Nothing had ever tasted so good. She began to take in her surroundings, the people scattered about the furniture and on the floor. She watched one of the girls allowing her knickers to be pulled down about her ankles before kicking them right off, while the man lying beside her sent his hands beneath her skirt. She watched a girl unzipping a man's pants and putting her hands inside. She kept thinking to herself, this is some kind of orgy, I must get out of here. But Dick was sitting beside her, caressing her breasts as he so liked to do, pushing up her jumper to get his hands beneath, sliding over the brassiere and trying to get round behind to release the catch, while she pressed her back as hard as she could against the settee. She hadn't allowed Howard to do this to her, so why was she allowing Dick? Then the weed was back. "No," she said. "I really don't want another."

"Yes, you do," Ron said. "You'll like this one better."

Amazingly, she did, and now he was sitting on her other side, kissing her mouth before joining Dick's explorations under her sweater. She was surprised Dick didn't object to that. Then Ron was really deep kissing her, and she gasped, while Dick's hands were on her knickers. "No," she said, but she had no idea how loud she was saying it, or if she was saying it at all. She seemed to have lost the will to resist them, found that she was rather enjoying what was happening to her, as the nylon was pulled down her thighs. It caught on her buttocks, and she raised herself to allow it to be pulled right off. Then they were both sliding their hands up and down her thighs, and between her legs, and she experienced a quite heavenly feeling of physical pleasure overlaid with a mixture of guilt and relaxed acceptance.

"Another drag," Ron whispered. "You really are a doll, Jo-girl."

Joanna began to shudder as impulses raced away from her groin. She didn't know whether she was being raped or they were using their fingers, but she didn't want them to stop. Then there came a thunderous rap on the door. "Shit!" Ron snapped.

One of the girls screamed. "Lights," said someone else, and the room was plunged into darkness.

Again came the rap. "Back," someone said.

"They'll be there too," another argued.

Joanna felt herself being dragged to her feet and hurried to the door. She couldn't believe this was happening, and the room was going round and round in any event. But at the door there was a large policeman. "Gotcha!" he said.

Dick had to keep his arm round Joanna's waist as they stood before the desk, or she would have fallen. "Name?" the sergeant said, without raising his head.

Joanna was taking deep breaths, as she had been all the way from Ron's house, trying to clear both her lungs and her brain. "Joan Smith," Dick said.

"Try again, son," the sergeant said. "She has a lot of sisters. All named Joan. All here tonight."

"My name is Joanna Grain," Joanna muttered.

The sergeant wrote it down. "Age?"

"Eighteen."

The sergeant raised his head to peer at her for the first time. Then he shook his head, somewhat sadly. "The charge is possession and use of cannabis. Don't say anything," he advised, as she would have spoken. "Now, you can have bail of twenty-five pounds. Do you have twenty-five pounds?" Joanna shook her head. The sergeant looked at Dick.

"Search me," Dick said. "Look, sarge, we weren't in possession of anything. We went to a party, and—"

"I'd save it, if I were you," the sergeant recommended. "You can make a phone call. Each of you. Twenty-five pounds each." He gestured to the phone.

Dick looked at Joanna. "My old man will beat the tar out of me," he said. "If he finds out."

"My sister will get us out," Joanna said. After all, she thought, I got her out once.

Matilda was in bed. "Do you know the time?"

"Listen," Joanna said.

"Oh, you little fool," Matilda remarked, having listened.

"Save it," Joanna said. "Get us out of here."

"Us?"

"Me and my boyfriend."

"Shit!" Matilda commented.

"I won't lock you up," the sergeant said. "Just sit down over there until your sister comes for you." He wasn't so gracious to the rest of the party, who had already been charged; it appeared that some of them were known to the police. But Dick was allowed to sit beside her.

"How did you get to *know* these people?" Joanna whispered.

"I get around." He seemed proud of being involved with them.

Joanna hunched herself into a ball, and suddenly realised that she was not wearing knickers. She hunched herself into a still smaller ball. If Mummy and Aunt Ethel found out . . . but they were certain to find out. "Over there," the sergeant said.

Joanna looked up, at Howard Edge.

Joanna stood up, then sat down again; her knees felt weak. "You're paid for as well," Howard told Dick. "Come along, the pair of you." They trailed behind him into the night; Billy opened the back door of the Rolls. "Where can we drop you?" Howard asked Dick.

He refused to be overawed by the car. "We're together."

"You," Howard said.

Billy started the engine and they drove away from the station. "Now listen," Dick said. "Where Jo goes, I go. Who are you, anyway?"

"I'm a friend of the family," Howard said. "And if you don't want to be put out on the pavement, I'd give Billy an address."

Dick looked at Joanna. "Please," she said.

"And leave you alone with this guy?"

"Like he said, he's a friend of the family."

Dick scowled, but gave his address. When they got there, he said, "I'll call you."

"Not tomorrow," Joanna said. "You could at least thank Mr Edge for putting up your bail."

"Thank you, Mr Edge," Dick said, and got out. Howard caught the door before it could be banged, closed it, and Billy drove off.

"Grass," Howard remarked. "What on earth made you do that?"

Joanna shrugged, preparing to defend herself. "We felt like some fun."

"Fun," Howard remarked, even more disparagingly. "These yours?" From his pocket he took her knickers.

Joanna pressed her knees together. "How did you get those?"

"The sergeant gave them to me when I paid your bail. He thought they might be yours. He'd spotted you weren't wearing any."

"Shit," she muttered. "Do you mind looking the other way?"

"Is that really necessary? After all . . ."

"You have seen me in the nude. That's not quite the same thing."

"You'll have to explain that." But he looked out of the window while she dressed herself.

"We seem to have been driving forever," she said, looking out of the window herself, and not recognising anything. "This isn't where I live."

"I think you need taking care of," he said. "And I can't do that if you go home to mother, who doesn't seem all that interested. So I'm taking you to my home. I'd have a nap, if I were you; it's a long drive."

"And suppose I demand to be set down, right now?"

"You can charge me with kidnapping."

She glared at him, but she was still too confused by the events of the evening to sustain a defence. "How did you know about me?"

"Tilly called."

"At your home in the country?"

"No, no. I was spending the night in town."

"And she knew how to get hold of you?"

"Well, of course she did."

"I really would like to go home."

"And I have said I think that would be a bad idea. Tell me about that young punk you were with."

"He is not a punk."

"He took you to that party."

"Well, yes. He's at the secretarial college with me. We date, sometimes."

"He take off your knickers?"

"I . . ." she bit her lip. "That is absolutely no business of yours."

"Listen. I'm going to marry you."

"With, or without, my consent?"

"You gave your consent, remember? On certain conditions. I'm prepared to fulfill them."

"With or without your present wife's consent."

"The divorce is going through. I'm afraid it'll take a little while. But until then—"

"I'm to be your mistress, right?"

"You will be my ward. I will not touch you until our wedding night . . . if that's how you want it."

She stared at him, unable to see his eyes properly in the gloom. "You're a romantic."

"Aren't you? Tell me if that chap has had you."

"If he had, would you put me out on the street?"

"No. I don't think I could ever do that. Jo, I want you. I want you on any terms you have to offer. But I also want to take care of you. That crowd you're running around with is no good. I'm not even sure you're still a virgin."

"Well, I am," she muttered.

"And the panties?"

"I know." She sighed. "I think I was going to be raped, without even knowing it. Then the police arrived."

"Hooray for the fuzz. But you understand why I want to look after you. Once you get hooked on cannabis—"

"What harm does it do?"

"Actually, not a lot. It induces unreality, but then so does alcohol, and cannabis at least isn't ruining your liver. The big risk is that once you get hooked on it, and the more you smoke the less effect it has, you start to want new sensations, new unrealities, and so you move on to the hard stuff."

"What's that?"

"Morphine. Cocaine. And ultimately, heroin. These are killers. Especially heroin. I don't want that to happen to you, Joanna. And the only way I can stop it is to have you in my care, always."

"And what about my mum? My studies?"

"We'll say, stuff your studies. As for your mum, I think we will have to get in touch with her, tomorrow, and explain the situation, and expect her to understand."

"She won't. She could take you to court."

"I don't think she will," he said.

Against her will, Joanna did sleep in the car. She was exhausted, and the cannabis fumes were still whirling around her head. Her brain was both active and feeling soporific, at the same time. If only she hadn't let Dick talk her into going to that party. But if she hadn't gone to the party, she wouldn't be here now, sitting next to Howard, feeling so warm and protected.

She blinked at the huge gates through which they were passing, and the curving drive beyond, bordered with oaks. And then, a blaze of light. She sat up, looked at her watch; it was four in the morning. Billy must be very tired. And Howard? He sat beside her and seemed not to have moved throughout the drive. But he turned his head when she stirred. "Home," he said. Joanna looked out of the window again. The house was at least three stories high, and there were lights on every floor. "They are expecting us," Howard said.

Joanna's heart and stomach seemed to roll over at the same moment. They! They consisted of a dozen or so servants, all eager to greet their master, and his new mistress. Because that was what she was, whatever he had promised. "I think the young lady wants only bed, Mrs Partridge," Howard was saying. "I'm afraid there is no luggage."

Mrs Partridge, a thin, somewhat severe-looking woman, did not allow her expression to register any emotion. Presumably. Joanna thought, she was used to this sort of thing. "Which room, Mr Howard?"

"Ah . . . the blue."

"Of course. Come along, my dear."

Joanna looked at Howard, who winked, and nodded. "I'll be up shortly."

Joanna followed Mrs Partridge into what could only be called a baronial hall, from, high chandeliered ceiling to potted palms and suits of armour. The grand staircase occupied the centre, and Mrs Partridge led her up this to a deep gallery, off which there opened several reception rooms. "There is a lift," she said over her shoulder.

"I can walk," Joanna said.

Mrs Partridge inclined her head, and led her along the gallery to a secondary staircase, which was as luxurious as any Joanna had previously known, and they went up to the next floor, where a corridor wide enough to be called another hall led between various doors. Mrs Partridge opened the third on her right, and showed Joanna into a bedroom which was definitely decorated in blue, from the bedspread and pillows to the walls and ceiling, and even the pictures. The housekeeper walked across the room, and opened an inner door, to reveal a bathroom that matched everything else, for both luxury and colour. "There's a shower, if you prefer." Mrs Partridge tapped the fitting. "I'm sure you will be comfortable. May I get you anything?"

Joanna licked her lips. "A toothbrush?"

Mrs Patridge opened a cupboard in the bathroom and showed her several brushes, still sealed in cellophane, and several unopened tubes of toothpaste as well.

"Thank you," Joanna said.

"Please ring if you require anything," Mrs Partridge said.

Did the woman never sleep? Joanna went to the window to look out at the dawn, which was just coming up. Everywhere there were trees, although she thought she caught a glimpse of water. Howard owned all this? And more. She turned as the door opened behind her. He was followed by a butler, carrying a tray with an ice bucket in which there was a bottle of champagne, and two flutes. The butler placed the tray on the table and withdrew without a word. "Or are you too tired?" Howard asked.

"When I go down, it's going to be for months," Joanna said.

"Then a drink won't do you any harm." He poured, and gave her a glass, touched it with his own. "Here's to happy days. Lots and lots of them." He drank, and she did also. Then he said, "You never did answer me. I'm talking about the short term."

Joanna drank some more, and sighed. "I couldn't possibly sleep in here alone," she said.

# Chapter Four

# The Mistress

Joanna supposed that as seductions went, hers was a disappointment. This was partly because she had been seduced long before they got to bed, had known it was going to happen for so long, had merely been flapping her wings against it like a bird caught in a closed window. Even more was it because her brain was still in a spin, from the marijuana, then the arrest and then the champagne, so that she was hardly aware of what was happening to her. When she awoke, it all seemed an almost surrealistic dream. She had enjoyed his stroking, had even tentatively stroked him back, wondering if he'd mind. There had been less pain than she had expected, but some discomfort remained.

But now she belonged. She was sufficiently old-fashioned, and sufficiently well brought-up, to accept that having given Howard her virginity, she was his. To have sex with anyone else would make her a whore, or at best a loose woman. Was that what she really thought of Matilda?

Matilda! She sat up in bed, for the first time truly realising where she was. She was alone, in this magnificent bed, in this magnificent bedroom, wearing . . . absolutely nothing! And the door was opening! She slid back beneath the covers, pulling them to her throat. It was Mrs Partridge, carrying a tray. "Breakfast, my dear," she said cheerily. "I hope you're hungry."

Joanna could only stare at her, speechless with embarrassment. Mrs Partridge placed the tray on the bedside table, lifted the covers off the various plates. "I told Cook poached eggs for today. Cold milk for your cereal, but hot milk for your coffee." She paused, anxiously. "You do drink coffee in the morning?"

Joanna licked her lips. It all smelt awfully good. And she wasn't going to tell this woman that at Aunt Ethel's they had always begun the day with tea. "Yes," she said faintly.

"Well, you just eat to your heart's content. You know where your bathroom is. There's no need to come down."

Was that a suggestion, or a command. "Is—?"

"Mr Howard has gone to town. But he'll be back for lunch."

There was so much that needed doing. "Did he—?"

"He said you were to have anything you wished, and that he would be back for lunch. That's not very far off, now," she added, and closed the door behind her.

Joanna sat up again. She was starving. She started with orange juice and cereal, followed by toast with the eggs and then more with marmalade and finished with two cups of coffee, feeling utterly replete. She had never had a breakfast like that in her life.

She drew a bath and wallowed for half an hour, then got dressed. Her clothes weren't as clean as she would have wished, but they were all she had. If only she knew what was happening in the outside world. Mums probably had the entire police force looking for her; save that the police would know where she had gone, or at least, who she had gone off with. To be a man's mistress!

She stared at the telephone on the bedside table. The temptation to use it was enormous. At least to call Tilly. But she couldn't call anyone, until she knew what was going to happen next. She went to the window overlooking the drive, and saw the Rolls-Royce coming towards her.

She turned with her back to the window, watched the door opening again. Howard carried a tray on which there was another ice bucket with another bottle of champagne, and two glasses. "I've already been seduced," she said, trying to be sophisticated.

"I always drink champagne before lunch," he explained, put down the tray, and came towards her. "Do you know you are quite the most beautiful creature on God's earth?"

"I think you're prejudiced." She was folded into his arms for a hug and a kiss.

"I'm sorry I had to dash off, but there were things to be done."

"I know. Where did you begin?"

"With your mum. She's waiting to see you. Are you up to it?"

He drove the Rolls himself. Joanna sat beside him, her knees pressed tightly together the whole way. It had to be done, of course, if only to collect her clothes. Although no doubt Howard would have bought her a complete new wardrobe, if she'd wanted it. But it had to be done. Trouble was, it was Sunday, and everyone in the close was home. Men were washing and polishing their cars, children were playing in the street; on Sundays, the close looked like a slum. An inquisitive slum.

All movement stopped as the Rolls slowly pulled up outside Aunt Ethel's house, except at the windows, where curtains stirred windlessly. But the door was opened for them, by Matilda! "I telephoned her to suggest that she might be useful," Howard murmured, walking beside her up the path.

"You look just super," Matilda whispered, hugging her, as if she had expected her to be a beaten-up wreck, Joanna thought.

Mums was waiting in the lounge, wearing the expression Joanna remembered from the day Daddy had been brought home dead. Aunt Ethel was nowhere to be seen. Neither was William, although Joanna knew he was home; his coat and cap were hanging in the front hall.

"Mrs Grain!" Howard kissed Mums' hands. "We've spoken on the phone."

Miriam goggled at him as if he were the devil. Then she looked at Joanna. "Are you all right?"

"I'm fine," Joanna said.

Miriam peered at her more closely.

"Perhaps we should all sit down," Matilda said, brightly.

"Yes, please," Miriam said, and chose the settee. The slight impasse was overcome when Howard sat beside her, causing her to withdraw to the far corner. Matilda and Joanna sat in chairs opposite. "Matilda said you had something to say to me," Miriam suggested, at large.

Howard cleared his throat. "I am here to ask for your daughter's hand in marriage. Joanna," he added hastily.

Miriam stared at Joanna. "Where did you spend last night?"

Joanna knew she was flushing. "At . . . at Howard's house."

"She was upset," Matilda said. "Well, after being arrested, and all that—"

"Had you taken drugs?" Miriam asked.

"I . . . I didn't know what it was," Joanna protested. "But, like Tilly says, I was upset. Then Howard came along and bailed me out—"

"Just like that," Miriam said, perhaps to herself.

"I telephoned Howard and asked him to help," Matilda explained.

"My solicitor will take care of the charge, Mrs Grain," Howard said.

"Just like that," Miriam repeated.

"Joanna, with your permission, of course, is going to be my wife," Howard pointed out.

"Just like that," Miriam said a third time. "How long have you known my daughter, Mr Edge?"

"Ah . . ." Howard looked at Joanna.

"Nearly two years now, Mums," Joanna said. "We met on the ship, remember?"

It was Miriam's turn to say, "Ah. And when will the marriage be, Mr Edge?"

"Well . . . as soon as my divorce comes through."

"I see. Thus your proposal of marriage is dependent upon . . . circumstances."

"Not really. My wife, my present wife, and I, have irrevocably split."

"Does your wife know you plan to marry again?"

"Well . . . no, not at this moment. I didn't want to tell her until Joanna had agreed, and yourself, of course."

"But you assume she will accept the situation?"

"Well . . . perhaps she may be unhappy with it."

"You mean *she* may not regard the split as irrevocable."

"I really don't know. It *is* irrevocable."

"But if she does not accept it, your divorce may be a long way off. And what exactly will the grounds be? Desertion is a matter of years."

"Well . . ." Howard looked embarrassed. "I think I can persuade her to go for adultery."

"With my daughter named as co-respondent?"

"Do you object to that?" Howard looked at Joanna, who knew her flush was deepening. "You wouldn't have to appear in court," Howard said. "Only your name would be used, and evidence would be provided . . . I know it's embarrassing, but that is the quickest way. And as for the name, well, as we are going to be married anyway, that wouldn't matter. Would it?"

"Perhaps not to Joanna, Mr Edge," Miriam said. "But the whole world would know that my daughter had committed adultery."

"Oh, Mums," Matilda said. "This is 1962!"

"In which everything goes. I could apply to have my daughter made a ward of court, Mr Edge. She is only eighteen."

"You have that right, Mrs Grain," Howard said. "In that case, we would have to wait for three years to get married. But we would get married, as soon as it became possible. And in the meantime—"

"It would estrange Joanna and myself," Miriam said thoughtfully. Her shoulders rose and fell, helplessly. "I do not approve. I think you have both behaved disgracefully, and intend to behave even more disgracefully. But as there seems to be nothing I can do about it, save have Joanna locked up . . ." Another shrug.

"Oh, Mums!" Joanna knelt beside her. "It's all going to work out, you'll see. Say you'll come to the wedding?"

"Ask me again, nearer the time," Miriam said.

There was really very little time to feel distressed by the estrangement from Mums. No doubt this was as Howard had intended it should be. First of all there was the establishing of Joanna in Caribee House. This was entirely painless. Mrs Partridge had undoubtedly entertained Howard's lady friends before, but she was able to take in her stride the fact that this lady friend was to be permanent, and to be her mistress. She recognised immediately that Joanna was entirely out of her depths, and took over as a sort of surrogate mother, aided of course by Matilda, who was wildly excited about the whole thing. But Mrs Partridge even managed to accept the constant comings and going of Matilda.

*Had* Howard and Matilda slept together, Joanna wondered? And did it matter if they had? It was she he was going to marry. But even with Matilda's hovering presence, and with Mrs Partridge always about to explain and convince, Joanna found herself somewhat lonely. The other servants were remote, and apparently regarded her with some suspicion. Was she really a permanency? But she wasn't sure of that herself. She was sure of only one thing, that she didn't want to leave the security of Caribee House and face the world, until she was Mrs Edge. And that promised to be a little way off. She viewed the world through Howard's television set.

She telephoned home several times in the first few days, but Mums was always busy. It was William she was really after. She and William had in many ways been closer than she and Matilda. She wanted William to visit, and perhaps spend a weekend. And he seemed quite keen. But he never came. Mums and Aunt Ethel had got at him.

Meanwhile, the divorce. A private detective came and inspected the wardrobe in the master bedroom with great care and even greater embarrassment. But there were her clothes hanging in the closet next to Howard's. This was apparently terribly important. "What happens now?" Joanna asked him.

"I make a report, miss. I mean, madam. I mean . . . it'll all be all right, you'll see." Just what she had said to Mums.

The great moment of every day was when Howard came in from the office; he had entirely given up using the London flat, and drove out every day, sometimes not getting home until eight. Joanna quite understood that the wheels of commerce had to keep turning, whatever his domestic problems, but with him home all the fears that overlaid her during the day disappeared. The principal fear of course was that he was deceiving her. She adored him, everything about him, but she was not a fool. He had had dozens of women in his time. He even, so Matilda suggested, went to clubs such as Anthony's to pick out the more attractive chorus girls and take them either to his flat or, if Alicia was away, to his house. Matilda even hinted that, had he not encountered Joanna that first evening, he might have chosen *her* instead, as a permanent companion. Except that there was a quality of immorality that lurked around Matilda like a miasma. Howard might well have considered her for a one-night stand – Joanna could not escape the feeling that he had in fact done so – but he would never have considered her as a mistress, much less as a wife.

But he had chosen her sister. Did that speak volumes for his perspicacity, or for her transparent innocence, or simply, as she was coming to accept, that she was so much better-looking than Matilda? Or, even more simply, that he had been looking for a reason to get rid of Alicia, and had found in this colonial hick the answer to his problems?

But as usual he seemed able to understand her every thought, and certainly her every fear. She had only been resident at Caribee House three weeks when he opened his briefcase on the bedroom table. "I have some things for you to sign," he said,

"Me? Sign? Sign what?" She was instantly suspicious.

"Certificates of ownership. These are shares."

She peered at the sheets of stiff paper. "Shares in what?"

"Caribee Holdings. My company. There are a thousand of them but you can sign for them in block."

"And what happens then?"

He kissed her, and poured champagne. "You own them, goose."

"A thousand shares in your company?" Cautiously she flicked the sheets. "Are they worth anything?"

"I sincerely hope so. We are currently quoted at six pounds, ten shillings on the Stock Exchange. So that pile is worth six and a half thousand pounds. At the moment."

Six thousand pounds? Just like that? "I don't understand."

"It's a gift, from me to you. A preliminary gift. It means you own part of the company. I have to tell you that at the moment it is a very small part. Caribee Holdings has one million shares, so you have a one thousandth stake in the company."

"A million shares . . ." Joanna had always been good at mental arithmetic. "You mean the company is worth six and a half million pounds?"

"At the moment."

"And you own it?"

"I control it. I have sixty-nine per cent of the shares, once you've signed."

That still meant he was worth . . . nearly five million pounds!

"Who owns the others?"

"Twenty-five per cent are owned by my three co-directors. Five per cent of those are owned by Alicia. And one per cent is about to be owned by you. However, I am going to see that increases. We are planning a rights issue in the next year or so, and you'll have the chance of increasing your stake."

Alicia had five thousand shares. That meant she had over thirty thousand pounds. Joanna was beginning to understand. "Who owns the house?"

"The company owns the house, as it owns my car, and all the ships."

"And you control the company," Joanna said thoughtfully. "But if Alicia now votes against you—"

"Her five per cent can have no impact whatsoever."

"But . . . can't she claim some of your shares in the divorce settlement?"

"No, because my shares are actually held in a trust company. It's managed by Billy. You remember Billy? The idea was thought up by my father, to avoid death duties. The shares are actually mine. I receive the income from them, and I can use them to control the company, but I cannot sell them or disburse them in any way without the agreement of the trustees. The trustees agreed to let Alicia have her five per cent. But she knows if she demanded any more they would refuse." He grinned. "They are all close friends of mine. Billy is in fact my closest friend."

"And you persuaded your trustees to give me this thousand."

Another grin. "Billy is very fond of you."

"Well . . ." She flicked the shares again. "You mentioned that they produce income?"

"Oh, indeed. I expect our next dividend to be one shilling and eleven pence per share. I'm afraid we are a little close-fisted, but the upkeep of the ships is high."

"One shilling, eleven pence, and I have a thousand of those . . . I'll have to work it out."

"It'll be just over ninety-five pounds."

"Oh, great. That's not two pounds a week. I could earn ten times that dancing at Anthony's club."

"It's not a salary, darling. It's all pin money. And incidentally, we pay dividends half-yearly, so it's really a hundred and ninety."

That sounded a little better. "And you have sixty-nine thousand, so . . ."

"Just over twelve. Thousand. From the shares. I am also paid a salary as managing director."

"So you're rolling in it?"

"Let's say I can afford you," he said, and opened a bottle of champagne.

Her initial feeling that he was treating her rather meanly was soon removed. He gave her an allowance of five hundred a year, on top of her dividends, and she began to feel a wealthy woman. And there was so much more. "There really is no necessity for you to lock yourself away out here, you know," he told her. "I have opened accounts in your name at Harrods and Fortnums, and at the following restaurants." He gave her a list; they were all the very best. "I have also opened an account for you at this firm of chauffeur-driven hire cars. All you have to do is telephone them, be picked up, go where you like, buy what you like, eat where you like, and be driven back here."

Instinctively she looked out of the window. "There's nothing to be afraid of, really," he said. "No one knows who you are. Listen, go out and buy yourself a mink."

She telephoned Matilda first. "Meet me at Fortnum and Mason's," she said.

"You're kidding."

"Eleven o'clock."

The car dropped her at the doors, which were opened for her. Feeling somewhat like a queen, she entered, looked right and left; she had not been here before. Needless to say there was no sign of Matilda. "Madam?" asked the young man in the morning coat.

"I'm looking for a fur coat."

"Ah . . ." He was taking her in. She was wearing her best day dress, but it had clearly not come from any couturier. Nor were her shoes absolutely right. "What sort of fur did you have in mind, madam?"

"I thought of mink."

"Oh, quite. I'll have someone take you up. Miss Loam?" The woman hurried forward. "Furs," the floorwalker explained. "And perhaps, well . . ."

"Absolutely," Miss Loam said.

"My sister was supposed to meet me here," Joanna explained. "Matilda Grain. I'm Joanna. Joanna Grain."

The name obviously did not immediately register. "I will tell your sister where you are to be found, Miss Grain," the floorwalker said.

Joanna was whisked upstairs. "Furs really need to be very carefully matched up," Miss Loam remarked.

"I know. I do need some clothes."

"Ah." Miss Loam brightened. "But we'll start with the coat." Languid young women surrounded her, but she was obsessed with the feel of the fur. "Pastel shades suit you best," Miss Loam suggested.

Joanna surveyed herself in the full length mirror, and looked past her shoulder at a horrified Matilda. "Whatever are you doing?"

"Choosing a coat."

"A perfect fit," Miss Loam suggested.

"I think so too," Joanna said. "I'll take it."

"Of course, madam. The price is a thousand pounds." Miss Loam waited, expectantly.

"I have an account," Joanna told her.

Miss Loam's eyebrows went up and down like yo-yos. "Then I'll just enter it up. Shall I take the coat, madam? To wrap?"

"Not necessary," Joanna said. "I'll wear it out."

Miss Loam hesitated, then said, "Of course, madam." She hurried for the exit, pausing for a quick word with the woman standing by the door.

"She's afraid you'll do a runner," Matilda whispered, stroking the fur. "But Jo . . . can you afford it?"

"I think so. Would you like one too?"

"Would I?" Matilda's eyes began to match Miss Loam's.

"Excuse me, miss," Joanna said to the waiting attendant. "May we have another of these? I think it should be a size larger." The assistant summoned another woman to keep an eye on them while she went for the other coat, but by the time she returned, Miss Loam had also returned, a different Miss Loam this, all breathless obedience to Joanna's every wish.

"We spoke of a new dress, perhaps . . . But it would be best to begin with lingerie, don't you think, Miss Grain?"

"Oh, yes," Joanna agreed. "Coming, Tilly?"

But Matilda was trying on her coat.

"Are you going to beat me?" Joanna asked spreading the sales slips before Howard.

"I might. But only because I think it might be rather fun. However . . . this is quite a whack for one day."

"You said to get a fur. Don't you like it?" She paraded in front of him, wearing the mink and nothing else.

"I think it's superb. But I didn't say anything about getting Tilly one as well."

"She was so jealous, Howie."

"I can imagine."

She knelt beside him. "Say you forgive me."

He stroked her hair, ran his hand over her shoulders and then down to cup her breasts. He was reassuring himself, she knew, that she really did belong to him, and that therefore she really was worth it. "I forgive you. But . . . no more days like today until your birthday."

Joanna giggled. "That's next month."

But she knew she'd gone right over the top, and did not repeat the spree. On the other hand, it was fun to be driven into the West End, to meet Matilda for lunch at a smart restaurant. She did this at least three times a week. She would have loved to entertain William in such style, but it simply wasn't possible through Mums' unrelenting hostility. She wondered how he was getting on. But then, she wondered how Dick was getting on. She heard nothing more about the cannabis charge; as he had promised, Howard got his solicitor to sort it out.

She heard nothing more about the divorce, either. Howard never spoke of it, and she saw no mention of it in the newspapers she had taken to reading from cover to cover. The important thing was that Howard seemed perfectly happy, and it was her business to keep him so. She enjoyed that. She was discovering that she was perfectly happy herself, did not want anything to change, until the day in the New Year she and Matilda were lunching together in the West End, and she looked up to find Alicia standing beside the table.

Joanna was so surprised she knocked over her glass of wine. "Well," Alicia said, loudly, "if it isn't the tart."

Joanna found herself sliding across the seat to come to rest against the wall, while Matilda goggled at Alicia in equal consternation. The maitre d' hurried up. Clearly he knew Alicia. "Oh, Mrs Edge," he said. "Is there something wrong?"

"I don't like the quality of customer you have in here, Jacopo," Alicia announced loudly, and heads began to turn. "Tarts belong on the street."

"But madam—" the maitre d' said.

Joanna stood up. She had had a couple of glasses of wine and was in no mood to be insulted. "You'll apologise for that remark," she said.

"Ha!" Alicia commented, and turned to her luncheon companion, another very well-dressed woman. "This is the little whore I was telling you about, the one Howard picked off the street to sleep with." She was still speaking very loudly.

"Madam, please," the maitre d' begged.

"You unutterable bastard," Joanna said.

"Don't you dare insult me!" Alicia shouted.

"I don't see how I can," Joanna pointed out. "You're beneath insult."

"Why, you—" Alicia swung her hand, but had it caught by Matilda, at last coming to life, and to the defence of her baby sister. "You—" Alicia turned to hit Matilda in turn, while the other woman looked as if she was going to take part.

The maitre d' seemed about to faint, and stepped back into the ranks of the half-dozen waiters who had suddenly accumulated. "Oh, no, you don't," Joanna said, and picked up the carafe of water from the table, upending it over Alicia's head. Alicia shrieked. By now everyone in the room was staring at them. "That's how we deal with loud cats at home," Joanna said.

Alicia stared at her through a watery haze, then turned and ran from the restaurant. "Oh, lord," Matilda said.

"You haven't heard the last of this," Alicia's companion said, and ran after her friend. Matilda sat down with a thump.

"Madam," the maitre d' said. "Ladies . . ."

"I'm sorry about the mess," Joanna said. "Would you like us to leave?" The maitre d' looked at her; they had ordered a very expensive meal. Then he looked behind the disappearing Alicia, sizing up the future. "I believe I have an account with you," Joanna said, sitting down. "It's in the name of Howard Edge, and my name is Joanna Grain."

"Oh. Ah. Mr Edge. Miss Grain! Yes, of course. Clean up this mess," the maitre d' commanded a waiter. "Dessert! Would you like dessert, madam?"

"Whatever is Howard going to say?" Matilda asked when they had placed their orders.

Howard knew all about it before he got home: Alicia had telephoned him at the office. "I suppose we're just lucky there were no reporters hanging about," he said. "But it's sure to make the gossip columns."

"Are you very angry?" Joanna asked. "I mean, she started it."

"Of course she did," Howard agreed. "It may all turn out for the best. She's finally got the message that you and I are a permanent item, and is prepared to take the divorce. For another two thousand shares. She wanted more, but we talked her down."

"Oh! Isn't that serious?"

"Not really. I told you, we're planning a rights issue in the next year or so. This is really to raise sufficient capital to upgrade our fleet, which is getting a little old. What it does mean, however, is that all individual holdings will be, if you like, watered down."

Joanna considered this. "Mine as well?"

"Not if you follow my advice. As an existing shareholder you will receive two for one anyway. But I suggest you also buy into the issue."

"I haven't any money."

"I'll lend you the money."

But her brain was racing away at another tangent. "If a whole lot of new shares are being sold, won't that lower the value of the existing shares?"

"Momentarily, perhaps. If we have a good reaction it should push the value up, in the long run, and we'll all be wealthier."

"But won't an issue of shares dilute your control of the company?"

"Not really. I also receive two for one. My stake will actually increase. But in any event, as long as I have fifty-one percent, I'm in charge."

"It all sounds terribly, well . . . nerve-wracking."

He grinned. "I've been doing it for years."

Joanna suddenly realised she had no idea how old he was – and she was going to marry him.

Howard was forty-one. This came as a considerable shock: Mums was only forty-five. "Age," he declared, "is a man-made mathematical formula. I'm as fit as many a man of thirty."

She also discovered that the first thing he did every morning on leaving the house was drive to a gym in London and exercise for an hour. "Do you think it's safe?" she asked Matilda. "At his age?"

"He always seems all right to me." Matilda giggled.

"Have you ever slept with him?"

"Well . . . a long time ago," Matilda said. "Does that make you mad?"

"Of course not. I always knew it, anyway. What . . . well, what is he like in bed?"

"Don't you know?" Matilda was astonished.

"Of course I know, as regards me. But you've had a lot more experience than me."

"Well, he always gets it up," Matilds said.

"You mean, some men don't?" It was Joanna's turn to be astonished.

"You'd be surprised," Matilda said. "But then . . ." she sighed. "I've always been in the weirdo side of the business. A, guys who are really past it but still want to try, and B, guys who are so high on booze or drugs they don't know which side is up." She giggled. "Or C, guys who do know which side is up, and don't want to know, if you follow me."

"I don't."

"Well, count yourself lucky. Although . . . Howard is very orthodox," she said seriously. "He doesn't even do fellation."

"Eh?"

"Where you suck him."

"Where I . . ." Now Joanna was horrified. "That's illegal. Isn't it?"

"Not between consenting adults."

"And you've done that?"

"When I'm doing what I'm doing, I'm a consenting adult. But he sucks you, right?"

"Well . . ." Joanna flushed. He did have a tendency to bury his head in her pubes, embarassing her as much as it had excited her. "That's not illegal, is it?" she asked anxiously.

"Not so far as I know, as long as you're a consenting adult." Another giggle. "Or a consenting wife. Listen, quit worrying. You're going to be Mrs Howard Edge, wife of the Chairman and Managing Director of Caribee Shipping. You're going to have the world at your feet. And in your handbag. You are never going to have to fear or want again."

Joanna shivered, and hugged herself. "Until Howard finds someone he likes better, and splits with me as he did with Alicia."

"If he ever does that, Jo, then you're a twit. For God's sake, you're eighteen, he's forty-one. You're young enough to be his daughter. All you have to do is keep him happy until he's too old to take on anyone else."

"Don't you think that's a trifle cynical? I happen to love him."

"You were the one worrying about him leaving you."

"It's a fact of life. He is a very attractive, very wealthy man. He's eligible, even if he is married."

"Now who's being cynical?" Matilda laughed. "You just follow my instructions, in everything. But mainly sex. You say he sucks you."

"I never."

"You didn't deny it. You have to do it back. Men like that. I'll bet you've never even touched his prick," Matilda said.

"Well . . . not really."

"Men like that," Matilda repeated. "Just go with him. And then you need a couple of pregnancies. Just a couple. He'll want children by you, but he won't want you out of action for too long."

"You mean it's all planned," Joanna said. "Whatever happened to spontaneity?"

"That's the biggest secret of all," Matilda told her. "Making him believe, now and always, that it is all spontaneous." She kissed her sister. "Enjoy it. Be happy. And make him happy too."

# Chapter Five

# The Tragedy

After the fracas at the restaurant, which made the gossip columns, the first time Joanna had ever seen her name in print, Alicia did decide to go for adultery, with the result that the whole business was settled within a year. Howard arranged the wedding for the very day the divorce became final.

It had been an incredibly busy year, too busy indeed for Joanna to feel any embarrassment about being painted a scarlet woman by the press. Actually, she was so young, and so patently innocent, she received more sympathy than criticism, and to her great pleasure even Miriam got swept up in the preparations, and moved into the house for the last month, ostensibly to oversee things like the gown, but in reality, Joanna knew, out of sheer curiosity. She was afraid that Howard might object, but he remained urbanely content, or so it seemed, and welcomed his prospective mother-in-law with open arms.

The reconciliation meant that William could visit as well. Joanna was delighted to be back in the company of her brother. William was now sixteen, big and strong, and seemed to be getting on much better at school. "What are you going to do?" Joanna asked him, one Sunday morning in late summer as they strolled in the garden.

"Go to university, I suppose," he said.

"Can Mums afford it?"

"Well, I'll have a grant, of course. I don't suppose there'll be much on top of that . . ." he paused.

"Would you like me to have a word with Howard?"

"Do you think he'd be interested?"

"Of course. You're going to be his brother-in-law."

"Let's see how it goes," William suggested.

Obviously he didn't want a hand-out. Joanna was pleased about that. She could of course give him some of her allowance, but Howard would be sure to know about it; she would prefer to tell him what she was doing. She was relieved that there did not seem any great urgency. William still had to pass the necessary examinations. She got the impression that he wasn't doing as well, scholastically, as he might; he seemed to be more interested in sport. But again, she supposed, early days.

He also seemed to have lost his earlier interest in girls. "That's odd," opined Matilda, who naturally saw a lot more of him. "Queer?" She gave one of her giggles. "Do you think he is?"

"Of course he isn't."

"Well, he only ever has boys about him, and some of them are definitely push-me pull-you," Matilda said, disparagingly.

"You simply have to face the fact that not everyone in the world relates their entire lives to sex, unlike you," Joanna pointed out, even more disparagingly.

She was having the time of her life, because now that the wraps were off, as it were, Howard wanted to show her off. He took her dancing, to concerts and the opera, and he held several cocktail parties at the house, where she was very definitely the hostess, wearing a succession of extremely expensive dresses. These occasions were at once exhilarating and disturbing. She could not help but respond to the open adulation of the men – Prince Hasim was always present, and as gallant as ever – or the envy of the women, to the champagne and the canapés and the feeling of being in control. But she was disturbed by the fact that Matilda was never included, and that they were never invited back to other people's houses. "It's a difficult time, for my friends," Howard explained. "Because they were all friends of Alicia's as well. Probably still are." He grinned, and kissed her. "I am the guilty party, you see. But it'll all settle down, once the divorce is final and we're married."

"If you're guilty, then I must be even more guilty," she said.

"You are guilty of nothing," he told her.

So far he had wanted only what Matilda would no doubt have described as the most orthodox of sexual responses from her. He liked to kiss her naked body from mouth to toe, and he liked to stroke her, but he demanded nothing back from her, and she didn't think she should take the initiative in that direction. He entered her in a perfectly straightforward manner, with her lying on her back. There too she thought she should wait for him to make the first move. He did not like wearing a condom, nor did he wish her to wear or use any protection herself, but she did not get pregnant. She wondered if this concerned him, but it did not appear to.

The fact was, they had a very odd relationship, she supposed. Although she was his fiancée, she was also his mistress. Although she had her charge accounts and all the money she could spend, the bills were paid, and no doubt scrutinised, by him; this knowledge had an inhibiting effect on her buying, and although she could, it appeared, go where she liked and meet who she liked, she rapidly realised that she was being overseen all the time, as everyone seemed to be in his pay, and thus that she really had no freedom at all. Not that she wanted to be any more free than she was; it was just the *feeling* of being caged. Her only friend was Matilda, and Matilda, she realised, was to be kept at arms' length from Howard's friends: she had a reputation, and besides, was a common-or-garden dancer. Matilda never indicated any resentment at her exclusion from her sister's social life, which was a great relief – but she had to be aware of it. Joanna entertained her to lunch at least once a week. They gossiped, and giggled and often got quietly tight, but did not again get down to any intimacies, while, inside her, she was aware of a growing build-up of resentment, that she should be so helpless, even to promote her own sister, who, so far as she knew, was still having to parade naked in front of a gaggle of lecherous old men and more, having to sleep with them afterwards.

The wedding date was set for the second week in December, a week after Joanna's twentieth birthday. On her birthday, the two sisters had lunch together as usual at a smart West End restaurant. "Where are you going for your honeymoon?"

"Do you know, I have actually no idea. Howard hasn't told me. I'm wondering if we're even going to get married."

"Eh?"

"Well, this Kennedy thing—"

"That's done, darling. We can't mourn him forever."

"Well, I can tell you that Howie has been very concerned, these past few weeks."

"And so you haven't asked him about the honeymoon." Matilda frowned. "You *are* going on a honeymoon?"

"Well . . . I imagine so. Unless he's too busy."

Matilda continued to frown as she played with her wine glass. "Do you and he ever talk? Or do you just make love?"

Joanna flushed. "Of course we talk."

"But only about his choice of subjects."

"Well . . . we can't talk shop, because I don't know anything about the business . . ."

"Have you ever been to his office? To Caribee Buildings at all?"

"Well, of course I haven't. As I said—"

"You don't know anything about the business. And Howard aims to keep it that way."

"I have no objection to that."

"Hm," Matilda commented. "I still think you should honeymoon, somewhere really exotic. And I think you should know where it is you're going."

Matilda was in many ways a troublemaker, Joanna reflected. But the nest had been stirred. Joanna felt more than ever thoroughly out of sorts as she dropped her sister after lunch. "Home, madam?" asked Wyndham the chauffeur.

"Oh, yes, home," Joanna said.

He engaged gear and the car moved to the corner, and waited for the traffic flowing by on the major road. Joanna regarded the passers-by without much interest; she had had a liberal helping of wine with her lunch and doubted she would stay awake until they reached Berkshire . . . and then found herself blinking at the face that was peering at her through the tinted rear window. "My God!" she remarked.

"Madam?" asked the chauffeur.

"Hold it a moment," Joanna said, and rolled down the window.

"Joanna?" It was Dick, looking untidy in an ill-fitting suit, with a battered-looking briefcase dangling from his left hand.

"Dick!" What a pleasure it was to see him again.

"But—" he looked left and right at the Rolls.

"I'm holding up traffic, madam," said the chauffeur.

"Oh . . . listen, get in," she said, and opened the door, and Dick half fell into the spacious car. Joanna banged the door shut. "Now you can drive," she told Wyndham.

"Yes, madam. Where would you like to go?"

"Just some place quiet," Joanna told him. He made no comment, filtered into the traffic.

Dick was scrambling on to the seat beside her. "I have to get back to the office."

Joanna giggled. "Tell them you had an accident."

It was so good to see him again, someone of her own social background, social structure . . . although Mums would probably say he was inferior. Aunt Ethel certainly would.

He was remembering their last meeting. "This is just like the car you drove off in after that drug bust . . . heck, two years ago."

"All but," she agreed.

"And since then . . ." he grinned. "The class was struck dumb when that old bag announced you wouldn't be coming back. You should've seen her face."

"And yours?"

"Oh, heck, Jo . . . you know, I damn near wept? Oh, what the hell . . . I did weep. I was so fond of you." Tentatively he touched her hand, and she squeezed his fingers. Damn that second bottle of wine, she thought. If I am not careful, I am going to do something very, very stupid.

But how she wanted to do something very, very stupid. With Dick. They had come so close to it, on so many occasions. "So," he said. "Now, I suppose . . . you're married or something." She pulled off her left glove, and realised, for the first time, that Howard had never even given her an engagement ring! "Well, hell," Dick said. "But this car must be costing a bomb."

"I am going to get married," Joanna said carefully.

"Oh. To that fellow?"

"Yes."

"But . . . he's, well . . ."

"Old enough to be my father," she agreed. "I suppose you could say that I have sold myself, hook, line, and sinker."

Wasn't that the absolute truth?

"Shit!" he muttered, and flushed.

They were out of the West End now, and the streets were quiet. "Can you find some place to park for a few minutes, Wyndham?" she asked. "Somewhere green. There has to be a park some place."

"Yes, madam." His ears were glowing.

"So, what are you doing now?" she asked.

"Well, I've left college, of course, and I have a job—"

"And you're married, and have kids."

"Chance would be a fine thing, on my salary. Listen, I have to be getting back, Jo. If I lose my job—"

"I'll make it up to you," she promised, with a wild idea that she might get Howard to give him a place at the shipping company.

"Right now, I want to . . . pretend. Pretend that it's two years ago. That there's nothing else."

"We're two years older," he said soberly. "We—"

"I know." They were suddenly in a green area, with trees and thick undergrowth. But she didn't need undergrowth. She had the car. "This is ideal, Wyndham."

The car pulled in to the side of a quiet lane.

"I don't suppose you'd care to go for a walk?" Joanna asked.

"It's a nice day for a walk, madam." Wyndham opened the door and got out. "How long a walk should I take?"

"Oh . . . half an hour," Joanna suggested. He touched his cap and walked away from the car.

"Gosh," Dick said. "To have that kind of power . . ."

"It's called money." She held his face between her hands and kissed him on the lips.

"Were you planning on a honeymoon?" she asked Howard that night at dinner.

"Of course."

"Oh! Am I allowed to ask where?"

He grinned. "It's a secret. My wedding present to you."

There really was no answer to that.

Nor was it his only present to her. On the morning of their wedding he gave her an enormous ruby solitaire. "Gosh," she said, as she flipped up the lid on the little blue box. "Oh, gosh."

"I never did give you an engagement ring," he reminded her. "So, better late than never."

She continued to goggle at the huge red stone. She had no idea what it might be worth, but it had to be a lot. Then a thought struck her. "You shouldn't be here at all."

"Eh?"

"It's bad luck for the bride and groom to see each other on the wedding day, until they're married."

"I never knew you were superstitious."

"Well . . ." she flushed. "I'm not."

"You just believe in old wives' tales. But I've always made my own luck."

As always, it was impossible to argue with him, and in any event the rest of the day was entirely taken up with the preparations. The house became filled with hordes of caterers and waitresses, with the dressmakers attending to last minute details, while Miriam fussed. Matilda arrived at ten. However much she might have been pushed aside during the past few months, Joanna had been determined her sister was to be her maid of honour, and Howard had not objected. Her first step into society, Joanna thought, giving her a hug and a kiss. "I'm so glad you're here," she said.

"Have you found out where you're going yet?" Matilda asked. "Oh, you ninny."

William turned up soon after, wearing a new suit – only the second suit he had ever owned – and looking terrified. Then the parson came. "It would have been so very nice to be able to marry you in the church," he said, squeezing Joanna's hand, "but there it is. Rules are rules. But I can bless you," he added brightly.

By then it was time for Joanna to get dressed, fussed over by Miriam and Matilda, and utterly surprised halfway through by the sudden appearance of Aunt Ethel. "What are you doing here?" Matilda asked.

"I was invited," Ethel said.

"Well, of course, but we didn't expect you to come."

Ethel merely snorted. "Can you really, in all conscience, wear white?" she inquired of the bride.

"You may not believe this, Aunt Ethel," Joanna said. "But Howard is the only man with whom I have ever been to bed."

Aunt Ethel clearly didn't think that was any argument.

The house was packed, partly with people Joanna had already

entertained at cocktail parties or met at dances, but also with people she had never met before, but who she gathered were staff from Caribee Lines. “Be nice to Young, Joanna,” Howard said, all smiles. “Without him we would be in deep shit.”

He passed on, and Joanna smiled, nervously, at the somewhat cadaverous looking man. “I thought I’d met Howard’s solicitor.”

“I’m not a solicitor, Mrs Edge. I’m chief accountant at Caribee Lines.”

“Ah.” It occurred to her that he might also be perusing all of her accounts. In which case he knew almost as much about her as Howard. “Then we have no secrets from each other,” she said with a bright smile.

“None at all,” he agreed, gravely.

Then there was Prince Hasim, resplendent in a morning suit, raising his topper and kissing her hand. “How I wish I were in Howie’s place at this moment.”

“Oh, come now, Your Highess,” Joanna said. “Don’t you have a full quiver of wives and concubines back home in Qadir? Or even here in London?”

“Concubines, yes. Wives, no, would you believe it? My English education, I suppose. I keep waiting for the right one. And when I find her . . . she belongs to another.”

“You say the sweetest things,” Joanna told him, and hurried away before he could say anything else. Not only did she not wish to think of any man save Howard on her wedding day, but the Prince gave her goose pimples . . . in the most erotic possible fashion.

The ceremony droned about her head. Howard had wanted music, even if they couldn’t be married in a church, and this was provided by a hi-fidelity phonograph, mostly stirring stuff. The wedding luncheon took upwards of four hours, with gallons of champagne and endless speeches. Howard’s was the most brilliant, that of his best man – the host of the bathing party that seemed so long ago –

the most boring. Then Matilda was ushering Joanna away to change her gown for a frock, and Mums was weeping, and Aunt Ethel was looking more po-faced than ever, before she was being hurried down an aisle of people, all reaching to touch her or kiss her. She hardly drew breath until she was seated in the back of the Rolls, and they were driving out of the estate.

"Do you know," Howard said, "there is only one person in the world who knows where we are going? No, two."

"Who are they?" Her head was still spinning from all the champagne.

"Peter Young. And . . ." he kissed her. "That's another surprise."

It was only four in the afternoon, but the day seemed to have been going on forever. She felt she should be full of scintillating conversation, or at least amorous intentions, but instead she fell fast asleep, only to awake a couple of hours later as they pulled into heavy traffic. She sat up with a start. "Gosh! I'm sorry, Howard."

He smiled at her. "I dozed off too."

"Where are we?" She looked right and left at the unfamiliar houses.

"Southampton."

"You don't mean . . ." She watched the docks approach. And alongside the Caribee dock, a ship . . . "That's the *Caribee Queen*!"

"Bound for the Caribbean and all places exotic."

"Oh, Howard!" She hugged him. "Where, exactly?"

"You know the itinerary. Out to Georgetown with dry goods, stopping at Bridgetown, load with rice and sugar, then back home, stopping at again at Bridgetown. Twenty-four days the round trip. Christmas at sea. It'll be terrific."

"Oh, Howard!" She hugged him again.

"You've no doubts about returning to British Guiana?" he asked in her ear.

"I don't think so. Anyway, I won't be Inspector Grain's daughter; I'll be Howard Edge's wife."

"Absolutely," he agreed.

He had of course told Captain Heggie that he would be travelling with his bride, but had issued the strictest instructions that there were to be no celebrations or undue attention. So he and Joanna took their places with the other passengers to board, although the purser could not help but be deferential as he showed them to the forward cabin himself.

The door closed, and Howard took her in his arms. "Just you and me, for twenty-four days."

"And a crew of thirty and ten other passengers," she smiled.

"Not one of whom is going to interfere with us in the least," he promised.

He was quite right. They unpacked their gear, as they were actually making the round trip and would not be leaving the cabin for those twenty-four days, and went on deck in the gathering darkness to watch the ship leave. Here they were just two of the group of passengers, mostly West Indian businessmen and their wives returning home after a summer in England. The purser did sidle up to Howard and mutter that the Captain would be happy to have him and Mrs Edge on the bridge if he wished, but Howard sent him off with a quick shake of the head. "Mrs Edge," Joanna whispered. "I like the sound of that."

At dinner as well, served at one long table in the saloon, they melded in with the rest of the passengers. As was traditional, the Captain did not join them on the first night out, but the first officer did. However, he too had been well briefed and paid Howard no obvious attention, although the special attention was there, had anyone cared to look too closely. But the talk was all about the Profumo Affair and changing conditions in the West Indies following the collapse of the federation, and both Howard and Joanna had to do nothing more than listen politely. And then at last the privacy and comfort of their own cabin. "Do you remember our first meeting?" Howard asked.

"I shall never forget it."

"Did you know that I wanted to bring you to this cabin, then?"

"I didn't," she confessed. "Matilda thought you did, and I told her she was an idiot. And," she added, "a married man. Actually, that's a lie. I didn't know you were a married man until we docked."

"And what did you think then?"

"That you were a lousy, despicable, but very typical man."

He kissed her, then eyed the nightdress she was carefully taking out of the drawer. "You're not meaning to wear that?"

"I bought it specially for tonight."

"I've never seen you in a nightdress before."

"Well . . . I don't normally wear one. I'll put it back."

"No," he said. "Put it on." Tongue between her teeth, Joanna settled the lace and satin on her shoulders, smoothed it down her hips. Howard had also undressed, but he didn't have any pyjamas. "You do realise," he said, "that these internal bulkheads aren't all that thick. No noise, or the neighbours will come rushing in."

"Do I usually make a noise?" she asked.

"There's always a first time," he said, and stepped up to her, digging his fingers into the bodice of the nightgown, and pulling down with all his strength.

It was in fact all Joanna could do to suppress a scream; he had never been violent before. She found herself backed against the wall while he proceeded to tear the beautiful garment into shreds, finally bursting the shoulder straps to let it gather in folds of tattered material about her ankles. Then he kissed her. "I've always wanted to do that," he said.

She didn't know whether it was the fact they were actually married, or the feeling of romantic isolation from normal convention inescapable from being on a ship at sea, but she had never known him in such a mood. His love-making took on a new and more vigorous aspect too, and having gone through his kissing and stroking routine, which always aroused her, as he knew, he rolled her on her face and lifted her thighs to enter her from behind. Another new experience, but one which quite transcended all the others, as he seemed to fill so much more of her, make her so much more aware of herself.

Suddenly she knew that she was indeed going to climax, and it was by far the best she had ever had. While just to lie there feeling him still in her and his weight on her back crushing her into the bunk, while the ship rolled gently as she made her way down the Channel, slowly because of the fog, and always behind her blaring horn, gave her the greatest feeling of security she had ever known.

The rest of the voyage was paradise, even if, by breakfast the following morning, it appeared that everyone on the ship, including the passengers, knew both who they were and that they were honeymooning. But as that also meant that everyone on board understood that they were in the presence of the Owner, when they clearly wished to be alone, as when lying in deck-chairs on the boat deck, they were left alone. Every night was a dinner party, in which at least one of the officers always joined. It was a happy ship with a happy crew, which made the passengers happy as well. "We've been carrying some of these people, to and fro, for ages," Howard told her, and she could well believe that.

The weather remained fine, as it was after the hurricane season and before the winter storms, the sea was unfailingly blue, as was the sky, and the *Caribee Queen* chugged steadily on her way before a broad white wake, passing through the Azores, and then making for Barbados. This was special, not only because of the attractiveness of the island itself, but because it was where Howard had joined the ship three years before, and thus where he had first met her. As they spent a day in Carlisle Bay, discharging cargo, he took her ashore, hired a car, and drove her up to the north of the island, where the sea caves were, and then down the west coast, past rockstrewn Bathsheba, past Sam Lord's Castle – "There's talk of turning it into an hotel,"

Howard said – and then on to the cliff above the Crane, where they could look at the huge rollers breaking on the Cobblers Reef, before racing in to churn up the beach.

From Barbados it was only a night's further sailing for British Guiana.

"Tell me something about the firm?" Joanna asked, as she lay in his arms.

"Planning a takeover?"

"I'm interested. Your life is my life, now."

He considered for a few minutes, then said, "It's not all beer and skittles. Like right now. We had huge hopes about federation, but since that has collapsed, and all the West Indian colonies are becoming independent states, trade has taken a downturn. Then we have two ships that need replacing . . . there are a few problems ahead."

"Oh," she said. It wasn't what she had expected, or hoped, to hear. "But it'll all be okay once you float your new stock issue, or whatever. Won't it?"

"Hopefully. If it's a success."

"But then you'll have a lot more shares. What do you do with them all? I mean, when it's dividend time?"

He grinned, and kissed her. "I don't actually own any shares in Caribee Shipping."

"Eh?" She rose on her elbow in alarm.

"It's a legal matter. Remember, I told you, the shares are all held by a trust company in Jersey. That's where Billy comes in: he manages the trust. That's to avoid death duties, you see, when I go. In the meantime, I get the income from them, and I control them for voting purposes within the Company."

"Just as the Company owns the house and the car . . . does it own me as well?"

Howard kissed her. "I own you, sweetheart. Do you object to that?"

She snuggled against him. "It's a comforting feeling."

"Excited?" Howard asked, as they picked up the pilot on the edge of the mid-flats, some ten miles off the coast.

"Oh, yes," she said.

"We spend three days here, so I've arranged a trip into the interior. Ever been to Kaieteur?"

"No, I haven't. You mean we're going up there? Can we afford it?"

"We're not broke yet."

They spent a morning in Georgetown, and she showed him the Eve Leary barracks, where she had lived with her parents before her father's murder. Then they drove up to Atkinson Field, the air base built by the Americans during World War Two, and there boarded the Grumman amphibian which would fly them into the interior. They held hands as they looked down on the endless reaches of forest, pierced only from time to time by the great rivers. "Most of that is still unexplored," Joanna told him, happy to be playing the mentor at last.

"It's not somewhere to come down," Howard agreed. They landed on the broad Potaro River, upstream of Kaieteur itself, and were led by their guide through a forest path to emerge on a flat rock that overhung the fall. "You don't suffer from vertigo, I hope?" Howard shouted, for now the noise of the cascading water was utterly deafening.

"Not till now," she assured him, and then held her breath as they emerged from the trees on to the rock and gazed at the most awe-inspiring sight in the world.

"When you think," Howard shouted, "of the way they carry on about Niagara and Victoria . . . they're cascades compared with this."

Joanna tried to take in the immensity of the scene, as the three hundred foot wide river, emerging from the trees about a mile to their right with a slow and almost purposeful intensity, rolling up to the lip only feet away from where they stood, and then plunging over, for . . . "How deep *is* it?" she shouted above the roar.

"The gorge is getting on for 1,000 feet," the pilot told them. "The sheer drop is 741; that is, two and a half times the drop of Victoria. The total drop is another hundred."

"A river the size of the Thames, dropping 800 plus feet," Howard said.

"It's been doing that for thousands of years," the pilot said. "Can you imagine the size of the cavern it must have dug out behind that water?"

Joanna couldn't. "Has nobody ever been there?"

"Not possible. There's no way anyone can get through that liquid wall. Unlike Niagara, it never freezes over here."

"Gosh," she said. "There could be all the riches of the world behind there."

"There sure is one vast cavern. One day, I guess, it'll have eaten back so far the river bed will collapse into it."

"But then there'd still be the fall," Howard pointed out.

"That's true. Anyway, it isn't likely to happen in our lifetimes. Not even yours, Mrs Edge."

They remained at the lip for an hour; the roaring water, plunging so far, had a mesmerising effect. But the biggest adventure was yet to come: taking off. They rejoined the Grumman, upstream, and taxied back several hundred yards. Then the engine was thrust up to maximum power, and the little aircraft raced over the surface of the river, water flying to either side. While ahead of them was the end of the world, where the river abruptly ended, and beyond, thousands of feet away, they could see nothing but the forest, huge and green and looming. "Here we go!" shouted the pilot.

Joanna closed her eyes, then forced them open again. This was something that had to be seen and remembered forever. She looked down through the window as they arrived at the lip. She saw the water cascading downwards, the immense rise of spray at the bottom, eight hundred feet away. She caught her breath as the plane dropped, level with the river behind them, before soaring upwards.

"Whew!" Howard said. "You should make your customers have a medical before this trip, just to be sure none of them has a heart attack." The pilot grinned. Presumably he did this so often he never even noticed.

"Where to, now?" Joanna asked. "Back to Atkinson?"

"We have two days left," Howard said. "I thought we'd have a look at the interior."

From Kaieteur the Grumman flew north-east for about a hundred miles before landing on another river, the Mazaruni, and before a settlement, Tumareng. "Ever been up here before?" Howard asked, as they taxied in to the bank.

"Not here. I've been up to the savannah, you know, the high prairie they call the Rupununi." He nodded, studying his map. "But as a young inspector, Dad was based up here for a few years," Joanna said. Howard squeezed her hand.

There was quite a crowd waiting for them on the bank, several black policemen, a couple of white men, and a large number of American Indians, descendants of the Arawaks who had used to own the country. Joanna had encountered them on her visits to the Rupununi; they were short, squat people, not terribly attractive, physically, but full of good humour and enormously strong.

"Mr Edge?" One of the white men shook hands with Howard. "John Dayton. I'm the DC. And . . ." he frowned at Joanna.

"Hello, Mr Dayton," Joanna said.

"Good lord," Howard said. "You mean you two know each other?"

"Gordon Grain's daughter," Dayton said. "My dear girl!" He embraced her. "How's your mother?"

"Very well, thank you."

"And . . ." he groped, mentally.

"Matilda and William," Joanna said. "I'm Joanna," she added, as he obviously didn't recall her name either.

Howard continued to look quizzical. "I've been to their house for dinner," Dayton said. "Oh, some years ago. You would have been . . . ?"

"Twelve, Mr Dayton," Joanna said.

"You've changed a bit. Well, this calls for a celebration. Oh, by the way, this is Inspector Calham. He's the local chief bobby." Calham, a young man wearing khaki uniform with shorts and stockings, shook hands.

Then they were hurried away to the Commissioner's bungalow for celebrations. Apparently neither Calham nor Dayton was married, and they thoroughly enjoyed the company of an attractive young bride; the meal was eaten on the bungalow verandah, behind mosquito screens, beyond which the Amerindians gathered to stare at them. "So, what would you like to do and see while you're here?" Dayton asked as they drank thick, sweet, black coffee.

"You tell us," Howard suggested. "Some gold workings, of course—"

"That's rather like watching a tree grow," Calham grinned. "Ever done any white water?"

"I'm not with you."

"He means rapid shooting," Dayton explained. "There's a river close by, a tributary of the Mazaruni, that has some spectacular falls."

"Now that sounds like fun," Howard said, turning to Joanna. "You game?"

"Isn't it dangerous?" she asked.

"Not if the boatmen know what they're doing," Dayton said.

"We'll give it a whirl," Howard said.

"Then we'll make an early start in the morning."

"I hope you don't think I'm chicken," Joanna said, when she and Howard were alone in their bedroom in the guest bungalow, isolated from the world by their mosquito nets, although the sounds of the village and the jungle beyond overlaid the evening, softened always by the constant swish of the river. The Grumman had returned to town, but would come back for them the day after tomorrow; the *Caribee Queen* sailed that night.

"Of course I don't," Howard said. "You have every right to be concerned. But these chaps know what they're doing."

"It's just that I'm not sure I should be bounced about too much." He had been looking at his maps, as usual. Now he slowly turned his head. "I missed last month. I put that down to all the excitement over the wedding. But I was due again four days ago," she explained. "I didn't say anything then, because, you know, with all this travel, it seemed quite reasonable to be late."

"Holy Hallelujah!" He hugged and kissed her.

"Only four days," she reminded him.

"Okay. But if there is a little fellow in there, we certainly don't want to bounce him about. You'll have to take a rain check on this one."

She squeezed his hand, then frowned. "But you're still going?"

"Darling, I'm not pregnant. It'll be the experience of a lifetime."

They slept in each other's arms, although Joanna was awake most of the night. She was not disturbed by the unfamiliar jungle sounds which drifted through her window, or by the sudden very heavy shower of rain just before dawn. It was merely a feeling of euphoria that swept over her from time to time. She had never been so happy in her life. She had been a little afraid that Howard might not really wish to start another family, but he had seemed over the moon.

And she would not have been human if she had not reckoned it would be one in the eye for Alicia.

They were up at dawn to breakfast with Dayton, before driving off along a rather bumpy track to look at some of the gold workings. As Dayton had warned, this was not terribly exciting, but Joanna was presented with a nugget, about half the size of her little fingernail.

"Pure, twenty-four carat metal," Dayton told her. "A quarter of an ounce weight."

"Which would be worth, how much?" Joanna asked.

"Oh, seventy-five dollars, maybe."

"I'm going to keep it, forever," she vowed.

Then there was an alligator farm, where they were shown hundreds of newly hatched babes. "Oh, aren't they just superb," Joanna cried, as one of the inch-long replicas was placed on her palm. Although born and bred in Guiana, she had never actally seen an alligator outside of a zoo; they were not normally to be encountered on the streets of Georgetown. Now the infantile reptile opened its jaws to yawn at her. "Can I have one, Howie? As a pet?"

"Of course you can," Howard said. "Just let's ask if it's practical."

"Well, sir, madam," said the black manager, "you can have one if you like. But you want to remember, these creatures grow. And then some."

"How big?" Howard asked.

"Well, sir, come a couple of years, if you was keeping him in your bathtub, you'd find his tail hanging over one end and his head over the other. His jaws would then be about three feet long."

"My God!" Joanna commented.

"I think maybe we should think about that one," Howard suggested. "Whatever would Mrs Partridge say?"

They drove over to the river, about half the size of the Mazaruni. "Listen," Dayton said.

It was by now a familiar sound, the road of water rushing downhill very fast.

A double-ended wooden boat was waiting for them, with a crew of eight paddlers. The boat was called a bateau, fittingly enough, but the word, in Guiana, denoted the specific double-ended construction rather than merely boat. They had by now been joined by Calham, and he and Howard got into the boat. "I'll take care of the little lady," Dayton said.

"See you in ten minutes," Howard said, taking his seat amidships, while the paddlers dug their blades in and the bateau moved away from the bank. Joanna felt she should say something, but nothing came to mind beyond the admonishment to take care, and that seemed rather puerile.

She got into the jeep beside Dayton and they followed the path down the gently sloping hillside. This was extremely bumpy, and she began to wonder if it would not have been more restful in the boat. Then Dayton braked and pulled off the track on to the bank. "There," he said.

Joanna gazed at the rocks, the tumbling white water. "How far is it?"

"It stretches about a quarter of a mile, but they'll be going so fast it'll seem more like a few seconds," he said.

They got back into the jeep and drove another hundred yards, then Dayton stopped again. Now they were virtually in the middle of the rapids, which went racing and bubbling past only a few feet away. "This is the easy part," Dayton joked, noticing her anxiety. "When they get to the end, the men have to haul the boat back upstream, overland."

Joanna was looking upriver, and at that moment the bateau appeared. It was already travelling quite fast, the eight paddlers' arms and blades moving in perfect unison. "They're a highly trained team," Dayton explained. "When they get to the rocks, it's a matter of adjusting their strokes to make the boat move with the current and avoid hitting anything."

"But they've done it before?" Joanna asked.

"Often," he assured her.

"How deep is it?"

"Only a few feet. If they do get tumbled, it's a matter of walking ashore."

She found that very reassuring, as the boat now came hurtling down towards them. Howard was grinning with excitement as they struck the white water. A rock reared in front of them and Joanna suppressed a scream, but a deft touch by one of the rear paddlers sent the boat slewing round. Before it could be picked up broadside by the rushing water, another deft stroke on the other side straightened it up again. Their technique was fantastic. Another two twists and they were level with the jeep. Howard waved. The bateau surged on.

"They'll be there before us," Dayton said, and turned back to the jeep. Joanna remained watching the boat as it did another twist. But the man on the left side did not respond quickly enough this time, and the bateau was picked up, broadside on, by the stream. There was a wild flurry of paddles, but she reached the next level before she could be straightened, and went over, still broadside on. "Shit!" Dayton commented, hurrying back to Joanna's side.

Joanna remained standing absolutely still, unable to move or speak. The bateau was upside down, racing on, out of control, striking a rock to splinter herself, and then again. Behind her were bobbing heads. "Rope," Dayton snapped, and ran back to the jeep to collect the coil of rope in the back. This he dropped on the ground, before hurling the end as far into the water as he could. But the heads were already scattering, shouting. "They'll be swept down," Dayton said, gathering up the rope. "Come on."

Feeling she was in a dream, Joanna got in beside him, holding on as he went bumping down the path, for another hundred yards. When he braked again, they looked at relatively calm water, although only a few feet further upriver it still tossed and stormed beneath clouds of spray. Already staggering towards the bank were several of the paddlers. "What about fish?" Joanna asked. "Piranha?"

"There are no piranha about here," Dayton assured her. "If any did get swept down the rapids they'd be suffering from shock. There's Calham." The policeman emerged, looking like a drowned rat. All eight paddlers were now sitting on the bank, gasping for breath. "Just Mr Edge," Dayton said, staring upstream. "Should be here by now."

Everyone was now looking, while Joanna's heart seemed to have stopped beating. The water was only five feet deep, Dayton had said. Well, all the other men had been able to stand. But . . . "Where is Mr Edge?" Dayton asked, his voice suddenly taking on an edge itself.

"He was thrown out with the rest of us," Calham said. "My God, you don't think—"

Dayton ran back up the track, two of the crew with him. "There!" shouted one of them.

"Oh, thank God!" Joanna gasped.

But there was no elation in Dayton's voice. "Fetch the rope," he shouted.

Calham led the others upstrean, carrying the rope. Joanna went with them, stopped to look at Howard, who seemed to be wedged between two of the rocks. He was neither moving nor holding on. Slowly she sank to her knees.

# Part Two

# The Heiress

'Why, I hold fate
Clasp'd in my fist, and could command the course
Of time's eternal motion'

John Ford

# Chapter Six

# The Widow

Dayton and Calham put the body in the back of the jeep for the drive back to Tumareng, Joanna sitting beside it. They had covered it with a blanket, for which she was grateful. Howard's mouth was open where he had gasped for the air that had not been available, and there were also bruises on his face where he had struck the rock. Joanna's brain was numbed. She had not been allowed to see her father's body. But she could only think, first father, now husband. And I am bearing his child. She had no doubt of that now.

Because of where they were, only a degree or two north of the equator, there were horrible connotations to death. There was a radio at Tumareng, and Dayton got on it right away, but it would still be four hours before the Grumman could be taken off its present assignment and got up to them, and now it was almost noon. Joanna watched as the big fridge at the DC's bungalow was emptied of its contents, and Howard's body placed inside, while the generator, normally run for only a couple of hours every evening – the fridge was mainly battery operated – clacked into life. She saw Dayton and Calham exchange glances, and could read their thoughts: this is going to cost a fortune.

But they had their duty to do. Joanna was invited to lie down on the Commissioner's bed, and when she declined, was seated in an armchair in the lounge and offered brandy. "I'd rather have coffee," she said. "Can't I have coffee?"

Coffee was brought. She sipped it, both hands wrapped round the red-hot cup, staring in front of her, only slowly becoming aware that people were standing around her, black men as well as white, and Indians too. "Please," she said. "I am all right."

Some of them left, shooed away by Dayton. Calham, having changed his wet clothes, sat beside her. "We were all thrown out," he said. "I didn't see Mr Edge after that. I don't know what to say. The drill is . . . well, every man gets ashore as best he can."

"Have you been capsized in a rapid before?" she asked.

"Yes. Yes, I have."

"And were lives lost?" He shook his head. "Then it was just an accident," she said.

They gave her another cup of coffee, and this she realised *had* been laced with brandy. She didn't really want to drink it, because she had so much to think about. But it did relax her, kept the unthinkable thoughts at a decent distance. She was a wife of just two weeks, and now she was a widow. And a mother. She was surprised, and somewhat ashamed, at how little grief she felt. But she had never loved Howard. She had been overwhelmed by him, from the moment of their first meeting. He had been a dream man, who had suddenly, amazingly, become reality. She had been swept off her feet, only managing a few faint flutters, like a butterfly caught in a jalousie. She had known all along that their marriage could never last. Howard had been a sexual rover, and soon enough he would have roved again, as she had been warned, in different ways, by both Alicia and Matilda. Both had recommended she make hay while the sun shone. Had she made hay? She had a thousand shares in his company, currently producing an income of just under two hundred pounds a year. But all her charge accounts would presumably end with his death. That man Young would see to that the moment the news reached him. She had not taken to Peter Young at all.

Well, she thought, I still have my mink. And the ring Howard gave me. That must be worth a fortune! She wondered if she had enough money to get home? But they would have to pay her passage; she would be travelling with her dead husband. Their boss. Who was their boss no longer. She realised that her fingers had curled into fists, and that her nails were eating into her flesh.

John Dayton, who would not leave her alone for an instant, gave her another cup of coffee, and offered her lunch, but made no comment when she declined. He ate himself; as the dining-table was on the far side of the lounge, he could still watch her. "The plane will soon be here," he promised her.

It took six hours for the plane to get to them, because the pilot had had some rounding up to do. With him were a doctor, an undertaker, and a man who introduced himself as Norman Peters. "I'm Caribee Shipping's agent in Georgetown," he explained. "My dear Mrs Edge, I don't know what to say. If there is anything you wish, you have but to tell me."

"I want to go home," Joanna told him. "With Howard."

"Of course."

The undertaker had a cold bag, into which Howard's body was loaded, rather as if he were a side of beef, Joanna thought. This was placed in the luggage compartment of the Grumman, with their suitcases. Then they flew back to the coast. No one spoke much, the exact tale of what had happened having been given to them at Tumareng. Inspector Calham would of course look after the local police formalities. At Atkinson Field there were reporters, but Peters ushered Joanna through the throng and into a car for the drive down to Georgetown. "I've booked you a hotel room—"

"I'd rather sleep on the *Caribee Queen*," she said.

Her last experience of being Mrs Howard Edge, she thought.

"Of course. Whatever you wish," Peters gushed. He obviously hadn't as yet been in touch with Peter Young.

Sailing was delayed for two days, to permit the autopsy and inquest. Joanna was required to appear in court, surrounded by sympathetic British expatriot officials, all of whom had known her father and remembered her as a little girl, who, with their wives and children – some of whom she remembered – wanted to hug her and kiss her and tell her how sorry they were at the terrible tragedy. She wanted only to be away from them, but had to sit and listen to how Howard's death had been caused by drowning while temporarily unconscious, he having apparently hit his head on a rock when thrown out of the bateau. No blame could be attached to anyone.

Then at last the *Caribee Queen* sailed, Howard now in the ship's refrigeration room. Joanna deliberately did not look at any newspapers or listen to any radio broadcasts, and the crew were clearly under orders not to disturb her in any way, so she had no idea how widespread was the news of Howard's death. She did observe that the *Caribee Queen* sailed with two empty cabins. This was because she was picking up two passengers in Bridgetown: Peter Young and Billy Montgomery.

Joanna was sitting on the boat deck beneath a broad-brimmed hat, looking across Carlisle Bay at the Careenage and the attractions of Bridgetown, when the launch came alongside. She did not look over the rail to see who was boarding, and thus was utterly taken aback when the two men, looking very hot and bothered, emerged at the top of the ladder. "My dear Joanna," Billy said, kissing both her hands.

"Mrs Edge," Young said. "My deepest sympathies." They were both wearing white tropical suits with black armbands, and white panama hats.

"I don't understand," Joanna said.

"We flew out yesterday, as soon as we heard the news," Billy explained, dragging a deck-chair alongside hers to sit down. Young did the same on the other side.

"I see," she said. "Business."

"That's about it," Young said. "The company."

"Yes," she said. "All I want is to go home. I won't trouble you any more."

Young and Billy exchanged glances. "We do understand your

feelings right this minute, Joanna," Billy said. "But . . . well . . . business must go on. It transcends death."

Joanna frowned. "What has that got to do with me?" Another exchange of glances between the two men.

"Did Mr Edge never discuss business with you?" Young asked.

"Sometimes. I have a thousand shares in the company. Do I have to give those up?"

Young took off his hat to scratch his head.

"Joanna," Billy said, "did Howard never discuss his will with you?"

"No, he didn't. We weren't into things like wills. He didn't expect to die."

"Of course he did not. But . . . there it is. We have a copy of his will with us. Do you want to look at it?"

"No."

"Well, with your permission, I'll tell you what matters. Howard left his entire holding in Caribee Shipping to you."

Joanna raised her head, slowly.

"That is," Young said carefully, "sixty-nine per cent of the shares."

For a moment Joanna could not grasp what he was saying. "That is to say," Billy explained, "you now own the company. Which means that you continue to own the house, and the apartment, and the car, and . . . well, everything. It's all in trust, of course. But you own the trust. Naturally, there are some provisions for his children by Alicia, but these do not affect your overall position."

"In effect," Young said, "he also willed you his authority as Chairman and MD. Now, of course, it is quite impossible for a girl of twenty to be chairman of a large company, much less MD, however . . ."

The calm sea suddenly appeared to be very rough, and the deck was going up and down. Howard *had* loved her, after all. He had left her everything. Every single, little thing. The entire world. Would you like to sail forever? he had asked her when they had first met. Now he had enabled her to do that, or anything else she chose. "Joanna?" Billy asked, having seen her eyes glaze.

"Who else knows about this?" she asked.

"Why, no one, at the moment," Young said. "We thought it correct that you should be informed first. As soon as I get back to England I shall of course acquaint all the other shareholders with the situation . . ."

Alicia, Joanna thought. My God, she'll curdle in her cornflakes! "As I was saying," Young went on, "while no one would expect you to take on the duties of Chairman and MD, the gift, shall I say, the choice, is within your keeping. The appointment."

He paused, and there was another exchange of glances. Because each of them is hoping for such an appointment, Joanna realised. "Is there any legal impediment whereby I should not be Chairman and Managing Director myself?" she asked, very softly.

"Well . . . no. But the difficulties—"

"Tell me about them."

"Well . . . apart from the day-to-day running of the company, an immense task, believe me, there is the effect the news would have on the shares. They would tumble."

"Would that matter, so long as we did not have to sell any? If the company continued to make the same profits as before, it would not affect the dividends, would it?"

Young and Billy gazed at each other; such a simplistic approach was unknown to them. "It's not quite as simple as that," Young said, wiping his neck with his handkerchief. "The value of the company affects the amount of money we can borrow. You are probably not aware of it, but there is an overdraft. Two million pounds. Also, Howard was planning a flotation next year. We need a considerable capital influx, you see."

"Why?" She continued to pretend ignorance.

"We need to liquidate our borrowings. In addition, of our four ships, two are coming up for replacement. In fact, they have really reached the end of their working life, and can only be disposed of for scrap. So we need that financing from the city. Now, this tragedy will certainly create a problem. I haven't told Miller & Sparks myself as yet, but they will certainly know of it by now. I imagine the wires are red hot right this minute. So—"

"Who are Miller & Sparks?"

"The brokers who were going to handle the issue."

"And you think they will refuse to do that, now?"

"No, no," Young said hastily. "But . . . well . . . they'll want to know that a responsible person is in charge of the company."

"Are you saying that I am irresponsible, Mr Young?"

Young mopped away, and looked imploringly at Billy. Who came to his rescue. "Of course Peter doesn't mean that, Joanna. But you must look at it from the point of view of these hard-nosed city analysts. You, we, Caribee Shipping, are asking them to invest several million pounds in the company. In return, they will wish assurances that the profits will be maintained at least at their present level, and will hopefully increase as the new, improved ships come on the route. Now, the key to the maintenance of profits is management, control, strength of will at the top . . ." his voice faded away as he looked into Joanna's eyes.

"I quite understand," Joanna said. "What you are saying is that I will have to find a chairman and managing director who can command the confidence of the City of London."

"Well, if you put it that way . . . yes."

"Then you must give me a little while to consider. But we have that time, haven't we? Until we dock?"

The *Caribee Queen* left Barbados that evening, steaming into the Atlantic. In five days time they would be home. And by then . . . Joanna lay awake in her bunk that night, listening to the growl of the engines. She was alone in a four-berth cabin, because this was the cabin the Owner always occupied when he, or she, was at sea. And she was the Owner. It had all been too sudden for her to grasp that afternoon. She had refused to join Young and Billy and the other passengers for dinner, had dined alone in her cabin. She was faced with an immensity she could only consider in total privacy.

What had she and Howard worked out he was worth? Four million pounds! So, she was now worth four million pounds. She tried to envisage what four million pounds, in bank notes, might look like, stacked up in front of her and couldn't. Well, then, she tried to envisage how it could be spent. The most she had ever spent in one day was two thousand, five hundred pounds, on that glorious morning she had bought both Matilda and herself fur coats, herself some new outfits, and then treated them both to a bang-up lunch. If she spent two thousand, five hundred pounds a day, every day, from here on . . . she got out of bed, switched on the light, and sat down with a pad of the ship's notepaper and a pen. It would take her one thousand, six hundred days to go through the lot. That was less than five years! That didn't seem very long. But that took no account of the income coming in and of course she wasn't going to spend two thousand five hundred pounds a day, not for a single day, much less a thousand odd.

So, approach it from the other angle. She was twenty. Supposing she lived until she was eighty, she could . . . she got busy with her pen. She could spend sixty-six thousand, six hundred pounds every year before the money ran out. That was more than five thousand pounds a month, or more than a thousand pounds a week. That suddenly put everything in perspective. Tilly! What was Tilly going to say? What was Tilly going to *do*? Tilly would need controlling. So would her spending, if she was going to remain a millionairess. But so would the company.

The company! No doubt it was self-perpetuating, even if astronomically in debt. But only with the right MD who would be able to gain the confidence of the city. Such a man should not be hard to find. She didn't altogether trust either Young or Billy, not for their honesty, but for their ability. But there had to be someone . . . Why *not* her? She could take over the chairmanship simply by announcing it. The other shareholders – including Alicia, delicious thought –

would have to accept her decision. They might all sell their shares and quit. She wondered if it might be possible to own every share? But the suggestion was that the company would go straight down the drain without the backing of its stockbrokers and its bankers. Her big task would be to convince the City that she knew what she was about!

She got out of bed, put on her robe, opened the cabin door. The saloon was empty, with dimmed lights. She crossed it and opened the door on to the deck. Immediately the breeze plucked at her clothes and hair. But it was a self-created breeze, caused by the speed of the ship; the sea remained calm. And they were still far enough south for it to be warm. She climbed the ladder to the bridge, stood for a moment on the wing, looking through the open door at the quartermaster standing at the helm, and the officer of the watch, who was on the far side, leaning over the high table and writing in the log.

She drew a deep breath and stepped into the house. Both men turned in the same instant, jaws dropping. "Good morning," she said.

"Good heavens, you gave me a start, Mrs Edge," the Second Mate said. "Thought you were a ghost."

Both her nightgown and négligé were white satin, given her by Howard as a wedding present; he hadn't got around to tearing them off her before his death. "Is all well?" she asked.

"Oh, surely, Mrs Edge. No problems." He gestured at the starlit night, the broad path of the moon across the sparkling water. "Perfect night." He tapped the radar. "Nothing within forty miles of us."

"Then do you mind if I talk with you for a while?"

"Why, it'd be a pleasure, Mrs Edge." He waited, perhaps expectantly. Presumably he had never before been in the position of entertaining, on the bridge, a beautiful widow . . . who also happened to be his employer.

"I want you to show me, and tell me, and explain to me," Joanna said, "everything about navigation."

Second Mate Mullin swallowed. "Navigation, Mrs Edge? That's a very big subject."

"I know. But we have five days and nights before we reach Southampton, don't we?"

"Yes, ma'am," Mullin said, with sudden enthusiasm.

At dawn Joanna returned to her cabin, showered, and dressed herself. She had a quick breakfast, then went down to the engine room. She had already had First Mate Crowther, who had replaced Mullin at two for the morning watch, and been equally scandalised at what he was required to do, and had then got every bit as enthusiastic, inform Chief Engineer Wilson that she wished to meet him in his kingdom, and he was waiting for her, eyeing her somewhat suspiciously. "It's not all that clean down here, Mrs Edge."

"That's why I am wearing jeans, Mr Wilson."

She had also tied her hair up in a bandanna, and for the next two hours followed him about as he explained about temperatures, ratios, gauges, pressure and oil consumption, while she tried to put thoughts of latitude and longitude, currents and leeway, sextants and logarithmal tables, Greenwich Mean Time and Ship's Time, out of her mind, and replace them with boiler pressure and designated speed, fuel consumption and induced horsepower. "You going to remember all of this?" Wilson asked when they had finished.

"No," she admitted. "But I am going to come down here again tomorrow, and the day after, and the day after that, and you can show me it all again and again." He scratched his head.

Captain Heggie was waiting for her when she returned to her cabin for a wash after the engine room. "You're being a busy lady, Mrs Edge," he said. "Suborning my officers." But he grinned as he said it.

"I didn't want to disturb your beauty sleep," she said. "But now that you're up, there's a lot you can teach me, too. About cargoes and costs, routes and alternatives."

"You mean to run this line yourself?"

"Just let's say that I am interested in how it works, at every level. But if I did decide to take over, would you object?"

"I think it would be the best idea since sliced bread. Let's go up to my office."

Young and Billy were up by now, breakfasting with the other passengers in the saloon. They looked at Joanna quizzically as she accompanied the captain up to the bridge, but preferred not to make any comment at that moment. Joanna spent the rest of the morning looking at manifests and cost sheets. "I hate to say it," she remarked, "as I was born there, but the trade with BG is the weakest."

"They have the weakest economy. But it should pick up when the territories recover from the failure of federation." Heggie said.

"Is that really going to happen, Captain?"

"Given time."

"Time we don't seem to have. You don't think we should be tempted to look for other routes, other markets? My husband has spoken of dwindling profit margins in the Caribbean."

Heggie scratched his head. "That's not my province, Mrs Edge. But I have to say it would be a hell of a gamble. We have these routes, we have these customers. You'd have to get both local permission and guarantees to go elsewhere."

"Just a thought, Captain."

"We're hearing rumours that you've been all over this ship, from top to bottom," Billy said, as he and Young finally cornered her in her favourite relaxing position on the boat deck.

"Don't you think I should know all there is to know about one of my possessions?" she asked.

There was the usual exchange of glances. Neither man had yet worked out how to take her, seriously or as an irrelevance. But her mind was fast hardening. The decision was composed of several things. She felt that Howard would not have left everything to her had he not intended her to succeed him eventually, although obviously he could not possibly have expected it to happen so soon or so suddenly. Thus she felt guilty for her earlier appraisal that she was just a passing fancy, and was determined to prove herself worthy of his trust. There was the matter of the child she was certain was in her womb, something known only to her. That child was the entire future.

Then there was the very real understanding that if she appointed a chairman and managing director, he would certainly shunt her aside as an ignorant young woman, and seek to run the company his way. While she had so many ideas on how to run the company *her* way. More than any of those, however, was the desire to meet, and beat, a challenge. To show the world, and particularly a few members of it, such as Aunt Ethel and Alicia, and even Matilda, who always treated her as a child, what she could do. She was a hick from the furthest possible sticks. But she wasn't stupid, and she knew what she wanted. Well, she was going to get what she wanted. Get? She would take.

She smiled at the two men. "By the way, I have informed the radio operator, through the captain, that I do not wish any business matters transmitted from the ship for the remainder of the voyage. As you said, Mr Young, the wires are no doubt red-hot in London. Let's keep them that way. After all, we'll be home in four days."

"While thousands are being wiped off the value of the company shares, every one of those days?"

She gave him a sweet smile. "That's my problem, isn't it? Tomorrow is Christmas Day. Lunch with me."

They wandered off, disgruntled, and she checked with Captain Heggie. "What time are we supposed to dock?"

"Six in the morning, Mrs Edge."

"On Monday."

"That's right. Sorry about the hour, but it means we can start unloading within a couple of hours of clearing customs."

"I think it's a splendid time to dock, Captain. Now tell me, do you have an up-to-date *Who's Who* on board?"

"I have last year's. We need to be able to identify our passengers, when we can."

"May I look at it please?"

She went into the radio shack, where the operator hastily stood to attention. "I have some telegrams for you to send. And I would like the replies brought directly to me."

"Of course, Mrs Edge." She wrote out the messages, gave themn to him. Then it was simply a matter of waiting.

Early as it was, Miriam, Matilda and William were on the dockside waiting for her. They were allowed on board by a sympathetic customs officer, now aware that he was dealing with the Owner's family. "Oh, my darling." Miriam held her close. "Howard . . . ?"

"He's on board," Joanna said. "He'll be buried in the family plot."

"You're so calm . . ."

"Well, I've had ten days to come to terms with the situation."

"Jo!" Matilda hugged her and kissed her. "I am so sorry for you." William said nothing, just held her for several minutes.

"You may go ashore whenever you please, Mrs Edge," Captain Heggie said. "We'll see to your gear. And—"

"We'll look after that, Joanna," Billy said. "There'll have to be an embalming, and, well—"

"What are you doing on board?" Matilda asked.

"Billy was Howard's man," Joanna said. "Now he's mine. Well, in a manner of speaking." The family stared at her. "I shall want to see you, whenever you've finished unloading, Captain Heggie"

"Of course, Mrs Edge. Just name the date and time."

"Keep in touch with the office," Joanna said. Once again the family stared at her. She smiled at them. "Shall we go?"

They followed her down the gangplank, to where the Rolls waited. Billy looked as if he would have liked to join them, but Joanna merely smiled at him, and closed the door. "Where to first, Mrs Edge?" asked the chauffeur.

"Harrods."

"Yes, ma'am."

"Harrods?" Miriam and Matilda spoke together.

"I need widow's weeds," Joanna explained. "I didn't take anything black on my honeymoon."

"But . . . Harrods?" Miriam was aghast.

"I think you should know," Joanna said, "that I am now the Chairman and Managing Director of Caribee Shipping. In fact, I own the company, to all intents and purposes."

Now their stares came at her as if she was a stranger. Well, she supposed, she was, now, to them.

"You own the company?" Matilda, predictably, was first to recover; Joanna could just imagine her brain tumbling over itself as she tried to determine what that might mean for her.

"Howard left me all his shares, yes."

"And you're going to run the company yourself?" William was delighted.

"I have that in mind, although there are certain things to be sorted out."

"Wowee!"

"But, you can't—" Miriam began.

"Don't say it, Mums, please. I can do anything I please, if I have enough guts and determination. Shouldn't you be in school, Willie?"

"They gave me the day off to meet you."

"Well, I'm sure you don't want to hang about women trying on clothes. Go to the games department and buy yourself something. Tell them to bill it to me."

William gulped and hurried off, and the three women swept inside, Miriam looking, as always when she entered this store, like a frightened rabbit.

"There's so much we have to talk about," Matilda ventured.

"I know," Joanna said. "We'll have a powwow after the funeral."

"Not till then?"

"I have a lot to do today," Joanna pointed out.

She bought herself three black dresses in varying styles and for varying occasions, and a black turban into which she could fit her hair. The assistant was most apologetic when she presented her card. "I'm not sure—"

"Telephone Caribee Shipping," Joanna told her. "Ask for Mr Young, and ask him if that card is still valid."

"How embarrassing," Miriam whispered.

"Not at all. It's correct business procedure. Everyone knows my credit is backed by Howard's. What they don't yet know is that Howard's credit is now mine."

The assistant came hurrying back. "So many apologies, Mrs Edge. It's just that—"

"Don't give it a thought," Joanna told her. "Now," she said, "I am going to drop you all home. I have some appointments."

"Aren't you going to come in?" Miriam asked. "There's so much—"

"Later," Joanna reminded her.

They dropped Miriam and William first, then drove to Matilda's flat. "I don't know whether to be over the moon or under it," Matilda confessed.

"Just remain absolutely calm," Joanna said.

"Like you. You really are something, little sister."

She was setting up to dominate. But Joanna just smiled. "I'm not little any longer, Tilly."

The car stopped. "About my work," Matilda said.

"Are you on tonight?"

"Yes. I'd like to quit."

"I wouldn't do that yet," Joanna said. "I don't have Howard's contacts yet. It might take me longer to find you a new job."

Matilda glared at her. "You are a bitch."

"I'm feeling my way," Joanna told her.

# Chapter Seven

# The Bargain

"His Highness will see you now, Mrs Edge." The secretary was English, very prim and proper, in her mid-forties. Hasim obviously did not mix work and play. Joanna was not sure if that was a good thing or not, in her position.

He was on his feet, standing in front of his desk, in a large, light office, huge windows overlooking London. "Joanna!" He came forward to embrace her. "I am so terribly sorry. When I got your wire, I just could not believe it." His eyes, as she had anticipated, roamed up and down the trim black dress she had just bought, settling on the black turban beneath which her hair was entirely concealed.

So here I am, she thought. Joanna Edge, *femme fatale*? Or Joanna Edge, blatant whore. That verdict would depend on how successful she was. "Thank you."

He held her hand and led her to a chair. "And you actually saw it happen? How terrible for you."

"It's all a bit hazy now."

"I can imagine." He sat beside her. "So . . . there is no trouble, is there? If there is anything I can do to help . . ."

"There is no trouble, Hasim. But I do need your help."

"You have but to ask."

"Well, I should tell you that I intend to manage the company myself."

Hasim's mouth made a small O. "Can you do this?"

"There is no legal reason why I should not. I suppose there is, in your country?"

"I'm not sure there is any legal reason there, either. It's just that no woman in my country would ever dream of attempting such a thing."

"But do you have any prejudices against dealing with a woman, in England?"

"Of course I do not. It is necessary all the time, nowadays. But there is also the question of your age . . ."

"I am legally an adult."

"Experience?"

"I shall get that. I'm working on it already. But I understand that almost everyone with whom I come into contact will hold your point of view."

He held her hands. "My dear Joanna, I wish only to help you. I was merely pointing out the obstacles."

"There are others. Caribee Shipping hasn't been doing too well."

He frowned. "Howie always gave the impression that he was on a roll."

"Howie was great at giving impressions. Trouble is, I think he believed them himself. I haven't seen the books yet, but as far as I can gather, the situation is this: profits are falling, partly because of the general situation in the West Indies, and partly because at least two of our fleet aren't up to it any more. They're costing us more to keep them running than they can possibly earn."

"Well, as to the West Indies, I know they are going through a period of uncertainty at the moment, since the collapse of the federation—"

"I don't believe they are going to recover all that quickly, Hasim. Not from what I've heard."

Hasim released her hand to ring a bell. "You must let me take you out to lunch."

She smiled. "I'm not that poor, yet."

"I would still be honoured." He gave his secretary instructions, and the door closed again. "But when you get your new ships—"

"Am I going to get new ships?"

"Howie spoke of a flotation—"

"We have a kind of chicken and egg situation," Joanna said. "There is no hope of us improving our financial situation, even if trade picks up, if we don't get those ships. At the present time, there is no hope of us getting those ships unless trade and profits pick up. What is more, there seems *absolutely* no hope of a flotation with a twenty-year-old managing directress in charge."

"So you would like me to underwrite some of the shares."

"Can you?

"I'm afraid it would only be a very small part of what you need."

"Then that is not the answer, although I am very grateful for the offer. But I think I have a possible solution."

"Tell me."

"When I leave here, Hasim, I must go to see, first of all, my stockbrokers, and secondly, my bankers. As we have agreed, they are both likely to take a very downbeat view of my situation. I need to present them with something that will make them believe that Caribee Shipping is going up, not down. We've agreed ships alone won't do it, while Caribbean trade is down. But if I could tell them that I have secured an entirely new trade route, one with a burgeoning and spreading economy, from which we could not fail to make a growing profit, that might just swing the odds in my favour."

Hasim released her hands, got up and sat down behind his desk. "You would be plunging into areas of which you and your captains know nothing. I mean, physically."

"They can navigate. So the waters around the Persian Gulf can be treacherous. You don't have hurricanes, right?"

Hasim pinched his lip. "There is also the matter that politically, the area is not as stable as the Caribbean."

"You reckon? What about the missile crisis a couple of years ago? And if that's been sorted out, Castro is still running riot."

"That is true, I suppose. One does tend to worry about personal problems to the exclusion of all else."

"Then you'll give me a guarantee, and slots?"

"It would mean treading on some corns," Hasim said, thoughtfully. "As it happens, the company that is presently handling most of our commodity trade – we are obviously not talking about oil here – has been letting us down somewhat over the past year or two. But it would cause quite a stir were we to put them out altogether—"

"I'm quite prepared to compete."

"You cannot compete, my dear Joanna. You can only replace. All shipping contracts in and out of Qadir are government controlled. So, you either have the backing of the government, or you have nothing."

"And you are the government."

He smiled. "I am a part of the government. Perhaps I could persuade my father . . . but it would be difficult."

Joanna drew a deep breath. "I'm not really any good at bargaining, Hasim. I have no experience of it. I know I have only one asset which I feel would be of any value to you."

"My dear Joanna," he protested, "you know how much I adore you. But . . . you are a widow of not yet a week."

"Then perhaps you would be prepared to wait a little while. I will not break any promises I may make to you, if you will not break any promises you may make to me."

His gaze drifted from her head down to her thighs, which were all of her he could see at the moment, and then back up again. "I would be prepared to wait a very long time for you." He gave a quick smile. "I already have done so."

"Then, do we have an understanding?"

"It will have to be a *little* while," Hasim reminded her. "I have my father and my uncles to persuade."

"I can be patient. If you can. But I will need some sort of time scale. For the bankers."

"I would say . . . four months. I will have to go to Qadir."

"Four months," Joanna said, half to herself. In four months time she would be showing.

"Will that be satisfactory?" Now he was anxious.

"Four months will be perfectly satisfactory," she said. "But . . . I also need ready cash. A good deal of ready cash. I must order the new ships right away. Will you back an increase in my overdraft? To be repaid out of the flotation?"

"Of course you may count on me."

"It's a large amount," she said. "I will need an additional four million." She held her breath.

Hasim waved his hand, and she realised she was moving into financial circles of which she had no experience.

"You mean, I can ask my bankers to call on you for an endorsement?" She had to get it absolutely straight.

"Of course. However," he said, "I would like it to be a confidential matter, between you, me and your bankers. At least for the time being"

"I will have to tell my board. And my stockbrokers."

"I understand that. I was thinking of the media." He stood up, came round his desk. Joanna stood also, and tensed herself. But to her surprise, he merely stroked her cheek and the line of her jaw with his forefinger, then stroked the bodice of her dress, knowing exactly where her nipples were, then kissed her gently on the lips. "Shall we lunch?" He had taken possession, in his own way.

Joanna only just made her next appointment; Hasim wanted to have champagne with his meal. "You understand," he said, "much as I would like to, I cannot marry you, Joanna. As the heir to the throne of Qadir, I must marry a Muslim. I don't suppose—"

"I'm afraid not," she said. "I take my religion very seriously."

How easy was it to lie convincingly, where someone was as sincere as Hasim ben Raisul abd Abdullah.

"But you will always be my first choice," he assured her.

"As you will be mine." In for a penny, in for a pound, she reflected.

* * *

"Mrs Edge. A terrible tragedy." Jonathan Prim's voice was just that, as well as a trifle cold.

"Thank you."

"Please sit down." Joanna did so, reflecting that neither the office nor the chairs were a patch on Hasim's. But then, Johnathan Prim was only a stockbroker. He was also an exact replica of his name, from long face and body to pince-nez. "Now," he said, placing his elbows on the desk and his fingertips together.

Joanna decided to take the initiative. "I assume Peter Young has been in touch with you?"

"Yes, he has. With some rather unusual, and, I may say, disturbing, intimations."

"You object to my taking over the company, Mr Prim?"

"My dear young lady, as you have a controlling share interest, you may do whatever you choose. But I am afraid you may find yourself a little short of support. I assume you have already spoken to the bank?" Of course he would know she had not.

"No, I haven't, Mr Prim. I have an appointment for tomorrow morning."

"I see. Well, then—"

"When I do see the bank people," Joanna said, "it will be necessary for me to have a firm assurance on the share issue."

"I'm afraid that will have to be left in abeyance for the time being, Mrs Edge. Until things have sorted themselves out."

"You mean, right now, no one will take it up. At least, in sufficient bulk to make it worth while."

"I'm afraid that is exactly the point, Mrs Edge. A flotation like this needs, as perhaps you are unaware, a substantial underwriting. A big insurance company, a big pension fund, these are the people we need to get in on the ground floor, to guarantee to us that they will take up a substantial proportion of the stock to be issued. City businessmen, well, they're a hard-headed lot, and while they may be personally sympathetic to you in your – ah – frightfully sad circumstances, they will still wish to see a viable return, at the end of the day."

"What exactly will they have against me, Mr Prim?"

"Well . . . apart from your age and inexperience, of course—"

"And my sex?" she asked, softly.

"Well, obviously it is unusual to have a woman, a very young woman, stepping straight into the chairman's shoes. But," he hurried on, "there is also the matter of the viability of your ships—"

"Which the share issue is intended to address."

"Oh, quite. But then there is the profit margin, steadily shrinking over the past three years—"

"But my husband, my late husband, was still intending to go ahead with the flotation, with your backing, I understand."

"Well . . ." Prim looked a trifle embarrassed. "Mr Edge had a way with him. He had planned a vast meeting of present and potential investors, at which he had intended to convince them that an upturn was just around the corner."

"Do you think he would have succeeded?"

"Yes, I do. Which is why my firm was prepared to issue the flotation."

"And you do not think I can do that?"

"Well . . . have you ever done anything like this before?"

"One must start somewhere," Joanna said, equably. "But Howard would have had to offer these potential investors some facts to support his case, would he not?"

"He would have pointed to an almost certain upturn in West Indian trade as the territories recover from the idea of federation."

"But he could not guarantee that would happen." Prim took off his pince-nez to stare at her. "My information is that it is not likely to," Joanna said. "At least in the short term."

"Did Mr Edge know this?"

"I think he must have done. But as you will know, Howie was always the supreme optimist. As you just said, he had a way with him."

"But . . . if the West Indian trade remains depressed, that would cause a very serious situation. For Caribee Shipping, certainly."

"I agree with you."

"Well, then . . . in the circumstances, Mrs Edge, I am going to have to advise my partners that in no way can we agree to handle a share issue in the name of Caribee Shipping."

"Not even if I told you that the Company is about to undertake a vast expansion, into new trade routes, with guaranteed profits?"

Prim allowed himself a self-satisfied smile. "Dreams are wonderful soporifics for tragedy, Mrs Edge."

"What I am going to tell you, and what you will soon hear from another source," Joanna said, "is entirely confidential. For the next four months. But you were not planning the issue for at least six, were you not? So that will not be a problem. What I wish you to do is prepare the issue and leave the rest to me."

"My dear young lady—"

Joanna refused to be annoyed by his constant use of the word young. "You have heard of the Emirate of Qadir?"

"Well, of course I have."

"It is one of the richest emirates in the Gulf, is it not?"

"Indeed it is."

"And I imagine you are aware that the Emirate's business affairs in the West are handled by Prince Hasim ben Raisul abd Abdullah, the heir?"

"Of course."

"Have you ever met Prince Hasim?"

"Yes, I have. May I ask—"

"I would like you to pick up your telephone, and dial Prince Hasim's personal number. I have it here." She opened her handbag and took out the card. "He will answer the phone himself. When he does, I would like you to ask him if it is being arranged for Caribee Shipping to take over the handling of the major part of Qadir's commodity trade. Providing, of course, that our new ships are on order. In this regard, Prince Hasim is prepared to underwrite a certain percentage of the share issue himself."

Prim continued to stare at her for several seconds, then he reached out his hand and picked up the phone.

The Rolls was waiting for her, and Joanna had Charlie drive her to the London flat. She didn't have keys, but he did. "You going to be all right here by yourself, Mrs Edge?" he asked.

"I'll be fine," Joanna said. "Just don't tell anyone where I am, Charlie."

"You can count on me, Mrs Edge. If there is anything I can do to help . . ."

A big handsome hulk of a man who was relishing his change of employer. And should he not, in view of what she was contemplating? What she had indeed set in motion? Save that she did not intend to go through with it, because of that saving grace in her womb. That would have to be confirmed right away.

"I know you will always be around, Charlie," she said, and closed and double-locked the door behind her, taking a deep breath. From the very start she had thought this flat the most elegant place she had ever seen. And now it was hers!

She kicked off her shoes, threw her mink across a chair, opened the fridge. Naturally there was a bottle of champagne in there. Several. Howie had always been prepared for a celebration. She opened a bottle, poured herself a glass, and sat down beside the phone. She was both curious and apprehensive. She wound the tape back to the beginning, let it play. Friends, condolences. Friends, condolences. Then . . . "I think you and I need to have a little chat, Joanna. Call me." Alicia. Of all the goddamed cheek.

"Joanna, oh my dear, dear Joanna. What can I do?" Andy Gosling! What could he do, indeed.

More condolences. She flicked the tape off, opened Howard's desk, hunted through his diaries and appointment books, found what she wanted, dialled. An Indian? Well, if he was good enough for Howie he had to be good enough for her. Save that the thought . . . but she was a big girl now, and growing bigger every moment.

Besides, now the idea had taken root, as it were, it was becoming more exciting by the second.

"Dr Alva's surgery."

"My name is Edge," Joanna said. "Joanna Edge."

"Oh, Mrs Edge," the receptionist gushed. "We are all so very sorry. What can we do to help?"

"I would like an appointment with Dr Alva, for tomorrow morning."

"Tomorrow morning? Oh . . ." There was the rustle of pages being turned. "Tomorrow is full. We could fit you in a week today . . ."

"Tomorrow," Joanna said.

"Ah . . ." There was an audible gulp on the end of the line. "Would you hold a moment?" Joanna waited. The girl came back on the line. "Dr Alva can fit you in, Mrs Edge. At eleven."

"Thank you," Joanna said. She drank some champagne. There was still so much to be done. Not least about Howie. She dialled Caribee Shipping. "Mr Young, please," she told the switchboard girl.

"I'm afraid Mr Young is in a meeting, If you will leave your name and telephone number—"

"This is Mrs Edge," Joanna said. "I wish to speak with Mr Young, now."

Once again the gulp was audible at the end of the line. "Of course, Mrs Edge, right away."

Am I being a bitch? Joanna wondered. But it was such fun. For so long she had been frightened of her shadow . . . now the shadows were all frightened of her.

"Mrs Edge! Where have you been? I have been trying to get hold of you all day."

She simply had to make him drop that didactic tone. "You mean Mr Prim hasn't called you?"

"No." Young's voice was flooded with curiosity.

"He's probably suffering from shock. If it is of interest to you, I had a meeting with him this afternoon, and Miller & Sparks will be handling our stock issue this coming summer. What I would like you to do, therefore—"

"Pardon me, Mrs Edge. Did you say they will be handling the share issue?"

"Is there something the matter with this line?"

"Do forgive me. But I spoke with them this morning, and they definitely declined."

"Amazing what a difference a few hours can make. Now, I've been rather busy today, but I would like to come in as soon as possible to have a look at the books, and other things. Can you tell me when the funeral is?"

"Ah . . ." She could almost hear his brain whirring. This woman doesn't even know when her husband is being buried? "Wednesday morning, at the village church."

"I see. Well, I have an appointment tomorrow morning, and another tomorrow afternoon. I assume you are going to the funeral?"

"Of course, Mrs Edge."

"Yes. Well, we can have a chat then. And I will be in the office on Thursday morning. But that is three days away, and there are things to be done. I wish you to put out tenders for the building of two new Caribee ships immediately. The designs can be roughly the same as the existing ships, improved where possible, but special attention must be paid to the refrigeration plants and the air conditioning."

Another telephonic gulp. "Are you sure this is wise, Mrs Edge? Whatever firm takes up the contract will require a down payment."

"How soon will the tenders be back? I wish you to emphasise that it is urgent."

"Well . . . within a few weeks, to be sure."

"Make it three weeks maximum, or there is no contract."

"Three weeks! Well, I suppose we could string along our decision for another month or two."

"We will make our decision in twenty-four hours, Peter."

"But . . . the deposit!" Now he was almost wailing.

"I will arrange it. Please get on with it, now."

Joanna hung up, drank some more champagne. There was still so much to be done. She telephoned a florist, ordered an outsize wreath. Presumably all she had to do was make her wishes known to Howie's secretary and all this would be taken care of for her, but she hadn't yet met Howie's secretary . . . and she was enjoying doing things for herself. Never had she been on such a high.

The doorbell rang, and she sat up straight. There were only about half a dozen people in the world who knew she might be in this flat at this moment, and she wasn't sure she wanted to see any of them. She took a deep breath, stood up, straightened her dress, adjusted her turban, which she had quite forgotten to take off, and opened the door.

"I've been looking everywhere for you," Matilda said.

"So, it seems, have a lot of people."

"I only just remembered where you probably were. Where you had to be, in fact, as you never went home. Or out to Caribee House."

"Well, come in." Joanna closed and locked the door again. "Champagne?"

Matilda gazed at the bottle in consternation. "Who's been here with you?"

"How many glasses do you count?"

"You've drunk nearly a whole bottle of champagne all on your own?!"

"I'm prepared to let you help me with the second one." Joanna took it from the fridge, and another flute from the cupboard, poured. "Or do you have to be sober?"

Matilda took the glass, sat down, and crossed her knees. "That's what I wanted to talk to you about."

"Tell me."

"Well . . . Jo . . . you can't really want me to go on parading around naked in front of a lot of old weirdos?"

"I thought you enjoyed it. Or at least, what came afterwards."

"I never did. I just wanted to make some money. Be independent. Didn't you always want that?"

"I suppose I did."

"Only you went about it the right way. Jo, let me quit."

Joanna raised her eyebrows. "Isn't that up to you?"

"I can't quit unless I have another job. Let me work for you."

"Can you type?"

"You know I can't type."

"Have you any experience of PR work?"

"Well, no."

"Then I don't see—"

"Jo, I'm your sister!"

"I know that, Tilly. But I have to be able to employ you as *something*."

"Well . . ." Matilda drank some champagne. "Let me be your bodyguard."

"My *what*?"

"Howie always had a couple of heavies knocking about. Where are they, by the way?"

Joanna shrugged. "Haven't a clue. I haven't seen them since I got back. And frankly, I've been too busy to look."

"But Howie felt he needed them."

"I think they just gave him a sense of power. Although, when you're a well-known and very wealthy man, I suppose there is always the risk of trouble."

"You are now a very wealthy woman," Matilda pointed out. "And I imagine you'll soon be fairly well-known, as well."

Joanna considered; she hadn't really thought about that aspect of things, as yet. "Mmm," she commented. "I suppose I'll have to keep them on."

"They went with Howie everywhere. Even to the loo, when he was out. You going to have them go to the loo with you? A bodyguard should always be there. You can't have men always there, unless you intend to sleep with them. And even if you did, as there's more than one, it would cause trouble. And think of the scandal. Whereas, I'll be with you, always, and no one will be able to say a word."

Joanna realised she was serious. She put down her glass, held Matilda's hands. "Tilly, you can't be a bodyguard."

"Why not?"

"Because you're a woman! What would you do if a heavy came in here now? Apart from screaming for help?"

"I'd lay him out."

Joanna stared at her with her mouth open.

"I'm a brown belt at karate," Matilda explained.

"You? You never told me. How did you do that?"

"I attend classes," Matilda explained. "Well, you see, a girl in my position needs to be able to take care of herself. You have no idea what weirdos sometimes ask me out."

"Have you ever had to use it?"

Matilda giggled. "Only once. Boy, it was fun. I'd go on and get my black belt if you'd pay for the lessons."

Joanna considered her for several seconds. But she had long been aware of the overwhelming loneliness of her position, a loneliness that could only get worse now she was the Chairman of Caribee Shipping. And Matilda was quite right in saying that a male confidante was only practical if he was also a bed partner, because that would be what he'd start thinking of very rapidly. Over the past couple of years she and Tilly had undoubtedly drifted apart, mainly because she didn't approve of Tilly's lifestyle. But they were still very close, as sisters should be. And if Tilly was prepared to give up her lifestyle and adopt *hers* . . . "There would have to be rules," she said.

"Tell me."

"No sleeping around."

Matilda pouted. "A girl needs her sex."

"Find yourself a steady. He doesn't have to be permanent. But while he's in situ, he's the one."

"Well . . ." Matilda frowned. "Is that what you're going to do?"

"I haven't decided yet. Whatever I do, it's not going to be for a while. I'm pregnant."

"You are what?"

"I'm having it checked out tomorrow. But I'm pretty sure."

"Holy Jesus! What are you going to do?"

"What do you mean?"

"You're not going to have the child?"

"Of course I am. I'm a married woman. It's Howie's child. The eventual heir to Caribee Shipping."

"You really think Caribee Shipping is going to be around in twenty years' time?"

"I have no doubt whatsoever of it. So here are rules numbers two and three. Whatever I tell you, whatever you hear within the company, is strictly confidential. That includes my baby, for the time being."

"But Mums—"

"I will tell Mums when I'm ready. If she finds out before then, you're fired." Matilda joined the gulping club. "Rule number three is total loyalty to me, and to the company, at all times. Got me?" Matilda nodded, brain obviously whirling as she wondered what she had got herself into. "And rule number four," Joanna went on, "is, when I am engaged in any business deals, you don't say a word. And I mean that."

She knew that would be the most difficult of the rules for Matilda to keep. "Is that all?" Matilda asked, somewhat sulkily.

"I'm sure there will be more, but those are all I can think of at the moment."

"What will you pay me? This club I'm at is paying me forty pounds a night."

"That is a hell of a lot of money," Joanna pointed out. "I will pay you thirty a week."

"Oh, come now, Jo! I'm your sister!"

"Which is why you're getting the job. And that is take home pay.

Your living, as you will be living with me, will be all found. I think that is a very good deal."

Matilda considered. "Well, I suppose it is," she said at last.

"Right. As of this moment, you're employed. How do you resign from your job?"

Matilda shrugged. "I suppose I just don't turn up."

"Right. You'd better prepare us something to eat."

"Oh. Right." Matilda got up. "What's our plan?"

"For tonight? Eat, and then get drunk, and then go to sleep," Joanna told her.

"Hm," said Dr Alva. "Hm."

Joanna rolled off the examination table and put on her knickers. "Don't worry about it. It's not diabetes. It's pure alcohol. My sister and I tied one on last night. I don't mean to make a practice of it."

Dr Alva sat behind his desk. He was older than she had expected, and wore horn-rimmed spectacles. But his smoothly brushed hair remained jet black, and he had lively eyes – as well as soft hands. "I will have to make a note of it."

"To show whom?" Joanna finished dressing.

"No one, Mrs Edge. But if I am going to be your doctor, I must have a totally accurate record of your health."

"Is anything the matter with it? My health?"

"At the moment, absolutely nothing. You are a very healthy young woman. However, if you consistently maintain a sugar level this high—"

"I've told you, it won't happen again. And if I were to come back and see you again tomorrow, it would all be gone, wouldn't it?"

"I would say so."

"Then there's nothing to worry about, right? Just tell me it hasn't hurt the baby?"

"I doubt very much that one such – ah – overindulgence would have any lasting effects."

"Thank you, doctor. Now tell me how old my baby is."

"Eh?"

"When would you say the baby was conceived?"

"Well, it is impossible to say, exactly. But from the size of the foetus . . . you say you have only missed two periods? And the next would be due next week. Yes. I would say your baby was conceived just under three months ago."

"Which would be early October last year."

"That would be about right."

"Will you make a note of that, please, on my records?"

He raised his eyebrows.

"I like to be exact about these things," she told him.

"What did he say?" Matilda had been forced to remain in the waiting room.

"That we should stick to one bottle a night, at least until the baby is born."

"But there is a baby?"

"I told you there was."

"Four million?" John Andrews scratched the back of his head, where the hair was thinning. "I think we need to consider this very carefully, Mrs Edge." He looked, somewhat apologetically, from Joanna to Matilda, seated in front of his desk. Apart from the introduction, he could tell at a glance that they were sisters, but it was always embarrassing to have to refuse a customer in front of other people, no matter how closely they might be related.

"There is nothing to consider, Mr Andrews," Joanna said. "I am in the process of ordering two new ships, and I will need to make a substantial down payment on them. There are also some other matters that need attending to."

"Don't you think that it would be a wise idea to hold off ordering the ships until after the share issue?" Andrews asked, looking as placatory as he could. "Then you – we – will know exactly how you stand. The fact is, you see, that with the overdraft currently standing at two million . . . you were aware of this?"

"I have been told," Joanna said. "I do not formally take control of the company until the day after tomorrow."

"Yes," Andrews said, getting a world of comment into the single word. "I am not sure that is altogether wise, either, Mrs Edge."

"Please don't start the inexperienced female business, Mr Andrews. I've had that. The present overdraft is secured by our existing ships, is it not?"

"That is so. But frankly, with two of them reaching the end of their useful life—"

"Which is why they have to be replaced."

"—and the last profit and loss statement so disappointing," he went on as if she hadn't interrupted, "we are not sure that our security is adequate. Certainly not for such a large increase in the loan."

"I am prepared to offer you my personal holding in the company. I think we are talking of four million pounds."

"Ah, no, not at this moment. These are early days, of course, but the shares have already been marked down by a considerable amount in view of your husband's death. What will happen over the next few weeks, when the rumour that you are taking over the company yourself becomes fact, well, I don't really know what to say. But I would certainly anticipate a sharp fall in the share price. A considerable fall."

"I see. Then I will have to offer you some other security, Mr Andrews, although I am bound to say that I consider your treatment of an old and valued customer to be disappointing, to say the least."

"Well—" Andrews' face reddened.

"However, I cannot let my personal feelings get in the way of my business," Joanna said, and opened her handbag. "You know Prince Hasim ben Raisul abd Abdullah?"

"Well, not personally."

"However, you may have some estimate of his personal wealth?"

"Well, yes, Mrs Edge. But—"

"He will endorse the loan for me. You may ascertain this by calling him on that number. He will receive your call, I promise you."

Andrews picked up the card and appeared to goggle at it. Matilda was goggling at them both. "The Prince will endorse a personal loan, from us to you, in the amount of four million pounds?" Andrews obviously felt a great need to get his facts straight.

"That is what I have said he will do, yes."

Again Andrews regarded the piece of cardboard rather as if it was a poisoned chalice. "Do you mind if I call him now?"

"I'd appreciate it."

Andrews picked up his private phone, dialled, waited. "Ah," he said. "I would like to speak with Prince Hasim, please. My name is Andrews, and I am calling on behalf of Mrs Joanna Edge." He listened. "I see." He looked at Joanna over the phone, cupping his hand around the mouthpiece. "The Prince is not in at this time." His tone was triumphant.

"Then find out when he will be in, and call him back," Joanna suggested.

He glared at her, but moved his hand. "May I ask when the Prince will be in? Not until tomorrow. Yes. Well then . . . excuse me?" Once again he listened. "Good heavens," he remarked, "will he really? That would be most awfully kind of him. Thank you." He replaced the phone, and gazed at Joanna with the air of a man who has just seen a miracle. "The Prince's secretary says he will call me. Prince Hasim, calling me! Tomorrow."

"Well, then," Joanna said, "I would be obliged if you would let me know the moment you have his consent to the loan. I shall be out in Berkshire tomorrow morning, attending my husband's funeral. But I shall be at Caribee Shipping on Thursday morning. Call me there."

Matilda managed to keep quiet until they reached the Rolls. Then she gasped, "This Prince—"

"You must remember Hasim? He was at that pool party we went to."

"I remember him very well," Matilda said. "He also comes to the club where I dance."

Joanna turned her head, sharply, as the car drove away. "You haven't let him have you?"

"Well . . ." Matilda looked sulky. "He's very rich. As you seem to have found out."

"As I seem to have what's left of every worthwhile man in London," Joanna snapped.

"And now you're letting him have you."

"I have promised to become his mistress," Joanna said, "in return for certain considerations, yes."

"You are a little . . . I can't think of the word."

"I am a woman who is making her way in the world. However, I do not become his mistress until after a decent period of mourning for Howard. Hasim knows and understands this."

"But—"

"Yes," Joanna said. "I think about four months is a decent mourning period. He has agreed to this."

"You'll be showing in four months."

"Absolutely."

"And you think he'll let you off the hook?"

"Of course. Hasim is both a gentleman and constrained by certain religous considerations. I will be unclean."

"And as such all bets will be off. Including his endorsements."

"Not in the least. My promise remains, to become his mistress as soon as possible."

"Which could be several months."

"At the very least. I intend to feed my baby."

Matilda shook her head in wonderment. "My baby sister. But I still think you're gambling for high stakes. He won't wait forever."

"He'll wait for a year or so. Who knows what may have happened by then? Anyway, what's the big deal? What's he like in bed?"

"Different," Matilda said.

They drove out to Berkshire that evening.

"Oh, Mrs Edge." Cummings, the butler, was there to great her. He and all the servants were wearing black armbands.

"I wish I could have been here sooner," Joanna said. "But there was so much to be done. My dear Mrs Partridge." She embraced the housekeeper. "It's so good to be home, even in these circumstances."

"It is good to have you back, Mrs Edge," Mrs Partridge said. "The – ah—" she looked at Cummings.

"The master arrived last night, madam," Cummings said.

"Where is he?"

Cummings led the way as if he himself were the undertaker. Joanna and Matilda followed, and then the servants. The casket was on the billiard table.

"I'm afraid that the undertaker advised us not to open the coffin, madam," Cummings said, as Joanna moved forward. "The journey, and, well—"

"Yes," Joanna said. "I understand."

"Would you care for a drink, madam?"

"A glass of brandy," Joanna said.

He nodded to one of the footmen, who hurried off, and then escorted Joanna to a chair in the winter lounge, Matilda as always following faithfully at her shoulder.

"I took the liberty of having the service orders printed up," he said. Joanna took the sheet of stiff paper and looked at it. "I hope you approve, madam."

"Oh, indeed I do."

The footman appeared with a tray. Joanna took her goblet and held it in both hands, Matilda anxiously following her example. "Would you care to see the dinner menu, madam?"

"I'm sure it will be fine, Cummings," Joanna said. "How many are we expecting for lunch tomorrow?"

"I'm afraid I cannot say for sure, madam. I am allowing for twenty. But we will be able to squeeze in more if necessary."

"Of course. Thank you, Cummings."

He bowed and withdrew, to be replaced by Mrs Partridge. "Excuse me, madam, but will Miss Grain be staying the night?"

"Miss Grain will be living here from now on, Mrs Partridge. Put her in the room next to mine." Mrs Partridge withdrew.

"I don't have anything to wear tomorrow," Matilda said.

"The service is at eleven. There'll be time for you to run up to town and get something," Joanna said, and drank some brandy.

"You know, you are quite frightfully relaxed," Matilda said. "About everything. I'd be having the screaming heebeejeebies."

"About what?" Joanna asked, getting up and prowling about the room. "Oh, it's all taking a bit of getting used to. I suppose I'm not quite *compos mentis*, at the moment."

"You certainly appear *compos mentis*."

"I figured out what had to be done. That's easy, when you've nothing to lose. It's coming to terms with what you actually are, at the moment; that's difficult, when there's been so much . . ." She whirled to face her sister. "You have no idea what I'm talking about, do you?"

"Not really."

"Well . . ." Joanna finished her brandy, set down the glass, whirled again, pointed at the full-length mirror on the opposite wall. "Howard told me that was a family heirloom. It's worth a thousand pounds."

"I can believe that," Matilda said.

"And now, do you know, I could walk right up to that mirror with a hammer, and hit it as hard as I like."

"Jo," Matilda said uneasily.

Joanna grinned. "I'm not going to. But I could. And nobody could stop me, or criticise me afterwards, at least to my face. And if the insurance refused to pay, well, who cares? You with me? It's to be in such a position. For the first time in my life. But with the knowledge that if I play my cards right, I'll be in that position for the rest of my life."

"It's called megalomania," Matilda muttered.

Joanna sat beside her on the settee, hugged her and kissed her. "Megalomania is when that feeling is uncontrolled. I'm under control, believe me. Whatever I have, whatever I see, whatever I do, is for this little fellow." She rubbed her stomach.

"And the shareholders?"

"The shareholders, darling, don't matter a damn. I have control. Shit!" she remarked, as headlights glowed in the drive. "I really do not want callers tonight."

She got up again, walked towards the door, then changed her mind and sat down again, waiting for it to open. Which it did, a moment later. "Mrs Edge," Cummings said. "Ah . . . Mrs Edge."

# Chapter Eight

# The Chairman

Remembering the last time she had met Alicia, Matilda gave a squawk and rose from her seat as if stuck with a pin. Joanna as usual remained quite calm; if she had not expected a confrontation quite so soon, she had known it had to happen, and better now than at the funeral. She couldn't invite her rival in, because Alicia was already in, striding towards her, followed at a safe distance by a nanny and the two children. "How nice to see you," Joanna said. "You've met my sister." Alicia gave Matilda a contemptuous glance. "And are these the children? We haven't met." The nurse was looking embarrassed, so Joanna knelt before the little boy. "And who are you?"

"I'm Howie."

"He is Howard junior," Alicia said, getting as much emphasis as she could into her voice.

"Of course. And this is Victoria, I suppose."

It was Alicia's turn to say, "Of course." Then she added, "Where is my husband?"

"Howard is in the billiards room," Joanna said. Alicia stalked out of the lounge. "I'd keep the children here, if I were you," Joanna told the nanny, and followed Alicia. "We are advised not to open the coffin," she said. "I gather the embalming wasn't a complete success."

Alicia turned to glare at her. "Another of your fouls-up, I suppose."

"I had nothing to do with it," Joanna said.

"Are you going to pretend you're not responsible for his death?

Taking him into the wilds of that country where you were born, and watching him drown?"

"I think, at some stage quite soon," Joanna said, "you will have to apologise for that remark." Alicia flushed. "Now, tell me where you are staying," Joanna invited.

"Why, here, of course. This is my home."

"I'm afraid you are wrong there," Joanna said. "This is *my* home. However, you are welcome to stay tonight, if you have made no other arrangements." She turned to the anxious Cummings. "Have Mrs Partridge prepare a room for Mrs Edge, Cummings. And one for the children and the nanny as well. I assume you'll join us for dinner, Alicia?"

"God almighty," Matilda said, helping herself to brandy. "What *are* you going to do?"

"About what? And go easy on that stuff."

Matilda, about to add a refill, put down her goblet instead. "She's here to make trouble."

"Of course she is," Joanna agreed. "But she can make all the trouble she wants. I'm driving." Alicia appeared in the doorway.

"Brandy?" Joanna asked.

"I'd prefer champagne."

"Then champagne it shall be, and we can all get drunk together. Cummings!"

"At once, madam." He hurried off.

"I suppose you have twisted them all round your little finger," Alicia remarked, crossing the room to straighten a painting on the far wall.

"I would like to think they are my friends," Joanna said, sitting down.

"Ha!" Alicia sat opposite her. "I really do not wish to have any quarrel with you, Miss Grain."

"Ah, Cummings, thank you." Joanna accepted a glass of champagne. "I'm sure you have no quarrel with my sister, Alicia."

Alicia glared at her as she took a glass herself. "I was speaking to you."

"But my name is Edge. Mrs Howard Edge. No, that's not right, with Howard dead. Mrs Joanna Edge."

"You can call yourself whatever you like," Alicia remarked. "The fact is that Howard inherited all of this from his father, and he intended all of it to go to his son when he died. Howard Junior."

"But he left it all to me," Joanna pointed out.

"You expect me to believe that?"

"The will is being read tomorrow afternoon. I'm sure you'll be there."

"I shall contest it. How dare you, a so-called wife of less than a fortnight, claim the whole of his estate?"

"I am not *claiming* anything," Joanna said. "I am accepting what I have been given."

"To liquidate the company! To liquidate everything Howard spent his entire life working for."

"Quite the contrary. I intend to build this company into something Howard never even dreamed of."

Alicia snorted. "A twenty-year-old girl?"

"Ahem," Cummings said from the doorway. "Dinner is served."

It was a frosty meal.

People started turning up very early the next morning, by the busload. Joanna had not really expected so many, but it appeared that the crews of all of the ships that were in port were attending; Howard had been a much-loved employer. With them were their wives and children. Joanna, who had herself been up early, went into the pantry in search of Cummings. "We have to feed them," she said.

"What, all of them, madam? That's about two hundred people, all told."

"It'll be a buffet. Use everything you have in the freezers, and send into the village for whatever else you need."

"And drink, madam?"

"Beer or shandy. Lemonade for the kids."

"But . . . where, madam? We can't have it out of doors in winter."

"We'll have it in the house, Mr Cummings. There's space."

"But the mess—"

"Messes can be cleaned up." To his consternation, she gave him a kiss on the cheek. "Don't let me down. You'd be letting Mr Edge down as well."

In the front room she found Howard Junior. "Well, hi," she said. "I hope you and I are going to be friends."

"Oh, yes," he said. "You're very pretty." A chip off the old block, she thought.

Miriam and Ethel arrived, with William, and a host of Edge cousins, some of whom Joanna had met at the wedding. She was conscious that they also felt somewhat askance at this widow of less than a fortnight's marriage being in control of their dead relative's estate, but unlike Alicia they were prepared to accept the situation. Peter Young and Billy Montgomery were there, of course, as well as Captain Heggie and Prince Hasim, who kissed Joanna's hand with great reverence. "I trust everything is working out to your satisfaction?" he murmured.

"Absolutely. I have put you beside me at lunch. We have so much to talk about."

"I look forward to it."

Alicia was last downstairs, with her children, but she insisted not only on driving in the Rolls to the church but also on sitting in the front pew alongside Joanna. Joanna didn't object, she didn't want a scene.

"Detestable woman," Hasim said, as they lunched; he might be a Muslim but he apparently did not include champagne as a wine. "I wonder you put up with her."

"I don't have much choice at the moment," Joanna said. "But things will change."

"My dear girl," Aunt Ethel said, "widowhood becomes you. You look absolutely ravishing."

"It's the black outfit with her yellow hair," Miriam explained.

"I've been hearing all sorts of things," William confided, when at last he managed to get her alone in a corner of the drawing room.

"All true, I'm sure."

"Are you really going to be Chairman of the Board?"

"I hope I shall be Chairwoman, actually."

He blew her a raspberry. "Any hope for, well—"

"When you've got your degree."

"At what?"

"Doesn't matter. Just get a few letters after your name."

"Yeah, Well . . ." he flushed and his shoulders sagged. "The beaks are making pessimistic noises about me getting to university at all."

"You'll just have to work harder."

"But . . . suppose I don't make it?"

"Try. I'll give you a job, regardless, Willie. But if you don't have a degree you'll have to come in at the bottom. Licking stamps."

"You're not serious? I'm your brother."

"And as such, I'm sure you'll work your way up. Now I have to see a man."

Peter Young was making gesticulating signs, mainly with his eyes, on the other side of the room. He had in fact been doing so almost throughout the service. "Have you seen the papers?" he whispered, as she stood alongside him.

"No. I hope they have said some nice things about Howard."

"As a matter of fact, they did. It's the share price. Do you know what it was when you and Howard set off on your honeymoon?"

"Something over six."

"Six pounds, twelve shillings and eleven pence. This morning they're opening at three pounds ten shillings."

"That's a bit of a drop."

"My dear girl, it's freefall. I've had Andrews on the phone. I gather your new loan is endorsed."

"Absolutely. So he doesn't have to lose any sleep."

"The rest of us do."

She squeezed his hand. "*Courage, mon ami.* When the news of the new ships becomes known, and our new trading route—"

"Eh?"

"I'll tell you all about it when I come in tomorrow."

He scratched his head. "Anyway, you can't possibly go ahead with ordering two new ships now."

"What do you suggest I do? Declare bankruptcy? You simply have to find some guts from somewhere, Peter. Or I won't be able to employ you any more." His head jerked as he stared at her. She smiled at him. "But I know you'll bounce back. I'll see you later."

It was time to locate Hasim again. This was the most critical moment since Howard had died. She had never doubted that Hasim would support her, financially, in return for the promise of getting her to bed. Now that promise had to be, at least, postponed. But her instincts told her that to string him along any further would be to risk losing everything – as she was about to do, anyway. "I've been talking with Peter," she said.

He nodded. "It is all gloom and doom in the City."

"But you're still going to back me?"

"Of course. Although selling you, if I may put it that way, to my father and brothers may take a little longer than I had anticipated. But I will do so, never fear."

"I wish the world had more men like you in it. No, I don't, on reflection. They'd be harder to do business with." She took a deep breath. "I would like to see you, alone, for a few minutes before you go."

"Of course. I am yours to command."

"Use the side staircase in half an hour."

She realised that she was intensely nervous. If he decided that he couldn't wait for the four months she had stipulated, which had now become more than a year, there was absolutely nothing she could do about it, having regard to the financial situation. She had set so much store by the fact that he was the ultimate gentleman.

She toyed with the idea of arranging for Matilda to burst in on her after a few minutes, then decided against it. It was she who was betraying Hasim. There was a limit to how far she could go. He even knocked, which was reassuring. "I'm here," she said.

He closed the door behind him, and she realised he was as breathless as she. "Are you afraid?" he asked.

"Of the future? No. Not with your backing. Of you . . . perhaps I am. I do not know what to expect."

He came towards her. "I always keep my bargains. It is as much a religious as an ethical code. But . . . sometimes, when I make a bargain as immense as ours, I need reassurance that there is substance to it."

She held out her hand, and he took it. "There is something I must tell you. Something I found out only yesterday."

"Tell me."

Another deep breath. "I am pregnant. Howard's last gift to me, I suppose."

He did not speak.

"I want you to know that this makes no difference to my bond with you," she said. "If you still wish me, when the baby is born . . . and weaned . . . I shall be yours without reservation." Still no reply, while his face never changed expression. "I'm afraid I really cannot contemplate an abortion," she said. "It is against my principles, anyway. And the child is Howard's. I did love him. I could not destroy his child." What an accomplished liar she had become, so very quickly.

"Do you know that I have never kissed you?" he asked. She slid her hand up his sleeve and round his neck, brought him against her, kissed him on the mouth. He kissed well, deeply and thoughtfully and hotly. She wondered what she had expected? Matilda had said he made love differently to westerners – perhaps she had expected him to kiss differently, too.

Suddenly she felt as randy as he obviously was. But her heart had to be ruled by her head. He could not be either sated or disappointed until her finances were restored. His hand slipped down her shoulder to caress her buttocks, then slid round in front to hold her through her dress. That took her by surprise. "Uh-uh," she whispered.

He stepped back. "I do apologise. When you and I finally get together, it shall be a night you will never forget. Until then . . . I must leave. Will you be all right? It seems to me that quite a few of the people here are after your blood."

"With you in my corner, Hasim, do I have anything to fear?"

This time he kissed her hand. "Absolutely nothing. Remember, I am only a telephone call away from you, at all times." He closed the door on the way out, and Joanna sat down. She felt quite breathless. As for the future . . . but the future was now far away.

Cummings was waiting for her. "There is a telephone call for you, madam. A Mr Richard Orton."

Dick? Reappearing at this moment? Like Andy, no doubt, seeking to grab what he could while he could. "Tell Mr Orton I thank him for his call, Mr Cummings, but I do not wish to speak with him at this time."

Lunch for the two hundred mourners occupied most of the afternoon. It was four o'clock, and with quite a few people still present, before Joanna managed to get herself and Alicia and a few other relatives into the study with Mr Parkins, the solicitor, and close the door. "I'm sure this is something we all wish to get over as rapidly as possible," she said, and seated herself before Howard's desk, presently occupied by the lawyer.

He cleared his throat and opened his briefcase. "This is really very brief," he said, looking somewhat apprehensively over the faces in front of him. "There is a list of small personal bequests . . ." he went through these with some speed. "Those apart, Mr Edge leaves his whole estate, which consists in the main of his control of the shares in Caribee Shipping held in trust and a few other outside investments, as well as his Jaguar car, to his wife, Mrs Joanna Edge, with the proviso that she will continue to make the allowances towards his two children, as agreed at the time of the divorce. These payments will be from her personal income, that is, five hundred pounds a year each until they are aged ten, one thousand pounds a year each until they are aged eighteen, and fifteen hundred pounds a year thereafter – so long as they remain living with, and in the care of, their mother. These payments are to be continued whether or not Mrs Edge marries again, and has issue by that second marriage."

"Just suppose Mr Edge and I had had any children," Joanna said. "Would the will be affected by that?"

"Well, yes . . ." Parkins allowed himself a cautious smile. "Mr Edge was a careful man when it came to money matters, as I am sure you appreciate. Should you have borne him a child, that child would take precedence over those by his previous marriage, and the allowances due to them would be reduced accordingly, by one half. But of course, that is academic."

"Of course," Joanna said.

"That is quite outragous," Alicia declared. "Do you mean he left nothing to me at all?"

"Ah . . ." Parkins looked embarrassed. But not that embarrassed. He had expected something like this. "You are divorced, Mrs Edge. That means that in the eyes of the law your marriage never was, except in so far as there were, and are, children. Mr Edge has made adequate provision for his children. However, as I am sure you both know . . ." he glanced from face to face. "Mr Edge held very little in his own name. This was of course to avoid death duties. All his shares are held in the trust company in Jersey, administrated by Mr

Montgomery . . ." he glanced at Billy. "Just as his house and his cars are owned by Caribee Shipping. Mrs Edge – Mrs Joanna Edge – has to pay taxes only on the money in Mr Edge's bank account. Thus the trust continues, under Mrs Joanna Edge's control. However, it is Mr Edge's intention, as stated in his will, that when his son comes of age, he shall be a full partner in both the trust and the business, sharing the responsibilities as well as the prerogatives with Mrs Joanna Edge."

"That is ridiculous," Alicia declared. "Howard is only ten years old."

"Then he will have to wait eleven years to become a full partner."

"I shall contest this will," Alicia announced.

"That is your right, madam. However, I must advise you that it will only cost you money. And should you contest the will, Mrs Edge, Mrs Joanna Edge, will be entitled to suspend all payments to the children until the case is settled, which may, of course, take some time."

Alicia opened her mouth and then shut it again. "What nonsense," Joanna said. "You go ahead and contest the will, Alicia. But I will commence my support for the children immediately. In fact, although Mr Parkins may feel the support is adequate, I shall double it, commencing with a thousand a year each now, to be increased when appropriate."

Once again Alicia looked like a fish out of water. "My dear Mrs Edge," Parkins protested. "This is most generous of you. But it is also quite unnecessary."

"I think it is necessary, Mr Parkins," Joanna asaid, allowing a touch of steel to enter her voice.

Alicia fled the room.

"Are you stark staring bonkers?" Matilda demanded, when they reached the privacy of Joanna's bedroom and she could strip off her sweaty clothes and stand in the shower. "There was no need to give away all that money. That bitch won't thank you for it."

"I'm sure she won't. But it'll undermine her case, if she ever brings one." Joanna stepped from the shower, towelled vigorously. "My God! My hair. Get me an appointment first thing tomorrow morning. I've called the board meeting for eleven, so I must be ready for that."

Matilda moved to the phone. "I still don't think—"

"Then don't, darling. Listen. I have given away nothing. By the terms of the will I can, if I choose, have the allowances for the children reduced should I ever have one of my own, by Howard. Now, everyone knows that is impossible . . . save for you and me and my gynaecologist." And Hasim, of course, she thought.

Matilda paused, phone in hand. "Are you really as ruthless as you sound?"

"I don't know. But I'm going to try," Joanna told her.

When she went downstairs the last of the guests had departed, save for Mums and Aunt Ethel and William; Alicia had apparently left with her children, without a word to a soul. Cummings and the staff were still clearing up, but he paused long enough to open a bottle of champagne and ensconce the family in the relative peace and quiet of the winter parlour. "What an experience," Aunt Ethel remarked. "What a lot of people. And that woman—"

"At least there wasn't a scene," William pointed out.

"What are you going to do now, dear?" Miriam asked.

"I am going to run my company," Joanna announced.

They all goggled at her, save for Matilda. "I meant, where are you going to live," Miriam said, keeping her feet firmly on the ground.

"Why, here, of course. It's my home." More goggling. "You are very welcome to come and live with me," Joanna said. "There's bags of room."

"Oh, yes, please," William said.

"Now don't be absurd, William," Aunt Ethel said, severely. "How can you possibly go to school in North London while living in Berkshire?" William looked at his sister for support.

"Of course he can," Joanna said. "I intend to run a business in Westminster from here. William and I will go in by car every morning, and I'll pick him up again in the evening."

"Wow!" William commented.

"What about you, Mums?"

"Well—" Miriam looked embarrassed.

"Oh, do move out too," Ethel said. "It'll be quite like old times, having my house to myself."

"I do think perhaps Joanna needs my support," Miriam ventured.

"I said, it's all right by me," Ethel repeatedly, huffily.

"I'll send the car to pick you up tomorrow," Joanna said. "I'll be out all day, but I'll arrange with Mrs Partridge to settle you in. Well . . ." she smiled brightly at them. "We'll all be together under one roof again. I'm so looking forward to that. And do please come to visit whenever you choose, Aunt Ethel." Aunt Ethel sniffed.

The door opened. "Excuse me, madam," Cummings said, "but there is a telephone call for you."

Joanna raised her eyebrows. "I think you can handle it, Cummings. It's probably someone else offering condolences."

"The gentleman said it was a business matter, and urgent, madam."

"Oh, well . . ." she followed him into the study, picked up the phone. "Yes?"

"Mrs Edge? Mrs Joanna Edge?"

"Yes."

"You don't know me, Mrs Edge, but would I be correct in assuming that you are the widow and sole beneficiary of the late Mr Howard Edge, Chairman and Managing Director of Caribee Shipping?"

"That is correct."

"And that you now own seventy per cent of the shares in the conmpany?"

"I would say that is my business," Joanna pointed out.

"That is," the man went on as if she hadn't spoken, "seven hundred thousand shares. These shares are presently valued at three pounds ten shillings each, but are expected to be marked down again when trading commences tomorrow."

"How very interesting," Joanna remarked.

"Mrs Edge, I have been authorised to offer you four pounds a share for the lot." He paused, waiting for Joanna's reply. But she did not reply; her brain was doing handsprings.

"That is, two million, eight hundred thousand pounds, cash on the barrel, Mrs Edge," the man said. "Think of it. No more trying to keep a sinking company afloat. Two million, eight hundred thousand pounds. Even if you did no more with the money than put it in a savings account at five per cent you would still have an income of one hundred and forty thousand pounds a year. I imagine you can live on that." Again he paused, and again there was no reply.

"Mrs Edge? I know this is a considerable decision for you to make. But the offer is there, and will remain on the table for the next twenty-four hours. All you have to do is ring this number . . ." he gave it to her, "and a meeting will be set up immediately between my principals and yourself." Another pause. "Are you there, Mrs Edge?"

"I'm here," Joanna said.

"Then we'll look forward to hearing from you."

The temptation was enormous. Nearly three million pounds, all for her. Not a worry in her life for the rest of that life. But . . . what about the rest of that life? An empty nothing. She would have failed Howard, and she would have failed the unborn son in her womb; she had no doubts at all that it was a son. Most of all, she would have failed herself.

"Mrs Edge?"

"I'm wondering why, if my company is on the verge of bankruptcy," she said, "you are prepared to pay nearly three million pounds for it."

"Well . . . my principal deals in collapsing companies, taking them over, building them up again—"

"So do I," Joanna said. "Tell your principal not to wait for my call, because his hair will go grey before he gets it."

"Now, look here, Mrs Edge—"

"And furthermore," Joanna went on. "Tell your principal I don't like undercover work. It's nearly always underhand. If he wants to make a hostile bid for Caribee Shipping, tell him to put it in writing and send it through the post. I will see that it is laid before my board. Good night to you." She hung up, and remained leaning on the desk for a moment, feeling quite weak. Had that really been Joanna Grain speaking? Then she went back to the lounge.

"Condolences?" William asked.

"In a manner of speaking," Joanna said, and drank some champagne.

She was on a high as she swept into the Caribee Building the next morning at half-past ten, Matilda at her shoulder. "Can I help you, madam?" inquired the receptionist.

"Yes, you can. Direct me to the boardroom, and tell Mr Young to meet me there," Joanna said.

"I'm afraid there is a board meeting this morning, madam. And Mr Young—"

"My name is Joanna Edge," Joanna said. "And yours is . . . ?"

The girl goggled at her. "H-Harriet Newsom," she whispered. "I do apologise, Mrs Edge, I had no idea—"

"You can take us up to the boardroom yourself," Joanna decided.

There was an elevator, but Joanna preferred to use the stairs. That way she passed through all the various departments. There was not a great deal going on; the staff were clearly anticipating redundancy notices as the firm went under or changed hands. The girl showed them into the boardroom, and hovered anxiously. "May I get you anything, Mrs Edge?" She looked at Matilda uncertainly. "A cup of coffee?"

"Thank you. By the way, this is Miss Grain, who is my personal assistant. You may consider anything she says as being said by me."

"Oh, yes, Mrs Edge. I'll get the coffee."

Peter bustled in, carrying a sheaf of papers and folders, and also accompanied by a young woman secretary. They introduced each other, while Peter chafed. "Have you seen the papers?"

"Now you know I do not read the papers, Peter." Joanna sat at the head of the table.

"Three even. They're expected to go down to two ten by tomorrow. Do you realise, Joanna, that the value of this company, and incidentally, your wealth, has been more than halved within a week? The City is saying that we are ready for a takeover."

"They are, are they? Well, some people have been jumping the gun." She told him of her phone call.

"And you refused it?" He was astounded. Matilda, hearing of it for the first time, looked on the verge of a collapse.

"Well, of course I refused it. We are not for sale, at any price. Now, I don't suppose you've heard from the shipyards yet?"

"No, no, there's no possibility of that for several weeks."

"I said one month, Peter."

"Yes, well . . . frankly, I should think they're waiting to see where the money is going to come from, before they bother to tender."

"Have the bank issue guarantees."

"Yes, well, the bank—"

"Peter, everything is under control. Ah, how about some introductions?"

The other shareholders were arriving. There were only three. And Alicia. "Quite a crisis, Mrs Edge," said John Donivan. "Have you seen the share price?"

"There'll be a suspension, I should think," said Clive Toogood.

"There will be a share recovery, you mean, when our plans are publicised, which they will be after this meeting. I intend to hold a press conference as soon as we are finished. Have you arranged that, Peter?"

"Yes, I have, Mrs Edge. Twelve o'clock."

"Well, then, we don't have too much time. Please be seated." She sat down herself. "Would you read the minutes of the last meeting, please, Marica?" she told Peter's secretary.

This was done. "I of course was not in attendance at that meeting," Joanna said. "But I hope you will agree it is a true record?"

They nodded their agreement, and she signed. "Thank you. Now, our business today is to outline and discuss our plans for the future."

"*Our* plans?" Alicia asked.

"You are a shareholder," Joanna said. "I would like from you all a unanimous vote of confidence in the company. Before," she said, as several people looked prepared to speak, "anyone says anything, let me tell you what we are about. Tenders have been put out for two new ships, which will update our fleet. Our two oldest ships, *Caribee Endeavour* and *Caribee Dream*, are up for sale. I'm afraid they are not likely to realise more than scrap value. This means that for the immediate future we will be down to our two existing ships, *Caribee Queen* and *Caribee Future*. However, I am hoping the new ships will be available within a year. This is stipulated in the tenders. These ships will have the latest in refrigeration equipment, and will be intended for operating in the tropical climates. However . . ." she smiled at them, "this does not necessarily mean the Caribbean." Now they were speechless, even Alicia.

"I am in the process of securing a new trade route for our vessels. This will be with the Emirate of Qadir, situated in the Persian Gulf. I will tell you frankly that this new deal has to be accepted by the Qadiri royal family, who own the emirate, but I have received assurances that it *will* be accepted, and that our ships will be welcome there just as soon as they are available. As you may know . . ." another smile, because they obviously did not know, "the Emir's family have a monopoly of all trade with Qadir. This is presently handled by the Ofgood Line. But the Emir, or at least his representatives, are dissatisfied with the service they are getting, and are prepared to give us sixty per cent of their handling. This will substantially improve our profit margins, as we do not intend to give up our Caribbean outlets. Now, are there any questions?"

There were several seconds of silence. Then Alicia asked, "And how are we going to pay for the new ships?"

"Our bankers are prepared to advance us, or I should say, me, the money."

"On what security?"

"The backing of the Emirate."

Another moment of scandalised silence. "Can you trust these people?" Donivan asked.

"Yes."

Alicia stroked her chin, thoughtfully; clearly she was remembering Prince Hasim's presence at the funeral. "Will this endorsement not involve the company in a very heavy loan structure?" someone asked.

"Only in the short term. Our new stock flotation will be launched this summer, and that will actually pay for the ships and liquidate our borrowings."

"It was my impression that the stock flotation would not now go ahead," Toogood remarked.

"Of course it will not go ahead," Alicia snapped.

"It is going ahead," Joanna said quietly. "I have spoken with the brokers, and they are happy. It will be launched this summer."

"Supposing you can find anyone to underwrite it," Alicia sneered.

"I already have. The Emir of Qadir."

"You seem to have this man eating out of your hand," Donivan suggested.

"His son, you mean," Alicia said. "I see it all now. You are, after all, nothing but a whore, Joanna."

"I have witnesses to what you have just said, Alicia," Joanna said.

"Would you care to retract and apologise?" Alicia flushed, while the men looked thoroughly embarrassed. Joanna glanced around their faces. "Prince Hasim is a friend, as he was a friend of my late husband. I assume you were aware of this, Alicia?"

"I did not care for Howard's friends," Alicia said. "I saw as little of them as possible."

"That was your decision. When I returned to England, I visited the Prince and put our situation squarely before him. As a result, he agreed to lend us his financial backing. There will be a profit in it for him and his family, and his state. It was a simple business transaction. Now . . ." once again she looked around their faces. The men were dumbfounded, Alicia was still licking her wounds. "I have outlined, down to the last detail, my plans for resuscitating this company and moving it ahead. I see a very bright future for us all. May I have a unanimous endorsement of these plans?" Everyone looked at Alicia. "Of course," Joanna said, "should any of you retain sufficient doubts about the future of the company as to wish to get out, I am perfectly prepared to buy his or her shares at the current market price."

"Ha!" Alicia commented. "I am not going to sell you my shares. I intend to be here, always, just to make sure you do not ruin the company. And when my son takes over—"

"There is one more thing I should tell you all," Joanna said, and took one of her deep breaths. "I am pregnant."

# Part Three

# The Phoenix

'Build me straight, O worthy Master!
Staunch and strong, a goodly vessel,
That shall laugh at all disaster,
And with wave and whirlwind wrestle!'
Henry Wadsworth Longfellow

# Chapter Nine

# The Proposal

This time the momentary silence was more scandalised than ever. Predictably, Alicia was the first to recover. "You expect us to believe that?"

"I believe we may share the same gynaecologist," Joanna said. "You have my permission to check with Dr Alva."

"And you're claiming the child is Howard's?"

"The child was conceived in the first half of October 1963," Joanna said, "at which time I was living, with Howard, at Caribee House. Incidentally, Howard is the only man with whom I have ever slept. I would think very carefully before you reply to that, Alicia. Or I will indeed see you in court." Alicia opened her mouth, then closed it again. Then she got up, gathered her papers, and left the room. The men looked more embarrassed than ever.

"Your unanimous acceptance of my plans, please," Joanna said. "I think I am right in saying that, as Mrs Alicia Edge declined to sell her shares, and indeed, made it plain that she plans to remain at the centre of the company's decision-making, she has already exercised her vote in favour."

"Will the announcement of your pregnancy be made at the press conference?" Davison asked.

"Of course," Joanna said.

"If I may say so, Joanna," Peter Young remarked, "you have the knack of living on the edge. Do you intend to continue that?"

"Only as long as it is necessary, Peter. Believe me, I long for a quiet life."

But she was as confident as ever at the press conference, smiled as she answered the most intimate of questions, both as to her financial arrangements and to the parentage of her child.

"As I understand it," said one young woman, "the fact that you are pregnant has no influence on the future of the ownership of the company, unless your child happens to be a boy?"

"That is the situation, yes," Joanna said.

"Would it then be fair to describe your late husband as a male chauvinist pig?"

Joanna continued to smile. "It is the privilege of certain members of the press to insult and diminish the dead, certain that they cannot be sued for libel."

The rest of the questions were more friendly.

"But," Peter said later, "you do realise that should the child be a girl—"

"That possibility is several months off, Peter. And meanwhile, we have a lot to do."

For the moment, everything was on the up. Her press conference, the bold announcement that the company was going ahead with considerable plans for the future, and that a new trade route would soon be announced, had an immediate steadying effect on the shares; her ability to announce that the route would be with the Emirate of Qadir, which she released the moment she received the cable from Hasim, had them moving upwards again. The tenders duly came in, and were given to the yard of Bramell & Hopkins, in the north-east. This brought favourable media reaction, as the north-east was so depressed, and even an invitation to lunch from the Under-Secretary for Trade and Industry. "The Government is very happy that you have decided to place these orders here in Britain," he told her. "I am sure there were some promising tenders from abroad."

"As a matter of fact there were," Joanna agreed.

"But you chose British. We are, as I say, very well pleased."

"Well," Joanna said. "If you felt up to making us a grant, we would be equally pleased."

He smiled. "I shall see what can be done."

The grant, for half the cost of the new ships, duly came though.

Then Prim was on the line. "Great news," he said. "Daley Direct are underwriting twenty per cent of the share issue." He paused, waiting for her reply. "You do know who Daley Direct are?"

"One of our biggest insurance companies," Joanna said.

"Absolutely. Now they have given the lead, others will follow. We may oversubscribe."

"I shall be delighted."

She had not told Prim about the surreptitious offer for her shares. Peter Young had promised to look into the matter, but as he said, there were dozens of potential culprits; nailing one down would be very difficult, especially as she had not heard from the mystery bidder again.

"And none of the other shareholders have been approached," she mused.

"Waste of time. Only your holding matters, because it controls the company."

"Well," she said, "keep looking. Or at least, keep your ears open."

It was three days later, that, as she was dropped before the Caribee Building, Joanna was knocked over. It all happened so fast she was taken entirely by surprise. Charlie the chauffeur had stopped, as he always did, immediately outside the great double doors to the building, and come round the car to open the door for her. As usual she was accompanied by Matilda, but again as usual, Joanna got out first.

As her feet touched the pavement there was a loud shout, and a figure cannoned into Charlie, sending him sprawling. Another body immediately cannoned into Joanna, sending her tumbling to the concrete in a scatter of arms and legs. Matilda, following her out, screamed, and immediately a crowd gathered, quickly dominated by a policeman. "What happened?" he asked.

Joanna lay half in the gutter, hands clasped to her stomach. Matilda knelt beside her. Charlie slowly clambered to his feet. "Two young tearaways, racing along the pavement, not caring who they upset—"

"I saw it all," an elderly lady said. "He's right. They were running along, laughing, pushing people aside—"

"Where'd they go?" the policeman asked.

"Round that corner."

He hesitated. "You all right, ma'am?"

Joanna was beginning to get her breath back. "My baby," she muttered.

"A doctor," Matilda said. "We must get her to a doctor. She's pregnant."

"I'll call an ambulance," the policeman volunteered.

"I'll take Mrs Edge," Charlie said, and swept Joanna into his arms to lay her on the back seat.

By now various people had emerged from the building, and Charlie hastily told them what had happened, so that they could report to Peter Young. Then he got behind the wheel. Matilda had already got into the back beside Joanna. "Are you in pain?"

"Yes," Joanna said. "My baby—"

"We'll be at the doctor in a few minutes," Matilda promised.

As they were. Dr Alva hastily had Joanna carried into a side room, as he already had a patient in his consulting room, but he gave Joanna priority treatment. She lay on the examination bed, gritting her teeth, less in pain than in fear. There was more than the life of her unborn child at stake; there was her entire future. "Hm," Dr Alva said. "Hm."

"For God's sake, doctor," Matilda snapped. "Say something coherent."

"It does not look as if any real damage has been done," Alva said. "No, no, I think, with rest, Mrs Edge will be perfectly all right."

"Oh, thank God," Joanna said.

"But . . . rest. You must go home and go to bed, and stay there for at least the next couple of days. I will come out to see you tomorrow."

Joanna looked at Matilda. "Tell Peter Young, I want to see him, today."

Charlie drove her home to an alarmed Mrs Partridge and Cummings. Mrs Partridge and the upstairs maid put her to bed, made sure she was comfortable, offered her aspirins and tranquillisers. "I don't want anything, until after Mr Young has been," she told them.

Peter arrived two hours later, sat beside her, looking grave. "Are you going to be all right?"

"I am going to be all right," she assured him. "And so is my baby. Although I'd like to see those two young thugs strung up and flogged."

"Yes, well, are you up to talking business?"

"Of course. What's the problem?"

"Well . . ." he cleared his throat. "There is a potentially serious matter which needs to be discussed."

Joanna moved, uncomfortably, in her bed. She was just starting to show. "Yes?"

"It has come to my knowledge that Alicia is having you investigated."

"You mean she's going ahead with contesting the will?"

"No. I think she understands, or has been made to understand by her solicitor, that she would be wasting her time there. No, no, she is having your private life investigated. Her hope is to prove that the child is not Howard's."

"Well, I don't see how she has a hope there," Joanna said. "As I said at the meeting, Howard is the only man I have ever slept with."

"Yes," Peter said, not altogether convincingly. "Sadly, in matters like this, it is often enough merely to muddy the waters, as it were, in order to bring a case. If, of course, we could carry out a blood test, well, the matter would be closed beyond all doubt."

"Are you suggesting we exhume Howard's body?" Joanna demanded, not sure whether she should be amused or angry.

"Well, of course I am not, Mrs Edge. Nor, at this distance of time, do I suppose it would be much good. The fact is . . ." He fiddled with his pen.

"Oh, come on, say it," Joanna invited.

"Well, there remains some doubt in people's minds as to just what – ah – inducement Prince Hasim received to persuade him to back Caribee Shipping so heavily."

"I see," Joanna said, grimly.

"There was also, I believe, a relationship with a young man named Richard Orton—"

"Tell me something," Joanna said, this time pleasantly, "have you been having me investigated too?"

"Of course not, Mrs Edge. What I have been doing is finding out what Mrs Edge – the other Mrs Edge – has turned up."

"I get the message. Well, there is a very simple method of proving that neither Dick Orton nor Prince Hasim can be the father of my child – that blood test you were talking about."

"As a last resort, I agree," Peter said. "The publicity would be unpleasant. Sadly, even if it were proved that neither Mr Orton nor Prince Hasim could be the father, well . . ." he glanced, surreptitiously, at Matilda.

"Jesus wept," Matilda commented, having got the message herself.

"Okay," Joanna said. "Let's have it all hang out, Peter. Alicia is working on the theory that because Matilda has slept around, I must have been doing it too. Right?"

Peter licked his lips nervously. "If it were just a matter of, as you put it, sleeping around, well . . . Mrs Edge has discovered that Miss Grain once worked in a nightclub which was closed down for being a brothel. And that you also frequented this place."

"That woman is clearly designed to be a garbage collector," Joanna snapped. "I went to Tony's once in my life, four years ago. Come to think of it, that was the night I met Howard. I suppose she also has found out that I was once arrested for being in possession of cannabis."

"I'm afraid she has."

"Which was the night I became Howard's mistress," Joanna pointed out.

"Ah, yes," Peter agreed. "She has also discovered that—" he flushed.

"That I was knickerless. But I was also a virgin. And I can prove that."

"Well—" Peter looked more embarrassed than ever.

"Because I lost my virginity that night, to Howard. Alicia can ask Mrs Partridge that – she had to launder the sheets. Anyway, I don't see what any of this can do to help her prove that my baby isn't Howard's. I didn't conceive for more than a year after moving into Caribee House."

"Absolutely," Peter said. "But what Mrs Edge is doing is accumulating a CV, if you like, to prove that you are the sort of woman who might well have had a lover even while living with Mr Edge and anticipating marriage to him."

"But she has to find the lover," Matilda remarked.

"Absolutely," Peter said again. "And if there wasn't one, well . . . you have nothing to worry about. But I thought you should be kept informed."

"I really am most terribly sorry," Matilda said, as they lunched.

"What for?"

"Well . . . if you didn't have a sister like me, your problems wouldn't exist."

"Don't be silly. That woman would have been a pain in the ass anyway. I am going to have to do something about her."

Matilda giggled. "Like hiring a hit man?"

Joanna frowned at her, and Matilda's eyebrows shot up. "You wouldn't!"

"Of course I wouldn't," Joanna said, wondering if she was telling the truth; at that moment she was so angry she would cheerfully look at Alicia down the barrel of a gun. "What gets me is her unmitigated gall. Stirring up all this dirt when she doesn't have a shred of evidence. I mean—" she paused with her wine glass on its way to her lips.

"What?" Matilda also stopped eating.

"Shit," Joanna muttered. "That day, my birthday, when I ran into Dick. I'd forgotten about it."

"So you ran into him," Matilda said. "I hope you're not telling me that something happened."

"Of course nothing happened," Joanna snapped. "Not what you're thinking of, anyway. And I was already two months pregnant, even if I didn't know it. But we were alone together. In the car."

"Oh, shit," Matilda said. "For how long?"

"Long enough to . . . well . . ."

"Have it off. But you didn't."

"No, we didn't. But you had put me in such a mood I wanted to. So we kissed and, well, played with each other. But I couldn't bring myself to go through with it. But that chauffeur . . . Wyndham . . ."

"Don't tell me he was there while this canoodling was going on?"

"No, I sent him for a walk. But the mere fact that I did that must have made him suspicious. So I got Howie to change hire firms. Maybe his nose was out of joint, the chauffeur's, I mean . . ." The more she thought about it, the more obvious it became. "Listen, I want you to handle this."

"Me?" Matilda squawked.

"Yes. You want to be my bodyguard. Then be my bodyguard. We have to spike that damned woman's guns. Find Dick, and get him to give a blood sample. That sample we'll store with Dr Alva. It may be possible for him to take blood from the foetus. In any event, the very minute my child is born, we'll know we have proof that Dick couldn't have been the father. But Dick must also be prepared to stand up in court and swear under oath that we did not have sex."

"Okay," Matilda said, slowly. "But if you are so innocent . . . why the agitation?"

"Just get on with it," Joanna told her.

Oh, what a fool she'd been, she thought, as the car stopped outside William's school. But how could one foretell the future? That day in the car she had no more foreseen her pregnancy than Howard's imminent death; she had, she recalled, even been doubting that they would ever get married! Of course, it would be obvious that Dick could not be the father of her child . . . unless it could be proved that they had also met in October. But it would still muddy the waters.

Had Alicia really tracked Dick down, through the chauffeur? Or had he gone to her? But he wouldn't have done that. He could know nothing of the in-fighting which was going on at Caribee Shipping. Or did he? He had no doubt been angry when she had refused to speak with him after the funeral. But what had he expected, that she would jump into bed with him with her husband hardly cold? Or was it much more serious than that, and he had felt that now she was a millionairess all of his troubles might be over?

As for Alicia . . . Joanna found herself frowning, as she remembered herself lying in the back of the Rolls on her way to the doctor, thinking that her entire future rested on the survival of the baby. Alicia knew that too.

My God, she thought. Two young tearaways, running along a crowded London street, pushing people left and right, but just happening to knock *her* down. If her baby had died, Alicia would have been guilty of murder. But her involvement could never be proved, as the police had never caught her two young agents. And she would have secured her own future. "Jesus!" she whispered.

"Hi!" William sat beside her, and the car moved off. She blinked at him, perhaps seeing him for the first time. She supposed that a baby brother is always a baby brother. That he may be growing all the time is hardly noticeable, day by day. But William was now just on six feet tall, with powerful shoulders and legs. He was frowning at her. "You look like a bear with a sore head."

"So life isn't all up."

"Care to tell me about it?"

She glanced at him. "How're things at school?"

"Well . . . not too good, I guess. Old Tommo says I don't have a hope of getting good enough grades for any university, much less Oxbridge. He's muttering about technical colleges and that sort of thing."

"I was really thinking of socially."

"Oh, you mean being picked up by the Rolls? And the beautiful sister." He glanced at her maternity dress. "Even if she is pregnant."

"You are going to get a thick ear in a minute."

"There were a few wiseguys at first, but I soon sorted them out."

Joanna was interested. "How?"

"I walloped them."

"Good lord. Didn't they object?"

"It's hard to object when you're lying on your back seeing stars with a guy's foot on your chest."

"Does Mums know about this?"

"I don't confide in Mums. Do you?"

"I suppose not. Do you *want* to go to a technical college?"

"Not really. I don't want to go to university either, even if I could. But I suppose I'll have to."

"I think one should avoid doing things one doesn't want to," Joanna said, a idea forming at the back of her mind. She needed all the help and support she could get, and where was she going to get it better and more loyally than from her own family? "You once had the idea of working for me."

"Licking stamps, you said, if I didn't have a degree."

"I've changed my mind. You would work for me, but not immediately. You'd have to attend another school, first, for six months."

"You mean some kind of crammer? No way."

"I was thinking of martial arts."

He frowned at her. "Martial arts? Holy hell."

"Don't you think you'd enjoy that?"

"Well . . . yes, sure I would. If I knew what came next."

"You'd come to work for me, as my personal bodyguard."

"Your . . . you need a personal bodyguard?"

"Yes," Joanna said.

William stared at her. "You're serious."

"Yes."

"Would I have to carry a gun?"

"You will not carry a gun. I just want you standing behind me, always."

His tongue came out and slowly licked his lips. "I'd get paid, for doing that?"

"Absolutely," Joanna said. "But, for the time being, this is our secret. Right? Let me down and you can forget it."

Another long stare. "I'm not sure I understand why a woman as tough as you needs a bodyguard at all," he said.

"Because I'm a woman, that's why."

Miriam didn't object to the idea. Miriam had long since given up objecting to anything. She had even gotten over the resentment at being about the last person in the world, it seemed, to know she was about to become a grandmother. She enjoyed gardening, and she had fifteen acres to play with. She spent her days wandering around the estate, usually with one of the gardeners at her shoulder, suggesting this, altering that, ordering this or that plant. Joanna gave her her head. She wanted her mother to be happy. Just as she wanted to be happy. That was difficult right now. She was waiting on so many things. But principally on her baby. By the end of May she was massive, and stopped going into work. Instead she had Peter Young come out to see her every day, with anything that needed signing, and with the latest update on how things were going.

Things were going very well. The new ships were well under

construction, the stock flotation, due in July, was already well subscribed, and the shares had recovered almost their original value. "They'll go higher," he opined.

"As I said they would," she reminded him. "Tell me about Alicia."

"All quiet there. I would say she's licking her wounds."

"Maybe," Joanna said.

She had never told Peter her suspicions regarding her accident, or the steps she had taken to make sure such a thing could never happen again; William was still at his martial arts training school, and she was paying his fees out of her own pocket, not from company funds. What was more disturbing was that Dick had apparently quit his job, and Matilda had been unable to find him. Alicia again? Or pure coincidence? In any event it was worrying.

She was overjoyed to receive a telephone call from Hasim, announcing that he was back in England. "I would like to see you," he said.

"Now? You would go right off me. I look like á house."

"A very lovely house," he assured her. "My house. May I come out?"

"Oh, please," she said.

It had of course been necessary to put William entirely in the picture. "You don't think he means to have it off with you?" he asked.

"No chance. I'm inviolate while I'm pregnant, and while I'm nursing. But he likes to look, and touch. After all, he does virtually own me."

"Ugh!"

"Your racism is showing," she pointed out. "Ḥasim is a very sweet and gentle man. And when he gets here, you just make yourself scarce."

"I thought I was to be at your side at all times?"

"Not in my bedroom."

She was pleasantly excited, as well as pleasantly reassured. For all the apparent equanimity with which he had taken the news of her pregnancy, she could not help but wonder if he might not have had second thoughts during his visit to his home, and no doubt his chats with his father. But he wanted her as much as ever. Which meant she did not have a care in the world. More than anyone else in the world that she had met, Hasim exuded a tremendous air of omnipotence, of certainty that no problem could arise that he could not handle with the greatest of ease. She needed some of that.

She had given instructions that he was to be shown right up, and a few minutes after his car, a Daimler, swept to a stop before the house he was tapping gently on the door. He wore a blazer and flawlessly pressed grey flannels, with a carnation in his buttonhole. She had forgotten how handsome he was. "Don't get up," he said as he closed the door behind himself. "I'm sure you must not exert yourself."

"I want to get up."

He leaned forward to kiss her. "You are looking very well."

"Considering?"

"No, no, I mean, seriously." He held her hands, sat beside her on the settee. "Now, is all going well?"

"On most fronts."

"You must explain that. Especially in the area where it is not going well. There is no trouble with the ships?"

"No, no. As soon as I'm in better shape, I shall go up to the yards and see how they are coming along."

"I will come with you. And the flotation?"

"Everyone thinks it is going to be a big success. I'm told you have a large part of the action."

"Oh, indeed. And yourself?"

"Well, I, or at any rate the trust company, gets two shares for every one we now hold, so I shall retain control."

"I never thought you would risk losing control, my dearest girl. And the baby?" He looked at her stomach.

She held his hand and placed it on the bulge. "I think he's happy you're here."

"No problems?"

"Well . . ." she told him about the accident. And about her feelings regarding it.

"Then the woman is dangerous," he said.

She rested her hand on his arm. "She's history, Hasim. The baby is fine, so Dr Alva says. And she hasn't tried anything else, since." She grinned. "I have surrounded myself with bodyguards."

"I have not seen any."

"That's because, like all the best bodyguards, they blend with the background. My brother William."

"That boy?"

"He's very capable in a punch-up."

"And he is good with a gun, also?"

"Now, Hasim, really. We do not do that sort of thing in England. It isn't legal."

"It may not be legal, but it is done in England."

"Well, I don't think I actually need that kind of bodyguarding."

"I disagree with you. I shall have to see what we can do."

"Hasim—"

"When you are my wife," he stated, "I must see that you are protected at all times."

Joanna's jaw dropped. "Was that a proposal of marriage?"

"Ah, yes. I am not experienced at these things."

"As Heir of Qadir, you merely tap someone on the shoulder and say, upstairs, tonight."

He kissed her. "Actually, I tap the father on the shoulder."

"You have never tapped me on the shoulder."

"I have wanted to, so very badly. But now—"

"You said you could never marry me, because I am not a Muslim. I am also not a virgin and I am soon to be a mother."

"Yes. We have discussed this, my father and I. The fact is, I *cannot* marry you, as the next Emir of Qadir. As you have just pointed out, it would be against all of my family's principles, and it would offend our people."

"Well, then—"

"However, if I am *not* to be the next Emir of Qadir, I can do what I like."

She stared at him, and again had to bring her jaw up, sharply.

"I have given my position to my brother," he said.

"But why? Not simply to marry me?"

"Yes. Simply to marry you."

"But . . ." Her brain was in a spin. How to tell this large, basically gentle, devoted friend that theirs was simply a business arrangement, that she did not love him, that she had planned not even to honour their agreement, certain that after waiting for more than a year he would simply tire of her and go elsewhere?

"I fell in love with you the moment I saw you, at that pool party, in that bathing suit. You know . . ." he grinned. "One does not have the opportunity of inspecting a woman in Qadir, if she is to be your wife. A concubine, now, that is something different. But a wife must be taken on trust. Most marriages, anyway, are undertaken for political purposes, a repayment of favours from the bride's family, or an anticipation of favours. To look at a beautiful woman, virtually naked, is a compelling business."

"Yes," she said. "But . . . what about all those concubines?" She had to clutch at straws.

"I have pensioned them all off," Hasim declared. "I have given them permission either to retire into private life, or go to the harem of another man, or even to marry, if they wish and can find a husband."

"Oh, Hasim," she said.

"Nor is there anything for you to worry about on the financial front," he said. "I am going to continue as Qadir's representative here in England, with the same income I now possess, and the same powers I now possess. The trading consortium we have agreed will stand, as will Qadir's support for your company, for as long as you need it. Your future is assured."

As indeed it would be, she realised, as Hasim's wife. Hasim's wife! What a fantastic prospect. He was certainly much more wealthy than Howard had ever been, or than she could ever be, she knew. She would never forget the dismissive gesture with which he had greeted her request for a four million pound endorsement. What would she be? A princess, no doubt. The Princess Hasim ben Raisul abd Abdullah. *That* would make Alicia squirm. But she did not love him. She had always intended, once she got things under control, to marry for love. And then, the company! "The Company," she muttered.

"I have said, it will remain secured," Hasim said.

"I meant, my place in it."

"Oh, well . . ." he shrugged. "If it pleases you to continue as Managing Director, I have no objection. It will be something for you to do. Providing . . ." he grinned, "it does not in any way interfere with our love life, or our social life. Or your life as a mother."

"As a mother?" she said, seeking another straw.

"Well, I wish to have many strong, fine sons. I will tell you a little secret. I may never become Emir of Qadir. But one of my sons will. My brother Mutil is, what do you call him in England . . . ? He is actually my half-brother, of course; we have different mothers."

"You're not serious. You mean he doesn't have a harem?"

"Oh, he does, but it is all young boys. So, you see, we have much to work for."

"Much," Joanna agreed feebly. "Hasim, my dearest Hasim, you realise that you have taken me entirely by surprise? I mean, I had never supposed that marriage between us would be at all possible."

"I know. I have sprung it on you."

"Yes," she said severely. "You have. And in my condition. I really cannot think about anything save my baby, at this moment."

"Of course. I am the most inconsiderate and wretched of men. Can you ever forgive me?"

"Of course I will forgive you," she assured him. "If you will promise to keep your proposal of marriage a secret, and not to raise it again until after the birth of my baby."

"Of course I will do that," he agreed. "It would not be right, in any event, for a pregnant woman to announce her engagement to a man who is not the father of her child. But you will allow me to offer you protection?"

"Protection? Oh . . . well, if you must. But it must be unobtrusive."

"You will not even know he is there. All you have to do is taken Wazir on your staff. As an underbutler. He is a very good underbutler."

"As an underbutler," Joanna agreed.

Had she actually said yes? Hasim assumed so, certainly. My God, she thought, what have I done? The first thing she had to do was persuade Cummings and William to accept the situation with Wazir. Cummings was far the less perturbed. "Will this gentleman actually be searching our guests, madam?" he inquired.

"Ah, not at the moment, Cummings," Joanna said, brightly. "We're not having any guests, are we?" Cummings bowed.

William was far less happy. "He's wandering about the place with a bloody great magnum under his armpit," he complained. "A butler! What happens if he shoots someone with it?"

"I'm sure that won't happen," Joanna assured him.

"How does he come to have such a weapon anyway? Is it legal?"

"You'll have to ask Hasim. But I wouldn't, if I were you."

He frowned at her. "What's this character to you, anyway?"

"He's my . . . protector."

"You mean you're his mistress? How can you be, with a bulge like that?"

"Hasim is a man who looks to the future." But then, so did she need to look to the future. A future she refused to contemplate until after her delivery. Yet that was soon enough. She had determined to have the child at home, and when she was about due Dr Alva moved one of his nurses in to be with her, just in case. Hasim also wanted to be present, but she talked him out of it. "You'd shock the neighbours," she said, thinking of Mums and Aunt Ethel. "And you'd be awfully bored. These things take time."

As it happened, the birth took twenty-four hours, and Dr Alva had ample time to be there, and give her a few whiffs of gas, which made it all very easy at the end and compensated for the extreme discomfort earlier. Then he was standing by the bedside, together with Mums and Matilda, smiling at her. "Well done, Mrs Edge," he said. "It was very simple, eh?"

Half drugged as she was, Joanna was only slowly registering. "My baby," she said. The child was placed in her arms.

"Isn't she sweet?" Mums said. "She looks just like her mother."

# Chapter Ten

# The Mother

Joanna gazed at her mother in consternation, then looked down at the child. She couldn't think, for the moment.

"Do you know," Mums said, "you have never mentioned a name for her? Have you decided one?"

Joanna looked at Matilda, who alone could possibly understand how she felt; she was the only one present who knew the contents of Howard's will. "I think Jo is very tired," Matilda said. "And needs to rest. Don't you, doctor?"

"Of course," Alva agreed. "Nurse!" The nurse hurried forward to lift the babe from Joanna's arms.

"Do not worry," Alva said reassuringly. "She will be well looked after, and returned as soon as you are rested. Your milk will not be in before tomorrow, anyway."

"I'd like Matilda to stay," Joanna whispered.

Mums raised her eyebrows, and left the room. Alva and the nurse did likewise, and Matilda sat in the chair beside the bed. "She's a lovely child," she said. "We were all so worried, after the accident. But she seems absolutely healthy."

"She needn't have bothered," Joanna muttered. "Alicia."

"Now, Jo . . ." Matilda smoothed the sweat-wet hair from her forehead. "You are going to love that little girl?"

"Oh, of course I am," Joanna said, irritably. "It's just that it leaves me with so much to do."

Of which Hasim was only one aspect. But he joined her as soon as he was allowed, held the baby, and then wanted to play with her nipples. "When does the milk start coming out?"

"Tomorrow," she said. "At which time you will have to leave them alone."

"I shall watch," he promised her. "We have so much to talk about, to do."

He didn't know the contents of the will either. But then, if he did, he would merely say, give it all up and just be my wife. She wasn't in the mood to contemplate either of those options.

Peter Young came down the next day, armed as usual with a sheaf of papers and letters for her to sign. Joanna lay propped up in bed, the baby at her breast, and he sat with his gaze carefully turned half away. "I am going to call her Helen," Joanna told him.

"A nice name, Helen. Any family connotations?"

"No. The only name I had considered before the birth was Howard. But Helen . . . wasn't she the face that launched a thousand ships? This Helen will launch at least two."

"Absolutely. Ah . . ." At last he looked directly at her. "I know these are early days, but have you given any thought to, well—"

"The future? I have given a great deal of thought to the future, Peter. But whatever we do must be done very carefully. First thing must be a reconciliation with Alicia."

"Are you serious? When you feel she almost had you killed? Or at least, the baby."

"She happens to be young Howard's mother. I can't get at young Howard except through her."

He stroked his chin. "And you mean to 'get at', as you put it, young Howard."

"There is nothing sinister about that," she pointed out. "If he is going to share the company with me in ten years' time, don't you agree that it would make sense to ensure that we are on the same wavelength?"

"That might be difficult to achieve. Wouldn't you say he has a good number of reasons for disliking you?"

"All planted by his mother. We have ten years to change his attitude, Peter."

"We?" he asked uneasily.

"I." She smiled at him. "But I would like to feel that you are on my side, and that this conversation will remain confidential."

"Absolutely," he said fervently.

As she had hoped, and indeed expected, Joanna received her first prospective breakthrough the next day, when the mail arrived. In the midst of several congratulatory letters was one from Alicia. *So happy for your success. I am sure she will be a lovely child.*

Alicia, of course, must be laughing all the way to her hairdresser, Joanna thought. But it was she who was laying the trap. She telephoned. "Thank you so much for your note." Alicia did not immediately reply, clearly surprised by the approach. "I wondered if you'd care to come here for lunch, whenever is convenient?" Joanna said.

"Me?"

"We have so much to talk about. I suppose Howard is at school."

"Yes. Yes, he is."

"But if you came on a weekend," Joanna pointed out. "You could bring him too."

"Just what are you planning?" Matilda asked. William was equally interested.

"I'm not exactly sure," Joanna said. "But there is no legal way I can beat them, now."

"I'm not sure I like the sound of that," William commented.

"Listen," she told them. "You are my brother and sister. Your business is to support me in everything I do. Don't worry. You are employed by me, not the company. So you cannot lose. Even if I were to lose control of the company, you have nothing to worry about. Hasim will see to that."

"Are you really going to marry him?" Matilda asked.

"It looks like it."

"He'll shake you up a bit."

"Perhaps I could do with some of that."

What *was* she going to do? She really didn't have any idea, save that she had to suborn Howard away from his mother and over to her, some time in the next ten years. She didn't want to contemplate what might be involved – because she found the idea exciting. She was, after all, still only twenty, only ten years his senior. And she knew she was a beautiful woman.

But he was only ten years old. She had to begin by being a most generously friendly older sister. Not for the first time in her life, she wondered if she was really as ruthless as she pretended, even to herself.

Alicia, predictably, was suspicious. But she did bring Howard to lunch, as well as his sister. "You'll be living here again, one day," she told the children, holding their hands as she escorted them into the drawing-room. William made a noise which sounded like a suppressed raspberry.

"Of course they will," Joanna said. "Or Howard will, at any rate. I expect Victoria will have married and set up house by then."

Victoria looked at her mother. "I'm sure she'd rather live here," Alicia said. Joanna signalled Cummings to serve champagne. "Is this all you ever drink?" Alicia asked.

"I'm afraid it was a habit taught me by Howard," Joanna explained. "Willy, be a dear and take the children for a romp in the garden." William made a face, but obeyed, and Matilda also mumbled an excuse and left. Both were under orders.

"Shouldn't your brother be at school or university, or something?" Alicia inquired.

"William has left school, and we have decided against university," Joanna explained. "He works for me. Oh, don't worry, he isn't costing the firm a penny; I pay him out of my personal income."

"Pay him to do what?"

"Why, to be my bodyguard."

"Your bodyguard? You, need a bodyguard?"

"It seems I do. Didn't you hear about my accident, in the spring? I was knocked over by two louts. I could have been badly hurt. And Baby could have been killed in my womb. William is around to make sure nothing like that ever happens again. But actually, I have two bodyguards. Did you notice the large Arab-looking man when you came in?"

"I thought he was a gardener."

"He's my real bodyguard."

"Where on earth did you find him?"

"He's a present."

Alicia's eyebrows shot up.

"From my fiancé, Prince Hasim ben Raisul abd Abdullah."

Alicia's eyebrows seemed totally out of control. "You're going to marry an Arab? So soon after Howard's death?" It was difficult to determine which shocked her the more.

"An Arab prince," Joanna pointed out. "He's very keen. As for when, we certainly intend to wait the full year But as I'm sure you remember, it is the House of Qadir that is backing the firm's expansion. As a matter of fact, that is something I wanted to talk to you about. As soon as I am out and about, which will be in another week or so, I am going up to the shipyard to see how the new ships are coming on. I think it would be a good idea to have Howard come with me."

"What on earth for?"

"They are going to be his ships, in ten years' time."

"Well . . . it'll have to be a time when he's off school."

"I'm sure you can arrange it," Joanna said sweetly.

She reckoned she had won round one. But she had to make certain of it. Three weeks later Alicia telephoned to say that she had arranged for Howard to have a long weekend. "Shall we meet you up there?" she asked.

"Ah . . . why not?"

Joanna summoned William. "I am going up to Newcastle next weekend to look at our new ships. But you won't be coming with me," she said. "Hasim will be doing that, so I shall be perfectly safe. Besides, I have a job for you. I am going up on Friday evening, and I believe Alicia and Howard will be doing the same. On Friday morning, I wish Alicia to have an accident. Nothing serious. I don't want her to be badly hurt. Just sufficient to prevent her travelling."

William gulped. "You mean—"

"Yes," Joanna said. "I do mean."

"Shit!" he muttered. "I could go to jail."

"If you do, I will see that you are well taken care of. But I am sure you won't, if you handle it right. You have a week to find out all about her movements, where and when she does what and with whom. If necessary, you can bring the accident forward to Thursday. But of course, you must remember that the further it is brought forward, the more serious it will have to be. The essential is that she cannot travel on Friday night."

"Do you have any idea what you're risking?"

"I hope I'm risking nothing, because you are my brother and you will never allow me to be involved. If you've a conscience about it, just remember that she tried to have me killed, or at least your baby niece killed, a few months ago."

He swallowed. "I'll see what I can do."

"No, no," Joanna said. "You'll do it. Buy or hire whatever you need in outside help. I just don't want to know about it."

"You frighten me," Hasim said, when he came to dinner. "In more ways than one. It would have been better to let my people handle it."

"I don't agree. William has to earn his spurs some time. And I wouldn't want you to be involved."

"But if he is caught—"

"I shall utterly disown him, and his action. He knows this. That is why he will not be caught out."

He shook his head. "I don't like it." Then he grinned. "But like everything else, I suppose you know what you are doing. This visit to Newcastle, will we share a room?"

The moment of truth, at last. "I am still feeding Helen."

"But she is not coming with us, surely?"

"No, she isn't."

"Then you will not be feeding her on this trip. You will still be carrying milk. I think I like that."

"You are an utterly obscene man."

He kissed her. "When two people are in love, it is quite permissible for them to be obscene together. In fact, it is important that they are. It makes a bond."

Then it was a matter of waiting. William had taken himself off, and Joanna did not hear from him for the rest of the week. But on Thursday night the telephone rang. "Joanna!" Alicia announced.

"Why, hello, Alicia," Joanna said. "When are you leaving for Newcastle?"

"I'm not," Alicia said, crossly. "I've had this stupid accident."

"Accident?"

"Well, you know I go riding every morning?"

"I didn't know."

"Well, I do. I canter my horse through the open ground near where I live. And this morning some absolute lout barged into me."

"On another horse?"

"Well, of course on another horse," Alicia shouted. "Just came out of nowhere, from behind some trees, totally without warning. My little Carrie took fright and reared, and got knocked over herself. Well, I came off, but my foot got stuck in the stirrup, and I've sprained my ankle. My doctor says it's lucky it wasn't broken. In fact, it may be. He's taken X-rays and will let me know tomorrow. But it's gone up like a balloon. And boy, does it hurt. Anyway, I can't travel. So that's it."

"Oh, what a terrible shame," Joanna cried. "But . . . the fellow who did this to you . . . was it someone you knew?"

"Of course it wasn't someone I knew," Alicia snapped. "I told you, it was some lout."

"But . . . what happened to him? Have you had him arrested?"

"Oh, it wasn't anything malicious. He was most apologetic. Seems he was only just learning to ride and completely lost control of his horse. He called an ambulance for me and was as helpful as he could be. Which doesn't mean he isn't a lout. Why any stable let him out on his own defeats me. They're the ones who should be arrested."

"Absolutely," Joanna agreed. "Well, we'll have to sort something out."

"There is nothing to sort out," Alicia said. "There is no way I can travel up to Newcastle."

"But what about Howard?"

"He can't travel on his own."

"He can come with me."

"With you?"

"I'll pick him up and take him up, and show him the ships. I mean, after you've arranged time off school and all—"

"With you," Alicia muttered.

"Doesn't he want to look at the ships?"

"Oh, he does. Very much. But . . . well—"

"I'll look after him," Joanna said. "Promise."

"Wow," Howard said. "I thought we were going by train."

"It's always better to travel by Rolls," Joanna explained. "This is Prince Hasim ben Raisul abd Abdullah of Qadir."

Howard goggled at Hasim. "Are you really a prince?"

"That's what they say," Hasim agreed. "Come and sit here between us."

He had been given his instructions, and the visit to Newcastle continued as it had begun. They had left Alicia's house very early in the morning, Joanna having been allowed into see the invalid, who was looking very pale and wan and obviously in some pain. "It *is* broken," she announced "Can you imagine? I'm going to be here for *weeks*!"

"Perhaps the rest will do you good," Joanna suggested.

They fed Howard on ice cream and crisps all the way up to Newcastle, where they were naturally staying in the best hotel. "Didn't your father ever take you away on business trips?" Joanna asked.

Howard shook his head, staring at the white-gloved waiters and the acres of silver cutlery. "Mine didn't either," Hasim said.

They put Howard to bed at ten o'clock. "Tomorrow is going to be a busy day," Joanna said.

Then she found herself in a bedroom with Hasim. "He seems a nice boy," Hasim said. "Is he really going to be your partner from the moment he's twenty-one?"

"According to Howard's will."

"And you don't think the accident should have happened to him instead of his mother? I mean, permanently."

She gazed at him. "You're not serious, I hope."

Hasim shrugged. "Didn't I once ask you the same thing?"

"What happened to Alicia was no more than what she had happen to me," Joanna pointed out. "Now we're quits."

"But you intend to seduce that boy."

"Just what do you mean by that?"

Hasim shrugged. "I'm easy."

"You mean you wouldn't be jealous?"

He grinned. "Of a ten-year-old boy?"

"He'll grow."

"By the time he does, you'll be my wife. The penalty for adultery is very severe in Muslim countries."

She blew him a raspberry.

"Now," he said. "I would like to make love with you."

It was an ordeal Joanna had dreaded, but which she found the most stimulating experience of her life. Hasim made her strip naked, and then get down on her hands and knees on the carpet. "Don't move," he said.

She made herself keep still, her hair flopping past her face, while he began stroking her, beginning at her neck, coursing down her back, sliding over in front to caress her breasts, all with the most gentle touch. Then he moved down to her calves and ankles and feet, separating each toe to caress it in turn, before coming up to her thighs. By then she was nearly bursting with suppressed emotion, as his hands went between her legs. "Don't move," he said again, and began stroking again. Then he was inside her, but not violently or even over-passionately. Instead the entry was slow and steady and maddeningly titillating. When she fell on her face as he allowed his weight to come down on her, she remained moving and gasping for several seconds.

"Do all Muslim men make love like that?" she gasped.

"There are seventy-eight different positions," he pointed out. "I know them all."

After a night like that, she presumed she had to be pregnant again, but it was Howard she needed to concentrate on. The three of them went to the yard the next morning and were shown over the ships, still in the very early stages of construction. Afterwards they took Howard out to lunch, and then shopping, buying him everything and anything he fancied. Then it was back to the hotel and another bang up meal, and another bang up night with Hasim as well.

For all her initial reluctance, and indeed, a residue of distaste she could not shake off, Joanna had to count it about the most enjoyable weekend she had ever had. But she knew she still didn't love Hasim.

They were married in December. There were two ceremonies, one Christian and one Muslim. There were large crowds at each. Joanna was now on a high, for the stock flotation had been a great success, the new ships were all but finished, and she was the darling of the city. And she was only just twenty-one.

Hasim was as handsome and as dominant as ever. Several of his relatives, but not his father or mother, came over for the occasion. "They don't approve, do they?" Joanna asked.

"I suppose they do not. But they will not stand in my way, now that the constitutional matter has been sorted out."

Amongst those who did come was Hasim's younger brother, Mutil, who was now heir to the emirate. "Be sure that you will always be welcome in Qadir, sister," he told Joanna.

But she didn't think he meant it.

To Joanna's surprise, and relief, she had not yet become pregnant, despite Hasim's vigorous sexual methods. "How many children do you have?" she asked him, while they were honeymooning in the Seychelles.

"None that I know of. Does this concern you?"

"Of course not," she said.

In fact, it was another relief.

"But I shall have children with you," he promised.

And suddenly she *was* pregnant.

But by now she was able to take things in her stride. Hasim's child was much less important than Helen, at least before it arrived. And meanwhile she could continue to run the company as she chose. Peter Young remained a tower of strength, as did Billy Montgomery. She received no more mystery telephone calls, and she could watch her share price climb as the new route came into operation, and Caribee Line ships were to be seen from the Gulf to Panama, while profits grew. Nor was being Hasim's wife as time-consuming as she had feared. Now that he was permanently stationed in London – she gathered it had been intimated that, for all Mutil's invitation, it would be best for the erstwhile heir and his bride to stay out of Qadir – he had his work to attend to, as did she. They met at his London flat in the evenings, during the week, before attending various soirées or going to the opera or the ballet, and spent weekends at Caribee House.

When she began to show, all engagements were cancelled, and as with Helen, she operated entirely from Caribee House. She gave birth to a baby boy in December 1965, very close to her own birthday. His name was Raisul, after Hasim's father. "Because who knows what the future may hold," Hasim said.

That was not the first intimation Joanna had had that he did not entirely count himself, or his family, out of the running as future rulers of Qadir. She found this disturbing. Hasim could do what he liked, but she had no wish for either herself or her son to become embroiled in Middle East politics. However, it all seemed rather remote, looked at from the comforts of Caribee House. She continued to employ both William and Matilda, although they now had very little to do, as Hasim's people took over the job of bodyguarding, although the mere fact that she was now the Princess Hasim protected her. She was therefore hardly surprised when Matilda announced her engagement to Billy Montgomery. If you can't get the best, take the second best, Joanna supposed. But she showered her sister with congratulations, and gave Billy a pay rise.

Her main energy was concentrated on young Howard, as the swinging sixties rose to a crescendo. She saw as much of the boy as was possible, and he always seemed delighted to see her. This entailed seeing a good deal of Alicia as well, but Alicia seemed blissfully unaware, or uncaring, that Joanna might have any ulterior motive than mending fences with both her and her children. Victoria remained somewhat sullen and distant, but Howard continued to be utterly charmed by his stepmother, and often spent weekends at Caribee House when free from school. On these occasions Joanna largely handed him over to William, with strict instructions to entertain his stepbrother to the hilt. She kept a low but very obvious profile, taking Howard for walks, watching television with him in the evening, from time to time letting him sit in on meetings with Peter

Young, being always the gracious, friendly, forward-looking friend and future partner, more than stepmother.

While all the time Howard grew, from a gangling twelve-year-old to a sturdy, good-looking teenager. And she wrestled with her conscience and her ambitions. She was playing a very dangerous game, she knew. But having embarked on it, she was more and more tempted to carry it to its logical conclusion. Amoral and immoral? Certainly. But then so was the entire business world. And so was her marriage. About which she became increasingly concerned. It was not that Hasim proved anything other than a loving and caring husband and father, to both Helen and to his own son. Equally he always seemed to welcome Howard, and even Alicia. But there were things going on that she did not like. Occasionally Arab men would come to Hasim's London flat, and they and Hasim would confer long into the night, while she was politely requested to go to bed. "I would like to know what is going on?" she asked.

"Nothing that need concern you, my darling girl," he assured her. With which she had to be content.

She had other things on her mind, as Mums began to sicken. Joanna reckoned she really didn't have enough to do, as even superintending the garden couldn't occupy her mind. She spent a lot of time just staring into space. Joanna consulted with Matilda, who was in the throes of her first pregnancy. "Make her see a doctor," Matilda recommended. "I'll do it."

But Dr Alva could find nothing actually wrong. "She's mildly diabetic," he said. "But we can keep that under control. She'll probably work it out." Joanna wasn't very happy with that.

It was a fortnight later that she was in her study at Caribee House on a Sunday morning – a weekend when Hasim had decided to stay in London, no doubt for another of his clandestine conferences, she supposed – when Cummings knocked. "There is someone to see you, madam."

"Out here? On a Sunday? Is it someone I know?"

"I cannot say, madam. But he says he knows you."

"Well . . . I think I'd better come down."

She followed the butler down the stairs and into the hall, frowned at the tall man who stood there. He was not much older than herself, she supposed, but very broad-shouldered and heavily tanned . . . "My God!" she exclaimed. Dick Orton.

He flushed. "I hope you don't mind my calling, Mrs . . . ah?"

"Princess Hasim," she said. "Of course I don't mind you calling." She held his hands, drew him forward for a kiss on the cheek. "It is so good to see you. But come in. Cummings, a bottle of Bollinger."

Dick looked uneasy. "At eleven in the morning?"

"I always drink champagne at eleven in the morning," she explained, quoting Howard. "Come in." She led him into the small parlour. "My God, it must be six years."

"Five, actually." He sank on to the settee beside her.

"The car!" But anyone less like the gangling youth she had canoodled with in the back seat of the Rolls all those years ago could hardly be imagined. "And then you disappeared."

"I got fired, for not going to work that afternoon."

"Oh, good lord! But I told you, if anything like that happened, to come to me!"

"I couldn't do that, Your . . . do I call you, Your Highness?"

"You call me Joanna."

Cummings returned with the bottle and two glasses.

"Leave it," she told him, and lifted her own. "Old friends. I should apologise for refusing to talk with you after Howard's funeral. I was a bit cut up."

"Of course you were. It was boorish of me to intrude. I just wanted to say how sorry I was."

"Thank you." There was a brief silence. "Where did you go?" she asked at last. "When you lost your job?"

"I emigrated, worked at various jobs."

"It did you good. Physically, at least."

"Oh, it cleared a lot of cobwebs."

"And now you're back. What are you doing now?"

"Well, nothing, actually."

"Right. So you want a job. You have one. Do you know anything about shipping?"

"Some. But I don't want any charity."

"You're not getting charity. You're getting a job, which I shall expect you to do well."

"Then I shall do well," he said.

"There's just one thing. I do not employ anyone on drugs."

"Oh, that." He flushed as he grinned. "I've never touched them since that night. If you knew how badly I felt about involving you—"

"I wouldn't. But for my arrest that night I wouldn't be here."

"Owning all this."

"In a manner of speaking. You start on Monday."

"Doing what?"

"Just turn up at Caribee Shipping, and you'll be told." She smiled. "Probably licking stamps. But Dick . . ." she rested her hand on his arm. "You'll progress, if you want to. I promise you that."

"Yes, well . . ." he finished his champagne. "I can't tell you how grateful I am . . . do I still call you Joanna?"

"While you're here. In public you'll call me Princess Hasim."

"That sound terribly grand."

"It is terribly grand."

"Well . . ." he stood up, looking awkward.

"Oh, sit down," she said. "There's half a bottle left."

She didn't tell Hasim about Dick's visit, but she didn't consider it necessary to swear the servants to secrecy: they were her servants, not Hasim's. She did, however, allow herself to think about it. She was delighted to see Dick again, for all his misdemeanours in the past. He reminded her of her own past, before she had risen to heights she still found dizzying. She was surprised at how happy a time she found it, in retrospect – she hadn't been particularly happy at the time, she recalled. But to have nothing more serious to decide every day than whether or not to go dancing or to the pictures, and whether or not to allow her escort to get too familiar . . . yet she knew she wouldn't have changed anything.

That was not quite true. Like Miriam. Who did not improve. Dr Alva became grave. "It is a mental problem," he said. "But it is a serious mental problem. I have given her tranquillisers, and stimulants, and nothing works. She just doesn't want to live."

"Why? Why should she feel like that? She doesn't have a care in the world." Joanna was quite angry.

"We have to try a psychiatrist," Alva decided.

But that didn't help either. No matter how hard Mr Hardisty tried, Mirian just wouldn't speak to him.

So there came the morning that Mrs Partridge hurried into Joanna's bedroom, without knocking, for the first time ever, to say, "Princess! Princess! Mrs Grain is dead."

"Why?" Joanna asked the parson. "Tell me why? She didn't have a care in the world."

The Reverend Enderby pulled his ear. "I didn't know your mother very well, of course, Princess Hasim," he said – his way of saying that Miriam had never been a regular church-goer – "but I sometimes wondered if she ever really recovered from your father's tragic death."

"That was eight years ago," Joanna said coldly. Was it only eight years? What a long way she had travelled in that time. But Mother had travelled further.

Hasim came down from London for the funeral, but apart from him and his bodyguards there were not many mourners, just Aunt Ethel, Matilda and Billy, William and the children, and – "Who is that fellow?" Hasim asked, as they left the church.

Joanna turned her head, sharply. Dick was keeping as far back as possible.

"A member of my staff," she said. In the commotion of Mums' dying she had quite forgotten Dick.

She found an opportunity to be alone with him during the reception after the funeral. "It was good of you to come," she said. "How did you get off?"

"I asked for time off," he explained. "I told them I was an old friend of your family."

"As you are," she agreed. "But you never met Mother, did you?"

"No. I had hoped to."

He was back to skating on thin ice. "So tell me," she said. "What are you doing?"

He grinned. "Licking stamps. Sort of."

"I'm sorry I've neglected you. Things have been a little fraught."

"Of course. In any event, you're the boss and I'm the office boy."

She felt like slapping his face, but then, she felt like slapping a lot of faces. She just could not believe that Mums had gone and died, without rhyme or reason, was almost inclined to demand a post mortem. Matilda forbade that. "Leave the poor old soul be," she insisted.

No doubt Matilda felt as guilty as she, Joanna realised. They had both followed their own agendas, leaving Mums to trail in their wakes. And now . . .

Two days later she got home from the office – as it was midweek she was staying at Hasim's flat in town – to find the flat unguarded. She unlocked the door, and found Hasim standing at the window, looking down on London with a pensive expression. "What's happened?" she asked.

"My father is dead."

"Oh, my God!" She put her arms round his waist to hug him. "I am so terribly sorry."

"He was pretty old," Hasim said. "Older than your mother."

"Will you have to go to the funeral?"

"It has been intimated to me that I should not. I have sent Wazir as my representative."

"I wondered what had happened to him. Oh, my darling." She released him and went to the bar. "Would you like a drink?"

"Yes. A whisky."

She raised her eyebrows. Hasim was not in the least a practicing Muslim, but he very seldom drank spirits. She poured two, gave him one, sat on the settee. "Will this, well . . ."

"Make any difference?" He turned, sat beside her. "Not in the least. All my arrangements, financial and shall we say, political, were made, with Papa's full agreement, to continue after his death."

"But Mutil is now Emir?"

"Yes," he said thoughtfully.

"Hasim . . ." she put down her glass to hold his hand. "You're not going to get mixed up in Qadiri politics, are you?"

"Why should I?" he asked. "I have no interest in Qadir any more. Except in so far as it pays me well." He put his arm round her shoulder to give her a squeeze. "And you, to be sure." Then he grinned. "They say these things always go in threes. I wonder who will be the third?"

Joanna supposed the best bet would be Aunt Ethel, who was several years older than Mums. But Aunt Ethel was in the best of health. Meanwhile she spent an anxious month wondering if Hasim was right that nothing would change, half expecting every morning to find an official letter on her desk informing her that Caribee Shipping's trading concession with the Emirate of Qadir had been terminated. But there never was one.

She found time, and some relief, from the anxieties of the situation by wandering through the vast building, finally discovering Dick on the ground floor, filling out invoices. "Is this what you do?" she asked, while the other clerks waited in hushed and reverential silence.

"I've been promoted, Princess Hasim," Dick said.

"How splendid. I have something for you." She placed the envelope on his desk, and returned upstairs to her office. It was an invitation to her twenty-sixth birthday party.

"I want it to be just a small, family affair," she told Hasim. "We are both still in mourning."

"Of course. I entirely agree."

"But you won't mind if I invite that new boy from the office? My old school chum?"

"Invite who you like," Hasim said.

She invited Aunt Ethel, who refused. Matilda and Billy Montgomery came, as did William with a young woman Joanna had not seen before, or even heard of. But she was delighted that William had accumulated a girlfriend. Her name was Norma. Alicia, Howard and Victoria came. And of course Dick.

It was rather a solemn occasion, but the ice slowly began to crack as the second round of champagne was served by Waqar, Wazir's stand-in as butler, even if Joanna did not suppose he would be much good as a bodyguard, for he was small and thin. "Well," she said. "It is so good, having you all here, and being just us. If you follow me."

"You are all the family I have now," Hasim declared. He was still somewhat gloomy.

"But not all you are going to have, eh?" Alicia asked. The two small children were out at Caribee House.

"Well . . ." Hasim actually smiled. "I hope not."

Joanna signalled Waqar to open another bottle. "Now," she said, seating herself beside Norma. "Tell me all about yourself."

"Oh. I . . ." She was tongue-tied with embarrassment. She was a small, dark girl, who looked nervous all the time.

"Norma works in a travel agency," William explained.

"How interesting," Joanna said.

"And she is twenty-two years old," William went on, grinning. "Unmarried, and drives a Mini. Her parents live in Cornwall. My sister," he explained to the still more embarrassed girl, "likes to have everything cut and dried. She'll grow on you."

"Well—" Joanna said, when the flat door opened, surprisingly, as it was locked. But it was Wazir standing there; he had a key. He also had a sub-machine-gun, as did the two men standing behind him.

# Chapter Eleven

# The Assassin

Joanna stood up, but in common with everyone else in the room, she goggled at the three men. Hasim and Dick were the first to react. Hasim spoke in Arabic, and Wazir turned his sub-machine-gun towards his employer and squeezed the trigger. In the same instant Dick threw himself across the room, catching Joanna round the thighs in a rugby tackle and hurling her right over the settee to the floor beyond with a crash that knocked all the breath from her body. Where her legs went she had no idea, but she suspected one of them caught Norma across the face and tumbled her too to the floor.

Meanwhile the guns continued to chatter, now overlaid by the shrieks of the people being hit as the bullets sprayed the room, while crockery and paintings dissolved, and wood from the walls, torn upholstery, and cascading blood filled the air. The whole thing lasted, Joanna realised in retrospect, a matter of seconds. It seemed an eternity at the time. She kept trying to rise and being held down by Dick's body; he had thrown himself on top of her. The sudden silence as the shooting stopped took them both by surprise, and after a moment he rolled off her and lay on his back, staring at the ceiling. "Are you all right?" Joanna gasped, aware of a weight across her legs.

"Yes," he said.

Joanna sat up, looked at Norma, who was the weight. But Norma was also rolling off her, equally protected by the settee from the flying bullets. "My God!" she whispered. "My God!"

Joanna turned on to her knees. She wasn't prepared to risk standing up, not only because Wazir might still be there, but because she didn't really want to look at the rest of the room, discover who had been hit. But as she knelt, she found herself looking at a stream of blood drifting round the end of the settee. She crawled forward, stared at her husband. She would not have known him save for his suit. The bullets had smashed into his face as well as his chest, shattering them both. She retched, and sank on to her haunches, unaware that the top of her head was now actually above the settee.

Now there was movement, all around her, dominated by a sudden high-pitched scream. Alicia!

Joanna scrambled to her feet, and looked over the settee at the doorway. But the doorway was empty. The three men might never have been, save for what they had accomplished.

William! William had been standing in front of her, joking about Norma. Now he lay on his face, the back of his jacket a mess of blood.

Matilda! Matilda lay against the far wall, screaming, being comforted by Billy; neither of them seemed to have been hit.

Alicia! Alicia sat by the settee, Howard cradled in her arms, while Victoria huddled against her for protection. They were surrounded by blood.

Waqar! Joanna looked at the bar and saw him just emerging from behind it, trembling.

"My God!" Norma kept saying. She had also reached her feet.

"Look after her!" Joanna snapped at Dick, and ran round the settee. "Waqar! Call the police!"

If they were not already on their way; the residents of the other flats had heard the shooting, and there was a great deal of noise and screaming coming from down the stairs and the lift shaft. Joanna knelt beside William, touched his head, realised he was breathing. "And an ambulance," she shouted. "Dial 999." Waqar was already at the phone.

"My son!" Alicia was wailing. "My Howie! Oh, my Howie." Joanna glanced at her, realised that Howard was dead. She couldn't take in what had happened, only that William might also be dying.

"We must stop the bleeding." Dick knelt beside her, ripping William's jacket open to find the wounds. Norma's knees gave way and she sank back to the floor.

"My Howie!" Alicia was screaming. "They've killed my Howie! You killed him, you bitch!"

Joanna merely looked at her. Dick seemed to know what he was doing with William. She turned on her knees, her stockings and dress now stained with blood, and gazed at Hasim. Billy held her shoulders and raised her up. "You should lie down."

"I'm all right," she muttered. "I'm all right."

Waqar stood at her other side with a glass of brandy, and she gulped it. "Will William live?"

"If we get him to a hospital," Dick said.

Sirens wailed, feet pounded on the stairs as the lift whirred. The flat was taken over. White-coated men clustered round William and administered various shots and medication before lifting him on to the stretcher. Hasim was left where he was while blue-coated men photographed and took measurements. Howard was gently extracted from Alicia's arms, and laid on the carpet, while more white-coated men gave her shots as well to calm her down. Victoria appeared to be struck dumb by what had happened.

"You all right, ma'am?" a police officer asked Matilda. Matilda just stared at him.

"She'll be all right," Billy said.

"You being?"

"I'm her husband. William Montgomery."

"Ah!" The inspector realised he had made a mistake and turned to Joanna, who remained kneeling beside Hasim. "Mrs . . . Princess Hasim?"

"Will my brother be all right?" Joanna asked, not looking at him.

"We're doing all we can," said one of the medics who had remained behind. "I think the princess is in a state of shock, Inspector."

"No," Joanna said. "No. It was a political assassination." The inspector pulled his ear. "I know one of the killers," Joanna said. "His name is Wazir, and he was my husband's bodyguard."

"Was? You mean he was sacked?"

"He returned to Qadir to attend the late Emir's funeral. They must have got at him, there."

"Who are 'they', Princess?"

"My husband's brother. His half-brother, anyway. Prince Mutil. I suppose you'd have to call him Emir Mutil, now. He was my husband's younger brother. When he married me, Prince Hasim renounced the throne in Mutil's favour."

"Then why should this Mutil have your husband murdered?"

"Because he feared Hasim might after all claim the throne."

The Inspector was clearly realising this business was a little out of his class. "You don't think this Wazir chap might have just have been disgruntled because he had been fired? Some of these Arabs are pretty hot-tempered. With respect, ma'am," as he recalled that her Arab husband's dead body was lying beside her.

"Inspector," Joanna said. "I told you. Wazir was not fired; he was sent back to Qadir to represent my husband at his father's funeral. And he was not alone; there were two other men with him. And of all the people in this room, only the three men who might have been involved in Hasim's claim on the throne were shot."

The Inspector scratched his head. "This lad," he looked at Howard's body, "was connected with your family?"

"Indirectly. He was my step-son."

"So he had nothing to do with the Qadir side of it."

"No, Inspector. But Wazir and his people did not know that. Their orders were to eliminate any possible claimant to the throne. They must have thought Howard was Hasim's son." But Wazir would have known who Howard was. "My God!" She ran to the phone.

"Who are you calling, ma'am?"

Joanna was punching the numbers. "My home in Berkshire. My son is there. Prince Hasim's son. They'll want him as well."

"We'll take care of it, ma'am." He attempted to take the phone from her fingers, and she jerked away. "Cummings! Listen! I want you to lock all the exterior doors, and windows, bar them, draw the curtains, and let no one into the house. No one, do you understand, until I get to you."

"Madam?" Cummings was clearly mystified.

"Just do it. I'll be there as soon as I can."

"You need to rest, ma'am," the police inspector said, at last managing to relieve her of the phone. He dialled himself, and began giving orders, obviously to the local police, to have Caribee House surrounded. "Yes," he said. "I think some of your people should be armed. I will have permission sent down to you, but do it anyway, now."

He replaced the phone. Joanna had sunk on to the settee. "Do you have any idea who would have given these orders, madam?"

"Prince Mutil, I would say."

"That's a pretty tall accusation, Princess. Like the doctor says, I think maybe you want to lie down for a while. We'll talk again later. Howick, get these bodies out of here."

"Listen," Joanna said. "Catch those men!"

"Oh, we'll do that, Princess," he said confidently. "Now, some of my men will remain here, eh? Just to keep an eye on things. They won't interfere, and they'll make as little noise as possible."

"Thank you," Joanna said. "I must get down to the house."

"The house is under police protection, Princess. No one is going to trouble your son. And you are in a state of shock. Please be sensible about this."

Dick and Billy helped Joanna and Matilda into the master bedroom. Alicia and Victoria had been put to bed in one of the other bedrooms, both having been given tranquillisers. "Norma," Joanna muttered. "What happened to Norma?"

"She went off to the hospital with William," Billy said.

Joanna sat on the side of the bed, her head in her hands, but she looked up as there was a tap on the door. It was Dr Grahame, the police doctor, looking apologetic. "I do feel that you should have some medication, Princess."

"How can I have medication?" Joanna said. "There's so much to be done. I must get home . . . My God! The children."

"You have other children?"

"My daughter and my son."

"Did you tell the police about them?"

"No. Yes. There was so much going on—"

"I'll make sure they have it under control," Dick volunteered, understanding that he was surplus to requirements at the moment. He hurried from the room.

"Believe me, Princess, you'll feel a whole lot better, more able to cope, if you can have a sound sleep," Grahame said.

Joanna sighed. "Oh, very well. You joining me, Tilly?"

"Oh, yes," Matilda said. "My God—"

"Don't start up again," Billy said. "Listen, I'll be in the lounge if you need me. Either of you."

"Should we undress first?" Joanna asked.

Grahame shook his head. "It'll take about ten minutes to work. So you can undress after the shot, go to bed, and have a solid night's sleep."

He injected them each in turn. "I'll stop in tomorrow. Or would you rather have your own doctor?"

"I think Dr Alva should come," Joanna said. She gave him Alva's card.

"I'll see to it." He closed the door behind him.

Matilda was already in the bathroom. Joanna joined her, and they stared at each other in the mirrors as they cleaned their teeth. Matilda's hands were trembling, and her toothbrush kept hitting her teeth. "Weren't you scared at all?" she said. "Don't you ever get scared?"

"I was terrified," Joanna confessed. But her hands weren't shaking.

"I never believed things like that really happened," Matilda said, throwing herself on the bed.

"Only to other people." Joanna lay down beside her. "But I suppose, when I married Hasim, I became one of those other people."

"But you never loved Hasim, did you?"

Joanna sighed. "No. It was always a business transaction. But you don't live with someone for several years without becoming at least fond of him. I'm going to get that bastard, Wazir, if it's the last thing I do."

Matilda giggled. "Some of his Arab blood must have rubbed off on you. And you still have little Raisul."

"Yes," Joanna muttered. Thank God the children had not come up for her party. She fell asleep.

Joanna awoke to a hum of sound, emanating from the lounge. She sat up, for a few moments unable to remember what had happened, looked left and right, expecting to see Hasim lying beside her, and then remembering that it should be Matilda. But Matilda wasn't there, either.

She rolled out of bed, went to the bathroom to splash the sleep from her eyes, looked out of the window. It was daylight. She must have slept for something like twelve hours. While . . . she pulled on a dressing gown and opened the bedroom door, gazed at a scene of ordered chaos, as cleaners removed the bloodstains, helped by Billy and Dick, both unshaven and jacketless, ties pulled down, looking exhausted. Matilda was with them, supervising, while two armed policemen stood about, looking helpless. "You look a whole lot better," Dick said.

Joanna ran back into the bedroom to use the phone there. Now at last her hands were trembling as she punched the numbers. "Cummings! Are you all right?"

"Madam? What has happened?"

"Listen! I'll be with you as quickly as I can. Until I arrive, keep all exterior doors and all the downstairs windows barred. Allow no one near the house."

"Even the police, madam? They are already in the house. But they won't tell us what is happening."

"Oh, thank God!" she shouted. "Well, they should be able to handle it. I'm on my way."

Matilda stood in the doorway. "They were on the spot half an hour after Hasim's death."

"Nobody told me."

"Well, you were asleep. But the children are safe. Believe me. Now, there's someone from the Foreign Office wanting to see you—"

"I'm going out to the house. If anyone wants to see me, they can come there."

She ran into the bathroom, showered, found Matilda still waiting for her. "Won't you have breakfast?"

"I'll have it at the house."

"You want me to come with you?"

"No, stay here. Go to William. Make sure he's all right. I'll be back as soon as I can."

"What about Alicia?"

"What about Alicia?"

"Well . . . she's still here." She gestured towards the other bedrooms.

"Oh, good lord."

"She's had to be sedated again," Matilda explained.

"What about Victoria?"

"She's in there with her. When she wakes up—"

"Give her breakfast. And if necessary, have her tranquillised again."

There was a knock on the door. "Dr Alva is here."

"Oh . . . let him come in." It seemed a waste of time dressing, as he would only want her to undress again.

He peered at her, lifted her eyelids, tested her pulse. "You're all right, Princess."

Am I still a princess? Joanna wondered. She didn't want to be.

"It's Mrs Edge you want to look at," she said. "She's in a hysterical state. Her son was killed."

"Oh dear, oh dear," Alva said. "Do you know that I delivered that boy?"

"See what you can do for her."

Matilda ushered him out, and Joanna dressed. Back to black. She knew that some time soon what had happened was going to get up and hit her straight in the face. But until that happened, she had to hurry, not keep still for a moment, and remarkably, as the medic had promised last night, her brain felt absolutely clear. She just wanted to be with her children, then she wanted to be with William, then . . . she went into the lounge. "Would you like me to come with you?" Dick asked.

She hesitated. "If you promise not to say anything."

He raised his eyebrows, but picked up his jacket.

"About this fellow from the Foreign Office—" Billy ventured.

"I told you, he can come down to Caribee House. Or wait for me to come back up. I'll be doing that this evening. Tilly, I want you to call me the moment you find out about William." Then she was in the back seat of the Rolls, Charlie driving, Dick beside her.

As promised, he didn't say anything, while she tried to get her thinking under control. The firm, the route to Qadir, the presumption that Wazir was still out there . . . had he tried to get at the children, on discovering that they weren't in the London flat? And been beaten to it by the police? But then he would try again. She buried her face in her hands. She had told Matilda that when she had married Hasim she had become one of the Other People. The people to whom things happened, terrible things. Which went on and on and on.

Dick rested his hand on her shoulder. "They'll catch those fellows." She gave him a wan smile.

"Were you very happy?" he asked. "I suppose that's not very tasteful."

"You're entitled to know. No, I wasn't *very* happy. It was a business deal. My body for Hasim's support and protection. Well, I had his support."

"Will this affect the firm?"

"I don't know. I don't know anything, right this minute. You said you wouldn't speak."

"I'm sorry. But you were looking so done up—"

She smiled, and squeezed his hand. "Don't worry about *your* job, anyway. I need friends. Are you my friend, Dick?"

"Always and forever." She lay back with a sigh. She could stand a little more of that sort of loyalty.

Caribee House was like an armed camp, in the midst of which Cummings and Mrs Partridge and the other servants were distraught. Raisul and Helen thought it was all great fun.

"I'm Inspector Garside," the tall thin man told her. "Local police. I was called last night and told to place my men and wait."

"Because those murderers are still at large," Jonna said. "You've heard nothing?"

"Only a confirmation of my original order."

"And no one has tried to get in here?"

"No, ma'am."

She held the children's hands and took them into the winter parlour. Dick was standing around awkwardly, so she beckoned him in as well. "You could do with a bath and a shave," she suggested.

"Where do I go?"

"The house is full of bathrooms," she said. "Just ask Mrs Partridge for one. She'll supply you with a razor and a toothbrush as well."

"What's happening, Mother?" Helen was five.

Raisul was only three. But there was no way either of them could be told the truth, right that moment. "There are some bad men in the neighbourhood," she said, sitting one on each knee, "so the police are going to stay with us until the men have been caught."

"Will they have guns?"

"Baddies always have guns. But so do the police. And the police always win. You've seen it on the telly."

"Why are you wearing black?"

The child was far too intelligent. "Don't you like me in black? It goes with my hair."

"I want to go outside to play," Helen said. "And the policemen won't let me."

"Play, play, play," Raisul chanted.

"You'll be able to go outside soon," Joanna said, and rang for Nanny.

Cummings produced a cup of coffee, and Dick joined her, looking much cleaner even if his clothes might have been slept in. "What do we do now?" he asked. "I suppose I should be getting in to the office."

"My God," she said. "The office. I wonder—" The phone rang. "That'll be Tilly," Joanna cried, as Cummings brought it to her.

But it was Peter Young. "Princess! I've just heard. I can't tell you how upset I am."

"Thank you, Peter."

"Is it . . . will it . . . well . . . ?"

"Business as usual, Peter. Until we hear otherwise."

"Ah . . . right. Will you be coming in?"

"Not today. Tomorrow. Is there anything urgent?"

"Nothing that compares with what has happened."

"Then hold the fort until I see you."

"Right. But by the way, do you know what has happened to young Orton? He's quite disappeared. He didn't come in this morning, and when we rang his digs he hadn't been in all night."

"He's with me," Joanna said. "He was present at the shooting, and he's pretty shaken up. He'll be in tomorrow."

"Oh. Right." Peter Young was clearly a puzzled man.

"I'm quite all right, really," Dick said. "I can go home, and change, and get down to the office."

"I want you here," Joanna said.

"I'm not much company."

"I don't want that sort of company. I just want you here. Right?"

The phone was ringing again.

"Tilly!" Joanna shouted. "Is he—"

"They've got the bullets out."

"Bullets!"

"There were three. Only one was in a dangerous place. They're using catch phrases: serious but stable. I think he's going to be all right."

"I'll be up to see him in the morning. I just don't feel I can leave the children right now, and I don't want to bring them up to London; they'd be asking where Hasim was."

"Of course. I'll hold the fort. There's just one thing."

"Tell me."

"Alicia."

"Don't tell me she's still at the flat?"

"No. She's gone off. But she's been on television, blaming you for Howard's death. That's slanderous, you know."

"Well, I suppose in a way I am responsible," Joanna said. "For being Hasim's wife."

"You don't understand," Matilda said. "She's suggesting that it was all a plot to stop Howard from taking over, as she puts it, Caribee Shipping."

"You're not serious?"

"She is. I think you have to do something about her."

If you knew how many times I have thought that, Joanna thought.

"I'll have a talk with John Giffard," she said. "Listen, don't worry about it. Tell you what, though, arrange an appointment for me with John for tomorrow morning."

"Will do," Matilda agreed.

"And give William my best love."

Joanna hung up, gazed at Dick.

"You live a fantastically exciting life," he said. And he had only been able to hear her answers.

"Sometimes it gets a bit much," she said. "I want to be with the children. Come with me."

It was about the most domestic day she had spent in a long while. Dick was actually very good with children, and he even managed to make them forget the presence of the policemen. While Joanna could sit in a chair and think. There was so much to be thought about.

Howard! Poor, poor Howard. *Was* she responsible for his death? Legally such a suggestion was absurd. Hysterically it might well attract a few sympathisers. Had she meant to seduce him? She had never been sure about that. She liked to regard herself as an utterly ruthless, determined woman, who would sleep with the devil if it would continue her control of the company, but she knew in her heart that was just dreaming.

Although she had regarded Hasim as the devil when they had first got together. Then he had turned out to be a very ordinary and loving man. Save that he could not forget he had once been the heir to Qadir. That was what had killed him. When she thought of Mutil, smiling, inviting her to visit him in his capital . . . My God, she thought, suppose I had gone?

That didn't alter her ambivalent attitude towards Howard, who was now lying on a slab in a mortuary. Just like his dad, six years ago.

Only Howard senior had never actually lain on a slab. Good God, she thought to herself, you are going round the bend.

"Lunch is served, madam," Cummings said.

The meal over, Nanny took the children away. "I am going upstairs to lie down," Joanna said to Dick.

"Right. Shall I—"

"You will come with me." She went upstairs, closed the door behind them both.

"The servants—" he protested.

"Are my most faithful adherents."

"Your husband—"

"Is barely cold. I do not wish to have sex with you, Dick. I may wish to do so, some time in the future. Some time quite soon. Right now I want to lie down and rest. And I need a man lying beside me. Does that concept hurt your feelings?"

"No," he said. "No. I—"

She unzipped her dress. "Please don't try to explain. You always talked too much. Just be there. Okay?" He gulped, watched her finish undressing. Naked, she crawled beneath the sheets. "Do you think I am a domineering bitch?"

"I think you are the most remarkable woman I ever met. Perhaps who ever lived." He was undressing now, as rapidly as he could.

"Do you know," she said, "this is the first time I have ever seen you naked?"

"Ah—" he checked.

"Oh, I like it," she said. "Very Grecian. But then, this is the first time you have ever seen me naked, isn't it?"

"Yes" he said, and raised the sheet to slide in beside her. "Not at all Grecian."

"Eh?"

"No Greek, including the Venus de Milo, ever looked like you."

"I think she was an Italian copy. No," she said, as his hand slid across to touch her thigh. "Not now. I am mourning my husband, and I don't know how I feel, about anything."

"But you want me to be here?"

"That's right."

The phone was ringing, constantly. Joanna stretched out her hand and picked it up.

"Joanna?"

"Peter?" she asked drowsily.

"I'm afraid things are on the move."

She blinked herself awake. "I take it that means down."

"I'm afraid so. Only a few points, and the market is about to close for the day. But I don't know about tomorrow. Especially . . ." he hesitated.

"Tell me."

"There is a communication from Qadir."

"Terminating?"

"With notice. Oh, very proper and businesslike. No reference to the Prince's death. But none the less—"

"When is it dated?"

"Oh, eight days ago."

"And Hasim was murdered yesterday. There's an admission of guilt."

"They'll claim the two events are unrelated."

"We'll see about that. All right, Peter. As you say, there is nothing more we can do today. I'll be in tomorrow." She hung up, stared at the ceiling.

"Bad news?" Dick asked.

"It wasn't unexpected. Do you know I have no idea where Hasim's body is? Or what funeral arrangements have been made?" She sat up, telephoned Hasim's office.

"Princess," said his male secretary. "We have been looking for you everywhere."

Which obviously wasn't true, as the man had to know exactly where she had to be, if she was no longer at the flat.

"The Prince's body is in a police morgue. They say there has to be an autopsy. But it will be released for cremation tomorrow. I have arranged it."

"And when will the cremation take place?"

"Tomorrow afternoon, after a service at the Qadir mosque."

"Do the police know this?"

"I do not consider that necessary, Highness."

"Well, I do, Nasir. The assassins have not yet been caught. They may well attend the funeral."

"I see. Will Prince Raisul be attending?"

"No, he will not," Joanna told him. "But I shall be."

"Of course, Highness."

She hung up, remained sitting on the edge of the bed. As usual, there was so much to be thought of. The news that the Qadir route was ended would have to be released tomorrow. That would cause another fall in the share price. She could only be grateful that for the moment the company was out of debt and totally viable. But it wouldn't stay viable long trading only with the West Indies. And she had no more strings to her bow. Save . . . she gave a little sigh, and lay down, on her back. Dick was propped on his elbow, watching her.

"Anything I can do?" he asked.

She gazed at him. "Yes," she said. "Cover me. Don't try to get between my legs. Just cover me."

He obeyed with alacrity, looked down into her eyes from a distance of a few inches. "May I kiss you?"

"I would like that."

It was a long kiss. "Do you know how much I love you?" he asked.

"Me? Or Joanna, Princess Hasim?"

"I was thinking of Joanna Grain."

"I know. That's why I want you around. I get so insecure."

"You, Joanna?"

"Me," she said. "Forget the façade. For Christ's sake, I've watched two husbands die, violently. Makes you think."

"So what happens now?"

"Now?" She inflated her lungs, driving her breasts upwards into his chest. "When I get some confidence back, I have a company to save."

# Chapter Twelve

# The Survivor

Joanna eventually sent Dick home to have a good night's sleep and get to the office the next morning; if she had him around too long they would have sex together, and that was unthinkable while Hasim was still lying on a slab. The trouble was, she was too confused about her emotions, her outrage at what had happened being overlaid by her continuing fear for Raisul, and even Helen, who was always at the side of her baby brother, and by her continuing apprehensions for William. She telephoned the hospital after Dick had left, and was told that her brother was stable but still unconscious following the extensive surgery. How she wanted to be at his side. But she dared not leave the children.

Inspector Garside did his best to be reassuring. "There is no way anyone can get into this house," he said.

"A determined man will always get in somewhere," Joanna insisted.

A car rolled down the drive. Joanna watched it from one of the upstairs windows, but the two men who got out were certainly not Arab. A few minutes later both men were in the house. "A Mr Norton, madam," Cummings explained. "From the Foreign Office."

Joanna had not bothered to dress after Dick had left. She put on a houserobe and slippers and went downstairs, aware that her hair was loose on her shoulders and that she must look as if she had just got out of bed. Which she had. "I'm afraid I was resting," she said, looking from face to face.

"John Norton, Princess, and this is Geoffrey Allan. My card."

She put the card on the table. "Please sit." She did so herself.

"You'll forgive us for intruding on your grief, ma'am," Norton said. "But this business, well, it does have ramifications."

"I'm sure it does. My husband was murdered by his half-brother, while living in this country."

"Ah . . . this is what you told the police last night. Have you any proof that Emir Mutil was involved in your husband's death?"

"Well, it's fairly obvious, isn't it? Prince Hasim was negotiating with certain people from his own country—"

"You have proof of this?"

"He was certainly meeting with people from Qadir, exiles like himself."

"But you do not know the subject of their discussions."

"Well, of course I do not."

"They need not have been discussing Qadir at all."

"Oh, for heaven's sake—"

"I wish you to understand the position of Her Majesty's Government, Princess Hasim. Great Britain has very important links with Qadir, both business and defence. It would be a serious matter indeed if those links were to be imperilled. Believe me, we have every possible sympathy with you in the horrible murder of your husband and your stepson, but you must understand that until and unless there is proof that the assassination was carried out on behalf of the present Qadiri government, we would not wish to take the matter any further, nor could we possibly approve of someone in your position throwing out accusations which have no substantiation."

"I had always assumed this was a free country."

"I hope it is. But freedom carries with it a certain responsibility."

"Mr Norton," Joanna said, "I can identify one of the three assassins. He was a man named Wazir, who had been in the employ of my husband—"

"Had been? You mean he had been fired?"

"Oh, God, I went through all this with the police last night. No, he had not been fired. He was highly valued by my husband. When the Emir Raisul died, a few weeks ago, as Hasim had agreed not to return to Qadir, he sent Wazir as his representative at his father's funeral. Something must have happened while Wazir was there. He was suborned, or something. So he came back to murder my husband. And my son."

"But you have no proof of this."

"I do not have any proof," Joanna shouted. "Only that I saw Wazir murder my husband in cold blood."

"I know. Very tragic. It would be unusual indeed if you were thinking clearly this close to such a horrendous event."

Joanna glared at him. "Just what are you trying to say?"

"I am merely trying to put it to you that you, we, all of us, need to think very clearly as to which direction we are going to proceed in this matter. The Arab world is riddled with blood feuds and ancient family rivalries. You say your husband was meeting with various Qadiris. You assume he was discussing politics. But they might have been personal matters, equally important to him, involving this man Wazir."

"Of course," Joanna snapped. "And Jack the Ripper could have been a milkman who just happened to be around when all those women were murdered. Am I to assume, Mr Norton, that you are going to stop looking for Wazir and his accomplices? I wish you to know that I want, and am entitled, to police protection until they are caught."

"We have no intention of ceasing to look for the murderers of your husband, ma'am. They will be caught. And until they are, you will continue to receive protection. And for your son, of course."

"Thank you."

"But in return, I would ask you most earnestly to refrain from making any statements to the press about Qadiri involvement in this matter. It would be far better for all of us, publicly at least, to indicate that this was a personal feud between Prince Hasim and his employee."

Joanna sighed. "I will be careful what I say to the press."

Because that ordeal was now upon her. The press had been besieging the flat and Matilda and the hospital where William was, as well as the Qadiri Embassy in London and even Caribee Shipping. Now at last they had gathered that Joanna was at her home in the country, and they came charging down, to be extremely put out when the police refused them entry to the grounds. Joanna was actually quite in favour of their getting uptight about that, as naturally they floated their own theories as to what was going on, theories which agreed with hers but which could not be related to her. She was, however, upset when she took the children for a walk in the grounds that evening and discovered all the fences lined with snapping photographers, using long-range lenses. It wasn't the photographs that bothered her as much as the thought that amongst those lenses there could be Wazir, armed with a gun.

She hurried the children back inside, had an early dinner. Now she wished she had made Dick stay, but she actually slept very soundly, and was at the office next morning at eight. It had been quite a decision to leave the children, although Inspector Garside swore they would be all right. And for her drive in she had an armed detective sitting in the front of the Rolls beside a highly nervous Charlie. She could see no necessity for his presence; had Wazir wanted her life he could easily have had it in the flat. Peter Young wore his usual long face. "The market isn't actually open yet," he said, "but I've been in touch with Prim, and he tells me the shares will definitely be marked down."

"To what?"

"Well, this time yesterday morning, before the news of the assassination broke, they were eight pounds, twelve shillings and four pence. At the close last night they were seven pounds, eighteen shillings and three pence. That wasn't too bad. But he suggests they may go as low as six this morning. And then, we simply have to release the news that the Qadir link is now broken. Irrevocably?"

"Yes," Joanna said.

"Well . . . we could be looking at five, even. Worse if we don't come up with a new route." He peered at her over the tops of his glasses.

"No new route, at the moment," Joanna said. "I shall have to work on it."

"You understand that this could be a most serious matter," Peter said.

"We've faced serious matters before."

"Indeed we have. But . . . well . . ." he looked embarrassed.

She knew what he was thinking; before she had had Prince Hasim waiting in the wings. "The ships need a refit, anyway," she said.

"Which will cost money we do not have."

"It is still necessary. And then put them on the Caribbean route. Advertise the extra sailings. We should attract some passengers. And contact our manufacturers and tell them we shall be placing additional space at their disposal."

"You do realise that there is a limit to how many washing machines and dishwashers one can sell in an area like the West Indies? It's geared to tourism more than anywhere else. A few live very well, and they have all the household appliances they require, and the rest live rather poorly, and they can't afford the latest models, or any models at all."

"I understand that, Peter. But we can at least ship more rice and sugar, can't we?"

"If they can grow more. I hate to be a merchant of doom and gloom, Joanna, but—"

"Listen," Joanna said. "Just do all the things I have told you, and let me worry about what happens next."

He looked as if he would have spoken again, then shrugged. "And the news from Qadir?"

"Oh, as you say, that must be released this morning, certainly the moment trading begins. Now I have a couple of funerals to attend."

First she went to the hospital to see William. He remained in intensive care, and with his oxygen mask and the mass of bandages she couldn't really identify him, until their hands touched and he squeezed her fingers. "We anticipate your brother will make a full recovery," Dr Alva told her.

Which was at least a crumb of comfort.

Billy and Matilda accompanied her to Hasim's funeral. They were not the only English people to attend, but the others were all very obviously plainclothes policemen, not only protecting her but looking out for Wazir. As if he would be foolish enough to turn up.

"You going back to the office?" Billy asked, when all the prayers had been said and chanted, the body had disappeared, and they stood on the steps of the mosque.

"No. I've had enough doom and gloom for the moment. And I need to brace myself for this afternoon."

"The funeral, or the share price?"

"Both."

"Well, if you want to have a chat about the shares—"

"I'll be in touch. Are you going to Howard's funeral this afternoon?"

"I think we should," Matilda said.

"Then will you pick me up?

"Two o'clock," Matilda promised.

Joanna had Charlie drive her to her own flat. Her ivory tower. There were, as always, several bottles of champagne in the fridge. She took one out, gazed at it for several seconds, then put it back again. Becoming an alcoholic was not going to help her situation.

She kicked off her shoes, lay on on the bed, stared at the ceiling. She was so tired. Mentally more than physically. She had thought the fighting was over, history. She had fought, and she had won. But her victory had been built on a mound of shifting clay. It was very easy for her to appear confident and commanding to Peter Young; she had a lot of experience at that. But the fact was, she had the strongest temptation to cut and run. Once the news from Qadir was released, and it should already have been released, no one could accuse her of insider dealing if she now placed her shares on the market. She almost felt that Billy had been hinting that might be the best thing to do. But that would drive the price through the floor. It would bankrupt the company. With no guarantee that she would clear anything worthwhile.

How considerations change, she thought. Nine years ago she had landed in England without a penny to her name. Now she was disgruntled because she might only clear a couple of million rather than the six she was presently worth. As for the company, who was she now working for? Young Howard was dead. Would Raisul be interested? That was a long time in the future. Helen? Could she possibly wish on Helen all the stress she had undergone over the past few years?

The phone was ringing. She let it go through to the ansaphone; she had no desire to speak with anyone at the moment. Then she played it back. "Joanna! Andy Gosling. I really would like to get together with you. Just for a chat. Give me a ring."

God almighty! What a pain. Quite apart from the lack of taste. But he had been as tasteless after Howard's death. But suddenly she didn't want to be alone any more. She telephoned Caribee Shipping, was put through to the downstairs deak. "Lunch with me," she told Dick.

"Ah . . . yes, ma'am. Where?" She gave him the address of the flat.

There was a supermarket on the corner. Joanna went down and bought a couple of steaks and a bottle of red wine. She was cooking when Dick arrived. "Who owns this?" he asked, looking around him.

"I do. Or, I suppose, the Company. It's my *pied-à-terre*."

"You know how to live."

"There's champagne in the fridge. Open a bottle and pour."

He obeyed. "Is this a wake?"

"Perhaps. But I'm not quite sure for whom."

He gave her a glass. "There's all kind of chat at the office."

"I believe it."

"So, what are you going to do?"

"Would you believe that I don't have a clue, Dick? I am teetering on the edge of financial collapse. Which could mean that you're teetering on the edge of losing your job."

"It's happened before. But you—"

"It's happened to me before. Nearly. This time . . ."

She served their meal while he opened the bottle of wine. "I'm sorry, I should have done that before."

He looked at the label. "Ten minutes breathing will do. We can finish our champagne." He sat opposite her. "Obviously now is not the time, and you're still the boss, but . . . when you've sorted all this out and finished mourning Hasim, would you marry me?" Joanna choked on a piece of steak, and he had to come round and pat her on the back. "Is that such a horrendous prospect?" he asked.

Joanna drank some wine and wiped the tears from her eyes. Horrendous, she thought. Dick worshipped her. And he was someone she could love. Perhaps. But . . . he wasn't in her league. He was basically a drifter. He had been as terrified as everyone else when Wazir had started shooting. Oh, he was kind and gentle, and she had thoroughly enjoyed the previous afternoon. But everything that had happened, or more importantly, had not happened, had been at her behest. He had obeyed her utterly and without question. Did she want, could she, risk a husband that subservient? There was no way she could have allowed either Howard or Hasim to lie naked on her body without having sex with them. Dick had just lain there, happy to accept that crumb from her table. "Of course it isn't horrendous," she said. "It's very flattering. But a little surprising. I assume you are not marrying me for my money?"

"It's your money."

"What's left of it. I think, as you say, that I have rather a lot on my plate right now, Dick. I need a little time."

"Of course." He grinned. "I just felt I should get my proposal in before all those other guys."

"What other guys?"

"The guys who'll be queueing up to get their hands on you once the fact of Hasim's death sinks in."

"Chance would be a fine thing."

He finished his meal, looked at his watch. "Do you wish me to stay?"

"No. I have to go to Howard's funeral. But . . . come back tonight."

"Here?"

"Here. We'll have supper together. I may be more settled in my mind by then."

"May I kiss you?"

"I'd like that."

Joanna wondered why all the decent, hard-working, gentle people in the world were failures. Simply because not one of those qualities worked in the real world. She telephoned the house, was reassured by Cummings. "Everything is under control here, madam."

"Are the police still with you?"

"Oh, yes, madam."

"And the children are okay?"

"Oh, yes, madam."

"Right. Well, Cummings, I'm going to spend tonight in town. But I'll try to get down there first thing tomorrow."

"Of course, madam."

There was no business news available on television at that hour, and she did not feel like speaking with Peter Young. Whatever was going to happen would already have started happening. She made up her face carefully while she waited for Billy and Matilda to collect her, checked her stockings. When this funeral was over, she thought, she was going to burn this entire outfit.

Then she telephoned John Giffard, her solicitor. "I know Alicia has been making slanderous statements," he said. "But in my opinion your best course is to ignore them. Everyone knows they're the ramblings of a hysterical woman. I'm sure you can do without a court case right now."

Joanna knew he was right, and accepted his advice. But she had barely hung up when the phone rang again. She regarded it for a few seconds before picking it up as the ansaphone cut in. "Joanna! I've been trying to get hold of you all day."

"I'm sorry, Andy, I just haven't felt like being got hold of. And right now I have to rush—"

"Listen! I want to have a meeting with you."

"I'm not in the mood."

"Do you know what's happening in the City?"

"I don't want to know, right now."

"Are you having a breakdown?"

"Possibly. Now I simply have to go."

"Jo—"

She hung up.

"You don't look too good," Matilda said, as they sat together in the back of the Rolls.

"I think I have every reason for not looking too good," Joanna pointed out.

"Absolutely. Therefore no one could possibly blame you for giving this one a miss," Matilda pointed out. "I can represent you."

"No," Joanna said. "He was my stepson. I am more than partly responsible for his death."

"Jo—"

"I am going," Joanna said fiercely.

But she accepted Matilda and Billy's suggestion that they remain at the back of the church, well away from the group of Alicia's family. Alicia herself, in black with a black veil, was a birdlike figure, flitting from group to group, up to the very moment the coffin was brought into the church. Predictably, she had refused cremation, and after the service there was a line of cars leading to the cemetery. Once again Matilda and Billy kept Joanna at the very back while the last words were spoken, then they would have hurried her away. But they had not reached the car when Alicia caught up with them, Victoria at her heels. "Murderess!" she hissed. "Whore! Husband-stealer!"

Joanna just stared at her, not certain what to say. Matilda stepped in front of her. "That is quite uncalled for," she said. "Our own brother was caught up in that attack."

"Your brother is *alive*," Alicia ground out.

"And my brother is dead!" Victoria shrilled.

"Get into the car," Billy muttered, urgently, at Joanna's shoulder.

"Bitch!" Alicia shrieked, and lunged forward. By now a considerable crowd had gathered, mostly mourners, while the road behind had suddenly become equally crowded with cars. Joanna could not stop herself stepping forward. It was quite against her character to back away from any crisis, and she could not believe that Alicia meant her any actual harm.

"Behave yourself," she snapped, and was utterly surprised when Alicia's body cannoned into hers. She stumbled backwards, her high heels caught in the gravel, and she went down with a thump that knocked all the breath from her body.

"Bitch!" Alicia screamed again, and hurled herself onto her, red-painted nails turning into claws. Gasping, Joanna got her hands up to catch the searing blows. She caught Alicia's wrists, even as Alicia's body again thumped into hers. As they were both wearing heavy coats the impact was less severe than it might have been, but Joanna's returning breath was again driven from her lungs. Desperately she forced her strength upwards, and in the same movement drove her assailant over on to her back.

Now it was Alicia's turn to gasp as she rolled in the mud, her hat coming off to expose her hair. Joanna gazed into the handsome, distorted face, and knew an almost killer urge, but was then struck a savage blow between the shoulder-blades, and went down herself, face into the mud. Yet again she lost her breath, but by now Billy had run forward and seized Victoria by the shoulders to stop her hitting Joanna again. Matilda was grasping Alicia, while other people crowded round to help.

Slowly Joanna pushed herself to her hands and knees, scraping mud from her face; mud clung to her mink, and there was mud in her hair. She was desperately angry, turned to find Alicia, blood pounding through her arteries. But she had her arm grasped as she was turned away from the shouting people. "You want to get out of here," a voice said, and before she knew what was happening she was bundled into the back of a Rolls-Royce that had drawn up alongside her own Rolls.

She fell on to the back seat, scattering mud, pushed herself up as the car drove away, blinked at Andy Gosling. He grinned at her. "You sure do make it hard for a guy to get hold of you," he said.

"Listen," she said. "Put me down."

"On the street? Do you have any idea what you look like?"

She blew mudstained hair from her face. "You are kidnapping me."

"I would say I am rescuing you from an embarrassing situation."

"All right," she said. "You have rescued me. I'm grateful. Now take me home."

"Which home?"

"My London flat will do. I assume you know where that is, as you keep telephoning."

He smiled at her. "You certainly need a bath." He tapped on the glass partition separating them from the driver. Who nodded. "He knows the address," Andy said.

"Thank you." Joanna gathered her mink around herself, suppressed a shiver. She was really quite shaken up. She knew Alicia was a fairly unstable character, but to be attacked like that . . . she had experienced more in the last couple of days than she could reasonably stand. "That woman needs to be locked up."

"I entirely agree with you," Andy said. She shot him a suspicious glance. "Do you know she's been making all manner of utterances to the press?" he asked. "She actually held a press conference this morning, just an hour before her son's funeral, mind you, to say that it was her inside knowledge that Caribee Shipping is effectively bankrupt? That the true facts are being disguised?"

"That's not true," Joanna snapped. "We have no financial difficulties until . . . well, until and unless I manage to find a new route for our ships."

"Of course," Andy agreed. "I know that. You know that. I hope your bankers also know that. But the press are always hungry for a story."

"Such as suggesting that I, and Caribee Shipping, are on our way out. They've tried that before."

"Indeed they have." The car was stopping outside the flat. "Mind if I come up?"

"Andy, I have today buried my husband and my stepson. If you make a pass, I shall break a bottle over your head." Because, she thought, I intend to have sex tonight, although you won't ever know that, with a man I could really love.

"I'm not going to make a pass. Word of honour. I wish to talk to you. And you need to talk to me."

"Tell me why."

"I will, upstairs."

She shrugged, got out of the car. They rode up in the elevator gazing at each other, but not speaking. She unlocked the flat, walked straight through to the bedroom to look at herself in the full-length mirror. There was mud everywhere, even on her face. "Minks can be cleaned," Andy said, from the doorway.

"So can human bodies. I intend to have a shower. Would you mind closing the door? There is champagne in the fridge."

"At three-thirty in the afternoon?" He grinned. "Don't tell me, Howard always drank champagne at three-thirty in the afternoon." He closed the door.

Mud had even managed to get under the mink, on her stockings. Even her knickers had mud on them, which must have meant that at some time during her fight with Alicia her dress had ridden up.

What a show for the public. And at the funeral of their son! Damn that woman.

She threw all of her clothes on the floor together with the coat, stood beneath the hot jet for several minutes, then washed her hair, which was also thick with mud. It was half an hour before she emerged, wearing a dressing gown, with her hair wrapped in a towel even after five minutes with the blower.

Andy sat on the settee, a glass in his hand. As soon as she appeared, he got up and poured her one too. "You look magnificent."

She made a face, sat beside him. "My idea is to have several of these, and then go to bed for a nap. I have a dinner engagement."

"Lucky chap. Are you able to concentrate?"

"I am always able to concentrate."

"I once made you an offer for your shares." She stared at him. "Oh, it was through an intermediary."

"You? You bastard."

"Why so? It was a straightforward offer. And more than the shares were worth, at that moment."

"You were a bastard for not coming straight out and telling me who you were. And for trying to get control of the company. So now you're back. What are you offering this time?"

"I have already bought out John Donivan. Only seven thousand shares, to be sure, but it gives me a stake in the company."

"When did this happen?" Surely she would have known.

"An hour ago."

"You really are a bastard. So, your speciality is buying up collapsing companies and restructuring them. Where do you get your money?"

"Have you never worked out that all of Howard's friends were millionaires? And he was at the bottom of the list, just about."

"You claim to be a millionaire?"

"I'm afraid I am one. I'm not quite in Hasim's class, but I am several times more wealthy than Howard ever was. Or than you are now."

"And now you reckon you have me across a barrel."

"I would love to have you across a barrel, Joanna. But as you said, you're not in the mood right now. But what's more important is that over the last few years I have developed a considerable admiration for you. I think you were magnificent when Howard died. I'm not going to pretend that I approved of your marriage to Hasim. Oh, he was a nice enough chap, and I knew you weren't going to be ill-treated in any way, but I know quite a lot about Qadiri politics, and it seemed to me that you were getting in over your head. As I am sure you realise by now."

"Yes," she muttered.

"All of which has persuaded me that you deserve to keep control of Caribee Shipping. But you do need help. We can work together."

"Oh, yes? With you employing me, is that it?"

"Not at all. You have something like seventy per cent of the company in that trust company of yours. I already have three per cent of the remainder. I would like you to sell me forty-four per cent of your shares at a mutually agreed price. But I do promise you it will be considerably over the current market value."

"And you will then virtually own the company. No deal."

"Hear me out, Joanna. If I am going to invest money, a lot of money, in your company, I need to have ultimate control, if only to be able to persuade my partners that the investment would be viable."

"You have partners?"

"Doesn't everyone?"

"I am not giving away my company, Andy."

"You still haven't let me finish. You will keep your company. There will be a clause written into the contract between us that as long as you retain a twenty-five per cent share holding, you are entitled to remain as Managing Director and Chairman."

She glanced at him, suspiciously. "And you will immediately take steps to have my share holding reduced below twenty-five per cent."

"I have never got the impression that you are a woman who can be persuaded to do anything she doesn't wish to. As it happens, I want you to remain Chairman. You know the firm, you know the ships, you know the men who sail them. They all worship you. No, no, there can be no change at the top."

"But you will tell me what to do."

"My God but you are a suspicious woman. I will not tell you what to do, Joanna. I shall merely control the finances."

"And you'll lose your shirt. Reduced to the Caribbean run, we are bound to lose money."

"I have a new route for you."

Her head jerked.

"Australia. There is a hole waiting to be filled. It is a small hole, but small holes often grow into big ones. There is a contract awaiting you for the shipment of dry goods in and sugar out of Darwin."

She gazed at him. "Suppose I tell you, no thanks, and take up that offer myself?"

He grinned. "Were you going to do that, Joanna, you would not have told me. But in any event, I control this contract as well. It's a company I acquired a couple of years ago. I've just let it tick over, waiting to see what was going to happen with your Qadiri connection. But I always knew it was right for Caribee Shipping."

"You're quite a guy, Andy Gosling," she said. "Talk about still waters."

"Then will you accept?"

"I'd need my head examined if I didn't. Providing everything you've suggested and offered is on the up."

"In my business, one has to be on the up." He refilled their glasses. "Well, here's to us."

"Partners," she said. "Business partners, Andy."

"Business partners, Joanna. For as long as you wish that."

He did not even kiss her. Odd. She couldn't believe a man like Andy Gosling could regard her simply as a business partner. But if that was how he was willing to play it, she was happy, because she couldn't play it any other way. She put on a pair of jeans and a shirt, so that she could go out to buy something for supper. But she had the wit to look out of the window first, and changed her mind. The paparazzi was gathering, and a few minutes later her doorbell was ringing. She ignored it, called Caribee Shipping. "Oh, Princess," gushed the telephone girl. "Mr Young was about to ring you."

"I'll speak to him in a moment," Joanna said. "Put me through to Richard Orton."

"Richard Orton. Right." If the girl was surprised at her boss's order of priorities, she concealed it well.

"Dick," Joanna said. "Listen, I have a problem."

"You mean dinner is off."

"Dinner is not off. But my flat is besieged by media people and I really don't want to face them. So I'd like you to go to the supermarket on your way here and buy whatever it is you feel like eating; I'll cook it. You'd better get some wine as well. Then go to the street behind mine, and find the interior fire door. Come in there and up the stairs. That way they won't see you."

"But surely that fire door is kept locked? Or at least, barred from the inside."

"Yes, it is. What time are you aiming to get here?"

"Well . . . sevenish."

"Make it six-thirty. We have a lot to do. I shall go downstairs by the fire staircase at six-twenty and hook back the bars, so the door can be opened from the outside. Be sure you put them back into place before you come up."

"Right. I'll see you then. Listen, did I ever tell you that I love you?"

"Could be. Hang up. I'll speak with Mr Young now," she told the switchboard, wondering if the girl had been listening in.

"Joanna! The roof's caving in."

"Tell me."

"We're down to five pounds fifteen, and there can be no doubt the slide is going to continue tomorrow."

"Perhaps. But the day after we'll be back on top."

"Eh? Don't tell me—"

"That I've found another sugar daddy? Not really, Peter, but we're back in business, with adequate financing and a new route."

"How in the name of God did you manage that?"

"I'll tell you tomorrow. And listen, call a board meeting for eleven, so I can put the facts before them all. Did you know John Donivan had sold his shares?"

"I had a call from Prim."

"And you never told me?"

"I couldn't get hold of you. Anyway, it's a symptom, rats and sinking ships and that kind of thing."

"He'll be sorry. Have a good night, Peter. I'll be in early tomorrow."

The bell had stopped ringing, but when she looked out of the window she saw there were still quite a few reporters there. They knew she was inside. Well, they were welcome to wait. She considered having some more champagne and decided against it; that could wait until Dick got there. She turned on the television, and sure enough on the local London news there was an item about a fight at the funeral, between the Princess Hasim and Mrs Alicia Edge. Thank God there had been no cameras about.

She switched off the set and moved restlessly about the room. She really was behaving very badly, she knew, so soon after Hasim's death. But she so wanted to begin a new life, with someone she genuinely liked, perhaps even loved, rather than someone who just happened to have accumulated her for her looks. And now that Andy Gosling had so strangely given her the opportunity to look to the future . . . She picked up the phone, called the house. "Everything here is fine, madam," Cummings assured her.

"The police still there?"

"Oh, yes, madam. I believe they intend to remain until those men have been caught. I shouldn't think it'll be long now."

"God, I hope not. Give them my love, Cummings. I can't come down first thing in the morning, but I'll be there tomorrow afternoon. Right?"

"Of course, madam."

She hung up, went to the window. It was quite dark now, but she could still see the cluster of people in the street, smoking cigarettes, gossiping. As it promised to be a cold night, they would surely push off, eventually. She looked at her watch: six-fifteen. He'd be on his way now, from the supermarket, laden with goodies, she hoped. She would have to pay him for them.

She made herself sit down. She was as nervous as . . . the first time she had gone out with Dick, she realised. That was stupid. He was a friend, not a stranger. They were going to make love. Have sex. But it would be loving sex. And then . . .

Her head jerked as there was a soft tap on the door. Again she looked at her watch. Six twenty-five. Where had the ten minutes gone?

She got up, made herself walk to the door rather than run. She drew the bolts and the safety catch, pulled it in, and Wazir placed his hand on her chest and pushed.

Joanna stumbled backwards, taken utterly by surprise. Her legs struck a chair and she fell over, missing the chair and sitting very heavily on the carpet. Wazir stepped inside and closed the door behind him.

Joanna gasped and got her breath back. "You bastard," she said.

He grinned. "And you are very beautiful, Princess."

Oh, my God, Joanna thought. The idea of rape had not entered her mind. But he couldn't have come here, with all the attendant risk, just to rape her. Anyway . . . "How did you get in?"

"I followed the man. Your lover. He opened the fire door for me. Very generous."

"You made him open the door?"

Oh, Dick, she thought, how could you?

"No, no, Princess. I waited for him to open the door, then I came in."

"Where is he?"

She was slowly pushing herself to her feet.

Wazir grinned again, and drew his finger across his throat. "He did not put up a fight. He was taken by surprise, and his arms were full of groceries."

"You killed him? Bastard!" she shrieked, and having reached his feet, hurled herself at him.

But Wazir was a big man, and caught her flailing arms without difficulty, forcing her back across the room and on to the settee, sitting beside her as he held her there. "You stop fighting," he said, "or I will hit you."

Joanna panted, but subsided. She needed to think. But she could only think, Dick is dead. This thug has killed him. As he killed Hasim and Howie, and nearly killed poor William. And thus I am alone, in my flat, with a killer. There was nobody else coming to see her tonight. There was nobody even going to telephone her. But there were those reporters in the street, waiting to see her. If she could reach the window . . .

Wazir released her arms, and she rubbed where his fingers had bitten into her flesh. "Now, you see," he said. "If you do not resist me, I will not hurt you. If you resist me—" he reached inside his jacket – he was, as always, wearing European clothes – and produced a knife, with a blade several inches long, "I will cut you. In my country, when a woman misbehaves, her husband has the right to mutilate her. I could cut off your nose, or take out one of your eyes, or cut off a breast. Perhaps both breasts."

Joanna found herself panting; he spoke so casually. "I am not your wife."

"You are my enemy. That is the same thing."

She looked past him, at the door. He had not replaced the bolts. If she could get to the door. But the window was a safer bet. "Now I will tell you what I wish you to do," Wazir said.

She got her eyes back to gaze at his. "My mission is to destroy the male house of Prince Hasim," he said. "To complete this, I must kill Prince Raisul. But I cannot get to him, in the house in Berkshire, because of all the police. You must get him out of there for me."

"You expect me to deliver my son to you, to be murdered?"

His left hand shot out so quickly she didn't have time to move. It closed on her throat, while his right hand thrust forward with the knife. For a moment she supposed he was going to stab her, but he merely slit her blouse, parting it to each side to expose her body: she was not wearing a bra. "You will do that," he said, his face close to hers, "or you will die, here, slowly and in great agony."

Joanna's brain seemed to have gone dead; there could be no doubt he meant what he said. So, play along with him and pray that something would turn up between here and Caribee House. But she couldn't give in too quickly, or he'd know she was planning something. "Here is what you must do," he said. "You must telephone your home, and tell your people there that the danger is now over, and that you would like your son brought to you here. You understand that?"

Joanna licked her lips. "I'll see you damned first."

He peered at her for a few seconds, then grinned, released her, and stood up. "Get up," he said. Joanna stood up in turn. "Take off that shirt," he said.

"Are you a rapist as well as a murderer?" he said.

He continued to smile. "I need to see what I am cutting, Princess." Joanna took off the shirt and threw it on the floor. "Very beautiful," Wazir said. "And you are twice a mother. Women who are twice mothers in my country are often fat."

He seemed absorbed. Joanna glanced at the window again. He would of course catch up with her. But if she could just open it and shout. "Go into the kitchen," he commanded.

Joanna turned as if to obey him, then turned back again, ducked under his arm, and ran to the window, fingers fumbling at the catch, other hand seizing the frame to throw it up . . . and Wazir caught her shoulder, pulling her back and swinging her round with a force that sent her scattering across the room. She stumbled into the settee and fell right over it, crashing to the floor beyond. While she lay there, breathless, he knelt above her, and slapped her face several times, sending her head to and fro. She thought she was choking, as she could not breathe. "You play games with me, eh?" Wazir growled.

Joanna blinked at him even as she tasted blood. "Well," he said, "I fix you good." Still kneeling above her, he began to unfasten her jeans.

And the door opened.

Both Joanna's and Wazir's heads turned together, staring in consternation at the apparition which stood there, a bloody mask of a face, into which blood still dribbled from the cut on his head; the blood had also stained his jacket and shirt and even his pants, and there was blood on his hands. But he was moving forward with a quite terrifying determination. Wazir muttered something in Arabic, and got off Joanna, drawing his knife as he did so.

"Dick!" Joanna screamed, both in relief and as a warning.

But Dick was already kicking, the toe of his shoe slamming into Wazir's wrist and sending the knife flying across the room. He immediately kicked with the other foot, catching Wazir on the side of the head and knocking him back to the floor. Joanna rolled away from him and reached her feet; pulling up her zip she scrambled over the settee and found the knife.

Wazir was attempting to get up, but Dick was on him again. They were much of a size, but Wazir was the heavier. For a moment they wrestled, Wazir trying to close his hands on Dick's neck, Dick slamming short-arm punches into Wazir's body, both men grasping and grunting. Their heaving took them against the settee, and it and they fell over together, the two men landing almost at Joanna's feet. She had the knife poised, but dared not use it at the moment, even if she could bring herself to use it at all, as the bodies beneath her were constantly changing position.

Then Wazir managed to thrust Dick away from him, and stagger across the room, back against the window. Panting, he thrust his right arm into the left side of his jacket, and drew an automatic pistol. It hadn't occurred to Joanna that he might have a gun as well as the knife. Now she stared in horror as Wazir levelled the gun at Dick, who was slowly getting to his feet. "No!" Joanna screamed, and hurled the knife.

She had never thrown a knife before, and it turned several times in the air. But the sight of it distracted Wazir, and his shot was wide. He tried to turn away from it, and struck the window heavily. The glass shattered, and he half fell through, desperately clutching at the frame to stop himself. From below there came shouts of alarm and excitement.

Dick hurled himself forward, seized Wazir by the belt, and jerked him back into the room. The pistol fell from Wazir's hand, and Joanna picked that up as well. "Oh, Dick," she said. "He told me you were dead."

"Well," he said. "He certainly hit me hard enough."

"Oh, Dick," she said again. "I thought—" she bit off the words. She could never tell him that she had always considered him a bit of a wimp. Because after all, he wasn't, and he had saved her life.

He grinned through his blood-caked lips. "Seems to me our evening together is ruined. Shall I let those characters up for their story?"

"I think they're entitled to it."

He pressed the street door switch. "Come on up, you guys," he said. Then he turned back to Joanna. "Give me the gun, and you'd better put something on."

Joanna hesitated, looking at Wazir, who was rolling to and fro on the floor, moaning, blood streaming from cuts on his face and neck and hands where he had shattered the glass.

"He's not going anywhere," Dick assured her.

Aunt Ethel's sniff could be heard throughout the church, quiet as the parson pronounced them man and wife. But she'd said it all already. 'Marrying one of her own clerks,' she had declared at large.

Joanna presumed there were a few people in Caribee Shipping who felt the same way, Peter Young amongst them. But she was the woman with the golden touch, even if none of them understood quite where the touch came from. She could marry whomever she chose. They moved slowly down the aisle, because William, although strong enough to act as Dick's best man, was still not fully fit. Joanna concentrated on walking straight; she didn't want to consider that at the age of not yet thirty she was on her third husband.

But she smiled at Andy Gosling. Andy had taken the news that she was not going to marry him with his usual insouciance. She had an idea that he was waiting, with seemingly endless patience, for her, the company, everything to fall into his lap.

Andy was perhaps a problem for the future. Her only problem for the present was Raisul. But the police had captured both of Wazir's accomplices, and felt sure there would be no further attempts on the boy's life for the foreseeable future, the more so as the Foreign Office had discreetly let Emir Mutil know they knew what he was about.

She had to believe that, just as she had to make sure Raisul grew up as an Englishman and the heir to Caribee Shipping, with never a thought about Qadir. She also had, she knew, to cope with Alicia's hysterical machinations. But she felt she could do those things. Thanks to Dick and Andy, to be sure, but most of all, herself. For the first time in her life, she was her own woman.

She had learned how to survive.

# THE PHOENIX

# THE PHOENIX

Caroline Gray

PAN BOOKS

This edition published 1999 by Pan Books
an imprint of Macmillan Publishers Ltd
25 Eccleston Place, London SW1W 9NF
Basingstoke and Oxford
Associated companies throughout the world
www.macmillan.co.uk



British Library Cataloguing in Publication Data

Gray, Caroline, 1930-
The phoenix
I. Title
823.9'14 [F]

ISBN 0 330 39652 8

This is a novel. All situations in this publication are fictitious and the characters are invented and are not intended to portray real people, living or dead. The events have not yet happened.

Typeset by Palimpsest Book Production Limited,
Polmont, Stirlingshire, Scotland.
Printed and bound in Great Britain by
Mackays of Chatham plc, Chatham, Kent

# CONTENTS

'Build me straight, O worthy Master!
Staunch and strong, a goodly vessel,
That shall laugh at all disaster,
And with wave and whirlwind wrestle!'

Henry Wadsworth Longfellow

# Part One

# Crisis

'Have ye sinned one sin for the pride o' the eye or the sinful lust of the flesh?'

Rudyard Kipling

# Chapter One

# The Storm

The knock on the cabin door had Joanna Orton alert in an instant. She had not actually been sleeping, she had been listening to the whine of the wind and the slapping of the waves against the hull, the reassuring growl of the engines beneath the deck. She sat up switched on the light. "Come."

The steward opened the door only a few inches; however attractive a woman Joanna Orton might be, she was the boss, and her privacy was not to be intruded upon. "Compliments of the captain, Mrs Orton. He says it will be necessary to alter course."

"Tell him I will come up." The steward closed the door, and Joanna thrust her feet out of bed. The motion of the ship was more severe than she had supposed when lying down, and she had to clutch the grab rail to stop herself from falling over, while she reached for her clothes, deciding against the dress she had worn for dinner in favour of shirt and pants and deck shoes. She ran a brush through her tangled golden hair, slid across the floor to the door. The cabins on board the *Caribee Queen* opened directly into the lounge and, as she had suspected might be the case, three of the passengers, two women and a man, were up, sitting in the armchairs anchored to the floor, drinking coffee and attempting to look unconcerned.

They turned sharply at the sight of the owner. "Oh, Mrs

Orton," exclaimed one of the women, "is there any danger?"

"None at all," Joanna assured her.

"Someone was talking about a hurricane," ventured the man.

"There is a hurricane, Mr Lamason," Joanna said. "But it is a good way off. We are about to alter course to make sure it remains a good way off." She smiled at them, brightly, and recalled that her first husband, Howard Edge, the man from whom she had inherited this shipping line, had reassured her in just that manner on the night of their first real meeting . . . was it really thirteen years ago?

She went outside, the door held for her by the steward. Instantly the wind plucked at her, scattered her hair, whipped her shirt to and fro. Even in the darkness she could make out the whitecaps racing by. She put the breeze at perhaps thirty knots, not yet half the strength of a hurricane wind, but sufficient to create lumps and holes in the sea, into which from time to time the freighter plunged or rolled, almost losing way with jarring force. She climbed the ladder to the bridge, where again the door was held for her by an anxious second mate. Once inside, the quiet was almost startling, but the sound of the gale still surrounded this little haven of peace. "Is there a problem, James?" she asked.

She and Captain Heggie had known each other for all of those thirteen years, as he had watched her grow from a frightened young girl into this confident, mature and most successful woman. Yet whenever she elected to sail with him, as she did whenever possible, he always knew a sense of responsibility that was almost disturbing. "I hope you approve, Joanna," he said, and spread the weatherfax print-out in front of her. She gazed at the chart of the North Atlantic, and the swirling angry mass that occupied the centre of it, several hundred miles north-east of Barbados, their last port of call. "Damn thing has dipped south in the last hour," Heggie explained. "So I've been forced to do the same."

Joanna nodded. She had been involved in Caribbean – and thus Atlantic – shipping long enough to know that they needed to keep the storm to their left to avoid the greatest wind strength. There had in fact been a suggestion from their Barbados agent that they should delay their departure from Bridgetown, but the *Caribee Queen* had a full cargo of rice and sugar from Guyana, not to mention eleven fare-paying passengers, and the route was a competitive one. Besides, all they had to do was keep their distance, which, with modern navigational aids and facsimile prints-out, was not difficult. "How far?"

"Two hundred miles."

Close enough for the outlying gales to batter them, but sufficiently far from any real trouble. "I approve. Tell me what you expect."

"Presuming the storm holds its present course and speed, we should pass it in about two hours' time, at a distance of about one hundred and eighty miles. Then we will be drawing apart at about thirty miles an hour, and we will be in the safest quadrant, so that by dawn we should be able to to resume our course. The whole diversion should take about eight hours, but that will, I'm afraid, make it probable that we shall be a day late arriving at Plymouth. Unless you wish me to increase speed considerably."

Joanna considered, as she glanced at the ship's chronometer; it was a quarter to three. But *Caribee Queen*, although her favourite of the six ships that composed her small company, was also now the oldest. She would not wish the old girl to tear her heart out. She had honeymooned, the first time, on board this ship. Besides, as this autumn of 1973 drew to a close, there was all this talk about fuel prices going up as a result of the Seven Days War between Israel and the Arab states in the Middle East and, perhaps as important as any of those, she was in no hurry to get home to the crisis she knew was awaiting her. "We'll be late, James," she said. "I'll explain it to the passengers. If I can be a few hours late, so can they."

"I'm sure they'll co-operate," Heggie said. His feelings for the owner were similar to hers for the ship: like most men who sailed for Caribee Shipping, he worshipped her.

"Call me again if there's any change in the situation," Joanna said, and went to the leeward door.

"Take care," Heggie advised.

Joanna blew him a kiss and went down the ladder.

By now all the other passengers had assembled in the saloon. There were eleven of them; four men, five women, and two children, all looking anxious despite the reassuring presence of Steward Demont, handing out cups of coffee and glasses of milk.

"Oh, Mrs Orton!" they seemed to chorus.

"Are we all right?"

"Will the weather get worse?"

"Should we put on our lifejackets?"

"Are there any ships close by?"

Joanna smiled at them. "I do assure you that there is nothing to be the least concerned about."

"But the captain called you to the bridge!"

"Captain Heggie wanted my approval of the course he is adopting, which is to give the storm the widest possible berth. I approved. I'm afraid this means that we may be a few hours late docking in Plymouth, but we will certainly have a more comfortable voyage. Now, I am going back to bed, and I strongly recommend that you all do the same. By the time you wake up tomorrow morning the storm will be behind us."

"Is it really a hurricane, Mrs Orton?" asked one of the children.

"Yes, it is. But we are not going to get involved in it. Good night."

Demont followed her to her cabin door. "Can I get you anything, Mrs Orton?" he whispered.

"Yes. Once they go back to bed, bring me a large brandy."

"Yes, madam." He closed the door, and Joanna kicked off

her shoes, but did not undress, instead lay beneath the covers, staring at the deck head above her.

Even in normal circumstances, she valued these voyages on board her ships. They were as much to revisit her Guyanese roots as to get away from Dick and her family, to rest from her job as Chairman and Managing Director of Caribee Shipping, and to escape the responsibilities of being one of the City's most exciting tycoons. This was at least partly because she was still so young – she would be thirty on her next birthday – and remained, she knew, an extremely attractive woman. With her golden hair, which she still wore long, at least in bed, and her clipped features, her full figure, which remained under control although she was twice a mother, she graced any gathering, or any newspaper or society magazine.

But it was also, she knew, partly because of the slightly sinister aura that surrounded her like a cloud. Because of her husbands, and their manner of departing this earth. Howard Edge, old enough to be her father when she had been a teenager and they had first met, had been widely known as a rake and man about town, as well as a successful shipowner. When he had divorced his wife to marry a girl less than half his age, and one who, in addition, came from no reputable English family but from a distant corner of the crumbling empire, it had caused a sensation. Which had grown when, only a few weeks later, he had died, accidentally but violently, and had, even more sensationally, willed his entire estate to his bride of a fortnight.

Poor Howard had, of course, not expected to die so suddenly and at such an early age. He had been looking to the future. And the future had suddenly been dumped in Joanna's lap, at the age of twenty. When, at such an early age, she had refused to concede an inch in her possession and therefore control of the company, even when it was revealed that Caribee Shipping was in a desperate financial state, sensation had piled upon sensation. The tabloids had rubbed their hands and waited for the coming catastrophe. And had been forced to bite their tongues. She might have been only twenty, but she had understood her assets as well as her liabilities. Arab money had put Caribee Shipping back on its feet. Perhaps the City was getting used to Middle Eastern investment. But they had not expected her actually to marry her Arab benefactor.

That had been to soar to the top of the tree. Many had wondered, sometimes audibly, just what a beautiful young English girl had to do to be the wife of an Arab prince. They would have been surprised, and no doubt disappointed. Hasim ben Raisul abd Abdullah had been the most perfect gentleman, in and out of bed. The most perfect husband too, in that, although enjoying a multi-millionaire income as Qadiri ambassador to Britain, he had allowed his wife to continue with her 'hobby', as he called it, of managing the shipping line; had, in fact, interfered with her life very little. Which was not to say he had not brought an utterly new dimension to her views on sex. But their marriage had been fatally flawed, as perhaps they had both always been aware. To marry a foreign, Christian woman, Prince Hasim had had to give up his rights to the throne of the Emirate of Qadir, owned by his family. He had seemed willing to do this, but when his father had died, to be succeeded by Hasim's younger brother, the intrigues had begun. There were many Qadiris who wanted Hasim rather than Mutil as their ruler. Efforts had been made to persuade him to re-enter the political arena.

Joanna had never been sure just what that would have entailed. The repudiation of his Christian wife? Hasim had loved her so desperately she did not think he would have done that, not even for a throne. In the event, the question had never arisen. The Emir Mutil had adopted the age-old Arabian method of dealing with his enemies and potential rivals – even if they were half-brothers. Joanna did not suppose she would ever forget the door of their London flat being thrown open while she was celebrating her twenty-sixth birthday, and the three men standing there, each armed with a tommy-gun. She would never cease hearing the shrieks of terror and pain from all around her as the room had been sprayed with bullets. She, and all the women present, had been unhurt; the assassins only wanted any man who could possibly be involved in an attempt on the Qadiri throne. But the slaughter had been sufficient. And she had once again been left a widow.

That had set the seal on her notoriety. And with the withdrawal of Qadiri money from her company – it had turned out that Hasim's millions were all Qadiri millions; he had had little to leave his widow – another crash had been expected. But she had again been saved, by another long-time admirer. With strings attached, to be sure, but nothing involving bed or marriage, at least for the time being. Thus she had married again, hastily. Dick Orton was her oldest English boyfriend, a relic from the days before even Howard had moved into her life. She had been certain that, at last, she was marrying for love. Third time unlucky. Because she now knew, as perhaps did everyone else, that this third marriage had been a mistake, and was now becoming a disaster. There was the real reason for her being on board this ship at this time; she had needed to think about her marriage. They had loved each other, at least in bed, for a while. But they lived, and moved, and above all, thought, on different wavelengths. She was managing director of a thriving little shipping line and, though he worked with her at Caribee Shipping as a co-director, he remained a clerk at heart, more interested in making sure the shillings and pence added up on a balance sheet than in considering how the pounds might be spent to best advantage. Dick existed in a miasma of apprehension at the risks of the shipping world, both physical and financial, and of the bubbling energy and vitality of his wife, which he did not possess and could not share.

Perhaps that was why she had not been a mother for him. She knew this had been a disappointment, although he was a good father to both Helen, her daughter by Howard Edge, and Raisul, her son by Hasim. But Dick viewed both the children with vague suspicion, as if fatherhood, even once removed, of such a disparate pair was bound to involve him, eventually, in catastrophe. Perhaps he was right.

But those uncertainties, weaknesses, became nothing compared with the report she had received two months ago. It had been like a slap in the face, although, as it had been she who employed the private detective in the first place, she had been pretty sure something was going on. But being pretty sure is not quite the same as being made certain. No wife can accept that a husband to whom she has given everything – too much, Joanna thought grimly, when she considered the share settlement she had made on him – is cheating. How she wished he had accompanied her on this voyage. She had invited him to. She had felt that a month alone together, or at least surrounded only by strangers, might enable them to level the mountain that lay between them. But he had declined to come, and beg she would not do. Nor would she change her mind about going herself. She found it important, even necessary every so often, not merely to voyage in one of her own ships, but to revisit the land of her birth, Guyana, the land where her father had been shot to death, where Howard had drowned. To suppose she received inspiration from such a sad background could never be right. Rather, these pilgrimages, made once a year, reminded her of who and what she was and, perhaps, gave her a sense of direction.

Dick did not like ships or the sea. Or far-off places. Or, presumably, hurricanes, even at a distance. And he did like being in London. He was wealthy, good-looking . . . available? Well, she thought, one of these days he might get a shock. Because a decision was hardening in her mind.

Demont brought her the brandy, and she sipped it, sitting up and trying to read a book, but too conscious of the weather outside to concentrate. Storms at sea gave her a feeling of exhilaration, of directly challenging nature. As if anyone could do that. One did what the *Caribee Queen* was doing; sneaked around the edges and hoped to go unnoticed, well aware that the force generated at the centre of a hurricane was more powerful than several hydrogen bombs all dropped at the same time. When she had finished her drink and switched off the light, she kept seeing that swirling white mass on the centre of the print-out, and she could imagine the wind strength, well over a hundred miles an hour, whipping even these deep and slow-moving seas into a frenzy of white-topped ferocity.

She awoke with a start, surprised at having been asleep, and was immediately aware of silence. The morning, for it was getting light beyond her ports, was exceedingly noisy, from the wailing of the wind to the battering of the waves on the hull, but that in itself was not disturbing. The really disturbing factor was the silence from below her, the absence of the reassuring sound of the engine, throbbing upward through the ship. She sat up, and was half thrown from her bunk with the violence of the movement. *Caribee Queen* seemed to be rolling scuppers under. Half the things on her dressing table had accumulated against the baffles; one or two had fallen over on to the cabin floor.

She switched on her light, dragged on her clothes. As she did so there came a buzz on her interphone. She fell across the bunk reaching for it.

"Joanna?" It was Heggie.

"What in the name of God has happened?" she shouted.

"The engine has been closed down," Heggie said, not altogether keeping a note of panic out of his voice. "There has been a burst fuel line. It may take an hour or two to repair."

"I'm coming up." Joanna slammed the phone down, staggered to the door, only then realising she was barefoot. But she didn't have the time to stop and look for her shoes; she could hear anxious voices from the saloon. The passengers had again accumulated, staring at her, only half awake and terrified, a huddle of pyjama- and nightgown-clad sheep. "Please," she said. "We have had to stop the engine for a few minutes. We'll be underway again soon enough. But until then, I strongly recommend that you return to your bunks; the movement may be violent."

To give credence to her words there was a roar as a larger than usual wave burst on the side of the now inert ship, forcing her over, while green water splashed on the saloon windows. The women started to scream, the children to wail, as they desperately clung to the chairs and tables to avoid being hurled across the room. "Bed!" Joanna shouted at the men. "Get them back to bed."

She left them to Demont, opened the lee door, and climbed the ladder to the bridge. In daylight the morning was terrifying. The waves were very big, looming monsters topped with several feet of foaming white, as she had imagined in her sleep. Normally those threatening waterwalls would fall behind as the ship surged ahead. Now they were hurling themselves at the vessel like a succession of infantry battalions, intent on destruction. As she reached the bridge, a wave broke over the bow, forcing it down, sending water curling over the forward hold to break against the lower superstructure. For a moment Joanna's heart seemed to stand still, as the ship hesitated before coming up again, but then she seemed to toss her head, sending the water flying to either side, and prepared to meet her next adversary. Joanna was clinging to a stanchion just inside the door. Now Heggie came towards her, and half dragged her across the heaving deck to the chart table. "Where is the storm?" she asked.

He prodded the chart of the North Atlantic, where he had made two marks. One was the hurricane, which in the four hours since she had last looked had advanced some fifty miles, more south than west. "My God," she muttered, peering at the little cross on the chart. "And this is us?"

Before the breakdown, *Caribee Queen*, her speed reduced because of the weather, had moved hardly more than the same distance, just north of east. She was now some hundred and fifty miles south-west of the storm. All things being equal, she should be east of the swirling mass by mid-morning, in the safe quadrant, but because of the breakdown she was fast entering the second most dangerous quadrant of the storm. "Will it keep on coming south-west?" she asked.

"Could be, at least as far as Barbados. Once they pass through the Windward Islands, hurricanes usually sweep up to the north, either for Cuba and the Bahamas and the East Coast, or for the Gulf of Mexico and then Texas or Mexico."

"None of which is going to matter much to us," Joanna said. "How long will the engine take?"

"Four, six hours, Chief Bartlett says."

"Shit," Joanna muttered, and looked at the clinometer on the bulkhead indicating the amount of roll. At the moment, *Caribee Queen* was rolling through a ninety degree arc, some forty-five degrees either way. Joanna knew that if a ship ever rolled sixty degrees she was unlikely to recover. That didn't bear thinking about. "But at least we'll be underway when that mess gets here. Supposing we don't move, how close will it come?"

"On this course, the eye would pass us about seventy miles to the north."

"Which means . . . ?"

"We'll have winds of over a hundred miles an hour, seas of maybe thirty to forty feet, rainfall measured in feet rather than inches."

Joanna took a deep breath. "Can we survive that?"

Heggie licked his lips. "Not without power." Then he grinned. "We'll have power."

"But it'll still be tight?"

"Oh, yes, Joanna, It's going to be tight. I've spoken with Barbados. Well, they're nearest. But they're two hundred miles away and expecting a direct hit. There's nothing they can do to help us."

"And London?"

"I've spoken with Peter Young. He's in a highly agitated state."

Peter Young was Caribee Shipping's company secretary. He had been Howard Edge's right-hand man when Joanna had first drifted into his orbit; since Howard's death he had remained at her shoulder, rather like a surrogate father. She sometimes felt that was how he saw himself. "But there's nothing he can do to help either," she suggested.

"We're rather in no man's land, out here in the middle of the Atlantic. Peter did say he'd have an ocean-going tug standing by at Gibraltar, just in case."

"Just in case of what?"

"Well . . ." Heggie pulled his nose.

Joanna went down to the engine room, escorted by Malan, the third mate; Heggie felt he should remain on the bridge. In the bowels of the ship the motion was not quite so severe, but it was difficult enough negotiating the ladders, and she was aghast when she reached the last catwalk. The normally pristinely clean chamber below her was covered in oil, and the men working on the broken piping looked like fugitives from hell, also smeared with oil and with their half naked bodies gleaming with sweat – the heat was intense. "You'd better stay here, Mrs Orton," Malan recommended, and himself went down to alert Chief Bartlett that the owner wanted a word.

Bartlett climbed the ladder to join her. He looked tired, and there was oil on both his uniform and his unshaven face. "What happened?" Joanna asked.

"Old age, I reckon. That engine has done a few miles."

"When was it last overhauled?"

"Last year, Mrs Orton. But it's not always possible to tell what's going on inside a pipe, if you follow me."

"But it can be repaired?"

"Oh, aye, it is being repaired. Trouble is, it's a longish job, and a messy one. To remove the fractured joint and replace it, we have to block off the pipe further down. We're doing that now. Hence the spillage."

"Captain Heggie said something like four hours," Joanna said, hopefully.

Bartlett pulled a face. "Nearer six."

She looked at her watch. "Just in time for lunch."

"If anyone feels like eating."

"Be a dear and have it done by then, Chief," Joanna said. "I suppose you know we have a whopper breathing down our neck. Nine hours to contact. That's three o'clock this afternoon. But we'll be feeling it long before then."

He grinned. "You mean we're not feeling it now?"

Joanna returned to the now empty saloon; the passengers had taken her advice. Demont was in his galley, doing various things; he seemed able to keep his balance no matter how violent the rolling. "All service is free, as of this moment and until further notice," Joanna told him. "Anything they want."

"Yes, ma'am," Demont agreed.

She sat at one of the tables, moving to and fro with the ship. She had long ago got over any tendency to sea-sickness, but she couldn't stop her stomach rolling every time a wave smashed into the ship and sent it, and her, reeling. If they came through this without some structural damage it would be a miracle. She breakfasted, precariously, then took her own advice and went back to her bunk. It was very tempting to be up on the bridge, but she knew everyone was doing all they could, and the presence of the owner would only be a distraction. Besides, she had no wish to look at those waves again.

She actually dozed off, wedging herself between the bulkhead and the leeboards with pillows, so that she was not thrown about, and awoke with a start at the sound of a crash. And that had not been a wave, she knew instinctively: it had come from inside the hull. She kicked the pillows away, sat up and promptly fell over again. The ship was well over. That was the normal extent of a roll, but she wasn't fully recovering. Oh, Jesus, she thought. She had to climb uphill to reach the door. Even in the galley things had shattered, and Demont was cleaning up.

"What's happened?" Joanna gasped.

"Something's gone below, ma'am." Demont was his usual imperturbable self.

"Mrs Orton . . ." one of the male passengers appeared in a doorway.

"Is everyone all right?"

"I think so. But . . . what happened?"

"I'm going to find out and let you know." The ship staggered under another blow, and Joanna slid across the saloon to the leeward door. When she opened it, she gasped in horror. The sea seemed very close, seething green and white only a few feet below the rail. She clawed her way up the ladder to the bridge, found First Officer Lewis in command. "Where's the captain?" Joanna shouted.

"He's gone below, aft," Lewis said. "Something's gone wrong down there. We think it's in the after hold."

Which was filled with bags of rice. Joanna grabbed the telephone, punched the number, looking at the clinometer while doing so. The ship was centred at ten degrees to starboard, and was still rolling through a ninety degree arc. That meant at the bottom of the starboard roll she was fifty-five degrees over. And the hurricane hadn't got here yet. She looked at the chronometer: ten-fifteen. The seas hadn't really increased a great deal, kept down by the pouring rain that was limiting visibility to the length of the ship. But they would over the next couple of hours. "Heggie," said the voice.

"Joanna. Report, please."

"Some of the cargo has shifted. We're working on it."

"Be careful," she told him, unnecessarily. If one of the crew, or the captain himself, were to be pinned by the mountainous rice bags shifting back the other way . . .

"It's under control," Heggie assured her.

Joanna hung up, clung to the nearest grab rail, as the ship rolled again. Now it was indeed scuppers under, despite the blanketing effect of the rain. "Ever been in a hurricane, Mr Lewis?" she asked.

"No, ma'am, that I have not. You?"

She shook her head and wet hair scattered across her face.

She realised she must look a sight. "Well," she said, "maybe we'll miss this one." The time was eleven.

Fifteen minutes later the rain stopped and visibility improved. Joanna wished it hadn't. Now they could suddenly see for miles, and there was nothing reassuring to look at. The sea was an unending vista of big, breaking waves, and the sky was crowded with lowering black clouds, racing by. "Fifty knots of wind recorded." Third Officer Malan was back on the bridge. "And rising."

*Caribee Queen* lay half on her side, like a half-tide rock, being buffeted by every wave, several of which were breaking right over her. She was in mortal danger, and the temptation to shout that to the world, to send a mayday, was enormous. But the radar revealed no ships within fifty miles of them, and they could not ask any vessel to enter a hurricane quadrant. She went back down to the saloon, where the passengers had reassembled. Uninvited by the crew, they had donned their lifejackets, and were sitting in a miserable huddle, being served drinks by Demont.

"Mrs Orton!" they shouted at the sight of Joanna.

"Is this boat going to sink?"

"I hope not," she said.

"Have you called for assistance?"

"There is no assistance," Joanna told them. "This is our problem, and we'll sort it out."

"I am going to sue," one of the men declared.

"That is your privilege, Mr Martin," she said.

"Engines breaking down," Martin said. "In a storm. That is criminal, Mrs Orton. Criminal. There are women and children on board."

"Yes, Mr Martin," Joanna said, wearily. A large than usual wave broke, and there was a chorus of screams. But *Caribee Queen*, after going right over again, almost righted herself. "Oh, thank God," Joanna said.

"What does that mean?" Martin demanded.

"That the cargo that shifted has been put right," Joanna

said. "Demont, I think I will have a glass of champagne." She smiled at her passengers, brightly. "Won't you join me?" They all accepted, even Martin.

"It's amazing how quickly they'll recover, once we're in the clear, Mrs Orton," Demont whispered.

But they weren't in the clear, yet. Joanna joined an exhausted Heggie on the bridge. "When I get hold of the bugger who loaded that rice," he growled.

"I don't suppose he allowed for this amount of rolling." She peered through the windows at the turbulence with which they were surrounded, at the massive waves smashing themselves against the hull . . . even inside the bridge it was necessary to shout above the whine of the wind. "How we've survived so far without structural damage . . ."

"We haven't," Heggie told her. "We've lost several lengths of railing, and both motor launches have carried away. That leaves two oar-propelled boats. Just enough for everyone on board. But they couldn't live in these seas anyway."

Joanna felt sick, for the first time that she could remember. Of course, even the motor launches would hardly survive, but just to know they were *there* . . . The phone buzzed, and Heggie picked it up. "This had better be good," he said. And then grinned as he looked at Joanna. "It is good. The Chief says he is ready to restart the engine."

Joanna's knees gave way, and she sat in the captain's chair, hanging on to the sides as the ship rolled deeply yet again. But a moment later there was a rumble from below. "Now," Heggie said. "I propose to run like hell, to the south-east. It'll mean a roller-coaster ride, but it's our only way out."

Joanna nodded. But she knew the dangers. *Caribee Queen* was three hundred feet long. In normal circumstances that was considerably more than the average wave length, and thus once she had power there was little chance of her being overwhelmed. But some of these waves were more than three hundred feet, and if, running before the wind, she were to bury her bows too deeply while her stern was being lifted by the following wave . . . of course there was no risk of the ship being pitch-poled, that is, capsizing stern over bow – she was simply too big – but if the propellers were lifted high enough so that they could not grip for longer than the average very brief cavitation period, she might well go out of control. The alternative was to risk being overwhelmed by the hurricane. "You do whatever you think is best, Captain Heggie," she said.

The captain called up two more coxswains to share the coming wrestle with the helm, then he spoke with Chief Bartlett, explaining exactly what he was going to do. "I will need instant responses, Chief."

"You shall have them, skipper," Bartlett promised.

"Shall I speak with the passengers?" Heggie asked.

Joanna shook her head. "I'll do it."

The ship was now gathering way, and the movement was vastly more easy, although still violent enough, but they were still steering across the face of the storm.

The passengers were again gathered in the saloon, where Demont was endeavouring to serve lunch, consisting of sandwiches and soup. "There's no way I could keep any cutlery on the table," he explained.

Holding on to a chair, Joanna faced them. "I know you'll all be pleased we're under way again. But I must tell you that the delay has meant we are too close to the storm. So we intend to run away from it."

"Won't running before this wind be very dangerous?" Martin again.

"It won't be as dangerous as trying to steam into it, Mr Martin."

"Because you're afraid that engine will break down again. I am—"

"Going to sue," Joanna said. "You've already promised that. I'll eat in my cabin, Demont."

He followed her a moment later with her meal. "Maybe he'll get washed overboard," he suggested.

"Then his family will probably sue," Joanna pointed out. "We can handle him, Demont."

"I reckon you can, Mrs Orton." Like all of Joanna's employees, he had over the years discovered a tremendous faith in her ability to handle every problem. "Mr Connor would like a word."

"Not another complaint?"

"Probably, ma'am. Shall I send him off?"

Joanna shook her head. "Must co-operate with the passengers, Demont."

Demont held the door, hanging on to the bulkhead as he did so, and Connor staggered in. "Oh," he said. "I didn't mean to interrupt your lunch."

"You are not going to interrupt my lunch, Mr Connor," Joanna said. "If you don't mind watching me eat. You'd better sit down."

As she was seated at the little table, he had no alternative but to sit on her bunk. She knew he was one of two men travelling alone: they shared D Cabin. He was a young man, somewhat younger than herself, she thought, a mining engineer from South America, who had found himself in Guyana, where he had joined the ship. He was tall and well built, although thinner than he should have been; she suspected malaria at some recent stage. This had also contributed to the gauntness of his features, the somewhat yellowish-brown complexion. His eyes glowed, certainly whenever he looked at her, and his mouth had an odd twist to it, which sometimes gave him an angry expression, as if he hated the world; that made him interesting. They had not spoken more than once or twice on the voyage: she had the impression that he had not spoken to anyone, even his cabin companion, a banking executive who had joined the ship in Barbados, very often. So she gave him an encouraging smile. "Do please feel free to complain, Mr Connor. Listening to complaints goes with being the owner."

"Do you sail on every voyage?"

Now the smile spread to her mind. She remembered a

sixteen-year-old girl asking the then owner that same question, thirteen years ago. So she made the same reply Howard had given her. "Chance would be a fine thing, Mr Connor. I sail when I can get away. Maybe once a year."

"Have you experienced a hurricane before?"

"No. And if things go according to plan, we're not going to experience one now."

"You're very confident."

"I have a good crew."

"But an old ship."

"You should have thought of that before booking your passage, Mr Connor. But old or not, she'll do the job."

"I didn't come to complain, Mrs Orton. I came to tell you that I have nothing but admiration for the way you are handling this situation. That if that moron, Martin, does sue, I'll be happy to give evidence on your behalf. So will several of the others."

"That's very kind of you, Mr Connor. Do you mean you'll be a character witness? Or that you are also an expert in marine engineering and meteorology, as well as navigation? Those are the areas where we will be challenged."

He flushed. "I was offering you my help."

"And I appreciate the offer." She drank her coffee. "You must forgive me. I'm a little tired." She gave him a bright smile. "I'm going up to the bridge to see how things are going. Would you care to accompany me?"

Captain Heggie raised his eyebrows as Joanna appeared with an escort, both windblown and wet with flying spray. He had already implemented his plan to run before the storm, and the scene was startling in the extreme. In front of them the ocean dropped away in a series of rolling hills with huge valleys beyond. Seen from behind the waves hardly seemed to be breaking, but the rolling effect was even more terrifying. Joanna moved to the wing to look aft, and wished she hadn't, because behind them the rollers were indeed topped with breaking white water to a height of several feet, tumbling over, roaring almost as loudly as the engine as they sought to catch up with the ship.

They had hardly gained the bridge when the first monsters had to be encountered. Joanna gasped, and instinctively clutched Connor's hand, both clinging to stanchions, as the bows went down into the deep trough before them, charging at the back of the water wall a hundred yards away. Heggie stood by the telegraph, and immediately he rang down for reduced speed. As promised, Bartlett responded immediately, and the ship checked, her bows only just entering the surging hillock, now so close. Even so, green water broke on the foredeck and showered aft, smothering the bridge, while from behind them the roaring increased as the wave behind them caught them up. But Heggie was already ringing down for an increase in speed, and *Caribee Queen* drove forward, scattering the wave breaking aft, driving her bows through the wave in front, to fly upwards, bows for a moment pointing at the sky, before they fell down again into the next trough, and the whole manoeuvre had to be repeated. "How long can she stand this?" Conner shouted into Joanna's ear.

"I hope as long as we can," she replied.

Afternoon drifted into evening. Heggie, exhausted, was relieved by Lewis, and the drill continued. Joanna was as drenched in sweat as any of them, but she did not wish to leave the bridge. Because now she knew they were winning. The seas were definitely getting smaller as they raced away from the eye of the storm, the movement was easing, and the engine continued to throb away reassuringly. But it was getting on for midnight before Captain Heggie stretched, and said, "I reckon you can turn in now, Joanna. I'm going to resume course in an hour."

"How late will we be?"

He made a face. "Maybe twenty-four hours. But the important thing is that we'll get there."

She stood on tiptoe to kiss him. "You've done a great job, James. You all have. I'll congratulate you properly tomorrow."

She staggered to the ladder, aware now of the stiffness creeping over her body, and only then remembering Connor, who was at her elbow. "Well, now," she said. "You've been in at the death. Only it was the life. Did you enjoy it?"

"I enjoyed being with you," he said. "At the death, and then the life."

She slid down the ladder before she replied. "Mr Connor," she said. "I'm going to bed. Alone. And I suggest you do the same." Shipboard adventures had this effect on people, as she knew only too well.

"I don't think you're going to sleep," he said. "I know I am not." They had reached the foot of the ladder, where they were for a moment sheltered from the wind. He opened the bulkhead door for her and had to catch her as they almost fell through.

Perhaps he knew that shipboard had as much effect on her as anyone. And then, the still surging exhilaration-cum-fear inspired by the storm . . . She wondered how much he knew about her, about her past, or even about her present. And did it matter? She knew what she wanted at that moment. Normally she would have rejected the thought out of hand. But if Dick was really having it off with some bimbo in London . . .

Most of the passengers had retired to their bunks; they would hardly know the traumatic events that had been happening on deck. But Demont was always there. "Mr Connor and I will have champagne, Demont," she said.

"Of course, ma'am. Worst over, is it?"

"You could say that."

He uncorked the bottle. "Shall I bring it in?"

"I think we'll have it as it is," Joanna said. Connor took the bottle, and she opened her cabin door. He followed her inside, closed the door behind him. "I think a hot shower is in order," she said. But she took the bottle from him first, drank from the neck. He did the same, watching her all the time. "Do you boast of your conquests, Mr Connor?" she asked.

"I never have."

"I would make it a rule." She stripped off her soaking jumper and shirt, kicked off her shoes, dropped her pants and knickers behind them. "Another."

He gave her the bottle, watching her all the while. She took a deep swig. The cabin was going round and round, but that could well be a combination of the movement and exhaustion, as much as the alcohol. "I should warn you," she said, "that the moment my head hits that pillow, I am going to pass out."

"Sadly, I think that's very likely to be snap."

Yet he looked interested enough, as he undressed himself. She stepped past the glass barrier into the shower, switched it full on, turned up her face to the flow. She felt rather than heard him come in behind her. "Did you wedge the bottle?" she asked.

"It's safe."

"I hate wasting champagne."

He was against her, and she could feel him. His arms went round her body, and his hands closed over her breasts, but gently, caressingly. The ship rolled and plunged, and they moved with it, to and fro. She turned into his arms and put her own arms round his neck. They kissed, savagely, while pressed against each other. And . . . "Ooops," she said.

"Damn," he said. "Damn, damn, damn. You will think me the most utter idiot."

"Actually, I'm flattered," she said. "And a shower is the best place for it to happen, wouldn't you say?"

"But . . . shit! I have wanted you so badly. I have dreamed of you every night this voyage."

She released him, finished washing him, stepped out of the shower and towelled herself dry. "Then come and dream some more. There's always tomorrow morning." Her hair was still wet, and she wrapped that in a towel too. It did not seem important.

She lay down with a sigh, waited for him to join her. "Do you know," she said, "I don't even know your name?"

# Chapter Two

# The Company

Peter Young was on the dock at Plymouth to greet Joanna as the *Caribee Queen* slowly nosed her way into her berth. So was all the family. Joanna had, of course, been in constant radio contact with both the office and the family since they had escaped the storm, and she had had a portent of doom. But then, she had had that before she had went away; now perhaps it was compounded by guilt. She waited on board while the passengers disembarked. Connor was the last to leave. He didn't want to leave at all. "What happens now?" he asked, having been allowed into her cabin where she was making up her face, wearing only bra and panties.

He had spent a lot of time in this cabin over the past week. He was, she supposed, a continuing moment of madness, born out of the storm and her despair at the collapse of her marriage – and the knowledge of the huge problems that lay immediately ahead. But now the moment of madness had to be ended, and the problems to be faced. "I have some things to sort out," she said.

"I'd like to see you again."

"I should hope you would. But . . ." she put away her lipstick and turned to face him. "As I say, there are things I have to do before I can take any time off, Sean. What about Gerry?"

"Well . . ." Sean Connor flushed. "He knows where I've been, nights. I didn't have to tell, it was pretty obvious."

"He's not likely to go charging off to a tabloid, is he?"

"I've sworn him to secrecy." Sean flushed. "It was the best I could do."

"We'll keep our fingers crossed."

"Would it mean a lot of trouble for you? I got the impression . . ."

"That my marriage is over? I think it probably is. But I intend to be the one who ends it, my way."

"You're one hell of a woman, Jo. May I call you?"

She shook her head. "Give me a number where you can be reached, and I'll call you."

"You will call?"

"I will call. Now, I have a lot to do. Like finishing getting dressed."

"May I kiss you goodbye?"

"Not without smudging my lipstick. But you can give me a hug and a squeeze."

He held her against him, and his hands roamed. She did not object when he unclipped her brassiere for a last caress, or slipped his hand inside her panties. It was odd, she thought, how things had a habit of turning full circle. Howard, old enough to be her father, could have had her in this very cabin – but he had been too much of a gentleman, whatever his reputation. Hasim had taught her almost everything she knew about sex, some of which she had passed on to Sean. Dick had always been somewhat in awe of both the beauty and the wealth that had so oddly fallen into his lap. Maybe he had just been unable to grasp it. And this boy, three years younger than she . . . as she had certainly seduced him, did that mean she was no lady? She thought there might be quite a few people who would agree with that.

A last caress, and he was gone. She put the slip of paper on which he had written down a phone number into her handbag, and pulled on her blouse, before concealing her untidy hair beneath a headscarf.

* * *

Once the passengers had left, the family came on board to greet her. "Oh, Jo!" Matilda, similarly blonde but more heavily built, her older sister, but one of her employees, was waiting to hug and kiss her. "We were so *worried.*"

Matilda's husband, Billy Montgomery, who managed the Caribee Trust in which all her wealth was secreted, as always looked embarrassed as he in turn hugged her; he had been one of her first admirers, but had had to settle for Matilda – he had also worked for Howard Edge. "Gosh, it's good to have you back." Always nervous in her company, today he was more uptight than ever. Their two small children jumped up and down.

William, Joanna's brother, as fair as his sisters, the youngest of the trio but at twenty-eight powerfully built and handsome, still moved awkwardly, even if it was three years since he had stopped one of the bullets meant for Hasim. He too worked for her. "I wish I'd been there," he murmured into her hair.

"I'm glad you weren't." She hugged and kissed his wife, Norma, a slender, dark and quiet young woman who never seemed quite certain that she belonged in the company of the boisterous Grain family.

"Darlings." She hugged and squeezed Helen – Howard's child, but with her mother's crisply handsome features and fair hair – now a sturdy nine-year old, then swept seven-year-old Raisul from the deck. How like his father he looked, from his dark complexion to long upper lip.

Peter Young, tall and cadaverous in appearance, hung back until the family greetings were over, then he embraced her. When they had first met she had instinctively disliked him. Now she knew his worth and valued him as a friend, and more, an important check on her wilder flights of fancy. "Tell me," she whispered.

"It's not good," he whispered back.

"Then save it for the car. Now, darlings," she said, "why don't you all go off home with Aunt Tilly. I'll be right behind you."

"But Mummy," Helen said. "We want to be with you."

"As I want to be with you," Joanna assured her. "But Uncle Peter and I have things to discuss." She frowned, for the first time realising someone was missing. "Where is Dick?"

"Ah . . ." Matilda looked embarrassed.

"He's in bed with flu," Billy said before anyone else could offer an explanation. "He's at home."

"Then I'll meet you up there."

She ushered them to the gangway, and was joined by Captain Heggie. "You'd better look at the damage," she suggested to Peter.

They walked along the deck, and he bent over the length of rail that had been crumpled up as if made of matchsticks, then they went up on to the boat deck to see where the launches had been torn away. "I've alerted the insurers," Peter said. "They've a man coming down this afternoon. He'll want to see the Log."

Heggie nodded. The insurers would, of course, be eager to pounce on any suggestion of negligence or navigational incompetence. Joanna's bags had been carried ashore and loaded into the back of the company Rolls. Now she said goodbye to Heggie, and, as was her custom, to each member of the crew. "You'll soon be shipshape again," she told them. "Meanwhile, have a good holiday."

She sat in the back of the car, Young beside her, as they drove out of the city and into the Devon hills. It was odd how memory kept coming back. She had landed at Plymouth, after crossing the Atlantic in that same *Caribee Queen*, then quite a new ship, at almost this same date in 1960. Thirteen years ago! That had been her first visit to England, for despite the fact that she had English parents, she had been born and had spent her girlhood, with her brother and sister, in the then colony of British Guiana on the South American mainland. In fact, she wondered if she would ever have come to England had her father, a superintendent in the Guyanese police force, not been murdered by a man he had sought for another murder.

That had been traumatic. As had been her first thoughts about England, so different in every way to BG. Had anyone told that sixteen-year-old girl that she would one day be sitting in the back seat of a Rolls Royce about to discuss pressing business matters with her company secretary she would have said he was mad. "Tell me," she said.

Peter Young sighed. "The price of oil has gone up seventy per cent. When we can get it. The Arabs are threatening a total ban on any country they consider an ally of the Israelis."

"That will affect everyone, surely. Not just us."

"Oh, quite. Although some companies are better able to take that kind of problem than others. Industry is in a mess. There's even talk that the PM may have to reduce the working week to conserve fuel. As for private cars, they may have to be phased out altogether."

"Especially gas guzzlers like this one," Joanna agreed. "What is Andy saying?"

"Andy has been trying to get hold of you. When I told him you were battling a hurricane in mid-Atlantic he all but blew a fuse."

"I'll have to see him right away." Andy Gosling was another old admirer, a one-time friend of Howard Edge's, who had come to her rescue, and that of the firm, when Prince Hasim had been murdered. The deal had been a hard one; he had insisted upon a fifty-one percent share-holding. But beggers couldn't be choosers, and he had at least guaranteed that as long as she held twenty-five per cent of the shares herself, she would remain Chairman and Managing Director. Nothing had changed there. But she had an inkling that he was going to be difficult. "I suppose the stock market is in a tizzy as well," she suggested.

"I'm afraid it is. There are bears crawling everywhere. Are you still going home?"

"I do have a home, Peter. We'll go to Caribee House as I

promised the kids. We can call Andy from there and set up a meeting. Anyway, I feel I should visit my sick husband."

"Mm," Peter agreed.

Joanna glanced at him. "You mean you don't want to be the one to tell me that he's a cheating bastard. Don't you think it's time I dealt with it?"

"It'll be nasty."

"Perhaps I'm in the mood to be nasty."

"Were you scared?"

"I think everyone was scared, Peter. I have never seen seas that big. But I suppose I was better off than most, because I was in charge. With Heggie, of course. He's a good man, Peter. He'll have first pick of the new ships."

"New ships?"

"Well, *Caribee Queen* is getting old. Her engines, certainly. That's why we got into trouble. But the whole ship is old. So is *Caribee Future*."

"I wouldn't make too many plans until you find out what Gosling has to say."

"He'll want the ships," Joanna said confidently.

How peaceful Caribee House looked. It was a large mansion, four storeys high, set in its own grounds in the Berkshire countryside, remote from the world save during Ascot week, when the cheers could just be heard from beyond the wood. It had been in the Edge family for two generations, even if the name was now lost, although no doubt her predecessor as Howard's wife, Alicia, was still dreaming of one day getting it back; as she had never remarried, she still called herself Alicia Edge. Alicia was an eccentric woman, to be as polite as possible in Joanna's opinion, who hated her replacement and indeed blamed Joanna for the death of her only son, shot in the same attack that had cost Hasim's life and so very nearly William's as well. Joanna had no desire ever to see her or hear of her again.

The car rolled to a stop before the portico, the dogs barked and surrounded them with wagging tails, and Cummings, the butler, and Mrs Partridge, the housekeeper, came out to greet them, along with the children. "We only just got here," Helen said importantly.

"Oh, Mrs Orton." Cummings seized her hand. "We were so worried."

"I'm a bad penny, Cummings," Joanna said. "I always turn up."

She embraced Mrs Partridge. Both Cummings and Mrs Partridge were old friends, who no doubt remembered the night Howard Edge had first brought the frightened young girl home. There had been other young girls before, but none after, and they had grown to respect and even, she thought, love her over the years. "Are you all right?" Mrs Partridge said.

Joanna smiled. "I've a few bruises. But they're all fading now. How is Mr Orton?"

"He'll be the better for seeing you, I'm sure," Mrs Partridge said, bravely; the servants were naturally aware of the gossip.

"Come along, kids, let's go see Daddy," Joanna said. "Mr Young will be staying for lunch, Mr Cummings." She looked at Peter, eyebrows raised. "And dinner too?"

He shook his head. "I think I had better get back to town this afternoon. But I'll make that call now, if I may?"

"Of course. Use the study. Tell him I'll be up tomorrow morning." She went up the stairs, holding the children's hands.

"Daddy has been very bad-tempered," Helen confided. She was, of course, perfectly well aware that Dick Orton was not her father, however confused Raisul might be.

"Then we'll have to cheer him up." Joanna opened the bedroom door. Her husband lay in bed. He had been watching television, but he switched off the set as she came in. Dick Orton was only a few inches taller than his wife, and had always been slight. Nowadays he sported a moustache, which was darker than his fair hair. His face remained as pinched as when she had first met him at secretarial college, thirteen years previously, for all the good living he had enjoyed recently.

"Home the wanderer," he said, and blew his nose.

"I won't kiss you, if you don't mind," Joanna said. "I can't afford a cold right now. Wherever did you get it?"

"God knows. I hear you've been having an exciting time."

Joanna sat down while the children roamed about the room; they didn't often come in here as Joanna maintained a separate bedroom – she liked to sleep alone, when the operative word was sleep. "It was more terrifying than exciting," she said.

"I can't imagine why you do it."

"I need to live, from time to time."

"Even if it might involve your dying, from time to time?"

"You weren't really going to die, Mummy, were you?" Helen asked.

"Of course not, darling. It was just Daddy's bad little joke. Now, I tell you what, why don't you run along and find out what there is for lunch. Take Raisul with you. I'll be down in a minute."

The children banged the door behind them, and Dick began to look apprehensive. "Okay," he said. "So it was a bad joke."

"Certainly in front of the children. When are you getting up?"

"The quack is coming this afternoon. He says I really should take it easy."

"What have you been doing recently that isn't easy?"

"Holding the fort, with you away."

"Odd. Peter Young didn't mention that to me."

"That doesn't surprise me. He doesn't like me. None of your people do."

"You should give them more of a chance, by letting them see you more often, at the office. You are aware that there is a crisis on?"

"Crisis, crisis, crisis. It's a bore."

"But a bore that has to be settled. I have a meeting with

Andy Gosling tomorrow morning. I'm told the share price has slipped."

"Several points. But that goes for everything. The FT Index is down like a mineshaft,"

"It's our shares I'm worry about." Caribee Shipping was not sufficiently large to be listed in the FT Index.

"I was meaning to talk with you about that," Dick said.

Joanna had followed the example set her years ago by Howard Edge, and made her husband a present of a block of shares in the company as a wedding present; this was to make him reasonably independent and less of a kept man. She had in fact been far more generous than Howard had been, and had made over five percent of her twenty-nine percent holding. Nor had she regretted it, even if he had used his private income to finance at least one mistress. When it came to the crunch, that was all he was going to get – that too had been written into their marriage agreement. Until now. Now she needed at least some of those shares back, if she was going to divorce him; she had to maintain that twenty-five percent control. But there again, he was obliged to sell them to her should they ever split, again by the terms of their marriage contract. It was just a matter of which came first, the chicken or the egg. "Forget it," she advised. "We've been through bad times before. We'll come back up." She smiled at him. "If you're bothered, I'll buy the shares back off you. Or at least some of them. At the price before I went away. Does that interest you?"

He glared at her. "No."

"Suit yourself. Well, I'd better get down to lunch. See you in the funnies." He switched the television back on.

"Andy is still in an agitated state," Peter Young told her over lunch.

"I'll cool him down," Joanna promised. It was splendid, after so long, to preside over a family lunch, even if the chair at the far end of the table was vacant. She was her usual bright and cheerful self, engaging both the children and her siblings in conversation, telling them about the storm, while her brain was concentrating on other things. She really needed to get some of those shares back. In fact, she had to, before she dared split with Dick. So then, why split at all? He had his floozie, while she . . . she had a phone number. What an absurdly immoral situation. Or would amoral be a better word? Or maybe just modern.

She needed to talk with Matilda. When they had first come to England, Matilda had been the most amoral woman she knew; Alicia Edge had gone so far as to call her a whore. But since her marriage to Billy she had been the soul of propriety and a good mother. The ridiculous thing was that it was *she* who had insisted upon the change. "If you're going to work for me," she had said, "there's to be no more sleeping around. I'm not asking you to give up sex. But choose one man and stick to him. One at a time, at any rate."

Matilda had taken the advice to heart, chosen Billy . . . and married him. At that time, of course, Joanna would no more have considered sleeping with any man save her husband than she would have tried flying without an airplane. How times changed. But Matilda was still her best source of advice . . . supposing she was going to carry things any further. But she had to do that. She had promised to contact Connor. If she did not, he would not have too much trouble in discovering where she lived. Besides, she wanted to see him again.

Peter Young departed after lunch to return to the office. Joanna paid Dick a courtesy call, then retired to her own bedroom, having invited Matilda to join her; the children were playing in the garden, and Billy was enjoying a siesta downstairs. "Must feel good, to be back in your own bed," Matilda suggested.

"It was quite an adventure. How have things been here?"

Matilda shrugged, kicked off her shoes, and lay beside her. "What were you thinking of, specifically?"

"Dick."

"Haven't seen much of Dick, while you were away."

"You know he's having an affair?"

Matilda turned her head, sharply. "You mean, you do?"

Joanna nodded, moving her head up and down the pillow. "That's one of the reasons I went, to think about things. I had a report last month."

"Shit!" Matilda remarked. "You mean you had a detective on him?"

"It seemed necessary. And it was necessary."

"What are you going to do?"

"I don't know."

Matilda raised herself on her elbow to peer at her sister. "You mean you're going to forgive and forget?"

"That's not my scene."

Matilda lay down again. "I didn't think it was," she agreed.

"But there are complications."

"You don't have any joint children. That's a plus."

"I was thinking in business terms. He has too big a holding. I have to get some of it back."

Matilda made a whistling sound. "That was careless of you."

"I know. I was in love. But we have a written deal. If things go bad, I can buy back the necessary to regain twenty-five percent."

"Then what's the problem?"

"The problem is that to implement the deal, I have to make the break. You with me?"

"But if that's what you want to do . . ."

"Do I, Tilly? I mean to say, to have one husband drowned before my eyes, another shot before my eyes, and now to divorce the third . . ."

"Stuff the tabloids."

"They penetrate through to the children. Or they will."

"So? As I said, Dick isn't their father. And I don't reckon they're all that fond of him."

"It'll still be nasty. And if I don't make the break, well, I have his shares supporting mine. Which is all I need."

"Isn't that going to leave you at his mercy?"

Joanna closed her eyes. There was more to it than the

children's attitude, of course. Dick, for all his vices, was her oldest living male friend – apart from William, of course. He had been one of the first boys she had met on coming to England, and they had romped together and indulged in all the excesses of the sizzling Sixties, from alcohol to coke. For her, briefly. For Dick just as briefly, he had sworn. From that degenerate scene she had been rescued by Howard Edge. Dick had gone his own way. But when they had got back together, he had been a strong, tough character, physically. He had proved that whilst defending her following Hasim's murder. Her mistake had been in supposing that physical strength and courage necessarily implied mental strength and courage as well. But still, to cast him off . . .

She had still not made up her mind when she drove into town the next morning, with Matilda, who was her PR. Secretaries and clerks gushed as she strode into Caribee Building, welcoming her back, exclaiming over the danger she had been in. Harriet, her secretary was waiting outside the lift shaft. "Mr Gosling is upstairs," she said.

Joanna raised her eyebrows; it was only just past nine. "He *is* anxious," she remarked, as they rode up.

"What are you going to do?" Matilda asked.

"Listen to what he has to say, first." The car stopped at the fifth floor, where Peter Young was waiting for her, having been alerted by the front desk.

"Gosling is here. With Townsend."

"So I gathered. You'd better let me see them alone, to begin with."

He raised his eyebrows. "Is that wise?"

"In the first instance, yes," Joanna said. "Don't worry, I'll buzz if I need any help. One buzz for you, Peter, two buzzes for Matilda, three buzzes for you both."

Peter and Matilda looked at each other.

"And stop worrying," Joanna advised. But she took a deep breath before entering the boardroom.

The two men stood as Joanna entered. Andy would be about forty now, she supposed; she had deliberately endeavoured to keep him at arm's length throughout their relationship. They had first met at a pool party in Howard's heyday, when she, on her first appearance at that kind of party, had been widely regarded as Howard's new mistress. That supposition had not then been correct, but as she had been only too well aware that it was going to happen, no matter how hard she resisted it, she had been left with a faintly defensive attitude to all the *aficionados* who had been at that party.

Principal amongst those, after Prince Hasim himself, was Andy, who had been the first to admire her bathing-suit-clad body. As he had been a friend of Howard's, he had not attempted to muscle in, but he had always been there. He had made what she had supposed to be a play following Howard's death, but on that occasion had been beaten to the post by Prince Hasim. Then he had reappeared following Hasim's death, when to her surprise, and considerable humiliation, it had turned out that he had not been after her body after all, but her company.

She had desperately needed the support following Hasim's death, thus she had accepted his offer and his plans. And in fact they had worked quite well together over the last four years. He had never overstepped the bounds of propriety, and had fulfilled his side of the bargain with meticulous honesty; his consortium had pumped sufficient funds into Caribee Shipping to keep it well afloat, and she had retained her position and authority as Chairman and Managing Director. She was puzzled as to what could have now so upset him. The situation was undoubtedly critical, but it was critical for the whole country, not just Caribee Shipping.

Now he smiled as he kissed her hand. He was a good-looking man, tall and only just beginning to run to a paunch, with distinguished grey wings to his dark hair. He dressed immaculately, and wore a carnation in his buttonhole. "Joanna," he said. "You are a sight for sore eyes, as always." He looked past her, as if expecting her to be accompanied by some of her entourage, but she had closed the door behind herself. "You know Tom, of course."

"I do." Joanna shook hands with Tom Townsend, a rather raffish looking character who wore a moustache.

"So you've been trying to commit suicide," Andy said, pleasantly.

Joanna took her chair at the head of the table, and they sat one to either side. "If you mean I have been taking a close look at how my crews, and my ships, stand up to bad weather, that is correct."

"You knew there was to be a hurricane?"

"We knew there was one about. We didn't anticipate actually getting involved with it."

Andy tapped the file in front of him. "Carton says there was an engine breakdown."

"A burst fuel line. The fact is, Andy, *Caribee Queen*, and all her equipment, is getting too old. The same goes for *Caribee Future*. One of the subjects we need to address, as soon as possible, are replacements." She saw the two men exchange glances. "I said, as soon as possible. I quite understand that in the present economic climate it may not be viable. But this situation can hardly last much longer. Can it?"

"I'm afraid it not only can, but it may well do so," Townsend said. "The Arabs have discovered that they possess a most formidable weapon, and seem prepared to use it. Your old friend Mutil is prominent in this."

"Well, he never did like us, anyway," Joanna said. "We must put our faith in the likelihood that they will start quarrelling amongst themselves. They always have in the past. And in any event, whatever the situation, whatever the costs involved, we have to live with it. The United Kingdom cannot just shut down. So our profits may be smaller for a while. So will everyone else's. And as soon as our own oil starts to flow . . ."

"Pie in the sky," Andy said. "It may happen, some time in the future. We have to consider the here and now."

"All right," Joanna said. "Let us do that. We have operated very successfully over the last six years, since this consortium was put together. Our profits have been good, our dividends satisfactory, our share price excellent. We have an adequate reserve fund."

"All of which are now in deep danger," Townsend commented. "And that reserve fund is adequate only in what might be termed normal circumstances."

"I repeat, we are in no different circumstances to anyone else," Joanna insisted. "Save that a lot of our competitors are not in such good shape. The one mistake we could make would be to give the impression we are panicking, as it appears so many other people are doing. I intend to place an order for tenders for two new ships, immediately, and to let the media know this."

"And how do you propose to pay for these vessels?" Andy asked.

"Let's get the quotes first. Then I'll have a talk with the bank. If they can't do it, we'll talk to Miller & Sparks about a flotation. Now is the time to think big, Andy. Not small. Then when this crisis ends, we shall be in a stronger position than any of our competitors."

"I'm afraid I don't agree with you," Andy said.

"We feel that now is the time to pull in our horns," Townsend said. "Lie low, for a while. Scrap the two out-of-date ships. If, as seems likely, world trade is going to be stagnating for a while, we can operate with the two newer vessels we already have. Cut the Caribbean and the Australian sailings in half."

"And the crews of the older vessels?"

"I'm afraid they'll have to go. Oh, we'll tell them that the moment things pick up and we can splash out on new ships they'll get their jobs back . . ." He paused as he gazed at Joanna's expression.

"Those crews are my oldest and most trusted employees," Joanna said.

"Well," Andy said, "we can mingle the best of them in

with the crews of the new vessels, and let some of *them* go."

"I have never heard such a load of rubbish in my life," Joanna said. "It's not even short-sighted; it's total blindness. You cut our work force, our fleet, and our delivery contracts, in half, and we'll never get them back again."

"Once we have made sure that we can stay viable, no matter how long the crisis lasts," Townsend said. "Then we will be in a position to . . . well . . ." he glanced at Andy, anxiously.

"I had dinner with Roger Petherick, a couple of nights ago," Andy said.

"Oh, yes?" The adrenalin was starting to pump in her veins.

"Well," Andy said. "Naturally Petherick Shipping is feeling the crunch too. He was thinking that perhaps the time has come for some of the smaller lines to merge." He paused, and watched Joanna's nostrils dilate.

"Makes sense to me," Townsend ventured.

Joanna gave him a look which had him leaning back in his chair. "And on what terms would we merge?" she asked, softly.

"He was thinking that if he and his partners bought fifty-one percent of our shares . . ." Andy said.

"Go on."

"Well, he is an active shipowner, unlike me. He would therefore expect to be Chairman. But I imagine he would agree to your remaining as MD, or at least, chief executive."

"You imagine?" Joanna said.

"He would also want the name to be Petherick Shipping," Andy hurried on. "Well, that again is logical, as he has more ships."

"Six," Townsend put in. "All reasonably new."

"Over my dead body," Joanna said.

There was brief silence, while Townsend and Andy looked at each other. "I know this is a bitter pill to swallow, Joanna," Andy said. "But it's not as if Caribee Shipping has been built up by your family over generations. It was founded by Howard's grandfather, brought to a viable concern by Howard's father, and began to decline under Howard. It is to your eternal credit that when Howard died you revived the company. You did wonders. But times change. And one must go with the times. I very much doubt whether in another twenty-five years there will be *any* small independent shipping lines about."

"There will be, and Caribee Shipping will be one of them," Joanna said. "Managed by my son."

"I think you are taking a rather limited point of view," Andy said. "With respect."

"I can take any point of view I wish," Joanna said. "By the terms of our legally-binding agreement, I remain Chairman, Managing Director, and in complete control of this company, so long as I possess twenty-five percent of its shares. Nothing has changed. The only decision that matters here is mine. And I am telling you that my company is not up for grabs. And just in case you have any funny ideas, gentlemen, I should remind you that, again according to our legally-binding agreement, you cannot sell your shares unless I agree to sell mine. And I am not going to do that."

Once again the two men exchanged glances. "I entirely agree with the situation as you have outlined it," Andy said at last. "But, as I say, times change. Perhaps you are unaware that you no longer own twenty-five percent of the company shares."

Joanna tossed her head. "Don't give me that rubbish. So I made my husband a gift of five percent when we were married. You agreed, in writing, Andy, that for the purposes of the company agreement, those shares remained in my possession, as I could buy them back from Dick whenever I chose."

"If he still possesses them when you wish to buy," Andy said quietly. "If I am correct, while, as you have just reminded us, we cannot sell our shares without agreement from you as chairperson, you did not make the same stipulation with regard to your husband. I assume you did not think that was necessary. But there it is."

"You're lying," Joanna snapped.

"My dear Joanna, that is slanderous, before a witness."

Joanna glared at him. "When is this supposed to have happened?"

"Two days ago."

"Two?" While *Caribee Queen* was approaching Plymouth. "Two days ago my husband was in bed with 'flu. He still is in bed with 'flu"

"One can buy and sells shares by telephone, Joanna."

"But . . . why should he do that?"

"I think it may have been intimated to him, by interested parties, that you had discovered his indiscretions, and might well decide to end your marriage. In which case, again as you have reminded us, you would be entitled to demand from him the return of all his shares. I imagine he decided that the best thing to do was get rid of them before that happened."

"You are unspeakable," Joanna said.

"Are you suggesting it was I who told him you knew?"

"Wasn't it?"

"My dear Joanna, really! But there it is. You no longer have a controlling share in this company, and we are therefore entitled to vote for your removal from the position of Chairman and Managing Director at the next shareholders' meeting. I have put this down for next Thursday. But I felt that we should have this little private chat first, so that you would be prepared, as it were."

Joanna looked from face to face. She was not sure she was seeing them clearly. But if there were tears in her eyes, they were tears of the sheerest outrage. They both smiled at her. "Of course," Townsend said, "if you feel, in all the circumstances, that you would like to sell out, we should be happy to buy your shareholding. I'm afraid the price is a little down, and may go further, but it's still over six pounds. That would be one point two million pounds for you. Not too bad, eh?"

"Once you offered me nearly three million," Joanna muttered.

"Ah, yes," Andy agreed. "But that was when you had seventy-five percent, and the price was somewhat better. Times do change, Joanna."

"Yes," Joanna said. "But they haven't changed yet. Until next Thursday's meeting I am still Chairman and Managing Director. So now you can get out. Both of you. *Allons. Vamoose. Scapa.* Leave my building."

"Well, I say . . ." Townsend protested.

Andy jerked his head. "I'd like a word alone with Mrs Orton, Tommy."

Townsend swallowed, then gave Joanna a stiff little bow. "No doubt we'll meet again on Thursday, Mrs Orton." He left the room.

"Another offer?" Joanna demanded. She knew that at any moment she was going to explode.

"Why, yes, you could put it that way," Andy said. "Are you really going to divorce Dick?" He studied her for a few seconds, then went on, as she did not reply. "If you don't, you need your head examined. You must know that he has a mistress?"

"Does all London know that?" she asked, wearily.

"I'm afraid it does. And then, he has behaved like the most utter bastard in quite literally pulling the rug from beneath your feet, in effect costing you your company."

"Does it matter to you, now?" she asked. "What I do?"

"It matters very much. You know how fond I have always been of you. As I have told you, I felt I couldn't compete with Howard. Not financially, but simply because you were his protégé. I will admit I was bit dashed when, after Howard's death, you upped and married that wog Hasim. But he had a lot of money to spend and I suppose a girl likes to have new experiences. I can't say I wept when I saw that he'd been done down by his Arab brethren. Now, I thought . . . and damn me if you didn't go off and marry some clerk. After I had put your company back on its financial feet. That was shocking."

"You congratulated me at my wedding, if I remember," Joanna said.

"Well, a chap has to show the right form, don't you know. But he was a total mistake. No money, no breeding. I suppose he's good in bed. You go for men who are good in bed, don't you, Joanna? But they do need to have breeding as well."

"You really belong crawling along a gutter," Joanna remarked.

"I always try to be a realist, to be pragmatic, and never to lose my cool. I think you should divorce Orton and marry me. I've waited a long time for this moment. How old were you when we first met? Sixteen? You were quite enchanting. I never doubted then that you would become an even more enchanting woman. I was quite prepared to let another man break you in. But that's all done, now. And I was right. You are quite the most enchanting woman in London."

"Listen," she said. "Go away. Please. Go far, far away."

"You need to think about it," he said. "Marry me, and you'll be richer than you have been since Hasim died. What's more, it won't just be income, it'll be capital. I'll still buy your shares for one point two, but that'll be your pin money. You'll have nothing more to worry about for the rest of your life. I will happily act the stepfather to your two children, although I will certainly hope to add to the happy home. If I say so myself, I am quite as good in bed as any of your past or present husbands. I'd be quite happy to give you a trial run, if you wish."

Joanna pressed her buzzer, three times. Andy raised his eyebrows, then turned sharply as the door opened to admit both Peter Young and Matilda. "This creature who masquerades as a gentleman is just leaving," Joanna said. "Will you kindly see him off the premises."

"Do you really think you can throw me out?" Andy demanded.

"I know I can throw you out, Andy," Joanna said. "And that is what I am doing. And just in case you get any funny ideas, I should inform you that Matilda is a black belt at judo. Her real purpose in life is not to act as my PR, as is supposed, but to act as my bodyguard. Now, are you leaving, or should Matilda reveal some of her talents?" Matilda, having got the drift, began to look suitably menacing. She was, Joanna knew, an expert at both judo and karate.

"Hicks from the colonies," Andy said disparagingly, but he got up. "We'll meet again on Thursday, Joanna, and by then I will have destroyed you. I am going to hold a press conference to tell the world that two of your ships are barely seaworthy, that your marriage is on the rocks, and that the future of Caribee Shipping is so grim as to be unspeakable. I am going to drive the share price right through the floor, so far they'll never see daylight again."

"But if you do that, your own shares will be worthless," Peter protested.

"Of course. But my share-holding in Caribee Shipping, however large and valuable on paper, is only a portion of my portfolio, and besides, I'll be able to do a deal with Petherick to buy my holding at considerably above the market price. But you, dear lady, will not have two cents to rub together. Nor will you have Caribee House, or the flat, or that Rolls you keep parked outside. Think about it." He left the room.

# Chapter Three

# Shares

There was complete silence in the boardroom as Joanna slowly sat down. Matilda was the first to speak. "Can he do that?" she asked.

"Probably."

"If he's engaging in some private deal with Petherick," Peter said. "We'll have him in court."

"If we could ever prove it," Joanna said. "Why wasn't I told that Dick had sold his shares?"

"Dick?" Peter and Matilda spoke together. They obviously didn't know what had happened.

"Your husband manages my trust company, Tilly," Joanna said. "You're not going to tell me he didn't know?"

"He never said anything to me," Matilda said. "Oh, the wretch."

"The world is full of wretches," Joanna said.

"Would you mind telling me just what has happened?" Peter asked. Joanna outlined her conversation with Townsend and Andy, and he gave a low whistle. "I would say they have us by the short and curlies."

"My short and curlies aren't for grabbing," Joanna said, and stood up.

"But what are you going to do? What *can* you do?"

"I am going to pay a visit to my sick husband," Joanna said. "I would also like to have a word with your husband, Tilly."

"He said he was flying across to Jersey today."

"Well, get hold of him and tell him to get his ass back here, on the next plane."

"Sorting them out isn't going to help," Peter said gloomily.

"I know that, Peter," Joanna said. "But I do intend to sort them out. Then I intend to regain control of my company. Arrange a press conference for tomorrow morning."

"What can you say to them?"

Joanna smiled. "I'll think of something."

"Home, Charlie," she told her chauffeur. He was a huge, bearlike man, an old friend, who had worked for Howard Edge, and was one of those who could remember his erstwhile boss taking that pretty, innocent, teenage girl out to Caribee House. Had that pretty, innocent, teenage girl ever existed? Now he made no comment, that having driven his employer into the city, with her sister-cum-bodyguard as always at her side, she was driving out again before lunch, without her sister.

Joanna was grateful for the long drive into Berkshire, because it gave her time for her emotions to settle down. And they were settling in the direction she wanted, a white heat of fury at the people who had betrayed her. How she could ever have supposed herself in love with that creep Richard Orton? But he was only a blip compared with what he had done. What she would now have to do. She had no option.

Cummings was as usual on the doorstep to greet her. "Is anything the matter, madam?"

"A lot, Cummings. But we'll sort it out." The thought that she might have to leave this house, her home for thirteen years, and people like Cummings and Mrs Partridge, her most faithful supporters in everything she had ever set out to do . . . it only hardened her resolve. She went upstairs, opened the door of Dick's bedroom.

"Well, hello, sweetheart," he said. "That was a quick trip. No problems, I hope."

Joanna advanced to the bedside. "Get up," she said.

"My dear Jo, I'm sick, I have a temperature."

"I don't give a damn if you have galloping pneumonia. Get up, get dressed, and get out."

"You can't throw me out. I'm your husband."

"Not any more, you're not. I am filing for divorce, this morning."

"Now, Jo . . ."

"You have fifteen minutes to be off my premises," she said. "Or I will have you dumped on the street."

He swung his legs out of bed. "You've found out about the shares!"

"I have found out about everything," she said.

"Listen. I can explain."

"Who did you sell the shares to?"

His face tightened. "I don't think I can tell you that."

"No matter. I will find out from Billy. But if you won't tell me, then you cannot explain. Anything." She slammed the door behind herself and went downstairs, grateful that the children would both be at school.

Mrs Partridge appeared. "Is there anything needs to be done, Mrs Orton?"

"Yes," Joanna said. "Don't ever call me Mrs Orton again." She went into the study, dialled her solicitor.

"Joanna?" John Giffard was another avuncular figure; the city, all London, was full of avuncular figures as regards her – she wondered how many of them she could trust? "I'm told you've been risking death on the high seas."

"John, I wish you to prepare papers for the divorce of myself and Dick." There was a moment's silence. "I wish them filed today," Joanna said.

"You wouldn't like us to meet and talk about it first?"

"There is nothing to talk about."

"There are, you know. Grounds—"

"I have proof of adultery."

"Ah. Yes. Messy. Now, a separation, followed by—"

"Adultery," Joanna said.

"Ah. Right. Now, settlement . . ."

"No settlement," Joanna said.

"My dear Joanna . . ."

"As I am sure you remember, John, when we married," Joanna said, "I settled fifty thousand shares of Caribee Shipping on Dick. They were then worth roughly a quarter of a million pounds, which was more money than he had ever had in his life before. He accepted that that was in full and final settlement of any claim he might have if we split."

"I don't think they're quite worth that now," Giffard ventured.

"He also accepted that the value of the shares would be subject to market fluctuation, and that if we split I would buy the shares back at the original price, or the present price, whichever was higher."

"And is that what you are proposing to do?"

"I can't," Joanna said. "He's already sold them."

Giffard was silent for a few seconds. Then he said, "But, now that I do remember the marriage contract, it was stated that he could not sell his shares without your permission. Did you give permission?"

"No I did not."

"Well, then . . ."

"What do you want me to do, John? Sue my husband for the money? He's probably already spent it. Anyway, I don't give a damn about the money. It's the shares that were important, and they're gone."

"Does that mean you lose control of the company?"

"Over my dead body," Joanna said. "Just prepare those papers and file them."

"I'll get on to it right away. Thank God there are no mutual children to complicate matters. But there is one more thing: co-habitation."

"Dick is leaving Caribee House, today," Joanna said.

He stood in the doorway, fully dressed, his expression a

mixture of anger and apprehension. "You're not going to get away with this," he said.

"Watch me. Where are your suitcases?"

"I haven't had time to pack. I'll send for my things."

"Make it soon. And don't come yourself."

"Jo . . ." he came into the room. "Can't we sit down and talk this over? I mean to say, I'm your oldest friend. Remember the good times we had when we were kids? And I saved your life from the Qadiri assassin. Remember?"

"I do remember, Dick," she said. "And I was, and am, eternally grateful. But now you may have cost me my company, Raisul's inheritance. And you did it in an underhand way. You have also found a sexual interest apart from me. I hate you for both of those things. Now please leave."

"Where am I supposed to go?" he asked, plaintively.

"Doesn't your girlfriend have a home?" He glared at her for several seconds, then left the room. Joanna discovered she was shivering.

There was so much to be done, so much of it really unpleasant. There was only one source from which she could obtain the shares to regain control of the company. The deal had been that Andy and his associates had bought enough of her stock to give them a fifty-one per cent shareholding. They had then bought out all of the remaining shareholders, save one, and their actual holding was sixty-three percent. Of the remaining thirty-seven percent, she held twenty-nine, five of which she had given to Dick and was now apparently lost to her, reducing her holding to twenty-four percent, one per cent below the figure required to give her perpetual control of the company. But there remained eight per cent, a matter of a hundred thousand shares held by Alicia Edge, Howard's first wife. Even half of those hundred thousand shares would put her back in control, by the terms of the original agreement. Andy had presumably not considered them important, because he knew that she and Alicia hated each other, that indeed the last time they had met

Alicia had physically attacked her; it had been Andy himself who had separated them.

So, whatever now needed doing, had to be done. And it had to be done before Andy reflected long enough to realise that there could just be a chink in his armour. She called Cummings. "Is Charlie still here?"

"Of course, madam."

"Very good. I am going out, possibly for several hours. I don't think I shall be back for lunch."

"Of course, madam. Should anyone call . . ."

"Just tell them I'm out, and you don't know where."

"Of course, madam."

Joanna telephoned her bank, was put through to Barry Andrews, the Area Manager. Like almost everyone else in the business world, Andrews had regarded her with acute distrust when as a twenty-year-old widow she had told him she intended to take charge of Caribee Shipping herself, and would need a good deal of financing to do so. His immediate rejection had been dissipated by the backing of Prince Hasim, and since then he had come to accept, and indeed, admire her, as a woman who meant what she said and who invariably got what she wanted. But today even his voice was worried. "Half a million, Joanna? This is a bad time."

"For everyone. I'm not going to buy a yacht, Barry. I need to buy some shares, and they are going to be expensive. You know I'm good for it. And you can have the new shares as additional security as soon as they're mine."

"Well, of course, Joanna, we'll back you," he agreed.

"You're a dear. I'll be in touch the moment I've actually written the cheque."

Joanna put on her mink, went out to the car. Charlie had already been alerted, and hastily stubbed out his cigarette. "Where to, Mrs Orton?"

"From now on I would like you to call me Mrs Edge again," Joanna said.

"Yes, madam."

"So let's go call on the other Mrs Edge. You know the address, I should think?" Charlie gulped.

It was a long drive. Alicia lived with her daughter Victoria on the south coast, just outside the Hampshire town of Lymington, in a small house which had views out over the harbour, principally a yacht haven and ferry terminus, covered with gleaming water at high tide and glutinous mud at low, with a glimpse of the Isle of Wight in the background. There was a small drive and a garage to the right of the building. Neighbours parted curtains to stare as the Rolls turned in, crunching the gravel, and stopped outside the door. "I don't know how long I'm going to be, Charlie," Joanna said.

"No problem, Mrs Or . . . Mrs Edge."

Joanna rang the bell, and after a moment it was answered by a maid. Alicia had not given up all of her creature comforts. "Is Mrs Edge in?" Joanna asked, pleasantly.

"Who shall I say is calling, madam?"

"What are *you* doing here?" Alicia was coming down the stairs; clearly she had seen the car from an upstairs window.

"A social call, my dear," Joanna said. "You're looking well."

Alicia was some ten years older than herself, and was a very well-preserved forty. She was a small woman, her pretty features somewhat tight, who wore her fair hair short, and had a compact figure. She wore a trouser suit, and as always several expensive rings. "So do you," she remarked, grudgingly.

"May I come in?" Joanna asked, as the maid stood by helplessly. The meeting was not getting off to a flying start.

"As you're here." Alicia came down to the foot of the stairs and held out a limp hand. Joanna gave it a quick squeeze. Alicia led her into a comfortable lounge. "Coffee? Oh, I forgot: you always drink champagne at twelve in the morning."

"I think coffee would be best, today," Joanna said.

"Coffee, Joanna," Alicia called, and smiled. "Her name isn't actually Joanna, but I call her that." Joanna sat down; this is simply not going to work, she told herself. But she had to try. Alicia sat opposite her. "So, what brings you down to this little neck of the woods."

"A business matter," Joanna said. Alicia raised her eyebrows. "I'm attempting to dot some i's and cross some t's," Joanna explained. "And I was wondering . . . how would you like to sell some of your shares in the company?"

Alicia's smile this time was more genuine. "You are attempting to be a smarty-pants, as always, Joanna. You are looking for a bargain while the price is down."

"Well," Joanna said, and waited while the maid served coffee and withdrew. "There is some talk that the price may not recover for a while. However, I don't want to do you down, my dear Alicia. I will pay the price the shares were before the Arab-Israeli War began. I think it was about eight. If you were to sell me half your shares at that price, you would realise four hundred thousand pounds."

"You have that kind of money to splash around?"

"I do."

"And it doesn't occur to you that if I needed, or wanted, that much cash, I would have already sold the shares?"

"You're not going to tell me you have?"

"No, I have not. That is my stake in Howard's company, and I intend to keep it."

"Selling half, you would still retain a considerable holding."

"And you would be increasing yours. You'll have to tell me why you want my shares."

Joanna drank some coffee while she got her thoughts in order. There was more than one way to play this, but Alicia had just indicated the most promising. She gave an elaborate sigh. "You may as well know the truth. Dick has stabbed me in the back. He has sold his shares, illegally, and left me with only a twenty-four per cent interest."

"Aha!" Alicia said. "So you have lost control."

"Not yet. The shareholders' meeting is next Thursday."

"I haven't been advised."

"I'm sure the advice is in the post. Andy is in a hurry."

"Well, well," Alicia said, all manner of expressions passing over her face as she considered the power she had just acquired. "And then you're out on your ass."

"Not quite," Joanna said. "I still have my twenty-four per cent."

"But no control. I suppose Andy intends to run the company himself. He should have done that long ago."

"Andy," Joanna said, "intends to liquidate the company, by selling it to Petherick."

Alicia frowned at her. "He can't do that."

"I'm afraid, if I am no longer Chairman and Managing Director, he can and he intends to, by the simple process of selling all his holding to Petherick. The deal has already been drawn up, I understand. The Caribee flag, the Caribee logo, will disppear, the Caribee ships will be absorbed into the Petherick line, and you and I, and Howard, of course, will be history. Forgotten history within five years."

Alicia continued to stare at her. "How do I know this is true?"

"You can ring Peter Young."

Another long stare. "I think I'd rather ring Andy."

"Oh, but . . ." Joanna bit her lip.

"You wouldn't like that, would you?"

"No, I would not like that," Joanna snapped. "My object is to save Howard's company. I thought you might feel the same way. Once Andy finds out I intend to fight him, he . . . well . . ."

"He'll come down here and make me a better offer." Alicia got up and began to walk around the room. "One thing I have always admired about you, Joanna, is your unmitigated gall. Howard and I were perfectly happily married when you appeared. You inveigle yourself into his life, make him think he is in love with you, get him to rewrite his will in your favour, and then carry him off to the wilds of South America to drown him in some rapids."

"Listen," Joanna said. "If there were a single other person present I'd have you in court for slander."

"Ha!" Alicia commented.

"You know as well as I that your marriage was over long before I ever met Howard. He was taking girls to the flat on a virtually nightly basis. He went for me because I wouldn't play."

"The oldest trick in the world," Alicia sneered.

"It happened to be genuine. I only ever moved in with him after you had left. I never asked him either to marry me or change his will in my favour. Those were his decisions, just as it was his decision to shoot those rapids. I begged him not to."

"Ha," Alicia commented again. "The fact remains, you had no right to the company, to Caribee House, to the flat, to that Rolls outside. By rights they were all mine. And young Howie's. Now, thanks to you and your Arab prince, my Howie is dead. I hate you for that. And now that you've gone in over your head you have the cheek to come here and ask me to bail you out."

"I have made you a perfectly fair offer," Joanna said, now also standing. "Most people would say it is a generous offer. More than generous, in the present circumstances. I am doing it to keep control of the company. Because that is what Howard wanted. If you can't appreciate that, you are a vicious, twisted woman." They glared at each other. Because she is, a vicious, twisted woman, Joanna thought. "Well," she said, "as I seem to have made a wasted journey, I'll say goodbye." She picked up her handbag. "Thanks for the coffee."

"What are you going to do?" Alicia asked. Suddenly she was genuinely curious.

Joanna shrugged. "Whatever I can."

"There's nothing you can do," Alicia said, "without my support."

"So, have a good gloat. In time you'll merely feel ashamed to have let Howard down."

"If I agreed to support you," Alicia said, "there are things I would require."

Joanna, almost at the door, checked. But there couldn't be any misapprehensions. "Your support is no good to me, Alicia," she said. "Merely having your shares voting with mine at the meeting won't matter a damn. We don't have enough. The only way we can save the company is for me to regain control as stipulated in my agreement with Andy. I have to have twenty-five per cent of the shares, in my name, by next Thursday."

"I wish the use of the flat. When you are not occupying it, of course."

Was it going to happen? Joanna felt a sudden glow of both confidence and energy, whereas five minutes before she had been absolutely drained of both. "I have no objection to that."

"I wish a seat on the board."

Joanna's jaw dropped. "You? You have never had a seat on the board."

"That was because Howard wouldn't let me. But you are going to let me, aren't you, Joanna? I think it would be a good thing for there to be two women on the board."

Joanna sighed. But having Alicia making stupid suggestions and raising irrelevant points, as would certainly be the case, would be nothing more than an irritation, compared with losing the company. "All right," she said.

"And for Stephen."

"Who?"

Alicia flushed. "So you don't know everything, after all. There is a man called Stephen Maddox, who I wish to have a seat on the board of Caribee Shipping."

Joanna sat down. "I'm surely entitled to ask who this man is? What are his qualifications?"

"Oh, he knows about boards and things. He's my financial adviser."

"You have a lover?" Joanna was astounded.

"What's so remarkable about that?" Alicia demanded, flushing more deeply.

"Nothing. I apologise."

Alicia sniffed. "You mean you are surprised that I, unlike you, remained loyal to Howard's memory for so long. But a woman needs love." Clearly, she meant sex.

"Absolutely," Joanna agreed. But the idea of having some toy-boy on the board . . . On the other hand, she had always worked on the principal of selecting priorities, and sticking to them absolutely. Priority number one was the company. If she didn't control it, it wouldn't matter to her who sat on the board. If she did control the company, well, she had always controlled the board as well.

"Well?" Alicia demanded.

"If that's what you want, my dear," Joanna said. "So, will you now telephone your broker and authorise him to sell half of your shareholding in Caribee Shipping to me, at the price quoted last November, and I will telephone my broker and tell him to complete the deal."

"Now?"

"Before I leave," Joanna said, and gave one of her bright smiles. "I wouldn't be able to digest my lunch if I thought you might be having seconds thoughts."

"Find me a nice pub, and join me for lunch, Charlie," Joanna said. It was past one, and she was hungry.

"It will be a pleasure, Mrs Edge," Charlie said, and obliged almost immediately. "I would say your meeting with the other Mrs Edge went well," he ventured as they sat together, drinking beer and eating cold meat sandwiches.

"As well as I could have hoped," Joanna said.

"So . . . all is well, then?"

She glanced at him. Charlie had been Howard's chauffeur before she had inherited him, and he had served her faithfully and well for the ten years since Howard's death. She had more than a suspicion that when Howard *had* died, Charlie had had a few ideas about taking advantage of the situation, but he had soon realised that Joanna was not the loose woman Alicia made her out to be. He was now over forty, she supposed, and delighted in their very real, but very chaste, intimacy; he knew nearly all of her secrets. "The water is still a little choppy," she told him. "But nothing the ship can't ride."

"I am very glad about that, Mrs Edge."

"You're a dear, Charlie. Now let's get home. There's still a lot to do."

Because a triumph like this morning always left her feeling randy, she needed to get home . . . and use that telephone number?

It was three before they reached Caribee House. "Mr Montgomery is here, madam," Cummings said.

Joanna had recognised the car parked in the drive. She went into the lounge, where Billy and Matilda were waiting, both looking anxious. "I came right back," Billy said.

"Thank you. When did you find out that Dick had sold his shares?"

"Well, I was advised when it happened, of course."

"That was two days ago. The day I got back."

"Well . . . yes, it was."

"But you didn't think to tell me?"

"Well, Jo, I meant to, but what with all the excitement of your homecoming, I'm afraid I forgot."

"You forgot to tell me something which might have jeopardised the company? What about yesterday?"

"There was so much going on . . ."

"Where is Dick, by the way?" Matilda asked. "Still in bed upstairs?"

"Dick has left."

"Just like that? I thought he had 'flu."

"He probably has raging pneumonia by now. But I no longer consider it my business."

Matilda goggled at her. "You threw him out? But . . . he's your husband!"

"The divorce papers are being filed now."

"Good lord." Matilda sat down.

"I'm most terribly sorry," Billy said. "Matilda has put me in the picture. What a mess. I can't help feeling that telling you two days ago wouldn't have changed anything. It would only have spoiled your homecoming."

"It would have saved me from being utterly humiliated by Andy and that creep Townsend," Joanna pointed out.

"Yes. As I say, I am most terribly sorry, but there was nothing I could do about it."

"Wasn't there? Those shares were held in trust. You are the manager of my trust company. Those shares could not be sold without our joint authority, in writing. Do you have such authority?"

"Well . . . no." He was flushing. "But Dick was your husband, and you weren't here . . ."

"You knew I was arriving, that very day."

"I . . . I was confused, I suppose."

"I am sure you were confused," Jonna agreed. "Who actually runs the trust company?"

"Jimmy Haddon. He's very good. I don't think you can blame him for what happened."

"I have no intention of blaming him for what happened, Billy. I am blaming you. I therefore wish you to get in touch with Mr Haddon, immediately, and inform him that he is now manager of the Trust Company."

"But . . . what about me?"

"You are fired," Joanna said.

There was a moment's silence. "You can't fire Billy," Matilda protested.

"I have just done so." Joanna went to her desk picked up the phone, dialled.

"He's your brother-in-law," Matilda shouted.

"Give me Mr Young," Joanna said into the phone.

"He's my husband!" Matilda shrieked.

"Peter? I am sorry to disturb you. This call is to inform you that Mr Montgomery is no longer in the employ of Caribee Shipping, or me personally. Will you please arrange for him to receive the correct amount of severance pay?"

She could hear Peter gulping on the far end of the phone.

"You are a bitch!" Matilda screamed. "Bitch, bitch, bitch!"

"Jimmy Haddon will be taking over the Trust Company. Would you please inform him?"

"Is this an act of vengeance?"

"I'm sorry you should think that, Peter," Joanna said. "I am firing someone who has proved himself to be incompetent and uninterested in the real interests of my company."

"Do you still have a company, Joanna?"

"Yes," Joanna said. "I, we, still have a company, Peter. Did you arrange that press conference for me?"

"They're coming in at nine tomorrow morning."

"I'll be there." She hung up, gazed at Matilda, who had advanced to stand on the far side of the desk

"You are a bitch," Matilda said again. "I ought to break every bone in your body."

"Then you'd better begin with my neck. Because if you lay one finger on me and I survive, I will have you, and him, sent to prison for a very long time," Joanna said, keeping her voice low and even.

Matilda burst into tears; she entirely lacked her sister's strength of character. "He made a mistake," she said. "One mistake. It was just an oversight. It was—"

"One oversight too many. I am sorry."

"We'd better go," Billy muttered.

"I will never speak to you again," Matilda said. "Never, never, never."

"That is entirely up to you."

Matilda glared at her a last time, then turned and marched for the door. Billy followed without looking at Joanna, who sat down with a thump and rang the bell absently. "Madam?" Cummings appeared in the doorway.

"Bollinger."

"Ah . . ." Cummings only just prevented his gaze from drifting to the clock on the mantelpiece. "Yes, madam."

Howard had always drunk champagne in moments of crisis. But she did look at the clock. It was half-past three, and Helen and Raisul would be in from school at any moment. She did not feel up to seeing them. She went into the study, called the bank. "The shares are being transferred now," she said. "I imagine the call will come through from Miller & Sparks tomorrow morning. I've told them you'll be sending across the papers making them security." She hung up, went into the hall, encountered Cummings, armed with tray, bottle and glass. "Upstairs, please, Cummings," she said.

He followed her up the stairs. At the top, Mrs Partridge waited. "Are you all right, madam?"

"No," Joanna said. "But there is nothing the matter with me a rest won't cure." She opened her bedroom door. "Just put the tray down, Cummings."

Cummings obeyed, and left the room. Mrs Partridge hesitated. "Is there anything I can get you, madam?"

"I have everything I want, thank you, Mrs Partridge. I don't want to be disturbed, please. Not even when the children come in."

"I'll tell Mrs Winshaw," Mrs Partridge said, and closed the door.

They had both, of course, heard Matilda shouting, Joanna supposed. She reckoned she was an endless source of gossip in the servants' hall. But they remained utterly faithful to her . . . or at least Cummings and Mrs Partridge did. She poured herself a glass of champagne, drank half of it, undressed, went into the bathroom and had a shower; she was wet through with perspiration. She towelled herself dry, finished the glass, refilled it, and sat on the edge of the bed.

Presumably she had now quite destroyed the family. She

had no sympathy for Billy. He had been in at the very beginning, regarding himself as Howard's right-hand man, whereas Howard had always referred to him, and regarded him, as 'my man'. He had been another who had tried to muscle in when Howard had died; he had even, she recalled with savage amusement, envisaged himself as the new Chairman of the company! And when she had politely informed him that was not on, and married Prince Hasim, he had married Matilda. It did not matter that Matilda had undoubtedly made the first move; Billy had seized the opportunity to stay close to the seat of power. Tilly, now . . . Tilly would come round, perhaps. If Billy would let her. She was given to strong statements and strong stances, without the strength of mind to carry either through. But they could never be close again. There was a shame. Joanna smiled as she recalled some of the escapades they had got up to in their youth. The time Howard had taken them to his London flat – her flat now – after Tilly had been arrested for go-go dancing in the nude, Howard had bought her an entire outfit from Harrods to replace the clothes she didn't have.

But even then, it had been *her* he had wanted, not big sister. She wondered if Matilda had always been jealous of that; it would have been against human nature for her not to be.

She drank some champagne. And William would have to choose sides, at least in the short term. She lay back, the glass held between her breasts, gazing at the ceiling. And as if she had used mental telepathy, the phone rang.

She stretched out her hand and lifted the receiver, just as Cummings answered from downstairs. "Jo?"

"Cummings here, Mr William. The mistress is resting."

"I'm awake, Cummings," Joanna said.

"Ah, yes, madam." Cummings replaced the phone.

"Jo? What the hell is going on?"

"Not a lot, save that I am trying to get some rest."

"I've had Matilda on the phone."

"I thought you might."

"Is it true you have fired her?"

"No, it is not true. I think she may have resigned. She didn't actually put it in as many words, but that was the gist of it."

"You can joke about it?"

"What am I supposed to do, cry?"

"You did fire Billy."

"Yes, for total incompetence and disloyalty. And I suspect a smack of dishonesty, although I can't prove it."

"Jo, these are your own flesh and blood."

"Billy isn't. God forbid."

"Jo, look, maybe I can sort things out."

"Did Tilly ask you to do that?"

"Well . . . not exactly. But I know she'd like to make it up. She really is in a bad way, Jo. She was crying, on the phone."

"I would give it a little while," Joanna said.

"Jo! This is family. Can we come down tonight?"

"Who?"

"Norma and I, of course. And we could bring Tilly. There'd be no need for Billy to come, if you didn't wish to see him."

"Not tonight," Joanna said. "I have had a pretty traumatic day. I have sacked one husband, one brother-in-law, and one sister. I have had virtually to crawl on my hands and knees to regain control of the company. Tonight I want to do my own thing, all right?"

There was a brief silence. "I'm not sure what that means," he said, apprehensively. "What are you doing?"

"Right now, I'm drinking champagne. Then I am going to have a nap. And when I wake up . . . I'll decide that when I wake up."

"But you don't want to see us?"

"Definitely not. Call me tomorrow."

Another hesitation. Then he said. "Well, take care."

"Oh, I shall do that," she said, and hung up.

But she had already decided what she wanted to do when she woke up. She got out of bed, refilled her glass, then opened her handbag and took out the slip of paper Connor had given her on board the *Caribee Queen*.

# Chapter Four

# The Crime

Joanna slept heavily, then got up and had a tub. She knew she was more nervous than she had been for a long time, but it was important not to allow anyone to see that. Equally, she had to recreate the atmosphere of the ship. That was going to be difficult. There was no storm raging outside, although it was threatening to snow. The important thing was to recreate her aura of total command. She hoped Sean wouldn't turn out to be a wimp like Dick, and require that aura always. But she felt it was important on this first occasion when they would meet in her natural habitat, as it were.

So she dressed in a pale blue evening gown with a deep *décolletage*, wore a choker of pearls and the huge ruby embedded between diamonds Howard had given her as an engagement present, and put her hair up – she could always let it down if the evening went as she hoped. The children were astounded. "Mummy, are you going to a ball?" Helen inquired.

"You look lovely," Raisul confided.

"Why, thank you, darling. No, I am not going to a ball; I'm expecting a guest for dinner."

"Oooh. May we stay up?" Helen asked.

"Not for dinner. But you may stay up and say good-night," Joanna said.

* * *

She had given Cook her instructions, as well as Cummings, and the huge refectory dining table was laid for two, a setting at each end, which meant that they would be separated by some fifteen feet of wood. She supposed she was being somewhat childish, wishing to awe him to such an extent, but she felt it was important to preserve their respective positions, at least in the beginning. But she was intensely nervous as seven-thirty arrived. He had said he would have no difficulty in getting to her, or in finding the house. As she heard headlights in the drive, and the crunching of gravel, Joanna remained sitting in front of the open fireplace, watching the flickering flames. The house was centrally heated, but she did like an open fire. The double doors opened. "Mr Connor, madam," Cummings said.

Joanna stood up, stared at him. He was better looking than she remembered, but he wore an open-necked shirt and a windcheater. On the other hand, she reminded herself, she had not asked him to dress. He was staring at her, in turn. "Sorry," he said.

"Why? Cummings?" Cummings served champagne. Joanna raised her glass. "Welcome."

"It's great to be here. Some place you have." Connor came into the room, and Cummings left, having placed the bottle on the sideboard in its bucket, closing the doors behind him. "I'm not sure of the drill," he confessed.

"I think we could kiss each other," Joanna suggested.

He held her in his arms, reaching past her to put his glass on the mantelpiece, then sliding his hands down the side of her gown to hold her buttocks. She didn't resist him; she felt the same way. He kissed her mouth for several seconds, then pulled his head back. "I was beginning to wonder if that ship wasn't a dream."

"Your first hurricane?"

"And yours, I seem to remember. But I gather you're still in one."

She released him, topped up their glasses. "You've been reading the newspapers."

"And some. Anything I can do to help?"

"You?" She smiled. "Oh, indeed. Just by being here. The papers don't know everything, you see."

She sat on the settee, and he sat beside her. "You mean things are worse than they appear?"

"That's a point of view. I'm divorcing my husband."

Just for a moment his eyes narrowed. "Why?"

"Oh, don't worry, it has nothing to do with you. I went away to get myself sorted out, attitudes and that sort of thing. And when I came back, I found my mind was made up."

"But I had nothing to do with your decision?"

"Nothing at all. Does that bother you?" She gazed at him.

"I was actually wondering if I could be of help in the business."

She smiled. "Thanks, but no, really. I've sorted that out as well."

"You've had a busy few days. So why am I here?"

He was definitely put out, and therefore aggressive. She rested her hand on his. "You are here because I wish you to be. I promised to call, remember?"

"I never thought you would."

"I always keep my word. Now you must meet the children." The door opened, and Helen and Raisul filed in, wearing their nightclothes and dressing gowns. Mrs Winshaw remained in the doorway. "This is Mr Connor," Joanna explained.

Helen held out her hand. "Hello, Mr Connor." Connor looked bemused.

Raisul took his sister's place. "Hello, Mr Connor." Connor shook hands.

"Say good-night," Joanna commanded.

"Good-night, Mr Connor," they chorused, and turned to Joanna to be hugged and kissed.

"I love your dress, Mummy," Helen confided, and then scampered to join her brother. Mrs Winshaw closed the doors.

"So you don't dress for dinner every night," Connor remarked.

"Only when I feel like it," Joanna said. "I do most things when I feel like it." She was being deliberately provocative, but the evening was not going as she had intended; she could sense waves of hostility beaming at her. But he had come, however resentfully, at her summons. "Will you fill our glasses?"

He obeyed, then sat beside her again "I had no idea you had children."

"Helen is nine, and Raisul is seven. They are by different fathers, but both fathers were my husband at the time. Raisul, in a perfect world, would be the present Emir of Qadir. No, I take that back. That would be a most imperfect world. He's better off where he is, the future Chairman of Caribee Shipping."

"You think very positively."

"I have found that necessary, from time to time."

"So . . ." he put down his glass. "What happens next?"

"Isn't that up to you?"

He shook his head. "Not in these surroundings. You're the boss lady. But then, you always are, aren't you?"

She considered him for several seconds. "I try to be," she said at last. "But tonight, I would like to surrender, absolutely. Just tell me what you would like to do."

She was remembering the little nibbles and sucks from on board the ship, so titillating. But those had been to the accompaniment of the howling wind and the gigantic slaps of the sea. In this drawing room there was no sound at all, apart from the guttering of the flames. "Anything?" he asked.

She raised her eyebrows. "Are you trying to frighten me?"

"I've an idea that might be difficult. I'd like to posssess you, for one short hour."

"There's a pessimistic point of view. Your wish is granted, sir."

"Now?"

"Dinner is in half-an-hour. But after that the night is yours."

"You know how to turn a man on."

"Don't sound so disparaging. It's what women were put on earth to do."

"There's a refreshing point of view in this bra-burning age. That butler fellow, is he likely to come back?"

"Cummings will knock on the door at eight o'clock to tell me that dinner is served. He won't come back before then, unless I ring."

"Then will you take off your gown?" Joanna stood up, released the zip, allowed the silk to settle about her ankles. She wore only panties underneath. "You are divine," he said. "All that beauty – and a brain as well." He himself slid the pants down, and she stepped out of both them and the dress.

"Do I keep my shoes?" she asked.

"I think we could do without them."

She kicked them off. "And my jewellery?"

"Oh, no, keep the jewellery. That makes you more exciting."

"And what about you?"

He undressed in turn. "I have always wanted to make love on a hearthrug in front of a roaring fire."

"Snap," Joanna said. "You mean you have never done it before?"

He grinned. "Not with a beautiful millionairess wearing all her rocks." He released her hair.

She could remember his caresses from on board the ship; they were divine. At the same time, she was realising that she didn't actually like him, or at least, the image he was presenting. On the other hand, as far as sexual therapy went, he was perfection. She did not object when, having brought her close to a climax by stroking her front, he rolled her on her stomach. He was kissing her neck as he did so, while his hands still roamed, then suddenly she realised something was wrong.

She had been so relaxed it took her a few seconds to understand what was happening, as he parted her cheeks and let his fingers roam between.

"We need a lubricant," he whispered. "What did they use in *Last Tango in Paris*? Butter, right. We need some butter."

"No." She tried to twist, and was suddenly held firm by his hand placed firmly between her shoulder-blades, pressing her to the carpet. "I'm not into that," she gasped.

"But I am. Possession. That's the name of the game. That's what you said you wanted." His face was close to her neck. "And this is the ultimate possession."

"You . . ." she tried to push herself up, but she was no match for him in strength, and was driven down again, face bumping against the floor.

"Hey," he said. "You promised I could do whatever I liked."

"So long as I liked it too," she gasped. "Let me up, you bastard."

"Well," he said, "without butter, this may hurt."

My God, she thought, I've got myself in the hands of a satyr. She felt him against her flesh, and still his hand was on her back, pressing her down. Desperately she flung out her own hand, found it virtually in the fire, touched a lump of burning wood, screamed with the pain of it, but still held it, and brought it back, stabbing it into his side. He gave a shout of anguish and rolled off her and away from her. Joanna rolled as well, dropping the piece of wood and rising to her knees as she gazed in horror at the smoke rising from her hand, the black mark across the palm.

That distracted her, and gave Connor time to recover and hurl himself at her. Instinctively she brought up her hands, still only aware of the searing pain shooting from her hand into her wrist and up the entire length of her right arm, for a moment knocked senseless by the swinging blow that caught her on the side of the jaw and sent her rolling across the carpet. Why aren't I being helped? she asked herself. I am in a house full of servants, who are *my* servants, who will do anything for me . . . but she had trained them all, most of all Cummings, never to interfere unless called for.

She had to reach the bell, before this madman destroyed her. Because she could no longer doubt Conner was mad, at least temporarily, with a mixture of pain and desire. He was at her again, kneeling above her, rolling her over as he wanted her to be. "Bitch," he growled. "Mistress of everything. Mistress of mine, too, bitch."

Joanna swung her arms, to and fro, behind her, and was rewarded with a grunt, then they were caught and forced down. But he needed at least one hand to hold her while he made his entry. She gasped for breath and waited for one of her wrists to be released, then swung again, connected with his head, sent him one way and herself the other, realised that her choker had burst and the floor was covered in pearls. On which his knees slipped as he came at her again, sending him thudding to the floor. Joanna reached her own knees, scattering pearls, clasped her hands together, and swung them against the side of his face. Her left hand was uppermost, the knuckles with the diamond and ruby ring exposed. The stones swung into his cheek, and as he shrieked and tried to pull away, they continued to bite and opened up a jagged cut down to his jaw, from which blood poured. "Aaaagh!" he screamed again, falling back to the floor, rolling on to his back on top of the scattered pearls, holding his face while blood seeped through his fingers.

Joanna reached her feet, panting and crying, and again he grabbed at her ankle. She freed it with a kick, and then jumped on him with both feet, landing on his lower abdomen. This time he gave a choking gasp and she was free. She stumbled and staggered across the pearls and through the mist clouding her mind, and pressed the bell. Then she fell to her knees, coughing and choking. The door burst open. "Madam!" Cummings clearly could not believe what he was seeing.

"Help," Joanna gasped. "You'll need help."

Because Connor was starting to recover; he was sitting up, still holding his face, moaning but also muttering curses. Blood still dribbled from his cut cheek, and she thought some was coming from his mouth as well – he must have cut his lips.

"Charlie!" Cummings bellowed, at the same time running

across the room to arm himself with the poker. Joanna also ran across the room, to reach her discarded gown. Connor reached his feet, staggering to and fro. "Now, sir," Cummings said. "Nothing foolish."

"Get dressed," Joanna told him, stepping into her gown. "And get out of here."

"Bitch!" Connor lunged forward, and Cummings stepped in front of his mistress, the poker thrust forward. "Listen, old man," Connor said, spitting blood. "I'm going to break your fucking head open."

Charlie appeared in the doorway. Connor checked, looking from the diminutive figure of Cummings to the very large and athletic chauffeur. "Get him out of here," Joanna panted, zipping up her dress.

"You," Charlie said. "Out!"

"Yeah?" Connor asked, and ran at him. His feet slipped on the pearls, but he wouldn't have stood a chance anyway. Charlie cupped his hands together and brought them up in a huge uppercut as Connor reached him. Connor arced backwards and struck the floor with a tremendous crash.

Charlie stood above him, and looked at Joanna. "Out," Joanna said.

Connor struggled to his knees. "I have to dress," he mumbled, pawing at the blood on his face, augmented now by the cut on his chin.

"He can dress outside," Joanna said.

Charlie seized him by the shoulder and threw him through the door. Connor landed on his hands and knees in the hall. Cummings gathered up the discarded clothing. "The gentleman may well catch cold, madam," he suggested.

"One catches cold from germs, not temperature," Joanna said. "And he's as much a germ as anything out there."

By now the rest of the household had been aroused. Cook stood at the far end of the corridor, Mrs Partridge and Mrs Winshaw at the head of the stairs, watching as Charlie grasped Connor's shoulders, heaved him to his feet, and thrust him at the front door, which Cummings, still grasping Connor's clothes, was thoughtfully holding open. The air outside was icy. "You can't do this!" Connor shouted. "I'll have the law on you." He tried to wriggle free to face Joanna, and Charlie pushed him through the door. Cummings threw his clothes behind him, and the door was shut.

Joanna found that she was sitting on the settee, knees pressed together, shoulders hunched. Mistress of all she surveyed, he had called her. She had been proud of that. But once again her relationship with men had turned out disastrously. That could never be allowed to happen again. "Madam?" Mrs Partridge sat beside her. "Are you all right?"

*No*, Joanna thought. *I am never going to be all right again.* But she nodded. "I'm all right, Mrs Partridge. Thank you."

"But . . . all this blood."

"His blood, Mrs Partridge."

Cummings appeared. "Will you dine, madam?"

Joanna shook her head. "I couldn't eat a thing. Apologise to cook for me, Mr Cummings."

"You must take something," Mrs Partridge said, severely.

"A cup of soup. I'll have a cup of soup, in bed. And a glass of brandy." Joanna got to her feet, unsteadily, and Mrs Partridge held her arm to help her across the room. "Charlie," she said, "you'd better collect up these pearls."

Charlie dropped to his hands and knees. Mrs Partridge help Joanna up the stairs and into her bedroom, helped her off with her gown and got her beneath the sheets. "The children didn't wake up, did they?" she asked.

"I don't think so, madam."

"Thank God for that." Joanna sighed, and closed her eyes.

But Mrs Partridge had seen her right hand. "Oh, dear me, madam. I must get something for that." She bustled off, and hurried back with antiseptic cream, gently coated the hand. "I won't bind it up," she said. "It's better to let the air get to it."

"Thank you, Mrs Partridge," Joanna muttered. The hand was actually quite painful.

"Did you know the gentleman very well, madam?" Mrs Partridge asked.

Joanna opened her eyes. "Know him? No, I don't think I knew him at all. We met on the ship, and I had hoped to know him better."

"I see, madam. It's just that, did you notice? He was driving a very expensive car. What do they call them? Italian. A Ferrari."

He probably stole it, Joanna thought, as she drifted off after her soup and brandy. But she didn't sleep well, her brain tormented with images and memories, her body with the very real bruises she had accumulated, and her hand intensely painful. How could she have been so stupid? No, she realised, not stupid, merely arrogant. Which was, of course, another word for stupid. She had been on a high, because she had again triumphed, had regained control of her company, had taken on the world and beaten it, so of course she could point an imperious finger, as perhaps Cleopatra had done when in the mood, and said, you, I will have you. But even Cleopatra had fallen on her face, or was it her asp, at the end?

"What was all that noise, Mummy, last night?" Helen asked at breakfast.

"Noise, darling? Oh, I am sorry. I must have had the television on too loud."

"Did that Mr Connor come here to watch television, Mummy?" Raisul asked.

"Yes, but I don't think he liked my choice of programmes; he left early." She watched Cummings pouring coffee, with never a change of expression.

"Was Mr Connor really driving a Ferrari?" Joanna asked, as Charlie drove her into town.

"Yes, madam."

"Where do you suppose he got it?"

"I can find out, madam. I made a note of the number."

"Thank you, Charlie. I'd be most grateful."

"I have all those pearls gathered up, madam. What shall I do with them?"

"Oh, when you have dropped me, take them to Garrard's and have them re-strung."

"Of course, madam." Like Cummings, Charlie was a master at maintaining a po-face, even at the thought of driving round London with several thousand pounds' worth of pearls in his pocket.

Peter Young was so agitated that Joanna almost suspected he knew about last night. "Joanna!"

"Peter? What new crisis?"

"Haven't you heard the news?"

"I'm afraid I haven't listened to the news this morning, Peter."

"The Prime Minister has declared a three-day week."

Joanna blinked at him. "You mean he's taken away four days? I'm not sure he can do that. Or anyone."

"No, no," Peter said. "He hasn't reduced the number of days in the week; he's reduced the number of days people can work. Offices can open, ships can do business. That sort of thing."

Joanna frowned at him. "Is that legal?"

"The government makes the laws. It's to save fuel while this crisis lasts."

"For heaven's sake, the crisis could last for months."

"I know. It's pretty grim."

"Has he thought of the unemployment that could result?"

"He, or his advisers, must have taken into account every possibility."

"You have more faith in advisers than I have," Joanna growled, and sat behind her desk. "When do we have to close?"

"Starting tomorrow."

"And suppose one of our overseas customers wants to get in touch?"

"I've arranged for any calls to be transferred to my flat. I'll handle them."

"You really are a dear." Joanna squeezed his hand. "What about Thursday's shareholders meeting? Is that an off day, or an on day?"

"Well, it would appear to be an off day, for us. But I'm sure we can hold the meeting somewhere not on the premises."

"Yes," she said. "We will. We'll hold it at Caribee House. That ought to be fun."

William came in to see her, peered at her. "Are you all right?"

"In a manner of speaking."

He studied her for several seconds, uncertain how to take her remark. "You look kind of uptight."

"I have a lot on my mind. Doesn't everyone?"

He peered at her hand. "What happened?"

"I rather stupidly picked a burning brand out of the fire. It'll be all right."

"Does it hurt?"

"Of course it hurts. Like hell."

"And what's that mark on your chin?"

She touched the bruise and winced. She had covered it with powder, but the make-up had worn off. "I fell out of bed, if it's any concern of yours."

He sat before her desk. "How does this three day week thing affect us?"

"Here in London? The same as everybody else. Overseas it doesn't affect us at all. We can't tell our ships to stop sailing every other day. Again, loading, or unloading, here in London or down in Plymouth may cause some problems. But rice and sugar aren't that perishable, and neither are washing machines or dishwashers."

"Crazy," he commented. "But not funny. Obviously, jobs are going to be at a premium."

"I think they probably are, in the short term."

"Billy may find it difficult." Joanna gazed at him. "They didn't ask me to say that," William added hurriedly. "But I know they really would like to make it up. They're very upset. So is Norma."

"May I ask what she has to do with it?"

"She's part of the family, now."

Joanna considered. Never had she felt so lonely, so vulnerable. Not that surrounding herself with family would really help; she had tried that before in times of crisis, with no great amount of success. She needed a man. Not necessarily for sex, although that helped. But she wanted someone strong and resolute, anxious to help her move forward. Howard had been like that. So had Hasim. Only Dick had lowered the level of the relationship she sought. But she dared not involve the family in her quest for a replacement for the two men who had made her what she was, neither of whom, she realised, she had really loved.

Was she the world's most selfish woman? Or the most unfortunate? That was a laugh. She had everything, beauty, money, power, perfect health . . . if she was feeling sorry for herself, if she had exceeded the bounds of good taste and morality in her search for private gratification, it was she who was the wimp, not any of the men in her life. She squared her shoulders. "Come out and have dinner, tonight."

"Who?"

"Oh, all of you. Even Billy."

"Gosh," William said. "I knew you'd come round. Thanks a million, sis. Tilly will be overwhelmed."

"Now let's get some work done, while we can," Joanna suggested.

She had barely delved into the contents of her in-tray when Harriet came in.

"I'm sorry to bother you, Mrs Orton, but there is a policeman outside."

Joanna raised her eyebrows. "Come to see we're not breaking the law? According to Mr Young, we don't have to close until tomorrow."

"This man wishes to speak with you personally, madam. There are two of them."

Joanna leaned back in her chair. "Then, you'd better show them in."

Her intercom buzzed. "Do you need me, Joanna?" Peter asked.

"I am going to find out what it's all about, and let you know," Joanna promised.

"You don't want me in there with you?"

"Not unless they've come to arrest me for something," Joanna said. "Then I'll buzz, and you come running."

She watched the door open, did not get up. Harriet was looking agitated. "Sergeant Welcom, and Detective Constable Woolley, Mrs Orton."

"Thank you, Harriet." Harriet hesitated, then closed the door. The sergeant advanced to stand before the desk; the constable remained by the door. Both men looked acutely embarrassed. "Well?" Joanna asked. But she pressed the button on the intercom, just in case.

"Mrs Joanna Orton?"

"That is my name. At present."

"At present? Do you mean that is an alias?"

"It is my present married name, sergeant. But I am in the process of divorcing my husband. Would you care to sit down?" Joanna invited.

"I will stand, Mrs Orton. Are you the the owner of this company?"

"I am the Chairman," Joanna said. "And Managing Director."

Almost, she thought he was going to remove his hat and scratch his head. "What is going on?" Peter Young bustled in.

"These gentleman are police officers," Joanna explained.

"Doing what?"

"They haven't told me that, yet."

Sergeant Welcom pulled himself together, visibly. "May I ask your name, sir?"

"My name is Peter Young."

"And you are . . . ?" he looked from one to the other.

"I am Company Secretary."

"Ah. Right, sir. This is a personal, not a company matter. So . . ."

"I would like Mr Young to stay," Joanna said.

"Very good, madam. I need to ask you one or two questions. Are you acquainted with a man named . . ." he took his notebook from his pocket and opened it. "Sean Connor?"

Joanna sat up straight, frowning. "Yes."

"Did you entertain Mr Connor to dinner at your house last night?"

"I did."

"Thank you, madam. I have a warrant here for your arrest for assault and battery, and grievous bodily harm, committed by you upon the person of Mr Connor."

"Are you out of your mind?" Peter shouted.

"That little bastard," Joanna muttered.

"Please understand, Mrs Orton," Sergeant Welcom went on, "that you need not say anything in answer to this charge, at this moment. But if you do say anything, we shall take it down and it may be given in evidence." Detective-Constable Woolley also produced a notebook, together with a biro.

"This is outrageous," Peter declared. "Joanna . . . ?"

Joanna stood up. Her brain was spinning. "Am I allowed to telephone my solicitor?"

"From the station, madam."

Joanna turned to Peter. "You do it." She turned back to the policemen. "Am I to be handcuffed?"

"Good heavens, no, Mrs Orton. You're not going to make a run for it, are you?"

"Not in high-heeled shoes, sergeant."

Harriet was waiting with her mink. "What shall I do?" she whispered.

"Mr Young is handling everything," Joanna said.

They rode down in the lift, past floors of amazed clerks, and emerged in the lobby. Charlie, as usual, was seated behind the front desk with the receptionist, and hurried forward. "Madam?" He looked quite capable of dispersing the policemen.

"Just relax, Charlie," Joanna said. "Mr Young will tell you what to do."

William burst through an open door on the left. "Jo!"

"Ah," Joanna said. "Dinner. I imagine I'll make it. But don't tell Tilly until then, William. My brother," she explained to the bewildered sergeant.

This was the first time Joanna had ever driven in a police car. In her extreme youth, on the one and only time she had been involved in a drugs bust, with Dick, she recalled, they had been thrust into the back of a Black Maria. And from that horrible misadventure she had been rescued by Howard – her knight in shining armour. Now she had to rely on Peter Young and John Giffard. But she knew she could. At the station she was ushered past a host of curious eyes, both officers and clients, into a windowless office. "One would suppose I was a murderess," she remarked.

"GBH can be a very serious offence, madam," Sergeant Welcom remarked. "Would you like a cup of coffee?"

"Not really. I'd prefer a glass of water."

Welcom nodded to his constable, who hurried off, and returned with the water at the same time as another plain-clothes officer entered the room.

"Mrs Orton? I'm Inspector Langridge. Do sit down." Joanna sat down and crossed her knees; she was still wearing her mink, and the room was rather warm. "You understand the charge?" Langridge asked. "And you have been cautioned?" Joanna nodded. "We will have to ask you some questions. Would you like to telephone your solicitor?"

"He's on his way," Joanna said, and a moment later John Giffard, looking extremely hot and bothered, was shown into the office.

"Joanna!" He kissed her. "I hope you know what you're doing, Inspector?"

"Are you prepared to let your client answer questions, Mr Giffard?"

Giffard looked at Joanna. "I am quite happy to answer the inspector's question," Joanna said.

"Thank you, Mrs Orton." Langridge nodded to the waiting constable, who switched on a tape recorder, gave the time, date, and the names of the people present. "Now, Mrs Orton," Langridge said. "Did you have dinner with Mr Connor last night? At your home in Berkshire?"

"Yes."

"This was at your invitation?"

"Yes."

"And after dinner, did you assault Mr Connor, and cause him severe facial injuries with a sharp instrument, as well as bodily injuries with a blunt instrument? These injuries including burning him? Following which you stamped on him?"

"Don't answer that, Joanna," Giffard advised.

"I cut his face with my ring," Joanna said, and took off her left-hand glove. "This one. And I seem to remember stamping on him, at some stage. And yes, I tried to drive him off me with a piece of wood I took from the fire." She took off her right-hand glove, showed him the scorch mark. Giffard sighed.

"You are aware that Mr Connor had to receive several stitches, and may well be scarred for life?"

"I was not aware of that. But I can believe it."

"And that he may have received internal injuries?"

"I am not aware of that."

"Will you tell me why you assaulted him?"

"I did not assault him," Joanna said. "I was defending myself against rape." Giffard's head came up with a jerk.

"You are accusing Mr Connor of attempting to rape you?" asked the inspector. "In your own living room, into which you had invited him?"

"Is that supposed to represent an invitation to have sex?" Joanna demanded.

The inspector flushed. "Forgive me for asking this, Mrs Orton, but it will come out: had you ever had sex with Mr Connor before last night?"

"Don't answer that," Giffard said again, his tone indicating that he had not the least hope of his advice being taken.

"Yes, I had had sex with Mr Connor before last night," Joanna said.

The inspector looked down at his notes. "Can you remember where and when this was?"

"It was on board one of my ships, the *Caribee Queen*, while we were on our way back from the West Indies."

"You have known Mr Connor for a long time, then?"

"Not at all. We met for the first time just over a fortnight ago. When he boarded the ship."

"And you first had sex with him . . . ?"

"It would have been ten days ago, I think," Joanna said.

"Four days after you had met him for the first time?"

"More like six, I should think."

"Six days." Langridge glanced at the constable, to make sure the the tape recorder was working. "Very good. You took a liking to Mr Connor, is that it?"

"If you weren't a policeman," Joanna said, "and I wasn't in your custody, I'd slap your face. The *Caribee Queen*, and that means both Mr Connor and myself, had just survived a hurricane. We were perhaps a little hysterical. So one thing led to another."

"But you had sex with Mr Connor on most of the remaining days of the voyage, right?"

Joanna sighed. "Yes, we slept together several times during the rest of the voyage."

"Then you will not deny that he – how shall I put it, Mrs Orton? – turned you on?"

"Yes, Inspector, he turned me on."

"But when, a few days later, he came to have dinner with you, at your invitation, and attempted to resume relations with you, the relations he had enjoyed on your ship, you scarred his face and stamped on his body, and burned him with a piece of wood. Mrs Orton, I must put it to you straight: did you or did you not invite Mr Connor to have dinner with you for the purposes of sex?"

"Joanna . . ." Giffard said.

"Whatever reason I had for inviting Mr Connor to have dinner with me, Inspector," Joanna said. "The decision as to what we did either before, during, or after dinner, was surely mine."

"You do not accept that, after what had happened on board your ship, he was entitled to believe that you had in mind a continuation of that relationship?"

"He was entitled to believe whatever he liked. That does not alter the fact that the decision had to be mine."

Langridge looked at his notes. "Mr Connor has said, in his statement, that you invited him to have sex again, on your drawing-room floor. Is that true?"

Giffard looked about to tear his hair out by the roots. "That is true, yes," Joanna said.

"But you suddenly changed your mind and scratched his face with your diamond ring."

"I changed my mind when he wished to sodomise me, Inspector."

There was complete silence in the room for several seconds. Langridge was the first to recover. "You are saying that Mr Connor tried to . . ."

"Bugger me," Joanna snapped.

Another brief silence. Giffard might have fainted. "Mr Connor makes no mention of this in his deposition," Langridge said.

"Would you have expected him to?"

"Well . . . Can you prove that he attempted such an assault upon your person?"

"No."

"Would you like to be medically examined by a police doctor? I can arrange it immediately."

"It would serve no purpose for me to have a medical examination, Inspector. Mr Connor did not succeed in his endeavours. I hit him first."

Once again a brief silence; the tape recorder whirred gently.

Again Langridge recovered. "You would be prepared to swear that this assault did happen."

"Yes, because it did happen."

"I am sure you can appreciate, Inspector, that it comes down to a simple matter of Mr Connor's word against Mrs Orton's," Giffard said. "I am sure you also appreciate that this case, should it come to court, has certain aspects which will appeal to the tabloid press."

"It is not my business to give an opinion upon that, sir," Langridge said. "I am required to deal with facts. And the facts are that Mr Connor was invited to dinner by a lady who he had every reason to believe was content to be his mistress, and when he endeavoured to continue their relationship, was very badly hurt."

"You did not expect my client to defend herself, against a perverted attack?"

"As to whether the attack was perverted, that remains to be proved. Mrs Orton has acknowledged that she cannot prove it. I entirely agree that she was entitled to change her mind about continuing her relationship with Mr Connor, but in that case, surely all she had to do was ring the bell for her servants, of whom, I understand, there were several in the house that night."

"I did ring for my servants," Joanna said.

"After having inflicted a most grievous wound upon Mr Connor."

"Therefore you intend to bring my client into court," Giffard said.

"I am afraid, sir, that will be necessary."

"Very well. Then I apply for police bail. Immediately."

"I'm afraid bail in this case is a matter for the magistrate, Mr Giffard. Tomorrow morning."

"You intend to lock my client up overnight?"

"That is the normal procedure, yes, sir."

"That is outrageous," Giffard declared.

"I am sorry, sir. Madam."

"I don't think you like me," Joanna remarked.

# Part Two

# Catastrophe

'All punishment is mischief; all punishment in itself is evil.'

Jeremy Bentham

# Chapter Five

# The Aftermath

At least Joanna was given a cell to herself. "You'll be comfortable here, Mrs Orton," said the WPC. "And it's just for the one night."

Joanna supposed it was not all that more confined than a cabin on board ship, save that in a cabin the toilet compartment was separate – and one could leave the cabin whenever one felt like it. It was, in any event, at the end of a humiliating half-hour, during which she had been photographed from every angle, and been required to give her fingerprints.

But it really was absurd that she should be locked up when she was totally innocent . . . but was she? The police clearly did not think so. Quite apart from their desire to make an issue of so well-known a personality, who had now, in their eyes, gone way out on a limb. What a field-day the media were going to have. As for the family . . . they were coming down for dinner tonight. She had forgotten to tell John Giffard that. He had promised to let Peter Young know exactly what had happened, he had promised to send in some things for her, but she had forgotten to tell him of her domestic arrangements. The constable was peering at her. "Are you all right, dear?"

Joanna's head jerked. "Eh? Oh, yes, I'm all right, Just thinking."

"I know," the young woman said sympathetically. "I'm sorry, but I have to search you."

"Whatever for?"

"A concealed weapon. Not that we imagine you'd try to break out, but if you did have one . . . and I have to take certain items. Some people get taken all queer when they're locked up."

"If you think I'm going to commit suicide, forget it."

"I'm sorry, Mrs Orton, but rules are rules." Joanna knew it was no use feeling resentful towards this poor young woman, who was only doing her job, and was very embarrassed by the whole thing. She submitted to the search, watched the belt being drawn out of her skirt. "I'm terribly sorry," the constable said, "but I have to have the bra as well." Her blouse was already open, Joanna took it right off, removed the brassiere. "And the stockings." Joanna sat down, rolled down her stockings. "You're being very co-operative," the constable said. "Some women, well, they get quite abusive."

"I am feeling quite abusive," Joanna assured her, buttoning her blouse. "But not towards you."

"It'll all turn out all right."

"Will it?"

"Well . . . of course, dearie. You just have a rest." The door closed and the key jangled as the lock was turned. For a moment Joanna was quite overwhelmed with the immensity of all the forces that were pressing upon her. That hurricane! Everything dated back to that hurricane. Because of the mood she had been in when the engine had failed, and the even greater mood she had been in when she had realised she, and her crew, and her passengers and ship, were safe. For a moment she must have been mad.

But the madness had continued for the rest of the voyage. Because she had wanted . . . not sex, so much, as the feeling of strength that a man's arms could provide. Dick's arms had never really provided that. And the two men who had provided that had both died, violently. She shuddered.

But at the end, she realised she had been brought down by her own arrogance. She was Joanna Grain/Edge/Princess

Hasim/Orton. She had been faced with disaster so often before, and had squared her shoulders and told the world, fuck off! And won! So she had supposed she could do anything she liked, and still win. She had to prove that all over again. But she thanked God she had got those shares from Alicia before this happened!

WPC Dearson brought in a bag of toiletries, nightclothes, and a change of day clothes with lunch. "Where did you get these?" Joanna asked.

"Your sister."

"Matilda has been here?"

"Mrs Montgomery. Yes. She asked to see you, but it's against the rules." But she was staking a place in the gratitude stakes, Joanna thought.

She was awakened just after dawn. Actually, she had appreciated the rest, the inability to do anything more than lie on her somewhat narrow bed and stare at the ceiling. She had been on the go since that storm. Now the world had to be faced. She put on the clean clothes, which included brassiere, belt and stockings, watched by Dearson, did the best she could with her hair, had breakfast, and was then escorted outside to the waiting Black Maria, in which there were three other women. She didn't think they had been as well-treated as herself; they looked scruffy and bad-tempered. But perhaps they always looked scruffy and bad-tempered. She was relieved that two policewomen got in to the back with them.

"Why ain't she cuffed?" asked one of the women. "She's on GBH. I'm on soliciting. How come she ain't cuffed and I am?"

"Just mind your own business," said one of the constables.

But the other leaned towards Joanna. "We will have to cuff you to take you in, Mrs Orton. It'll only be for a few minutes."

Joanna said nothing; she could not imagine the day could

possibly get any worse. And then realised she was wrong; as the van stopped outside the doors of the magistrate's court, it was surrounded by the media, men and women, screaming questions, flash-bulbs exploding. "Would you like a blanket?" asked the constable, affixing handcuffs to Joanna's wrists.

Joanna hesitated, then tossed her head. "They know what I look like."

"Hey," asked one of the prostitutes. "You famous, then, darling?"

"Very," Joanna told her.

The rear doors were opened, and she was assisted down by the two constables. The driver and his mate had got out and were trying to push the media back, but it was an impossible task.

"Joanna! Look this way!"

"Joanna, show us the ring!"

"Joanna, how's the bum?"

"Well, really," commented one of the policewomen, pushing her forward.

"Joanna! Give us a smile!"

"Joanna, is it true you bit him where it hurts?" Then they were inside, and the doors were closing.

"Now I think I know what it feels like to be lynched," Joanna gasped. They had come close enough to touch her, and she felt quite breathless.

"Did you really bite him where it hurts?" the woman constable asked.

"I never had the chance," Joanna said, regretfully.

Then the cuffs were taken off, and she was with John Gifffard.

The hearing lasted one minute, and she was required to state only her name and address. What was more embarrassing was having to sit there while the prostitutes were heard, and fined; they happened to be first on the case sheet. Then John applied for bail, which was immediately granted, in her own cognisance of a thousand pounds.

Joanna wasn't sure whether to be pleased or sorry that Connor was not in court. But she had been committed for trial, on his say so. The bastard. William and Norma, Matilda and Billy, and of course Peter, were waiting for her as she was escorted through an inner room to a back door. "I'll come out tomorrow, Joanna," Giffard said. "And we'll talk things over."

"Not tomorrow," Joanna told him. "I have a board meeting."

He glanced at Peter, eyebrows arched.

Peter shrugged. "You know Jo, John."

"Where do you want to go?" William asked.

"Home," Joanna told him.

"I should've hit that character harder," Charlie commented, as they threaded their way through the traffic.

"Then you'd have been in the dock beside me," Joanna commented, "What about the children?" she asked William, who was seated in the back beside her, together with Norma. Matilda was in the front beside Charlie. Billy had sensibly decided now was the moment to keep a low profile – no one was sure of Joanna's mood.

"Well," William said, "because it all happened yesterday morning, it's in all the papers today. And it was on the TV news last night."

"I told Mrs Winshaw to keep them home from school today," Matilda said.

"Why did you do that?" Joanna demanded.

"Well . . ." Matilda stared through the front window; her ears were pink.

"She did it on my recommendation," William said quietly.

Joanna turned her head, but he met her gaze. She had no means of telling whether or not he was lying.

"They could have been put through an unthinkable ordeal," he said.

She sighed. "I suppose you're right."

"You know what I think?" Matilda asked brightly, at last turning round as she felt sure of her brother's support. "The case doesn't come up for a couple of months. I think you should take a holiday, away from it all."

"But she can't leave the country," William objected. "Those are the terms of the bail. They've taken her passport."

"Well, she can go to some remote island, off Scotland, or the Channel Islands. You don't need a passport to go there. Just to lie low."

"While my children take all the flak and my company collapses," Joanna mused. "Forget it."

"Mummy!" Helen was in her arms. "Oh, Mummy! Were you really arrested?"

"It's something everyone should experience," Joanna told her. Not, she remembered, that it had been the first time she had been arrested. But before there had been Howard, waiting to rescue her.

"Did that man really attack you?"

"Yes," Joanna said. Fortunately, the fact that it had been a sexual attack did not seem to have penetrated the girl's awareness.

"I'd like to kill him," Raisul said.

Joanna hugged him in turn and ruffled his hair. "Next time he comes to visit I'll let you."

"Oh, madam." Cummings looked ready to burst into tears, as did Mrs Partridge. "Shall I . . . ?"

"Oh, indeed, Cummings. Bollinger."

"Is it going to be all right, madam?" Mrs Partridge asked.

"Of course it is." But she couldn't be sure.

Next morning she was at the office early. Harriet had bought every newspaper, and the headlines made some pretty ghastly reading, varying as they did from the sedate; "COMPANY DIRECTOR AND CITY WHIZ WOMAN COMMITTED

FOR TRIAL ON GRIEVOUS BODILY HARM" of *The Times*, to "HE TRIED TO BUGGER ME, SAYS GLAMOUR-GIRL, JOANNA ORTON" of the tabloids. Presumably Dick would be having a quiet chuckle. "Mrs Edge is here," Harriet said.

"You'd better show her in."

"She has someone with her."

"Her toy-boy. Yes. I'll see them both."

"Joanna!" Alicia announced. "You are absolutely impossible!"

"I find a lot of people impossible," Joanna said.

"Ha! This is Stephen Maddox."

It had to be. Stephen Maddox had a moustache and glowing dark eyes, but he also had good shoulders and a powerful body, which presumably was what Alicia was after. She shook hands. "May I say that we are entirely on your side, Mrs Orton," Maddox gushed. "The fellow should be castrated."

"My own feelings entirely. Shall we talk a little business?" She gestured them to chairs in front of her desk. "I have been looking up the company rules, and it is not possible for anyone to have a seat on the board who does not have shares, so . . ."

"That's all right," Alicia said. "I have sold Stephen one percent of my holding."

"Ah. Right. Well, brace yourselves for a battle. I want your full support."

"And we'll have yours."

"Agreed. But there is still going to be a battle."

Andy and Townsend arived with their partner, a man called Amalia, who was Greek, who Joanna hardly knew at all. They had also brought their solicitor, but Joanna would not accept him in the boardroom. "You can nip out and talk to him whenever you wish," she said. "If he comes in, I'll have to get hold of John Giffard, which will not only be time-wasting but even more tedious when he gets here, as the two of them will spend the morning arguing."

"Quite on top of the world, aren't we?" Andy asked. "You do understand that we intend to turf you out?"

Joanna smiled sweetly. "I know that's what you wish to do, Andy."

"What's it feel like to be raped?" Townsend asked.

"Being raped feels slightly more attractive than talking to you two," Joanna said. "Shall we get to business, then we can maybe have some fresh air in here. Alicia, you know. This is Stephen Maddox."

"Who?" Andy inquired.

"He's a shareholder," Alicia snapped.

Andy frowned, and glanced from Alicia to Joanna, for the first time realising that he might have a united opposition. "Yes," he said, "let's get to business."

Joanna sat at the head of the table, Peter Young sat at the bottom. The five other shareholders seated themselves, but before Joanna could invite Peter to read the minutes, there was a knock on the door. "A Mr Holroyd, Mrs Orton," Hariet said. "Says he's a shareholder."

Joanna looked at the man coming through the door. He was massive, with shaggy hair that badly needed cutting, and heavy features; he made her think of a bull mastiff. "You'll be Joanna," he said. "Sorry to barge in like this. No one notified me of this meeting."

He looked around the staring faces.

"Just who are you?" Joanna asked.

"James Holroyd. I bought your husband's shares."

"Good lord!" Joanna commented. "You and I need to have a chat."

"Can you prove you hold those shares?" Peter inquired.

"I can, sir. I have the certificates with me."

"Well, we knew Dick sold his holding to someone," Andy said expansively. "You'd better sit down, Mr Holroyd. Can we get on?"

"Of course." Joanna nodded, and Peter read the minutes. Joanna signed them, and leaned back as she looked at the itinerary.

"This was drawn up at the request of the majority shareholder," Peter explained. "Mr Gosling. I tried to get it to you yesterday, Joanna, but . . . well . . ."

"She was all tied up," Townsend said. "Haw haw haw."

"Item number one, the position of chairman to be resolved," Joanna read, and looked up. "I have no objection to that. Although I am not sure what is to be resolved."

"Now, Joanna," Andy said, "prevaricating is not going to help. We all know the situation. Or . . ." he looked at Maddox and Holroyd, "perhaps we do not. Just to put you gentlemen in the picture, when the company was restructured a few years ago, while I became the majority shareholder, I agreed, with my partners, here, that Mrs Orton should remain Chairman and in complete control of the Company for as long as she owned twenty-five per cent of the shares. As it happened, Mrs Orton wished to alter that agreement very shortly, when she married Mr Orton. She wished to make him a present of a percentage of her shares, which would reduce her holding below the twenty-five percent we had agreed, but which she claimed would actually remain hers because she had the contractual right to buy the shares back whenever she wished. I was quite happy to agree with this; I and my associates have always had the greatest confidence in Mrs Orton's handling of the company, till now.

"Now things have changed. Mrs Orton's plans are, in the present economic circumstances, unacceptable. As Chairman she might be able to push these plans through, but now it also turns out that Mr Orton has sold his shares. Apparently to you, Mr Holroyd. The sale was illegal, I suspect, but that is a matter between Mrs Orton, her husband, and you, sir. The fact is that Mrs Orton no longer possesses twenty-five percent of the company shares, and therefore has no right to remain as Chairman. Now, my associates and I might have been willing to continue our present arrangement, providing Mrs Orton would agree to certain proposals put forward by us. This she flatly refuses to do. In these circumstances therefore, I propose, indeed I and my associates insist, that Mrs Orton be removed from her position as Chairman and a new chairman be installed." He paused for breath.

"Thank you so much for that succinct appraisal of the situation, Andy," Joanna said. "There is just one small error in your summing up. You have just said that you have no right to remove me as chairman as long as I hold twenty-five percent of the shares." She picked up the phone and held it out. "I suggest you ring Jersey, speak with James Haddon of my Trust Company, and ascertain my exact shareholding."

He guessed immediately what had happened, looked at Alicia, who smiled at him. "You wretched woman," he said. "You sold out."

Alicia sniffed. "I did what I felt was right. I am Howard's wife. I have no intention of seeing the company disappear." Andy's mouth opened and shut.

"I imagine you have already informed Roger Petherick what would be the outcome of this meeting," Joanna said. "Well, I suggest you give *him* a ring, and inform him that nothing has changed, that Caribee Shipping is not for sale, under any circumstances, and that I look forward to not hearing from him again. Now, ladies and gentlemen, shall we move on to more important matters: the ordering of two new ships for the company, to take us through the seventies and hopefully into the eighties."

"Champagne, I think," Joanna said.

"It's on ice." Harriet hastily fetched a bottle from the fridge.

Joanna smiled at her new associates: Alicia and Maddox had joined herself and Peter in her office; Holroyd had indicated he would like to stay, but she was not in the mood for recriminations at this moment – she'd agreed to a meeting the following day. "You were so calm," Alicia said. "While that thug was trying to destroy you."

"Well, it's easy to be calm when you know exactly what the opposition is doing, and when you know you hold the last trump," Joanna pointed out.

"I think you were brilliant," Maddox said admiringly. Alicia gave him a dirty look.

"They'll still be fighting," Peter reminded them.

"What with?"

"Well, this court case . . ."

"Is a straightforward business of self defence," Joanna said. "We may leave that with John Giffard."

"What exactly happened?" Alicia asked. "The papers said this man Connor was a friend of yours."

"The operative word is was," Joanna told her. "He attacked me. It is as simple as that."

She had no intention of going into the gory details. "Now, I feel quite exhausted, and I have the family coming out for dinner. Peter, I'd like those tenders put out immediately."

"I shall do that. I suppose you have taken financing into consideration?"

"Actually, I haven't," Joanna said. "I simply have not had the time. Get some figures together, and we'll have a meeting with Prim and Barry Andrews."

"It could be tight."

"Whenever wasn't it tight? Alicia, thanks a million for your support. Maybe we could get together for a meal some time. With Stephen, of course."

"Of course," Alicia said, and squeezed Stephen's hand. "Don't look so frightened, darling; her bark is worse than her bite."

"Well . . ." Joanna stood up, and her buzzer went.

"I have Mr Giffard on the line, Mrs Orton. He says it's urgent."

Joanna sat down again, picked up her private phone. "John?"

There was a kind of gulp on the end of the line. "Joanna, I'm afraid I have some bad news. Sean Connor died in hospital, an hour ago."

He had been speaking as quietly as he could, and Joanna was quite sure no one else in the room had heard what he had said. For a moment she couldn't think what to say, remained with the phone held to her ear. "Joanna?" he asked. "Are you all right?"

"Yes," she said. "I'm all right."

"I think we need to talk. Are you available this afternoon?"

"Yes. But not here. I'm going out to the house. Can you come out?"

"I'll be there . . ." a brief hesitation while he checked his diary. "About five. And Joanna, please don't discuss this with anyone until we've spoken."

"I understand that." She replaced the phone, smiled brightly at the people seated in front of her.

But Peter was frowning. "Nothing wrong?"

"Oh, no," she said. "But I really must be getting home. You're in charge, Peter."

"Of course. Will you be in tomorrow?"

"Of course," she said. She kissed them all, then went down to Charlie and the waiting car.

"All well?" Charlie asked, as he threaded his way through the midday traffic.

*No*, Joanna wanted to scream. *All is not well. Nothing is well.* "Everything is fine, thank you, Charlie," she said.

I have killed a man, she thought. But so have you, Charlie, on my instructions. He had not been charged with assaulting Sean Connor, because Connor had only brought charges against her. Now Connor was dead . . . had he had time to add Charlie, and perhaps Cummings, to the list? And did that matter beside the fact that Connor was dead, dead, dead? She had been too closely associated with death, too often, in her life. And it hadn't been all that long a life.

And now? What was John Giffard going to tell her? The police had intimated that they felt she had gone over the top in her response to Connor's assault. She had denied that. Now the police had a great deal of ammunition to support their claim. My God, she thought: I could lose the case. And then what? But they couldn't possibly send her to gaol, for defending herself against an attempted rape?

Her hands were clammy inside her gloves, and she took the kid off to rub her fingers together. Just when she had again triumphed, when she was again in command, of the company and of her destiny. Had she ever been in command of her destiny?

"You sure you're all right?" Charlie asked, studying her in the rearview mirror as they began to leave the traffic behind. "You don't look so good."

"I feel sick," she said. Charlie pulled over to the side of the road and stopped. "Must be something I ate," she said.

"For breakfast?"

She hadn't realised the time; just coming up to twelve. She smiled. "Must be something I need to eat. Just pour me a glass of brandy and get me home, Charlie."

Caribee House was quiet; the children lunched at school. But Cummings was every bit as observant as Charlie, even though Harriet had telephoned to tell them the mistress was on her way. "Is everything all right, madam?" he asked.

"Everything is fine, Cummings," she assured him.

"Cook has prepared lunch. And if you'd like a word about the dinner menu . . . ?"

"I'm sure it's perfect, Cummings. As for lunch, I think I'll skip it. I just want to lie down."

"Of course, madam." His gaze drifted past her, and she knew Charlie was signalling in the background. But neither would press her too hard.

Mrs Partridge was at the top of the stairs. "Is everything—"

"Everything is fine, Mrs Partridge," Joanna lied. "I'm just exhausted."

"Of course, madam. Would you like me to cancel dinner?"

"No, no," Joanna said. "I'll be all right if I have a few hours' sleep."

"Of course, madam."

She stumbled into her bedroom, stripped off her mink and her sweat-wet clothing, had a hot shower, and fell across the bed. Oil shortage or no oil shortage, the central heating was maintained at seventy degrees Fahrenheit in the house. She closed her eyes, and saw Connor's face in front of her. The Connor from the ship, who had seemed a kind and caring person. Although even then she had recognised in him a streak of almost vicious anger. At her? Or the world? Or just at his own desires? Had what he wanted been so terrible? Had she over-reacted? Or had her reaction been caused by the underlying sense of shame and guilt, that she, Joanna Orton, should have had to send out for a man?

She wasn't going to sleep. So, pill, or drink? She thought a pill would be safer and took two. Then it seemed only a moment later that she was awake, sitting up and pulling hair from her face, as she listened to the gentle knocking on the door. She got out of bed, pulled on her dressing gown, opened it. "I'm sorry to disturb you, madam," Mrs Partridge said, "but Mr Giffard is here. He seems sort of agitated."

"I knew he was coming. I should have told you. God, is it five o'clock already? Tell him I'll be right down. And ask Cummings to bring some tea." Her mouth tasted like a sewer. She had another shower, cleaned her teeth, pulled on jeans and a loose blouse and thrust her feet into slippers, went downstairs. Giffard stood looking out of the French windows at the traces of snow on the croquet lawn. "Well?" she asked.

He turned, came towards her, held out his hands. She took them. "There's to be a post mortem, of course. Either tonight or first thing tomorrow morning. At the moment, it seems he died of pneumonia."

"Because I had him thrown out into the snow?"

"Not entirely. Everyone dies of pneumonia, Joanna. It's a condition which overtakes one as the heart ceases to beat; the lungs collapse. But the bleeding suggests that he had a serious internal injury."

"Which I am supposed to have caused?"

"That is something that will be determined after the post mortem. The hospital recognised the symptoms of an internal injury right away, but initially they were more concerned about the gash in his face, which appears to have been quite considerable. Then Connor's general condition was so poor they were hoping to improve it somewhat before operating. In the event, he didn't improve. And, sadly, the police have it on tape that you admit jumping on his stomach with all your weight."

"God, what a mess. I didn't mean to hurt him, John. Not badly enough to cause internal injuries. You know that."

"Of course I know that. You were acting in self defence. That's our defence. But the police claim, as they have done all along, that you over-reacted, and kept over-reacting until Connor was a hospital case, and then just threw him out."

"Okay, so I went over the top. I was frightened, I was disgusted, and I was angry. You get enough women on the jury and they'll know exactly how I felt."

"Of course. Unfortunately, you see, this is no longer a case of grievous bodily harm."

"I know. It's manslaughter. That doesn't alter the facts, does it? That Connor tried to rape me, and that I defended myself. Perhaps a shade too vigorously."

Still holding her hands, Giffard guided her to the settee and made her sit. He sat beside her. "I had a visit from Inspector Langridge just after I'd spoken with you this morning. You remember him? He was handling the investigation."

"I don't think he likes me."

"Possibly not. But that's neither here nor there. He's on his way down here now."

"Here? I don't want to see him here."

"I'm afraid you will have to. You see, the police have decided not to charge you with manslaughter; they're going for murder instead."

# Chapter Six

# The Prosecution

Joanna knew her fingers were tightening into claws; she could tell by Giffard's expression that her nails were biting into his flesh. "But . . . that's not possible," she whispered. "Murder . . . that implies pre-meditation. I invited Connor here to sleep with him. That was all. I had no idea he was going to turn out to be a satyr."

"The police think they can prove otherwise. You see, they obtained an order to search Connor's digs, as they were entitled to do. They found it filled with cuttings of you since your return to England. They also found various notes he had made, including items regarding money, indicating that he intended demanding some off you. They reckon he was doing that when he came here. And that you knew what he was planning, and were prepared for it." Slowly Joanna released him to clasp both hands round her neck. "Their theory," Giffard went on, speaking slowly, "is that you and he had an affair on board the ship, as you say, but that it was strictly a shipboard romance, as these things so often are, and that you had every intention of ending it the moment you reached dry land, again as so often happens in these affairs. And you thought you had done that. But Connor by then knew all about you, how wealthy you were and where you lived, and he contacted you and demanded to see you again, or he would take the story to the papers. The police reckon you agreed to see him, with every intention of ending the affair for good. And that that is what you did. They reckon the story of the attempted rape, and attempted, ah, bestial assault, is all make-believe."

"That is ludicrous," Joanna shouted. "He never mentioned a word about blackmail. He even offered to help in the company's difficulties, if he could."

"Can you prove that?"

"Of course I can't."

"There's our problem. The police do have proof that he was planning blackmail. Or so they claim."

"For God's sake, John, if I had intended to kill him, wouldn't I have had a gun or a knife or some poison? Would I seriously have assaulted him with my bare hands? I'm a woman, not an all-in wrestler."

"They reckon you were too smart for that. They reckon you invited him down here, provoked him into attacking you, preempted the situation, and then had your staff beat him insensible and throw him into the snow to die. There are warrants out for Charlie and Cummings as well; they will be served this afternoon."

"Oh, my God! Oh, Jesus! They were only doing what I told them to do."

"Joanna, please don't ever say that again, not even to me."

"I can't let them take the blame for my decisions. Listen!" She held his hands. "They say Connor demanded to see me to extort money. But he didn't know where I lived. I invited him down, John."

"Can you prove *that*?"

"When we left the ship, he gave me his address and telephone number, so that I could contact him if I felt like, well . . . seeing him again. He wrote it down. He did. Surely the police can match up the writing."

"I would imagine so. Let me see the piece of paper."

"Oh, gosh! I've just remembered. After I'd called him, I threw it away." Giffard sighed. Joanna held his hands again. "John! How much trouble am I in?"

"It's not good. But, as you said the other day, we have to see how many women we can get on the jury."

The new hearing lasted no longer than the first, only this time there was an increased grimness about the proceedings, and bail went up to twenty-five thousand pounds. Joanna went straight from the court to Caribee Shipping, where Peter Young had, as she had requested, set up a meeting with Jonathan Prim, the senior partner at Joanna's stockbrokers, Miller & Smart, and Barry Andrews. "Good of you to come," she told them. "Do sit down. Harriet, coffee."

"Was it very wearing?" Andrews asked. They had all known her for a long time, watched her climb to stardom in the city, But with them, too, she sensed a certain grimness.

"Not really," she said. "The wearing part comes later. But we're not here to discuss my personal problems. As you may imagine, we need some financing."

"So does everybody," Andrews pointed out.

"Then surely old and loyal customers come first."

"Of course. What are we talking about, apart from the half million last week?"

"That was to regain complete control of the company. The shares are your security."

"Yes." His tone was doubtful. "They are dropping. Quite fast."

"That is the problem I wish to address. We have to show the world that we are totally confident, not only in *the* future but in *our* future. We had a bad press because of that mid-Atlantic breakdown. But we brought the ship home, which must count for something. However, the breakdown was caused by age, and the same goes for *Caribee Future*. So the first thing we need to do is order, and let the world know we have ordered, two new, modern vessels. You put out for those tenders, Peter?"

"Yes, I did. Early days yet, of course. But . . ." he looked as if he would have continued, but changed his mind.

"How much were you thinking of spending?" Andrews asked again.

Joanna looked at Peter. "To get what we want, ten million."

Prim gave a low whistle.

Andrews sighed. "Not on, I'm afraid, Joanna. Certainly not at this time."

"Well, then . . ." Joanna looked at Prim.

He shook his head. "It won't work, right now, Joanna. For several reasons. We are about to enter a period of extreme recession, if not worse. I also believe we are about to enter a period of extreme inflation as well. To have both depression and inflation at the same time may sound absurd, and it may well turn out to be catastrophic. But the fact is that the price of oil has already gone through the roof and is going to go higher. And almost everything the civilised world does, makes, sells or consumes is based on oil. So, the economic outlook is grim in the extreme. People are not in the mood to take up substantial share issues. Add to that, well . . . you don't wish to discuss your personal problems, and I respect that, but they are there. People are asking just who will be running Caribee Shipping in a month or two."

"I shall be, Jonathan."

"I sincerely hope you will be, Joanna. But it needs to be proved to the public, and especially the institutions who we need to take up substantial parts of any issue."

Joanna looked from face to face. "Just what are you telling me?"

"That you just have to be patient," Andrews said. "Sit it out."

"We are about to start losing money, Barry."

"You have a reserve fund. Use it. This situation can't last very long, it's too serious. Another few months." He looked at Prim.

"After your trial, when you are clear of all charges, people will be back on your side."

"Meaning they are not on my side now?"

"Now, Joanna, you know what I mean."

"And suppose, just suppose, I am *not* cleared of all the charges against me?"

Again Prim and Andrews exchanged glances. "That's impossible, surely," Andrews said.

Joanna and Peter, left alone, gazed at each other across the boardroom table. "What a mess," he commented.

"Can we go on as we are, for a few months?"

"A few months, yes. As Andrews said, we can dip into our reserves, but they are not going to last forever. Our share price is dropping. So of course is everyone else's, but ours is travelling a bit faster. That has to do with, well . . ."

"My being charged with murder."

"I'm afraid so. But again, as Andrews and Prim said, once that is out of the way . . ." he paused, looking at her face. "Are you scared?"

"Yes," Joanna said. "I'm scared." It was the first time in her life that she had made such an admission.

"I can't tell you how sorry I am about this," Joanna told Charlie and Cummings. Both had been charged as accessories, and released, like herself, on bail; she had stood the bail.

"It's you we worry about, madam," Cummings said, while Charlie merely looked embarrassed.

"In my evidence, I shall of course entirely exonerate you both."

"There is no need for that, madam," Charlie protested. "The bastard, begging your pardon, deserved everything he got."

"But whatever you did, it was because I told you to do it," Joanna insisted. "I do promise you that neither of you is going to jail." Even if I go myself? she wondered. But that was impossible. Whatever theories the police might dream up, she had acted in self defence. But she was still frightened. "Give it to me straight, John," she told Giffard, when he came down to see her. "The very worst."

"Well . . ." he sipped his champagne. "As you know, I

have already asked the charge to be reduced, from murder to manslaughter, and the magistrates have refused. I shall make the same request of the judge, when we come to trial. Hopefully he will show more sense."

"I want to know what happens if he doesn't."

"Well, then, I'm afraid we are going to have to go through the whole business of your relationship with Connor. I have people working on his background, which appears to be rather mysterious. It would seem that he is, or was, fairly well connected."

"The Ferrari."

"Yes. He actually did own it. Now that is odd for a mining engineer who has been invalided home. Where did he get the money to buy, apparently outright, a car like that? As I say, I have people working on it, but at the present time it looks rather as if he might have been a remittance man."

"Say again?"

"A remittance man. That is, the scion, probably a child of a wealthy family, who decided to get rid of him by sending him to the 'colonies' as they would consider it. The question is to find the family, as he does not seem to have confided in any friends as to his real background, or even his real name, supposing Connor is not it. In fact, he doesn't seem to have had any friends at all."

"Isn't that something in our favour?"

"Well, slightly. The fact that a man does not have many, or any, friends, does not necessarily make him a criminal. It just suggests that there may have been something abnormal in his personality."

"Well? Can't we use that?"

"We can and we will. But merely getting too close to someone with a personality disorder is not a reason for killing him. No, I'm afraid if the worst comes to the worst, I am going to have to put you in the witness box and take you through your relationship, step by step. And when I have done that, the prosecution will do it all over again, only from a more hostile point of view."

"Every word of which will be reported in the papers for my children to read."

"Sadly. The prosecution are going to set out to prove, from the various episodes in your life, that you are an immoral woman who, when for the first time in her life was threatened with blackmail for her immoral activities, reacted like a vicious animal and murdered the would-be blackmailer."

"Sounds terrific," Joanna muttered.

"Our only defence is going to accept that you have behaved immorally from time to time in your life, but that you have never revealed the slightest vicious streak, or indeed engaged in the slightest physical violence. That is, of course, not quite true, but on both the previous occasions you were the attacked rather than the attacker. I shall also, of course, make a great deal of the point you raised earlier, that there is simply no evidence that you had made any preparations for killing Connor, if that is what you had in mind. There was no trace of a weapon, unless your ring can be so called, your servants will testify that they responded to your call for help and had not been briefed in any way as to what to expect."

"What about Charlie and Cummings?"

"Their fate really depends on yours. You will be tried first. If you are acquitted, then the cases against them will be dropped. If you were to be convicted, their trials will go ahead. But their positions are infinitely less serious than yours, if you do not require them to say anything more than that they were called upon for help and told what to do."

"Which happens to be the truth."

"Yes," he said pessimistically. "However . . ." he brightened. "I think you will do very well in the witness box. I am expecting an acquittal. It's just a pity that at the very minute you are being tried for murder, you are also divorcing your husband. I don't suppose . . . ?"

"No," she said. "Absolutely not."

"Well, we'll have to see if that cannot be somehow used to our advantage." His tone indicated that he didn't quite see how.

"I want to know what happens if there is not an acquittal, John."

"Well . . ." he finished his drink. "If that were to happen, you would have to be condemned and sentenced. But it can't possibly happen."

"Condemned and sentenced to what?"

"Well . . ." he looked longingly at the bottle, and she refilled his glass.

"I assume I can't be hanged."

"Oh, good lord, no, That went out years ago. But there would probably be a custodial sentence. A few years . . ."

"A few *years*?"

"Joanna, you simply have to get it through your head that, were you to be found guilty, it would be of murder. Now, of course, we should appeal, but . . ." He shrugged.

Joanna refilled her own glass.

"What are you going to do?" William asked.

He was dining alone with his sister. Norma had understood there were matters to be discussed with which she had no business. Matilda would have liked to be present but William had talked her out of it; Joanna had shown no sign of wishing to re-employ Billy. "There is nothing I can do, save wait. It's all in John Giffard's hands now."

"You're taking it very well."

"I'm not, really. I'm a gibbering wreck, inside."

"You can't possibly be convicted. Can you?"

"I can, Willy. I'm claiming self-defence, but I am the only surviving witness to what actually happened that night. Just as I am the only witness to what I had in mind. So it's going to come down to whether or not the jury believe me. That jury is going to be composed of twelve men, and hopefully women, who are going to be given an image of me, if they didn't already have one. The women may be sympathetic towards a rape victim, but was I a rape victim? They're going to be told how I was Howard Edge's mistress for a year, and then, when he finally married me, I mysteriously inherited his entire business empire only a fortnight later. They're going to be told how I married Prince Hassim for his money. I can't deny that. Telling them that I grew to admire and respect and love him afterwards isn't going to do all that much good. They'll be told how I am in the process of divorcing my third husband. They'll be told how I fired my own brother-in-law. They'll be told how I had an affair with Sean Connor on board my ship. I can't deny any of those things. At the end of it all, they're going to be told how I planned his murder, because he was getting in my way. That's the only thing I can deny, and having been depicted as an utterly ruthless woman who will do anything to get her own way, that denial isn't going to sound very convincing, is it?"

"You're being too pessimistic," William argued. "The prosecution can't bring in anything about your previous life, surely."

"Yes, they can, once I take the stand. And I have to take the stand, because I'm my only witness. Right?"

"What a fucking awful mess."

"What about afterwards? Assuming the worst. I may have to go to prison, for a while."

"You can say it, that calmly? Have you any idea?"

"What are you trying to do, send me into a nervous breakdown? Yes, I have an idea what it may be like. It's something I have to accept. But I'll be back, soon enough. Someone will have to hold the fort until then. It has to be somebody I can trust, absolutely. Can you do it?"

"Well . . ." he flushed. "What about Tilly?"

"I can't trust Tilly, and you know that. She's entirely at the mercy of Billy, and I wouldn't trust him to sell my clapped-out washing machine for the best possible price and give me all he got for it. I want you to come in and sit on the board next week.

It's grim, I know. The money people tell me we can't have any new ships right now. But we simply have to have the new ships just as soon as it is possible. You have to keep pressing. Peter Young will give you maximum support, I know."

William licked his lips in a mixture of anticipation and uncertainty.

"You'll also have control of all my personal finances, including the trust company. I'll make out all the necessary authorities. But I don't want to come out of prison worth a penny less than I am now. Right?"

"I'll do my best. But Jo, it isn't really going to happen, is it?"

"Of course it isn't," Joanna assured him.

"Did you really kill Mr Connor, Mummy?" Helen asked.

"Of course she did," Raisul said. "It says so in the papers."

Joanna regarded them across the breakfast table. "You don't want to believe everything you read in the newspapers, darling. I didn't kill Mr Connor. Not intentionally. It seems I may have hit him a little too hard, and he died."

"Will you be hanged?" Helen asked. "One of the girls at school said you will be hanged."

"No, darling, I won't be hanged," Joanna said. "They don't hang people any more."

"But you'll be locked up, for ever and ever and ever," Raisul said. "One of the boys at school said you would be."

"And I'm sure he knows best," Joanna agreed. "Charlie's waiting."

They kissed her and scampered off. They didn't really understand what was going on, she supposed. But . . . she looked at Cummings, standing by the sideboard.

"Should I keep them home, Cummings?"

"I think you are doing entirely the right thing, madam," Cummings said, as loyal as ever.

But she needed more than loyalty. She summoned Mrs

Partridge to her bedroom. "You understand that I may have to go away for a while," she said.

"Oh, no, madam. I will never believe that," Mrs Partridge declared.

"I don't believe it either," Joanna said. "But it is a possibility that we have to face. Now, in that eventuality, I do not wish anything to change here." Mrs Partridge looked terrified. "Mr brother will be handling all of my affairs, with full powers of attorney," Joanna said. "He will therefore be handling all the expenses of Caribee House, together with all staff salaries, of course. Including yours, naturally, Mrs Partridge. But yours will be doubled."

"Madam?" Now she looked about to faint.

"Because I am going to appoint you legal guardian of the children until I return. Don't look so alarmed, it will only be for a few years, at the very worst."

"But, madam, the children . . . ?"

"Adore you, Mrs Partridge."

"Yes, but . . . Mrs Montgomery . . ."

"Mrs Montgomery has her own children to worry about," Joanna pointed out. "I know I can rely on you, and trust you, Mrs Partridge." She gave a brief smile. "Molly."

It was the first time she had ever used the housekeeper's first name.

"Oh, madam!" Mrs Partridge burst into tears.

"Well!" Matilda declared. "Of all the ways to treat your own sister."

"I'm sure you have enough to do with your own two, Tilly," Joanna said.

"You think I'm irresponsible," Matilda declared.

"Well, since you have raised the subject, I do not think you are a hundred percent reliable," Joanna acknowledged. "What I wish, should the very worst happen, is that my children be brought up, until I can come back to them, in the most sane and uneventful manner possible. God knows, should I lose my case, they will be subjected to enough pressure, both at school and from the media. They need always to be able to return here to an atmosphere of the utmost safety and tranquillity. I believe that Mrs Partridge and Mr Cummings are the people most able to provide that safety and tranquillity."

"This is all because of Billy," Matilda stormed. "You hate him."

"I do not hate him," Joanna said, keeping her own temper with difficulty. "But I certainly do not intend to allow him any say in the upbringing of my children."

"You can talk like that," Matilda snapped. "What kind of a mother have you been? Swanning about the world, marrying and remarrying, and now, inviting some layabout to come here and spend the night, and then killing him . . . you're not fit to be a mother."

"My dear Tilly," Joanna said, "You are sounding just as I expect the prosecution to."

"It's strange how things turn out." Alicia, as she always did when visiting Caribee House, moved restlessly about the drawing room, checking for dust here, straightening a picture frame there, as if she still owned the place, Joanna thought. Or as if she intends to own it again.

"I'm sure you're right," she said politely. She had not asked Alicia to call, could only wait to discover what was on her mind.

"I mean, when you came down to see me . . ."

"I had not yet killed Sean Connor, Alicia."

"Of course I know that. But you were already setting up to meet him." She gazed at her rival, eyebrows arched.

"I was already setting up to do nothing," Joanna said. "The reason I got in touch with Connor that night was because I was feeling on top of the world, after seeing you."

"Those shares." Alicia sat down. "I'll buy them back from you, if you like."

"Why on earth should you want to do that?"

"Well . . ." she gave a little smile. "You're going to have no use for them where you're going."

"All cut and dried, is it? Alicia, even if I am sent to prison, which everyone agrees is highly unlikely, I will still be Chairman and Managing Director of Caribee Shipping."

"That's absurd. How can you run a company from prison?"

"Someone will run it for me, pending my return. The only necessary requirement is that I retain my controlling interest."

"Ha," Alicia commented. "And who *is* going to run the company, pending your return?"

"My brother, William. He is already a director."

"That boy? What does he know about running a shipping company? Do you suppose Andy Gosling will put up with that?"

"He'll have to."

"Ha," Alicia said again. "I really don't want to quarrel with you, Joanna, but it would make far more sense for someone more experienced to act for you."

"I see. Someone like your Stephen, for instance."

"Well, he's been in the City all his life."

"What as? Someone's messenger?"

Alicia stood up. "I did not come here to be insulted."

"Then I apologise. I have a lot on my mind. But I have made all the necessary arrangements for the conduct of the company during my absence. Just as I would have done had I been told that I needed a serious operation that would keep me out of circulation for some time. This is exactly the same thing."

"It is not at all the same thing, "Alicia said. "Going into hospital for an operation is an honourable thing, whereas going to prison . . ."

"I think you had better leave," Joanna suggested.

Alicia got up again. "You don't have so many friends that you can afford to throw them away."

"Are you my friend?" Joanna enquired. "I never knew."

Alicia snorted, and left the room.

* * *

"Appearance is very important," said Jeanette Corder. She was one of John Giffard's juniors, and the senior woman in his partnership. She was somewhat older than Joanna, very smart and handsome in an efficient sort of way. "May I look?" she asked.

Joanna waved her hand at the wardrobe, and Jeanette opened the doors. "Their idea will be to convince the jury that you are a brazen hussy," she said over her shoulder. "We must present you as what you are, a hard-working, talented businesswoman. This is ideal." She took out a grey wool suit, and then frowned. "Oh dear. Trousers. Don't you have a skirt for it?"

"I'm afraid not. Won't trousers do?"

"Definitely not. The trial judge is old Crowther. That's bad in any event. He's the sort of old-fashioned MCP who doesn't believe there is such a thing as rape in the first place. Trousers on women are definitely a guarantee that she is loose."

"But that's outrageous," Joanna said. "I mean, his point of view. Can't we get him changed?"

"It happens to be his turn on that particular bench. But it's not all down. If, in his misogynistic fervour, he misdirects the jury, or even shows extreme prejudice, it could be grounds for an appeal against your conviction . . . supposing you are convicted, of course." She paused to give a bright, and quite unconvincing, smile. "Here's what we want."

It was a blue suit, with skirt, and a thin white pin-stripe. "Wear this with a white blouse, buttoned right up, plain stockings, court shoes, and a modicum of jewellery – just a pearl necklace and your wedding and engagement rings."

"I don't have an engagement ring, at the moment. It's exhibit A."

"Ah. Right. Then just your wedding ring. That's probably better, anyway. Now, hair . . . you should put it up. I mean, that hair, worn loose it'll have every man in court dreaming of being in bed with you, and that can be a short step from believing that they could be, if you are the sort of woman depicted by the prosecution. Do you always wear it loose?"

"Not when I'm in a business meeting."

"Regard this as a business meeting. I assume you have your own hairdresser?"

"Of course."

"Not everyone does, you know. I want you to have it put up in a tight bun. That'll serve two purposes. One, it will again lessen the allure. Two, you have superb bone structure. With no hair about that will heighten the suggestion of total innocence. Right?"

"Right," Joanna said. "I never realised presentation was so important."

"Presentation is everything, Mrs Orton. The prosecution are going to do their damndest to present you as a guilty woman. We are going to do our damndest to present you as an innocent woman. And you are going to do your damndest to help us do that. Right?"

"Right," Joanna said.

"Brandy, madam?" Cummings asked.

"Why, not, Cummings?" Joanna asked. The children had been put to bed, and the servants had disappeared into their quarters. All but faithful old Cummings. Because in precisely twelve hours she would be standing in the dock at the Old Bailey accused of murder. Tomorrow, tomorrow, tomorrow, she thought. Cummings brought the drink, waited for any further orders. "Go to bed, Cummings," she told him. He looked doubtful. "I will switch off the lights."

"Yes, madam." He sounded more doubtful still, and she presumed that when she finally went upstairs he would immediately reappear to check that everything was in order.

Now she waited for his footsteps to die away along the hall before standing up, glass in hand. She kicked off her shoes, walked through the double doors into the hall, then across the hall into the billiards room. A room that had hardly been used since Howard's death. It was on that table that his coffin had been laid, after their return from the West Indies, as it had been here that the funeral had commenced and the wake had followed.

She went on, into the dining room, with its huge refectory table and its row of chairs. Again, a room seldom used since Howard's death. Hasim had preferred to entertain in his London flat, had used this house as a weekend getaway. Dick had not really been up to a great deal of entertaining.

She had, she supposed, never used this house sufficiently. She had camped here, for thirteen years. Was she now going to have to move out? Nobody would tell her. She went upstairs, prowled through the bedrooms, the Blue Room, where she had first surrendered to Howard, the other guest rooms, and then the master bedroom, where she had slept in solitary splendour since her honeymoon. Even then she had not really enjoyed sharing a bed with Dick. All behind her, now.

She slept heavily, waking with a start as the telephone jangled. She picked it up, but Cummings had already answered, downstairs. "Madam is asleep, sir," he was saying. "I do not think—"

"I'm awake, Cummings," she said.

"It's Mr Orton, Madam."

"Jo! Listen! I have to see you."

"Why?" she asked.

"I've been subpoenaed. By the prosecution."

"Then to see me would be incorrect. I'm not sure it wouldn't be illegal."

"Stuff that. Listen, they'll want to ask about, well . . . your character, I suppose."

"Tell them the truth."

"If they were to manage to bring out something about that drugs bust . . ."

"Tell the truth," Joanna said again. "I was totally innocent, and you know it."

"Of course I do, but they could still manage to make it look bad."

"So?"

"Well . . . I could deny it."

"It's a matter of police record, Dick. Your denying it would only get you charged with perjury."

"I'm trying to help you, Jo. I will help you, if . . ."

"If what?"

"If you'd drop all this stupid divorce thing. That isn't helping you much, either, you know. If we were to show a united front . . ."

"It would have so many cracks in it we'd both fall flat on our faces. I won't thank you for the offer, Dick, because I don't think you really had me in mind."

"Bitch!" he said. "I hope they—" She hung up.

She had not expected the court to be so crowded. But, of course, not only was the case sensational in itself, it promised to be salacious as well. She stood in the dock, flanked by two policewomen, and although John Giffard and Jeanette Corder both smiled at her encouragingly, she felt more lonely than ever before in her life. Grahame Long, seated in front of them, did not look at her at all. When would British courts become civilised and allow the defendant to sit at a table with his, or her, lawyers? After all, she was supposed to be innocent until she was found guilty. Standing isolated in the dock, surrounded by policewomen, was an indication of guilt.

It all came down to Grahame Long. The best man in the business, John Giffard had assured her. She could only hope he was right. At least he looked like a lawyer, and a successful man, medium height, somewhat stout, with a sharp nose, reeking of good tobacco and wearing a Savile Row suit. They had had three meetings, and he had clearly studied the evidence very carefully. He had asked her various questions about her past life and previous marriages, noted the answers, and made no comment. So she had asked him. "Well?"

"On the evidence that I have been shown, Mrs Orton, both for and against, there should be an acquittal. I say should rather than will. The jury system requires that, even in a case in which all the odds are stacked on your side, you still have to convince them that you acted only as any decent woman would have done." At last he had smiled at her. "Just be yourself."

She had been so reassured. "What about this terrible judge we have?"

"If the jury believe you are innocent of murder, Mrs Orton, Crowther can foam at the mouth, but there is nothing he can do about it."

Total reassurance, however, was prevented by the media, who were not a hundred per cent for her. In fact, they seemed pretty well divided. And the division was simply along the lines of whether or not she had indeed acted in her own self-defence, as any decent woman might have done. The newspapers, and television, were pretty well agreed that she had proved herself to be a hard, and ruthless businesswoman over the past thirteen years.

The prosecution case was a simple one, and it was exactly as Long had suggested it would be. "The Crown will prove," said Mr Horton-Smith, QC, "that on a voyage home from England, in November of last year, Mrs Orton, Managing Director of Caribee Shipping, travelling in one of her own vessels, had an affair with the deceased, Sean Connor. The Crown will contend that when the voyage ended, Mrs Orton assumed that this romance had also ended, as shipboard romances are wont to do. However, the Crown will prove that Mr Connor did not see it that way, that he wanted to see Mrs Orton again, and that, having discovered that she was a wealthy woman, he intended to blackmail her by threatening to reveal their affair to the press. With this purpose in mind, he visited her at her home on the night of sixteenth December, last. He had informed Mrs Orton that he was coming, and she was waiting for him.

"The Crown will prove that she sent her children to bed and told her servants that she was not to be interrupted unless she called for them, so that she could be alone with him. But after only a little while, Mrs Orton attacked Mr Connor, so viciously that he received extensive injuries. She then called her servants and had the injured man thrown out into the snow. The Crown will show that despite his injuries, Mr Connor managed to regain his car and drive away, but that he collapsed before he could reach his home. He was taken to hospital, where, forty-eight hours later, and after making a statement to the police, he died of the internal injuries he had received, aggravated by the extreme cold to which he had been subjected when ejected from Mrs Orton's house."

The jury listened intently, and Joanna was disturbed that they seldom looked at her; she had been told this was a bad sign. She was also disappointed that despite Long's efforts, there were only three women, and none of these looked particularly sympathetic, either. She preferred not to look at the judge, a large, red-faced man who seemed to glower at her.

Long's riposte was savage. "The prosecution's case," he told the jury, "is entirely built upon supposition and circumstantial evidence. The defence will not deny that Mrs Orton had a shipboard romance with Mr Connor. But she did not wish it to end when the voyage was over. Rather, she wished it to continue. It was she who contacted Mr Connor and invited him to her home for dinner. When he arrived, he was introduced to her children before they went to bed; we have the evidence of the children's nanny, Mrs Winshaw, to prove this. Hardly, you might say, the procedure of a woman who is about to carry out a brutal murder.

"The defence will not, it cannot, pretend that Mrs Orton is a woman of great moral stature; she is, however, as is well known, a highly successful businesswoman who must be given credit for her clear-sightedness and determination. We thus again ask you to consider whether such a woman would plan a murder in her own home, virtually in the presence of her children, when there would be no hope of concealing the crime.

"We will admit freely that she invited Connor to visit her with a continuation of their relationship in mind. She only turned against him when he wished to indulge in sex of the most perverted kind. When she requested him to stop, he refused to do so. She therefore defended herself, as would any woman in those circumstances. As a result of her spirited defence of her person, Mr Connor was injured. The prosecution have contended that it was from those injuries, and the way he was manhandled by Mrs Orton's servants, that he died. Sadly, this may well be so. But there is not the slightest indication that Mrs Orton pre-meditated or planned this tragedy. She acted in self defence, and we shall prove this to your satisfaction."

The prosecution evidence was mercifully brief. They were biding their time. After the various routine evidences of arrest had been given, Demont the steward was called and, clearly very embarrassed – he kept glancing apologetically at Joanna – established that he had served drinks and coffee to Mrs Orton and Mr Connor, in her stateroom, not only on the night of the storm but on several occasions afterwards. In view of the fact that the defence had conceded that Joanna and Connor had had a shipboard romance, this seemed a rather unnecessary crossing of t's and dotting of i's to Joanna, especially when Demont was followed by Connor's cabin mate, Gerald Aston. But Mr Smith-Horton had his reasons. Aston could only testify that Connor had never again slept in their cabin after the night of the storm, and that Connor had said he was sleeping with Mrs Orton. The Boss, he called her. But then Mr Smith-Horton asked him: "When the ship had docked in Plymouth, Mr Aston," he said. "What happened then?"

"We cleared customs and immigration on board, and then we went ashore," Aston said. He had not looked at Joanna at all.

"You and Mr Connor went ashore together?"

"No, sir. Mr Connor hung behind. He said he had to say goodbye to the boss."

"And when did he come ashore?"

"About fifteen minutes later."

"And what did he say to you?"

"He said that she was the most exciting woman he had ever known."

"And what else did he say?"

"He said that he was going to have a lot more of her."

The spectators gave the required gasp of appreciation, Judge Crowther the required tap of his gavel.

"He did not specify what he meant by that statement?" Smith-Horton asked.

"No, sir."

Smith-Horton did not call for speculation on the part of the witness, which would have led to an objection. Long did what he could. "In his conversation with you, Mr Connor did not mention that he had given Mrs Orton his phone number, and expected her to call him?"

"No, sir," Aston said.

There were various police officers to testify that they had searched Sean Connor's room and found a good deal of material to indicate that he was planning to blackmail Joanna. This material was produced as evidence. There was also the medical evidence, outlining Connor's various injuries. The doctor described the beating as severe, and concluded that Connor had died of a ruptured peritoneum caused by being stamped upon with extreme force, and that he had then been subjected to exposure that had gravely weakened his condition.

"How healthy was Connor when he visited Mrs Orton?" Long asked in cross-examination.

"I would say perfectly healthy. He had had a bout of malaria a few months previously, but had made a complete recovery."

"You are saying that there was no trace of any existing stomach problem before sixteenth December last, or any other internal complaint?"

"None at all," the doctor said, with total certainty.

Then the prosecution got down to its real business. Captain Heggie was called. "For how long have you worked for Mrs Orton?" Smith-Horton asked.

"Ever since Mr Edge died sir. Thirteen years, now."

"Has she been a good boss?"

"Oh, yes, sir."

"Would you describe her as firm?"

"Oh, yes, sir."

Grahame Long began to frown at the ceiling.

"No doubt during those thirteen years there have been many crises?"

"Well, sir, that's the nature of the shipping business."

"Through all of which Mrs Orton has triumphed. By her firmness? Her determination? Her courage?"

"Absolutely, sir."

"Her ruthlessness, would you say? In letting nothing stand in the way of her gaining her objective?"

"Objection, m'lud," Long said. "The introduction of this witness has no bearing on this case, which is a matter of facts, not opinions." He allowed himself an important smile. "However favourable."

"With respect, m'lud," Smith-Horton argued. "The only fact we possess about this case is that Mr Connor is dead, as a result of an assault upon him by Mrs Orton. It is the prosecution's contention that this attack was pre-meditated and planned. Mrs Orton denies this. Thus the case hinges upon what was actually in Mrs Orton's mind at the time. She is unlikely to tell us the truth about this. It seems to me, therefore, that learning about her state of mind, on various previous occasions of a critical nature, is very relevant indeed."

"That is preposterous," Long said.

"I will see you gentlemen in chambers," Lord Crowther decided. "Court is adjourned."

Long was furious when he joined Joanna and Giffard for lunch.

"He's going to admit the evidence. And anything else that may indicate your ability to make critical and perhaps ambiguous decisions. Well, that is grounds for an appeal, for a start. And I have told him I will object to every one."

"What did he say?" Gifffard asked.

"He said that was my privilege." Long squeezed Joanna's hand. "Don't worry, my dear. They are playing entirely into our hands."

"Mr Montgomery," Smith-Horton said. "For how long have you worked for Mrs Orton?"

"Ever since Howard . . . Mr Edge . . . died. Thirteen years."

"And before then you worked for Mr Edge?"

"For eight years, sir."

"I believe you were in a position of some responsibility?"

"Mr Edge had a trust company in Jersey which I managed. Mrs Orton inherited that, and I continued to manage it for her."

"I believe you are related to Mrs Orton?"

"I am her brother-in-law, sir."

"And do you still work for her?"

"No, sir. I have been fired."

"How sad. When did this misfortune take place?"

"In December of last year. Right after she returned from her Caribbean voyage."

"May we ask why you were dismissed?"

"Well . . ." for the first time Billy looked at the dock, his cheeks pink. "She intimated that she was not happy with the way I was running her company."

"Just like that? After twenty-one years in the employ of Mrs Orton and her late husband, she sacked you?"

"I'm afraid she's like that," Billy conceded.

"You mean she acted in a totally ruthless manner, because you had, perhaps, failed her in one small direction. Did you suspect that she might have acted as she did because she had another grave matter on her mind?"

"Objection," Long said, wearily.

"How long have you been married to Mrs Orton?" Smith-Horton asked Dick.

"Four years."

"But you have known her longer than that?"

"Oh, yes. I knew her since she came to England, thirteen years ago."

"You were friends. Close friends?"

"I thought so."

"But your friendship was interrupted. How did that happen?"

Dick shrugged. "She took up with this wealthy guy, Edge."

"Were you upset by this?"

"Very."

"But you understood that Mrs Orton, or Miss Grain as she then was, would always go for the main chance, with a ruthless disregard of whoever might get hurt in the process."

"Objection."

"Now, Mr Orton, I understand that you and Mrs Orton are in the process of getting divorced."

"She has filed for divorce against me, yes," Dick said, choosing his words carefully, as he had no doubt been coached to do.

"Do we take it that you not wish for this divorce?"

"Heavens, no," Dick said. "She's my wife. I love her." The court smiled.

"But Mrs Orton is determined to divorce you. Why?"

"She found out that I had had an affair."

"Did she ask you for an explanation? Or perhaps even a promise that it would not happen again?"

"Joanna isn't like that."

"You mean she just announced she was divorcing you?"

"She threw me out of the house," Dick said.

"This being a day or so after her return from the Caribbean?"

This time there was no need for an objection.

"Mr Orton," Long said, "is not the real reason Mrs Orton is dvivorcing you is because you sold a block of shares in her company, held by you, and which, by the terms of your marriage agreement, you were not entitled to sell without her permission?"

"That may have had something to do with it."

Joanna felt her barrister might have made a tactical error, as that was just another example of her presumed ruthlessness.

But there remained Alicia. "When did you first meet Mrs Orton, Mrs Edge?"

"I have no idea. It was some time in nineteen sixty-four."

"You were, at that time, married to Mr Edge?"

"Yes, I was."

"And Mrs Orton, or Miss Grain as she then was?"

"Was one of his floozies. Or so I thought. I soon realised my mistake when he moved her into Caribee House."

"You had, of course, moved out?"

"Of course."

"And Mr Edge then divorced you to marry Miss Grain?"

"Yes."

"Did you wish to divorce Mr Edge?"

"Of course I did not. But when that woman gets her claws into someone—"

"Strike that remark," said Lord Crowther. "Please confine yourself to answering the questions, Mrs Edge." But he smiled at her as he spoke.

Smith-Horton was happy enough. "I do not suppose you have seen a great deal of Mrs Orton since your mutual husband died?"

"Not a lot," Alicia said. "She attempted to be friends, but I found it difficult."

"Quite. Will you tell the court when last you met up with Mrs Orton?"

"Well, we've seen quite a lot of each other over the past few weeks."

"This was after Mrs Orton called on you at your home,

on the morning of . . ." he checked his notes, "sixteenth December last."

"Yes."

"Why did she visit you?"

"She wanted to buy some of my shares."

"Did she tell you why?"

"She needed my shares to replace those sold by her husband. So that she could retain control of the company."

"And you agreed to this?"

"Well . . ." Alicia glanced at Joanna. "She made me an attractive offer. She offered both myself and a friend of mine seats on the board of Caribee Shipping if we would agree to sell her the shares."

"Would it therefore be correct to say that Mrs Orton was going to allow nothing, absolutely nothing, to stand in the way of her retaining control of the company?"

Again Long did not even bother to object. Then the prosecution case was closed.

For only the second time in their acquaintance, Joanna saw Grahame Long smile. "I am amazed that they have had the effrontery to put up such a case," he said. "We, you and I, dear lady, will utterly destroy them."

"They've painted the picture they wanted," Joanna pointed out.

"In many ways it is a flattering one," Long said. "They have depicted you as a strong-willed and determined businesswoman. All right, so they may have got across the idea that you are also a ruthless woman. That doesn't make you a murderess. Rather does it make you a woman who would in no way jeopardize her company, and her place within that company. All you have to do is be yourself and tell the absolute truth when I put you on the stand, and we will have nothing to worry about."

Joanna wished she could be as certain. William and Norma

came down for dinner, but it was a sombre occasion. "How are the children taking it?" Norma asked.

"They think it's great fun," Joanna said. "Mummy against the world."

"And Mummy always wins," William said. Joanna made a face at him.

Cummings appeared. "There is a phone call, madam."

"If it's another reporter, tell him to take a running jump."

"The gentleman does not claim to be a reporter, Madam. He merely says that he would like to speak with you on an important matter."

"I have no wish to speak to anyone tonight, Cummings," Joanna said. "You may tell him so."

"Yes, madam." Cummings withdrew.

"Don't you think you could at least have found out his name?" William asked.

"His name is irrelevant. Nothing is relevant, William, until after tomorrow." Norma squeezed her hand.

Grahame Long had a fairly full quiver even before he got to her. Mr Cummings was very embarrassed. "Yes, sir," he agreed with Long's question. "There are several telephones in the house, but only the one number. I normally answer the telephone downstairs. If it is for Madam, and she is not downstairs, I can switch it to her bedroom."

"But you cannot remember Mr Connor telephoning Mrs Orton?" Long asked.

"No, sir, I cannot."

"Well, then, will you tell the court when you first were informed that Mr Connor was coming down to dinner."

"That very evening, sir."

"Did you usually receive such short notice about providing for a dinner guest?"

"Well, sir, yes and no. There is always plenty of food in the house. All we, Cook and I, need is the necessary notice to prepare it."

"But on this occasion the notice was something like two hours."

"Yes, sir."

Charlie was even more helpful. "No, sir," he said. "I had received no instructions for that evening at all."

"But you were still in the house at eight o'clock," Long said.

"Yes, sir, I often stayed late, had a bit of supper with Cook and Mr Cummings and Mrs Partridge, before going off."

"Had you ever seen or heard of Mr Connor before that night?"

"No, sir."

"So, what actually happened, as far as you were concerned?"

"Well, sir . . ." Charlie gave Joanna a quick glance. "I was with Mr Cummings and Mrs Partridge, and we heard Mrs Orton calling for help. Mr Cummings and I ran along to the drawing room, and we found Mrs Orton and Mr Connor fighting. And Mrs Orton told us to throw him out, which we did,"

But Smith-Horton had a telling response available. "Mr Hatch, you said you found Mrs Orton and Mr Connor fighting. Will you describe what you actually saw?"

"Well, sir . . ." Charlie hesitated. "Connor was lying on the floor, like."

"And Mrs Orton?"

"Was standing over him."

"What was she wearing?"

"Well, sir . . ." now Charlie's cheeks were pink. "She wasn't wearing anything."

"You mean she was naked."

Charlie licked his lips. "Yes, sir."

"And she told you to throw Mr Connor out. Was he moving, did he resist you in any way?"

"He tried, sir."

"What did you do?"

"I hit him, sir."

"You knocked him down?"

"I knocked him out, sir."

"You mean, as far as you could see, he was unconscious."

"He wasn't moving, sir."

"Then tell us exactly what you did?"

"We . . . Mr Cummings and I, took him down the front steps and across the courtyard to his car."

"Took him? You have just testified that he was unconscious?"

"Yes, sir – we dragged him."

"I see. You dragged him across the courtyard to his car. But you didn't actually put him in it?"

"No, sir. We didn't have the keys."

"Where do you suppose the keys were?"

"In his pocket, I suppose, sir."

"But you made no effort to take them out. You dragged an unconscious man across the courtyard to his car, and then you . . . what exactly *did* you do?"

"We left him there."

"Was it snowing?"

"Yes, sir, it might have been snowing."

"You dragged an unconscious, bleeding man across the courtyard to his car, and you left him, lying in the snow. Did it occur to you to call for an ambulance?"

"Well . . . no, sir. But he really was all right. After a few seconds he got up and got into the car and drove away."

"You saw this?"

"Oh, yes, sir."

"Where from? Were you still standing beside the car?"

"No, sir, We had gone back to the porch."

"So, having dropped Mr Connor beside his car, literally, in the snow, you retired to the porch to watch. And after some time . . ."

"A few seconds, sir."

"How many seconds?"

"Well, sir . . ."

"Five, ten, twenty . . . a minute?"

"Oh, it was less than a minute, sir."

"What was Mrs Orton doing while you were watching Mr Connor drive away?"

"I don't know, sir."

"What was she doing when at last you went inside?"

"She was standing in the drawing room. She told me to pick up the pearls; Mr Connor had broken her necklace."

"How do you know?"

"Sir?"

"How do you know that Mr Connor had broken Mrs Orton's necklace?"

"Well, sir, she told me he had."

"Quite. Just two more questions, Mr Hatch. When you returned inside, was Mrs Orton still, ah, naked?"

"Oh, no, sir. She had put on her dress."

"Of course. Tell us about the dress."

"Sir?"

"Was it torn? Damaged in any way? You have just testified that Mrs Orton told you to gather up the pearls scattered about the floor as a result of Mr Connor having torn the necklace from her neck. I imagine you, or I, could have burst a pearl necklace, and 'torn' it from Mrs Orton's neck, without very much difficulty. But removing her dress, against her will, would have been a somewhat more difficult matter. If the pearl necklace had been snapped, as Mrs Orton resisted the alleged rape, the dress would almost certainly have been torn. Did you notice any tear, or rent, in the dress Mrs Orton had put on?"

Charlie gulped, started to look at Joanna again, and changed his mind. "No, sir."

"Thank you, Mr Hatch."

Lord Crowther looked at Long.

"I will now ask the defendant to take the stand, m'lud."

There was a stir around the court. This was the moment for which they had all been waiting.

# Chapter Seven

# The Defence

"Joanna," Long said. "The prosecution has made a determined effort to depict you as a hard and ruthless woman, who would do anything to maintain her position. Is that how you see yourself?"

"I was given a hand to play," Joanna said. "And I felt it my duty to play it to the best of my ability."

"This has to do with your first marriage. Will you tell us exactly what happened?"

"Howard Edge asked me to marry him," Joanna said. "His first marriage had broken down. I accepted his proposal. I had known him for several years, and I was in love with him. I was twenty years old and I had no vision of the future other than as his wife. But he died on our honeymoon, and to my astonishment I learned that he had willed his entire stake, a controlling stake, in Caribee Shipping, to me. I was pregnant with his daughter. I felt it was my duty to maintain and use that controlling stake in the company for the sake of his memory and my unborn child."

Long looked pleased. This was jury convincing stuff. "And this is what you have done?"

"To the best of my ability, yes."

"Did this have any influence upon your second marriage?"

"I suppose it must have done. I approached Prince Hasim, whom I knew was an old and valued friend of Howard's, and asked him to back me while I got the company back on its feet. He agreed to do this. I was totally surprised when, some time later, he proposed marriage."

"Why were you so surprised?"

"Because it entailed such a great sacrifice on his part. He was heir to the Emirate of Qadir. He had to renounce this if he was going to marry a woman who was both a foreigner and a Christian. I asked him to consider the matter most carefully, but he insisted."

"And it cost him his life. What was your reaction to that?"

"I was totally shattered."

"And then you married for a third time. Did this have anything to do with the preservation of your stake in your company?"

"No. Dick was an old and treasured friend. I thought we were in love."

"And then you found out that he was having an affair, and you reacted as I suspect most women would have done. But then you had an affair yourself. May I ask, was this your first extra-marital affair?"

"Yes," Joanna said.

"And was it undertaken in a spirit of revenge against your husband?"

"Not really. There had been a severe storm. We were perhaps lucky to have survived it. I think we were all on a high when we realised we were safe, and Mr Connor and I just got together. Perhaps having made up my mind to divorce my husband made it easier for me."

"This affair with Connor was therefore entirely fortuitous. But you wished to continue it."

"Well . . ." Joanna gave the jury a surreptitious glance. "He seemed a nice man. And I was very lonely."

"So, you invited him to spend the night with you at your home."

"I invited him to dinner," Joanna said. "I was going to let the evening take care of itself."

"Had you any idea that he might be going to blackmail you?"

"The thought never crossed my mind," Joanna said.

"He gave no indication of it?"

"None at all."

"But you found it necessary to attack him?"

"I found it necessary to defend myself," Joanna said in a low voice.

"This man was already your lover, but on this occasion you found it necessary to reject his advances. Violently. Why?"

Joanna licked her lips. "He . . . attempted to perform a perverted act."

"He wished to sodomise you." There was a rustle of comment around the court, and Lord Crowther used his gavel. "And this assault you would not permit."

"No, I would not," Joanna said.

"You asked him to stop, but he attempted to persist, and you defended yourself. Tell the court exactly what happened."

"I hit him. I had forgotten I was wearing my ring. It cut open his face and he went berserk, and came at me again. I managed to knock him down, and I jumped on him with both feet. I was trying to stop him from attacking me again."

"Of course. And then?"

"I rang for my servants and told them to throw him out."

"Did you realise he might be badly hurt?"

"No, I did not. I was too upset."

"Was he bleeding?"

"There was blood on his face, where my ring had cut him. And there was some on his mouth."

"What did you suppose caused that?"

"I thought he must have cut his lips."

"You had no idea that he might have been bleeding internally?"

"No, I did not."

"So you had him thrown out. What did you do then?"

"When I had recovered a little, I asked my servants what had happened to him, and they told me he had driven away."

"What did you do then?"

"I went to bed."

"Joanna, you are under oath. Did you, at any time that evening, or at any time before that evening, plan, or even contemplate, killing Sean Connor?"

"I did not."

"Did you, at any time that evening, or at any time before that evening, plan, or even contemplate, seriously injuring Sean Connor? Or injuring him at all?"

"I did not."

"Your attack on him was an instinctive, violent reaction to the perverted attack he was attempting to inflict upon you?"

"It was."

"Thank you, Joanna," Long said.

"I'm afraid I do not feel able to call you 'Joanna'," Mr Smith-Horton said, "because I do not know you as well as my learned friend. But I am afraid I must go over the ground that counsel for the defence covered so carefully, but yet, I suspect, not carefully enough. You have stated, under oath, that the only extra-marital affair you have ever had was with Sean Connor. Will you deny that, when you were plain Joanna Grain, you were the late Howard Edge's mistress for a year before your marriage?"

"I was Howard's mistress," Joanna said. "I became his mistress when he asked me to marry him. The year's delay was caused by the divorce proceedings against his first wife. As we were not yet married, that can hardly be classed as an extra-marital affair." The court smiled.

But Smith-Horton was not put out. "No doubt. However, you moved into Caribee House as if you were his wife, a year before your marriage. And a fortnight after your marriage, Mr Edge was killed in a boating accident, following which you discovered, almost equally by accident, that you were heiress to his entire fortune. Is that correct?"

"Yes," Joanna said in a low voice. "That is correct."

"Now you have testified . . ." Smith-Horton ruffled his notes as if he did not know by heart what was in them, "that having inherited Mr Edge's estate, and his controlling interest in Caribee Shipping, you discovered that the firm's finances were in a bad way, and so you applied to an old friend of Mr Edge, Prince Hasim of Qadir, for help. Am I right?"

"Yes."

"And Prince Hasim most generously gave you this help. A noble fellow. I'm afraid I must ask you this, Mrs Orton, or Mrs Edge as you had by then become, were any favours offered to Prince Hasim for this remarkable act of generosity on his part?"

Joanna bit her lip. "We were old friends."

"How charming. Mrs Orton, you are under oath: did you or did not not have sex with Prince Hasim in return for his investment in your firm?"

"I . . . it was not for a year after his investment." She looked at the jury. "I was pregnant." This time they did not smile.

"However," Smith-Horton continued, relentlessly. "You did have sex with Prince Hasim before your marriage. But of course, as you were by then a widow, this was not an extra-marital affair either. And obviously you had sex with him after your marriage. What a silly question. You bore him a son! And then, following Prince Hasim's tragic murder, you married your old friend Richard Orton, and have now decided to divorce him." He looked at the jury. He would not dare put into words the obvious implication, that to be married to Joanna Grain did not imply longevity as a husband, but he was inviting them to read his thoughts.

"Following which," he went on, "you had an affair with Sean Connor. One of these romantic shipboard events. One which, you have testified, you wished to continue. But one which, you have also testified, could not stand any attempt at perversion. This shocked you to such an extent that you attacked Mr Connor with, if I may so put it, tooth and claw.

Now, Mrs Orton, I hate to be indelicate, but I'm afraid I must probe the secrets of your marriage bed. I find it difficult to comprehend how a woman who has admitted to having shared that bed, in and out of marriage, with several men, should suddenly react so violently to an attempt to, shall we say, extend the bounds of lovemaking."

"I did not wish it to happen," Joanna insisted.

"And it was not something that had ever happened to you before?"

"Of course not." Long snapped his pencil in two; he had suddenly realised where Smith-Horton was heading.

"Mrs Orton, you are under oath. You were mistress and then wife to an Arab gentleman over a period of some four years. Once again, I hate to be indelicate, but . . . well . . ."

"Prince Hasim was the most perfect gentleman I have ever known," Joanna snapped.

"And his sexual habits were those of a gentleman. But also those of an Arab."

"Of course. But he would never do anything I did not wish."

"He never attempted to, ah, enter you from the rear?"

"If this noise does not cease," remarked Lord Crowther, "I shall clear the court. I am not sure in any event that this evidence should not be heard in camera, Mr Smith-Horton. Is there much more of it?"

"I think just two more questions, m'lud, if Mrs Orton will answer the last."

"Very well. Mrs Orton?"

Joanna had had the time to recover. "Yes, he did."

"But you did not consider this an ungentlemanly act, between man and mistress, or husband and wife."

"It is not an ungentlemanly act," Joanna said. "It is the way many people suppose we are intended to have sex."

"No doubt it is. And you were happy to humour your husband, or even your would-be husband. Now, will you answer the court this: supposing your husband had elected to use yet another method, the method attempted by Sean Connor, would you have resisted him?" The court was absolutely quiet as Joanna stared at him. "Would you have turned on Prince Hasim like a tigress? Would you have split open his face with your ring? Would you have stamped on his stomach, rupturing his peritoneum? Would you have called your servants and had the prince thrown out into the snow?"

Joanna licked her lips. "You are under oath," Smith-Horton reminded her.

"It would have been different," Joanna muttered. But her defence was in ruins, and everyone in the court knew it.

Not that Grahame Long intended to lower his flag without a fight. "The prosecution case," he told the jury, "rests upon two very debatable points. The first point is that Sean Connor intended to blackmail Mrs Orton, and that she killed him to prevent that happening. We cannot deny that it seems to have been in Mr Connor's mind to blackmail the defendant. But we do deny that Mrs Orton ever knew of it, or that she in any way planned Mr Connor's death. Her assault was that of a woman defending her body from the most foul kind of rape.

"Which brings us to the second point upon which the prosecution has based its case. Mrs Orton was defending herself against sodomy. No one is arguing about that. The prosecution has seized upon the fact that she may, or may not, have endured this from one of her previous husbands. Ladies and gentlemen, this is irrelevant. A woman's relations with her husband do not imply that she is bound to accept such relations from any other man, against her will. That is rape. The prosecution have implied that as Mrs Orton and Mr Connor were lovers, he was in the position of a husband. But that is not so and cannot be so. When a woman marries, it is implicit that she has taken on certain obligations towards her husband, including that of sharing and giving comfort in the marriage bed. This does not apply to an affair. For a woman to have an affair may be morally reprehensible, but it does not bestow upon the lover any of the rights of a husband, or upon the woman any of the obligations to submit to his requirements that may be the case in a marriage.

"Mrs Orton was defending herself against rape. That she defended herself too successfully is a tragic misfortune. But under no circumstances can she be found guilty of premeditated murder." But he was not happy. The jury were looking uncommonly grim-faced.

"I do not think anyone can truly deny that Mrs Orton, née the Princess Hasim, née Mrs Howard Edge, née Joanna Grain, has lived a very full life," Mr Smith-Horton told the jury. "She has had, one might say, a singular penchant for marrying both well, and fortunately. She lived with Howard Edge for over a year until he finally married her, divorcing his own wife to do so. She inherited his considerable wealth, but when she discovered that the company which was the foundation of that wealth was in financial difficulties, she promptly married again, to an even more wealthy man, with whose assistance she was able to put Caribee Shipping back on its feet. Again, this marriage took place approximately a year after Prince Hasim first guaranteed Mrs Edge's, as she then was, finances. Then, when Prince Hasim was assassinated, she married again. This time she did not marry for money; perhaps she had enough of it, by then. She married for what she hoped would be love, but when that did not materialise, without the slightest hesitation she sacked her third husband, as she might have sacked a clerk in her office. Of course she was, is, entitled to do this; Mr Orton has admitted adultery. But it is a measure of the woman's character that, having landed in England from her adventurous voyage to the Caribbean, on fourteenth December last, the very next day she gave Mr Orton his marching orders. Mrs Orton is clearly a lady of great decision.

"By then she had embarked on an affair, which might have been intended, she says it was so intended, to progress. Let us not forget that Mrs Orton has testified, almost proudly, that she never slept with a man she did not then marry. Was Mr Connor to be the fourth in line? But she very rapidly found out that he was perhaps not a suitable husband. I think we are entitled to ask ourselves why. One may confidently assume, as Mr Connor spent eight consecutive nights in Mrs Orton's cabin on board the *Caribee Queen*, that it was not a matter of sexual inadequacy or sexual delinquency. We do know that Caribee Shipping is again in financial difficulties. Possibly Mrs Orton had discovered that Mr Connor had no money. She says she still wanted the affair to continue. But the evidence suggests otherwise.

"We have proof that Mr Connor intended to blackmail her, and this proof has been presented to you. When he visited Mrs Orton with the intention of implementing the blackmail threat, he was beaten so badly that he died from his injuries. The fact that he drove his car away from Mrs Orton's home in no way alters that fact. It may be a testimony to Mr Connor's strength of both body and mind, but the fact remains that even as he carried out this act of will, he was dying, of the injuries he had received at the hands and feet of Mrs Orton, and of Mrs Orton's servants, as instructed by her.

"Ladies and gentlemen, Mrs Orton has said she attacked Connor in self-defence while resisting an attempted rape. This with a man with whom she had spent eight presumably blissful nights, on board her ship. Had there been anything distasteful about any of those nights she had merely to end the affair there and then, without any recourse to violence. They were on her ship, surrounded by her most faithful and obedient employees. But she did not wish to end it. Yet, surprisingly, she did wish to end it as soon as Mr Connor visited her at her home. She says this was because he attempted to commit an unnatural act. Ladies and gentlemen, we need to keep a sense of perspective about this. Any woman is entitled to defend herself against rape. She is not entitled to kill to do so, unless her own life is in danger. Could Mrs Orton really have supposed that a man with whom she had spent eight blissful nights was about to murder her?

"She further claims that she did not intend to resist having sex with him. She wanted that. That actually rules out any consideration of rape. But she refused to accept the unnatural act. Ladies and gentlemen, are we to believe that this woman, who, as I say, has lived a very full life, in and out of bed, and who in the course of that life has married outside of what might be called the English norm, with apparently total contentment, is going to react so viciously to an attempted unnatural act as to kill her lover? I think not.

"Ladies and gentlemen, we have before us a bold, determined, mentally brilliant woman. The facts of her life speak for themselves. She is regarded by many in the city as the ultimate entrepreneur. She has used her beauty, and her brains, and her charm, and her determination, to succeed in business. She has never let anything stand in her way. Anything! Her first husband died at the beginning of December, nineteen sixty-three. He died in South America, and his widow brought his body home by ship. A matter of ten days. Then he had to be buried, and she had to pick up the pieces of his business. Yet at the beginning of January nineteen sixty-four, less than a month after Howard Edge's tragic death, Prince Hasim was guaranteeing her borrowing with her bank. Prince Hasim himself died in December, nineteen sixty-nine. Again, less than a month later a consortium of businessmen was injecting capital into Caribee Shipping to make sure it stayed afloat.

"Mrs Orton returned from her Caribbean voyage in December of last year, her mind made up to divorce her husband, with all the trauma that was going to involve. Within two days she was negotiating to buy shares from Mrs Alicia Edge. If there is one thing of which we can be certain with regard to Mrs Orton it is this: if the centre of London were to be blown up tomorrow, the day after she would be opening an office for her company in Birmingham or Bristol. We cannot help but admire a woman of such single-minded determination to succeed.

"But let me ask you to consider this: what then would be the reaction of such a woman when an itinerant lover with whom she has had a few enjoyable nights informs her that he is going to blackmail her? I have to say that we also have to admire Mr Connor's courage in taking such a risk. But then, perhaps he did not know her as well as we now do. Sean Connor is dead. He was killed in a vicious, and we believe we have proved to your satisfaction, a pre-meditated attack, planned and carried out by the defendant. I thank you."

"It's so unfair," Joanna said at dinner. "That attack upon Hasim's character, simply because he was an Arab. How could they *do* that?"

"Because he's dead," John Giffard pointed out. "If he were alive, we could have called him in evidence."

"If he were alive," William pointed out, "this situation could never have arisen."

"If only he *were* alive," Joanna muttered. "What's going to happen, John?"

"I very much fear that will depend a great deal upon Crowther's summing up," Giffard said.

"The task before you," Lord Crowther told the jury the next morning, "is one of the most difficult with which a jury, any jury, has to cope. Only the defendant knows the truth of what happened that night last December. Only she knows what was in her heart when she launched that vicious attack upon Sean Connor. She claims it was an instinctive reply to being attacked in a perverted and obscene fashion. The prosecution claims it was a carefully planned and meticulously carried out murder. You have to decide whether or not the defendant is telling the truth, or whether, as a continuation of that carefully planned and meticulously carried out murder, she is now defending herself with that brilliance to which both sides have attested." Joanna, sitting in the dock, stared at him in consternation, while icy hands closed on her heart and stomach.

"In most murder cases," Lord Crowther went on, "there are

at least one or two points of evidence which are incontrovertible. And there are just a few points of evidence which you may care to consider here. Firstly, it is incontrovertible, accepted by both sides, that Mrs Orton and Sean Connor were lovers. It is for you to determine whether a woman could so viciously attack a man with whom she has shared her all, and with whom there does not appear to have been any differences, either of a sexual or a social nature, before that dreadful night, unless there was some ulterior motive preying on her mind. Secondly, it is incontrovertible that the police found evidence in Sean Connor's lodgings that he was planning to blackmail Mrs Orton. Thirdly, it is incontrovertible that Mr Connor visited Mrs Orton on the night of sixteenth December last year, that she sent away her servants with instructions not to return unless called, and that within half an hour of their being alone together, Sean Connor was attacked. These are the only facts we possess. It is your duty to interpret them and determine whether or not Mrs Orton is guilty of murder, or of involuntary killing – manslaughter – in self-defence.

"In arriving at your verdict, there are several points you need to consider very carefully. One is the relationship between Mrs Orton and her lover that I have already mentioned. Then you need to consider the various facets of Mrs Orton's life that have been revealed to you in this court. You need to determine just how susceptible this woman, this enormously successful, experienced, and sophisticated woman, was to an event which might, or might not, have been outside of her previous experience. You need to consider the events of that night. The defence have made much of the fact that it was Mrs Orton who telephoned Mr Connor, and not the other way around. But Mrs Orton has made no secret of the fact that she wished to continue the affair. Therefore why should she not have made the first move to ensure that continuance? It was what was said on that telephone call, and more importantly, what was said after Mr Connor had arrived at Caribee House and the servants had been sent away, that you need to consider. Mrs Orton has denied that anything was said about blackmail. It is your duty to determine whether she is telling the truth, or not.

"But it is also your duty to consider the behaviour of the defendant *after* the event. You may wish to consider the analogy of a hit and run driver. If a man driving a car knocks down a pedestrian, and kills him, he is guilty of involuntary manslaughter. If he then stops his car, renders what assistance he can to his victim, calls for help, accepts his error of judgement, we may sympathise with his misfortune, and although evidence must be taken as to how fast he was driving, and whether or not he had been drinking alcohol, he remains an object of some sympathy. If, however, instead of stopping, he drives away and leaves his victim, perhaps dead, perhaps dying, perhaps able to recover from his injuries if given sufficient help soon enough, then he is guilty of a crime. You may wish to consider why Mrs Orton, if her attack upon Mr Connor was totally unpremeditated, did nothing to offer him any assistance, even when supported by two of her servants, which would surely have prevented any risk of a further attack. She has said she did not know how badly he was hurt. But she could certainly see that his face was split open. She could also see that he was only half conscious. Yet she had her servants throw him out into the snow. I should remind you that a few minutes later she asked what had happened to him. And on being told that he had managed to get into his car and drive away, Mrs Orton went to bed. As she had earlier dismissed her husband from her house, so now she calmly dismissed her lover. You may wish to consider all these points."

"That old buzzard virtually directed them to find you guilty," Grahame Long said as they sipped coffee in the small office just off the courtroom, under the watchful eye of a woman police constable.

"Well, you said he wouldn't like me," Joanna reminded him.

"I can tell you . . ." his head turned as the door opened.

"Ready for you, Mrs Orton."

"Gosh, that was quick," William said.

"Is that good?" Joanna asked.

"Ah . . . not really," John Giffard said. "Keep your fingers crossed."

Joanna was led away from them, down beneath the courtroom, and up the steps into the dock. For the last time, she thought. She was curiously calm. She had accepted the fact that she would be found guilty. It was a matter of bracing herself for what came after that. She hardly heard what they were saying, as the forewoman handed over the piece of paper on which she had written the verdict, and it was passed up to Lord Crowther, who peered at them as he read it. "The verdict is unanimous?"

"It is."

The woman police constable standing beside Joanna gave her a little nudge, and she came to attention, at the very edge of the box, the panel eating into her waist. "Joanna Orton, you have been found guilty of the pre-meditated murder of Sean Connor on the night of sixteenth December last," Lord Crowther said. "Have you anything to say before I pass sentence?"

For a moment Joanna couldn't speak; even though she had guessed what was coming, her tongue still seemed to be stuck to the roof of her mouth. Desperately she found some saliva. "I did not mean to kill him," she said.

Lord Crowther waited, to see if she would add anything, but as she didn't, after a few seconds he continued. "You have been found guilty of the crime of murdering your lover. We do not know, because you will not tell us, whether it was because he was trying to blackmail you, or whether it was simply that you had grown tired of him. The fact remains that you determined on his death, and you carried out the crime with an efficiency which only those who have no knowledge of your business methods would consider unusually ruthless.

"You are a woman who has spent her adult life reaching for goals which many might suppose unattainable, but in which you have always attained your objective by a single-minded determination to succeed, and a willingness to take extreme risks to achieve that success. Perhaps it was inevitable that such a life, a life that has been, more than once, touched by violence and death, should culminate in a determination to be rid of a man who had become, at the very least, a nuisance and, at the worst, a positive danger. However, those that take the law into their own hands must be prepared to suffer the severity of the law when they are found out. Joanna Orton, it is my decision that you will go to prison for twenty-five years. Take her down."

# Chapter Eight

# The Prison

There was a moment's total silence in the courtroom, then Matilda, seated in the public gallery, screaned, "Oh, my God!"

Her comment was caught up in the swell of noise from the body of the court itself, against which Lord Crowther banged his gavel in vain in an attempt to gain the silence necessary to discharge the jury. "Let's go," said the woman constable, holding Joanna's arm.

Joanna felt about to faint. Twenty-five years! Giffard had said a few years. She had anticipated ten, which with remission might mean she was out in no more than six. Twenty-five years! Even with remission she'd be past forty! An unimaginable age! Giffard was waiting for her downstairs. "We'll appeal, of course." Joanna stared at him. Did he really exist?

"Come along, dear," said the woman constable.

"No, wait," Joanna said. "There are people I have to see. My company secretary . . . my accountant . . . my children, for God's sake!"

"I'm afraid that isn't possible, right now," the woman said. "It'll all be arranged later. Now you must go to prison."

Joanna turned to Giffard, her eyes suddenly opaque as they filled with tears. "I'll see to everything," he promised her. "Joanna, we'll appeal. Don't give up."

Joanna was hurried along the corridor and down a flight of

steps to where a Black Maria waited. The rear doors were opened, but to her enormous relief there was no one else inside. She stepped up, and was followed by two women constables. The van drove off, into a crowd of reporters who had assembled outside the gates. "Parasitic swine," remarked one of the policewomen.

"Where am I going?" Joanna asked.

"Liddleton."

"Where is that?"

"Just outside London. It's not too bad. Overcrowded. But then, where isn't, nowadays?"

"Overcrowded? I won't have to share a cell?"

"I'm afraid you will, dear. At least for a while."

Joanna licked her lips. She had always been such a private person. Even in her marriages, she had slept alone when sex wasn't involved. My God! When sex wasn't involved! "Can't I . . . well, I'd be willing to pay . . ."

"Hush, dearie. You want to forget that you used to buy everything you wanted. Find your feet, first."

Joanna hunched her shoulders. This can't be happening, she thought. It just can't. I have to wake up some time soon and discover it's all a nightmare.

"You all right, dear?" asked the policewoman.

"My head hurts."

"Try to relax. When you go to prison, you have to take each day as it comes. You start thinking about the future, you'll go bonkers. Same thing if you start thinking about the past. Live each day as it comes, minute by minute."

"For twenty-five years?" Joanna shouted.

The woman sniffed. "Just trying to help, dear. You did kill a man, you know."

Joanna hunched her shoulders and closed her eyes. Live each day, each minute, as it comes. God, she should be driving back to Caribee House, sitting in the back of the Rolls behind Charlie, looking forward to a glass of champagne and a romp with the children . . . would she ever see them again? Right that minute, if she had a knife or a gun or a bottle of poison, she thought she would cheerfully end it all.

Liddleton might only have been just outside London, but the drive took a couple of hours. In the back of the van, Joanna couldn't see out to gain any idea of where they were or where they were going. But at last the van stopped, and she heard voices. Then they drove beneath an archway into a yard surrounded by high walls in which there were small windows. It looked just like every prison film set she had ever seen. But this was real. "Here we are, dearie," said the policewoman, as the doors were opened.

Now the policewomen were replaced by female guards, large, strapping women with jangling keys hanging from their belts. They did not look particularly aggressive, merely frighteningly efficient and cold-spirited. "Joanna Orton," one said, reading from her clipboard. "Murder." She raised her eyes to gaze at Joanna, who was little more than half her size. "Mrs Anstey is waiting to see you. That way."

Joanna glanced at the policewomen, wondering if she should say goodbye, but they had already got back into the Black Maria, and were lighting cigarettes. I'm a non person, she thought. Joanna Orton, murderess. I'm a statistic. She followed the wardress through a door set in the wall, and along a corridor. Another wardress followed. Presumably I'm dangerous, she thought. Murderesses are dangerous.

Around them were the sounds of people; hundreds of people. All women. All criminals. To whose ranks she now belonged. They climbed several flights of stairs, marched along a corridor. Now the sounds were muted, as they were left behind. They reached a door, and the wardress knocked. "Come," a quiet voice said.

The door was opened, and Joanna was ushered into a large office, cosy with book-lined walls. The only chair was behind the desk, and it was occupied by a small, gray-haired, quiet-looking woman who wore her hair in a tight bun. Her face was a trifle pinched, but was not unkind. "Orton, ma'am," said the wardress.

Mrs Anstey leaned back, and gazed at Joanna, who realised that her eyes were colder than they had first appeared. "Trouble," the governor remarked.

"I'm no trouble," Joanna protested.

Mrs Anstey leaned forward again. "You will address me as ma'am, Orton. And you will speak when you are spoken to. Do you understand me?"

"Yes . . . ma'am." Joanna had never addressed anyone as ma'am in her life before.

"And you can take it from me that you are trouble," Mrs Anstey told her. "Looks, grooming . . . oh, trouble." She looked down at a large chart on her desk.

"If possible, I would like a cell to myself," Joanna said. "Ma'am." And then realised she had not actually been addressed.

Mrs Anstey looked up. "You would like? If possible? You have a lot to learn, Orton. Number twenty-seven."

"Twenty-seven, ma'am," said the wardress.

"I will see you again when you've settled in, Orton," Mrs Anstey said. "I'm sure we will have things to discuss."

"She likes you," remarked the wardress, as Joanna was led away. "You could do all right."

"If she likes me," Joanna said, "I'd hate to be someone she dislikes."

"What you want to remember," the wardress told her, "is that in here you're someone everyone will dislike. Just because you're different. Twenty years ago they'd have hanged you. Times change, they do."

"Were you a wardress, twenty years ago?" Joanna asked, innocently.

The wardress stopped, and turned to face her. She made to step back, but found herself against the second woman, who held her arms. "My name is Angie," said the wardress. "You want to remember that. I'm the difference between hell and purgatory in this place. You want to remember that too."

She dug her fingers into the bodice of Joanna's dress and pulled down, very hard. She was a strong woman, and the material split as if made of paper. She kept on tugging until she had reached Joann's groin, exposing petticoat and underclothes. "Oh, dear," Angie said. "Now you've torn your dress. But you won't be needing it again, not for twenty-five years, darling."

Joanna knew nothing but the killing fury she had experienced when Connor had assaulted her. She could not free her arms from the woman holding her, so she kicked with all her strength, slamming her high-heeled shoe into Angie's ankle. Angie yelped with pain and doubled over. With a supreme effort Joanna tore her arms free, and was hit a mind-shattering blow in the kidneys. She gasped and retched, and fell to her own knees, feeling that she was choking with pain. Dimly she heard a whistle, and then she was surrounded by uniformed women, who dragged her to her feet, and half carried her along the corridor, before bundling her through a doorway into a large storeroom, where several more women waited. "What the shit is going on?" one of these asked.

"She's gone berserk," Angie panted.

Joanna straightened as the pain began to wear off, tried to brush hair from her forehead, and only then realised that her wrists had been handcuffed behind her back. "You wouldn't think she was the type," said the woman behind the counter. "Not looking at her."

She came round the counter and fingered the material of Joanna's torn dress. "Nice." She pulled Joanna's head forward, looked at the label inside the collar of the dress. "Harrods, no less. What about the undies?"

"Listen," Angie said, putting her face close to Joanna's. "We're going to release your wrists. You start any more trouble and we'll put you in a straitjacket. You hear me?" Joanna hated herself as tears rolled out from her eyes. She nodded, biting her lip. But she was still aching too much to consider the possibility of being hit again. She could only think, when John Giffard comes to see me . . . "So take them all off," Angie said. "Don't worry, darling; you'll get a receipt."

Joanna stepped out of her dress and her shoes, took off her petticoat and underclothes. "And the watch," said the storekeeper. "And the wedding ring."

Joanna laid them on the counter, terribly aware of the eyes, watching her, seeming to investigate her every nook and cranny without actually touching her. But they were going to touch, sometime during the next twenty-five years, she knew. Some time soon. "Rolex," remarked the storekeeper. "You're a right toff, darling. Height?"

"Five foot six," Joanna whispered.

"Weight?"

"One hundred and twenty pounds."

"That seems about right." She began taking clothes out of the shelves behind her, while Joanna shivered. The room was suddenly chill, and the eyes were still there.

The woman laid two pairs of drawers, two brassieres, and two very plain blue dresses on the counter, together with a pair of trainers. To these she added a toothbrush, a tube of toothpaste, and a pack of sanitary pads. These are all I now own, Joanna thought. "Get dressed," Angie said.

Joanna pulled on the somewhat coarse drawers, added the brassiere, dropped the blue denim dress over her shoulders, thrust her feet into the trainers, stooped to tie the laces. "Now pick up the changes," Angie commanded. There were also two flannel nightgowns – how long was it since she had worn anything in bed? – and two bandannas. "Tie it up," Angie said.

Joanna tied the large square round her hair, gathering it into a mass. "All the wisps," said the storekeeper, and held a mirror for her. "You keep it out of sight at all times. That's the rule."

Joanna didn't really want to look at herself, at the vestiges of make-up left, at her expression . . . She tucked the stray golden wisps beneath the cloth. "Come along," Angie said.

"Mind you keep them clean," recommended the store-keeper.

From the storeroom the corridor led to one of the cell blocks. They entered this on a catwalk, some twenty feet above the floor of the block itself; Joanna was reminded of walking the catwalks above the engine room on board *Caribee Queen*, and again her eyes filled with tears. She heard shouts and whistles, and opened her eyes again, looking down now. There were some twenty women on the floor beneath her, looking up, waving table tennis bats or magazines, cheering and cat-calling. "They like you too," Angie said. She led the way along the catwalk, then on to a more solid corridor, away from the noise beneath them. "Number twenty-seven."

The door stood open, as did all of the cell doors during this recreation period. Joanna stepped inside. There were two bunks, an upper and a lower, again reminiscent of a ship's cabin; there was even a wash basin and an exposed toilet, together with a table and two chairs. That the cell was already occupied was indicated by the book on the table, together with a couple of magazines, the toothbrush and a few other toiletries on the basin surround, the folded flannel nightdress on the lower bunk, and above all, the faint smell of humanity that hung on the air, not offensively, but very noticeably. "Enjoy it while you can," Angie said, enigmatically. "And remember, the watchword in this prison is cleanliness. Nothing upsets the boss so much as lack of personal hygiene. You shower every day, right?"

She left the cell, the other wardress followed. Joanna remained standing in the centre of the cell for several seconds. Her home, for twenty-five years? She went to the window, which was above the table. By climbing on to the table and kneeling there she could see out, but the window looked down on to the prison courtyard, and did nothing to cheer her up.

She heard movement behind her, and turned her head, sharply. Three women had come into the cell. Two of them were older than herself, she could see at a glance, one considerably so. Her face was hard, but not vicious; she was overweight and had straggly gray hair. The other was in her middle-thirties, thin and pinch-faced, her figure totally concealed by the blue dress. The third was hardly more than a girl, Joanna reckoned. She was tall and had a very full figure, with long legs, and a mass of curling brown hair – obvious even beneath the required bandanna. She was the first to speak. "You're Joanna Orton," she said. "We saw you on the telly. I'm Cindy."

She held out her hand, and Joanna squeezed it. Could she possibly have found a friend? "I'm Betty," said the thin-faced woman, and also shook hands.

"I'm Mary," said the older woman. "Get down." Joanna climbed off the table, no longer quite so sure that she had found any friends. "Let's have a look at you," Mary said, and pulled the bandanna from Joanna's head to allow her golden hair to drop to her shoulders.

"I thought we had to wear these at all times," Joanna protested.

"Not in the cell, you don't have to. Nice hair." Mary thrust her fingers into Joanna's hair. "Wait outside."

She was speaking to her two companions. Betty immediately stepped outside to stand in the corridor. Cindy hesitated. "Not so soon, Mary," she begged. "Give her a chance to settle in."

Mary snorted. "So you can have first go, eh? They'll all be after this one."

Joanna looked from one to the other. "Would someone mind telling me what is going on?"

Mary smiled at her; Joanna thought of a large cat surveying a small mouse. "Think of it as an initiation," she said. "I'm just going to find out if you're going to be one of us."

"And suppose I'm not?" Joanna asked.

"Then you won't enjoy your stay here, darling. And if it's going to be for twenty-five years, that's a long time not to enjoy. Right?"

Joanna stared at her, feeling the killing anger beginning

to well up inside her again. "Please don't hurt her," Cindy begged.

She didn't specify to whom she was speaking, and she left the cell to stand beside Betty and ensure Mary had privacy. "You really are a looker," Mary said, sliding her hand down from Joanna's hair to caress her neck. "Strip off, and let me look at the rest of you."

"Bugger off," Joanna told her.

"Listen, you little stuck-up runt, I run this floor, see? People do what I tell them to, or suddenly they ain't good-looking any more. You got it?"

"Then get this," Joanna said, clasping her hands together and swinging the combined fist into Mary's midriff. Mary gasped, and bent double, and still keeping her hands together, as she had been taught by Matilda, Joanna struck her on the nape of the neck. Mary crashed straight down to the floor, her head hitting the concrete with a terrible crack. Betty screamed.

Cindy ran inside to kneel beside the older woman. "Oh, my God," she said. "You've done her."

People crowded the doorway, and were then thrust to left and right by Angie, followed by several other wardresses.

"I am sure you will be pleased to know," said Mrs Anstey, "that Mary Eldridge is not going to die. But she certainly has concussion and a nasty cut. Have you anything to say?"

"She made an obscene advance," Joanna muttered.

"And whenever anyone makes an obscene advance you attempt to kill them, is that it? You have not yet been in my prison for twenty-four hours, and in that time you have assaulted one of my guards, and another inmate. Are you going to claim that Angie also made an obscene advance?"

"Yes," Joanna said stubbornly.

"As I said, Orton, the moment I saw you, trouble. Well, we don't want that kind of trouble here. I was going to give you a spell in solitary in any event, for the attack on Angie. Now this second matter . . . two weeks. Two weeks to allow you to think, Orton, and come up straight. Otherwise you will find it very hard."

Joanna thought she had never heard anything so reassuring in her life. Two weeks in which she didn't have to speak to a soul, or react to a soul, either. Angie grinned as she was marched down the corridor to the punishment block. "Two weeks," she said. "You'll have rubbed yourself raw by the end of it." Joanna looked at her, and Angie flushed, and looked away.

Joanna lay on her bunk and stared at the ceiling. If she played her cards right she could spend the entire next twenty-five years in here. All she had to do was assault someone the moment she got out. That was all she felt like doing, at the moment. Twenty-five years! Two weeks! What difference did it make, really?

"Well, Orton?" Mrs Anstey asked. "How are you feeling?"

"I am feeling fine, ma'am," Joanna said.

"Good. Then may we hope for some co-operation?"

"Yes, ma'am." Because she didn't really want to be left alone for another two weeks. She had never been utterly alone in her life before, and the initial relief of not having to respond, not having to *feel*, had quickly worn off.

"Good," Mrs Anstey said. "Your lawyer was down to see you, last week, but as you were in punishment he could not. He is coming back today. Do try to keep out of trouble until you have spoken with him. Who knows, it might be good news."

"Well, hi," Cindy said. "How's the celebrity?"

"Am I a celebrity?"

"Oh, yes. Everyone's scared about what you might do next."

"You mean no one is going to try to rape me?"

"Chance would be a fine thing."

"But you're all queer. You too?"

Cindy flushed. "It's a matter of, well, you've been here a fortnight. I've been here a year. And I have four to go."

"Lucky you. What did you do?"

"I knifed my boyfriend. I thought he was my boyfriend."

"But he didn't die."

"No, worse luck. But five years . . . my solicitor says I'll be out after three. That's still two years off. So what do you do? I was used to it pretty regular. If a man was dropped in here today I'd lead the rush. But there's no chance of that. So you form . . . relationships." Again she flushed, attractively. "You and I could have a pretty good relationship." She fluttered her eyelashes.

"I'll look forward to that," Joanna said. "But I'm not in the mood for sex right now. With anyone." She still had hopes.

Kept alive by thoughts of revenge. She received, within her first month, a considerable amount of mail.

*Couldn't have happened to a nicer person*, Alicia wrote.

*London won't be the same without you*, Andy Gosling wrote.

*Strange how apparent winners can wind up losers*, Dick wrote.

When I get out of here . . . Joanna thought.

John Giffard smiled, as brightly as he could. "Our grounds are going to be prejudice on the part of the trial judge," he explained. "Leading to mishandling of the case in that much of the evidence he accepted should have been inadmissable, and also to misdirection of the jury. I think it's pretty strong grounds."

"When?" Joanna asked.

"Fifteenth of November."

"But that's four months away!"

"It's as quick as can be."

Her shoulders hunched. "Tell me what's happening outside?"

"Well, Labour is getting the country back to work, gradually. But it's tricky without a real majority. There's talk Wilson will go back to the country later this year to gain more support.

The economic situation is still pretty poor, with the price of oil set to go higher still. They're talking about twenty per cent inflation this year."

"And the company? I'm so out of touch."

"I believe Peter Young and William are coping. At the moment."

"I want to see William. And I want to see Mrs Partridge, and the children."

"You'll have to give me an order of priorities. You're only allowed one visit a week. I suppose the children and Mrs Partridge could be counted as one, but do you really want Helen and Raisul coming here? Seeing you like this?"

"Am I supposed not to see my children for twenty-five years?"

"Of course not, Joanna. I'll arrange it."

"I want Peter to write to me, on a regular basis, at least once a month, to keep me up to date with company business."

Giffard was writing busily. "Will do. Anything else? Matilda?"

"She can come and see me, after the children, and after William. What about Charlie and Cummings?"

"The trial comes up next month. Not for Cummings. The charges against him have been dropped. But I suspect Charlie is for it."

"That's very unfair."

"If you are acquitted on appeal, or even if your sentence is reduced, we'll be able to do something about him. In any event, I imagine his sentence will be no more than half yours, if that."

Joanna reached across the table to grasp his hand. "What did you say?"

He looked embarrassed. "It may be just a reduction. You see, there can be no argument about the fact that you caused Sean Connor's death. The only argument is about what was in your mind when you did it, and whether or not Crowther influenced the jury into believing you had planned it."

"So whatever happens, I'm still going to be stuck in here for years," Joanna said thoughtfully.

"Not so many years, perhaps. But it's important that you behave yourself." She raised her head, frowning. Giffard flushed. "I've been told about the fights and the solitary. You really want to avoid those, if you want to get out of here at the earliest possible moment. Parole boards take things like fighting very seriously."

"Parole boards," she muttered. She was going to be judged by a bunch of stuffy twits who wouldn't know the meaning of life if it got up and bit them in the leg.

"But that's some time in the future," Giffard said. "You have time to make up for what has happened by exemplary behaviour from here on in."

"Exemplary behaviour meaning I accept being raped, is that it?"

"You're not serious?"

"Listen, there are over two hundred women in this dump, with not a man in sight. What do you suppose they do for kicks?"

"Good lord. I'll have a word with the governor."

"I wouldn't waste your time. I suspect she needs her kicks as much as anyone. Listen, John – just get me out of here. I don't care how you do it, but get me out!"

"Letter for you," Angie announced. Joanna had been lying on her bunk – the upper bunk as Cindy, for all her youth, was the senior inmate at the moment – sat up and swung her legs over. Cindy took the letter and passed it up. "Overseas," Angie remarked.

"This has been opened," Joanna protested.

"All mail addressed to inmates is opened, darling," Angie pointed out and closed the door.

Joanna frowned at the envelope; she had supposed it would be from Peter Young. But it was postmarked Vancouver, Canada. She took out the pages inside. The handwriting was neat and educated. '*We have never met, but I followed your trial with interest. As I should. Sean Connor was my son.*'

"Jesus," she muttered.

Cindy was on her feet, leaning against the upper bunk. "Bad news?"

She was genuinely solicitous. She was, in fact, a very nice girl, Joanna had discovered, even if she had nearly killed her lover in a fit of jealousy; her clever lawyer had got the sentence reduced on the grounds of provocation. It all seemed a matter of luck. Now she was enjoying having the famous businesswoman-cum-murderess Joanna Orton as her cellmate. She enjoyed it even more during recreation; although she had made to move to cement her position, Joanna had taken over from Mary as boss of the block, and everyone wanted to be seen speaking with her, but Cindy was the one who was closest. That she wanted to be more than just friends was fairly obvious, but like everyone else in the cell block she was afraid of Joanna's reaction, which could be so violent, and she was also very patient. She reckoned that by providing unfailing support while Joanna remained so much on edge, they would have to get together some time.

"A hate letter," Joanna said, and gave it to her. "You read it. I'm not in the mood for that kind of muck."

Cindy perused the sheet of paper. "You have it wrong." She read:

> "'*Sean was the product of a liaison which I bitterly regretted. I brought him up as my own, but he proved so difficult I was happy to see him go out on his own, even when he took his mother's name. I continued to finance him, but we did not see each other over the last few years of his life. I wish you to know that you have my deepest sympathy, as I have no doubt that every claim you made in court was true. My son was a vicious monster. I tried to be in touch with you before the trial to ask if I could be of any assistance to*

*you, but you declined to take my call. I cannot blame you for that. Now, I cannot of course do anything to help you while you are in prison. I have been informed that as I am neither a relative nor a member of your legal team I am not even allowed to visit you. But I shall be watching over you with great interest, and if you need any assistance when you are released, I hope and believe you will contact me. With every good wish. Michael Johannsson.*'

"Sounds a really decent guy."

"Sounds a right crank, you mean," Joanna said. "We don't even know if he really was Sean's father. In any event, some hick from a Canadian town . . ."

"Vancouver," Cindy said. "That's a big city."

"I still don't see how he's supposed to help me," Joanna said.

"What shall I do with the letter?"

"Flush it."

As the summer wore on, her tension grew. William's visits were an embarrassment. He avoided meeting her gaze, and muttered about how things really were bad and getting worse. "I'm not sure I can cope," he admitted.

"Just hang in there," Joanna told him. "I'll be back in charge by Christmas." If only she could believe that. But she had to, or she would go stark raving mad. Matilda's visits were even more of an embarrassment, as she was obviously mortified by having to come to the jail at all. Peter Young's letters did nothing to dispel the gloom, but he had always been a pessimist.

Only the children lifted her spirits, but it was very briefly. They were doing their best to grasp the fact that somehow their beloved mother had turned into a wicked woman, who had to be locked up for the good of everyone who wasn't locked up, but they still apparently assumed she would be coming home any day, as they were told by Mrs Partridge. Mrs Partridge herself burst into tears every time she saw her mistress. But the days ticked by, the cruel combination of boredom and tension only slightly relieved by the October election, which again returned Labour with a sufficient majority to govern. But only November mattered.

As the appeal revolved around legal arguments, Joanna was not required to go to court on the first day. When the time came for the justices to hand down their decision, however, she was taken up to London. Giffard and Norma had brought her some of her own clothes to wear, and Norma herself did her hair was well as she was able. Wearing a good frock and some jewellery, stockings and high-heeled shoes, and wrapped in her mink, Joanna suddenly felt like a million dollars again. The only discordant note were the two wardresses seated to either side of her. But to be driving through London, seeing the shops and the people, being again part of the real world, was a delight; the past six months need never have been. She felt so good she even smiled at the justices, three of them, seated in a row facing her as she sat in a chair in the centre of the room. They did not smile back.

The judgement was very long, detailed and involved. Joanna kept drifting off and not properly listening to what was said by the Lord Chief Justice. She did gather, however, that the court of appeal felt that Lord Crowther might have allowed his prejudice against the accused to influence his directions to the jury. On the down side, they felt he had not been wrong to allow aspects of her earlier life to be given in evidence. "The case rested almost entirely upon the accused's motives for killing Sean Connor," concluded the Lord Chief Justice, "and her motives could only be understood by an understanding both of her character, and of the events that led up to that fateful night. It is however, the opinion of this court that the sentence imposed by Lord Crowther was unreasonably severe, and it is our intention to reduce the term."

Joanna sighed, audibly; she had been holding her breath. The entire courtroom was shrouded in a mist of tears. "The term of imprisonment will, accordingly, be reduced from twenty-five years, to twenty," said the Lord Chief Justice.

Joanna could hardly see the man, or his colleagues, because of the tears, which were now flowing very fast. But these were tears of anger. She wanted to shout abuse at them. She wanted to pick up the chair and hurl it at them. She felt the killing rage she had known when assaulted by Mary, or by Connor himself. How dare you three old fuddy-duddies lock me up for twenty years? she wanted to scream. I have worked so hard, sometimes in great danger, to get where I am, and you can take it all away from me with a word and a stroke of the pen. Twenty years! "That is very disappointing," John Giffard said.

Joanna stared at him. "*Disappointing*?"

"We can go to the Lords, of course. But I'm afraid it would get us nowhere. I suppose you are paying the price of notoriety. Because you're so good-looking, so confident, so successful, and because you've lived such a . . ." he hesitated, "a full life, people just feel you *have* to be guilty."

"I thought judges weren't supposed to feel," Joanna said, "just interpret the law."

"They're human." He held her hand. "I'm terribly sorry it had to turn out like this, Joanna. But, twenty years . . . you'll be out in eight, if you do nothing stupid."

She withdrew her hand.

Cindy could tell at a glance that the appeal had not been successful. She sat on her bunk, hands dangling between her knees, and watched Joanna use the loo. Gone were the high heels and the fur coat, the stockings and the expensive lingerie. Gone forever, perhaps. Would she ever want to wear them again?

"They're a set of bastards," Cindy said. Joanna sat at the table. "Coffee?" Cindy asked, brightly, getting up. Joanna looked at her, and she sat down again. "You have to—"

"Just don't say it," Joanna said. "Say it, and I'll break your neck."

It really was quite unreasonable to take against Cindy, Joanna knew. The girl was only trying to be helpful. But she was part of the world, and Joanna hated the entire world at that moment. For the next week she hardly spoke to a soul, and ate sparingly. Cindy was clearly worried, but she kept her thoughts to herself.

Then she was summoned to the interview room, ten days after the appeal, to find both Giffard and William waiting for her. For just a moment her spirits soared. Something good must have happened. But a look at their faces convinced her that it hadn't. "How're things today?" Giffard asked.

Joanna had never seen William looking so miserable. "Tell me," she said.

"We had a shareholders' meeting, three days ago," William said.

"The week after the appeal. They had been waiting for that. "And?"

"The fact is, Jo, it simply isn't going to work. I mean . . . well . . ." he looked hopefully at Giffard.

"Things are in such a state of flux it needs a great deal of positive thinking, and positive action," Giffard said.

"William has full power of attorney," Joanna said. "Can't he be positive?"

"I'm afraid it isn't as simple as that," Giffard said. "Gosling is making a formal application to the high court to have you removed from the position of Chairman and Managing Director."

"We have an agreement."

"Which he claims is invalid in the case of a convicted criminal."

"You'll fight it."

"I shall oppose it, certainly. But my information is that the application will be granted."

William looked about to burst into tears. Perhaps she was

near to tears herself. But she was far more angry than tearful. "What will happen if he wins?"

Giffard sighed. "He will take over the company to do with as he sees best."

"You mean he will sell out to Petherick."

"I'm afraid that is a possibility."

"The bastard."

"I'm afraid there is more," Giffard said. "Once you cease to be Chairman and Managing Director, you lose control of everything. That is, Caribee House, the London flat, the car . . ."

"My children!"

"Oh, there's nothing to worry about there. No one can take them away from you."

"I meant, where are they going to live?"

"We'll find somewhere," William said. "I mean to say, you'll still be a wealthy woman, Jo, owning twenty-eight per cent of the company shares . . ."

Joanna looked at Giffard. His face was red. "One needs to be as optimistic as one can. The shares really have gone on a slide since your conviction. They're just on two at the moment, but they may go lower. This is what is going to influence the High Court judgement."

"Apply to have trading stopped until after the judgement."

"We shall try, of course."

Two pounds a share, she thought. Once she had been worth six million pounds. Now it was just on half a million, and dropping. I am ruined, she thought. My family is ruined. And my company is ruined. All gone. As a result of a moment's madness.

"We'll sort something out, sis," William said. "Really we will."

Joanna looked at him, and he flushed.

Giffard gathered up his papers and put them into his briefcase. "We must be going. I really am sorry about this, Joanna."

"You knew all along it was going to happen," Joanna

said. "Oh, get out. Both of you." She pointed at William. "And take care of my children." The room was empty, save for the wardress. And at last she could allow herself to weep.

# Part Three

# Out of the Pit

'Life may change, but it may fly not;
Hope may vanish, but can die not;
Truth be veiled, but still it burneth;
Love repulsed, – but it returneth!

Percy Bysshe Shelley

# Chapter Nine

# The Proposal

"Recreation," Cindy said. "Let's play table tennis." Joanna did not reply. Cindy scratched her head. Joanna not speaking was nothing new. She very seldom spoke. She very seldom did anything, except lie on her bunk and stare at the ceiling. Cindy thought she might be going quietly mad.

Outwardly, she was a model prisoner after her uneasy start. She did exactly what she was told to do by the guards. She went to the showers, she took her exercise, but in a zombie-like state, as if she had no idea who was around her or even where she was. And once in the cell she became totally withdrawn. It was eerie, and a little frightening. Even the other inmates were aware of it. None of them would dare interfere with her after the beating she had inflicted on Mary, but they were well aware that she was not one of them.

"Gives me the creeps, she does," Betty said.

"I reckon she'll top herself one of these days," Carrie suggested.

"In my cell?" Cindy cried in alarm.

"You don't want to leave her alone."

Cindy had been so terrified she had run up the stairs; Joanna had, as usual, refused to join them in the recreation area. But Joanna continued to lie on her bunk and stare into space.

Cindy sighed, and sat at the table. She was just as afraid of her cellmate as was everyone else in the block. But she had also grown to like her, and sympathise with her. To have had so much – in the terms of Cindy's life and background to have had *everything* – and then have it all ripped away, and be left with four walls and a single change of clothing . . . she felt something had to be done to bring her back to the real world. But to risk arousing that searing temper . . .

Cindy was not the only one who was concerned. A few days later she was called into the office, where the guard was dismissed. This was not unusual. Mrs Anstey was fond of têtes-à-tête; the other girls called them tits-à-tit. Mrs Anstey was a closet lesbian, but she was also the Boss and there were always a dozen reasons she could provide for looking, touching, enjoying, providing the inmate was attractive enough. Cindy had herself had to endure an hour's 'physical examination' when she had first come to Liddleshall. But she instinctively knew that she had not today been summoned to satisfy any of Mrs Anstey's suppressed desires. "How is Orton?" Mrs Anstey demanded.

"She just lies there. She doesn't speak."

"But she eats?"

"Oh, yes, ma'am. She has a good appetite."

"Therefore her problem is entirely mental. She's applied for none of the jobs."

"No, ma'am."

"She has to have one. What do you suppose would suit her best? Garden or library?"

"She's very well-educated. She'd enjoy the library. I shouldn't think she's ever worked in a garden in her life, going by her hands. But the fresh air might be better for her."

"Hm. What's she like as a cellmate?"

"Most of the time I don't know she's there."

"But you like her," Mrs Anstey suggested.

"Oh, yes," Cindy said enthusiastically. "She's so . . . so elegant. Even without make-up or proper clothes. Just elegant."

"Yes," Mrs Anstey said thoughtfully. "Have you, ah . . ."

"Good lord, no," Cindy said. "You saw what happened to Mary, ma'am."

"I did indeed. But that was a symptom at her despair at being in here at all. I think she has now surrounded herself by a cocoon, meant to resist the world in which she finds herself, until she can escape."

"Escape, ma'am?" Cindy positively squeaked.

"I do not mean physically escape from Liddleton, silly girl. I hope she has more sense than ever to attempt that. I should punish something like that most severely, and anyone who attempted to assist her." She glared at Cindy. "I meant ultimate release. But she cannot remain inside that cocoon for what may well be ten years or more. She would never re-emerge. I wish you to break into her mind, Cindy. Release her mind. And her body, of course."

"She'd scrag me if I laid a finger on her," Cindy muttered.

Mrs Anstey was flicking through some papers on her desk. "Let me see. You are due to come before the parole board in twenty-two month's time, Cindy. Should I feel that I could ask for, and obtain, your full co-operation in certain matters of internal discipline, I have an idea I could have that date brought forward by six months. Think of that. Just over a year. Wouldn't you like to be out of here in just over a year?"

Cindy licked her lips. "I'll never be paroled if I'm put in solitary for fighting."

Mrs Anstey raised her head and gazed at her. "I give you my word, Cindy, that should there be a fight in your cell, no blame whatsoever will be attached to you. Nor will you be punished in any way, and no entry will be made upon your record, the record that will be submitted to the parole board."

Cindy swallowed, and Mrs Anstey smiled.

"However, obviously it would be best if there was no fight. Handle the matter any way you like. Take your time. But not too much time. I want that cocoon removed."

"Do *you* like Orton, ma'am?" Cindy asked, as innocently as she could.

"Come here," Mrs Anstey said.

Cindy bit her lip, but stepped round the desk to stand next to the governor's chair. Mrs Anstey rested her hand on Cindy's leg, then moved it up, under the skirt, up the back of her thigh, to reach her knickers. Cindy found she was holding her breath; the trouble with Mrs Anstey was that one never knew what she was going to do next. Then she suddenly squeezed. However little in actual size, she was a very strong woman. Cindy gasped with the pain of it, and her mouth sagged open, remaining open as Mrs Anstey released her.

"I look forward to liking Orton, Cindy," Mrs Anstey said. "When her cocoon has been removed. But do not tell her I said so."

"Look at that," Cindy said. "That woman is an absolute thug." The cell door had clanged behind her, and now she bent over, hoisting her dress so that Joanna could see the mark.

For a moment it did not appear as though Joanna was going to react at all. Then the bunk creaked as she rolled over. "Shit," she commented. "Who did that?"

"Old Anstey."

"Can she do that? Can't you complain?"

"Who'm I to complain to?" Cindy asked. "Mrs Anstey?"

"Aren't there visitors? Inpectors?"

"Sure there are. And she knows when they're coming. Not for another month. What am I going to have to show them by then?" She sat down, and got up again immediately, to lie on her bunk, on her face. "All we can do is grin and bear it." She sighed. "It's better when we're buddies. When you have a buddy. Everyone needs a buddy."

Joanna hung her head over the bunk to look at her. "You'd like us to be lovers, right?"

"Well . . ." Cindy flushed. "Buddies. And if we got physical, well, why not? We both have feelings."

"You'd have to show me," Joanna said.

Cindy couldn't believe her ears. Was it actually going to

be this easy? But . . . she frowned. "You never been with a woman? Not even when you were a girl?"

Joanna gave a savage smile. "I was always kind of busy, when I was a girl. Going with men."

To have sex with Cindy was actually to defy the world. Or so Joanna told herself. The world had gathered itself into one immense fist, and smashed that first into her face, sent her reeling out of its orbit into this specially man-made hell. Of course the world, all of those people who had spent the last, thirteen years reading about Joanna Edge, the city whizz-kid, or Joanna the Princess Hasim, the society beauty, or Joanna Orton, the city's most glamorous and successful widow, had also spent their time building up a mountain of envy, perhaps lust, certainly in many cases hatred. More importantly, they had taken refuge in the old Anglo-Saxon streak of puritanism, which still persisted whatever the breakdown in moral values during the swinging sixties. Joanna Orton had stuck out her chin time and again, and anyone who had tried to hit it either missed or fell flat on their faces. Ergo, Joanna Orton must one day fall flat on her own face, and then everyone could have a good laugh. She could almost hear them.

But there was no doubt that Cindy was right, and one simply had to share. Where one shared so little physical space, and so much of everything else, sex had to come into it. And she wanted, and needed, sex as much as anyone. At one level, therefore, life became almost tolerable. The level was when one was actually *doing*. Joanna was given a job in the prison garden, where Cindy also worked. Here was another exercise in full circles, she thought, remembering how, when her mother had come to live with her at Caribee House following Howard's death, she had allowed her to take over the huge garden – with the aid of several gardeners, of course – because Mums had liked gardening and Joanna had not known one plant from another.

Mums had been happy in that garden, perhaps for the first time since her husband's murder. And actually Joanna discovered that she too could be happy in the garden, even as she watched her beautifully manicured nails and her soft white hands become discoloured, and in the case of the nails, cracked and broken.

"Well, at least you'll be able to get a job when you leave," Cindy joked, and then gulped, as she saw the expression in Joanna's eyes. Because the hate, the desire for revenge on all those who had done her down, was still there.

She would have liked to shut out the outside world altogether. But that was not possible. The children's visits were the most traumatic moments of the week. Joanna desperately wanted to see her children, but at the same time she didn't want them to see her, to see her broken fingernails, to pick out the gray strands in her hair, because these were gathering, to see her without her make-up and her mink, her aura of total authority. To see the real Joanna Orton, perhaps.

But seeing them was traumatic enough. William had managed to rescue something from the crash, and they weren't destitute, but they certainly weren't as well off as they had been, and she quickly spotted when Raisul's blazer was beginning to look brassy and Helen's dress had obviously been darned. As for where they were living . . . "It's very small," Helen confessed.

Joanna looked at Mrs Partridge. "Well, madam, it's smaller than Caribee House, to be sure," Mrs Partridge said. "But Mr William said it was all we could afford."

At least the children looked healthy and well-nourished. "I do wish you'd come home, Mother," Raisul said. "I miss you quite a lot."

Out of the mouths of babes and sucklings, Joanna thought. "I'll be home as soon as I can," she promised. "But I'm rather tied up here at the moment."

She still possessed a macabre sense of humour.

Businesswise, things were even more traumatic, seen from a personal point of view. The Labour administration seemed totally unable to control inflation, which had soared past twenty per cent during the great oil crisis and had not dropped far below it since. Shipping costs had soared too, but that was no concern of hers, save that it made thoughts of ever getting back into business, the only business she knew, more difficult than ever. The general air of depression was accentuated by the share plunge following the collapse of Burma Oil early in the new year, and in the spring unemployment shot past the million mark for the first time since the end of the War. Inflation was now twenty-two per cent. She received one letter from Peter Young, and one from Harriet. Both had been made redundant by the Petherick takeover, and while Harriet had quickly found another secretarial job, Peter was very gloomy about his prospects. He was fifty-five and had spent almost all his working life at Caribee Shipping. Matilda did not visit her at all, or write, but she gathered from William than Billy had found himself a job, albeit at nowhere near the level he had known at Caribee. William himself had also managed to find a job, but he too had had to accept a lower status, both in position and pay.

Dick Orton had disappeared following the decree nisi. Charlie was in gaol, like her, although his was a comparatively brief, three-year sentence. And poor old Cummings had died, some said of a broken heart. Something else to be avenged.

John Giffard wrote to her from time to time, always encouraging, but as nothing ever evolved in the direction of any other appeals she soon ceased to feel the least excitement when she saw one of his envelopes. Her past life was dwindling to nothing. As that policewoman had said on her very first day, only today mattered. And the day she got out, and could begin her revenge.

Today was cleaning the cell, showering, gardening, recreation, exercise, meal, lock-up, gardening, showering, recreation, meal time, lock-up. It was an unfailing, unceasing routine, varied only on visiting day, when the second gardening period was replaced by a chat with the outside world, and on Sundays, when the first gardening period was replaced by church parade.

It was so unchanging an existence that keeping track of the days, much less the weeks and the months, and then the years, became very difficult. But for the use of the library she thought she would have gone mad. Joanna had always considered herself a very well-read person; now she discovered there were lots of authors, and lots of subjects, she had never touched, simply because she had been too busy. Now she found them a boon. Was she ever going to be able to use her mind, or her mental attitudes, again?

She depended very heavily on Cindy, who kept a very careful tally of the days and weeks and months. In many ways the younger woman, and Cindy was seven years her junior, was like a mother to her. Cindy had grown up in poverty, conditioned by the sixties, during which she had been a young teenager, enjoying the current philosophy of it you can get it, grab it, then spend it. She had been remanded twice, given two suspended sentences, and had actually spent six months in prison before the near fatal argument with her boyfriend. He had apparently been a petty thief and occasional pimp, and Joanna felt that if Cindy hadn't stabbed him, someone else would probably have done so eventually.

But that background meant that Cindy was well able to take care of herself, with the necessary caveat that she also understood when the odds were too heavy and she simply had to submit and hope to get away as lightly as possible. As she was an extremely pretty girl, with an impish sense of humour, she had been drawn into Mary Eldridge's orbit immediately on entering the cell block. This she had accepted as being a force too powerful to resist, just as she had accepted without protest the occasional summons to the Office, and the occasional hazing by the guards.

But she had not enjoyed any of it, and to have unearthed a real-life heroine of her own was, to her, paradise. She knew that the secret of Joanna's success was not physical; Joanna was only five-foot-six inches tall and she was a slender woman. It lay in the mind. Joanna dominated those about her simply because of the intensity of her personality. Any of the other inmates, and certainly more than one of them acting together, could have taken her apart. But they were all afraid of what she might do while being taken apart, or even more, after they had finished. Joanna was consumed with passion – and more than half of the time that passion was hatred, anger, an overwhelming desire to hurt. She had nothing to lose. Because she had already lost everything, and now she had only twenty years within these walls to look at.

"Don't you ever look back, and think, Christ, if it could have been different?" Cindy asked, as they lay together in her bunk after lights out.

"Sometimes," Joanna said. "And then I think, could it ever have been different?"

"If you hadn't jumped on that Connor's guts . . ."

"It had to happen," Joanna said. "That's how I figure it. The way I was, the way I thought I could do anything, it had to happen. Connor was just in the wrong place at the wrong time. His name could have been Smith."

"Don't tell me you're feeling sorry for him?"

"Not in the least. Because he wasn't *there*. You follow me?"

"You mean, it was some kind of karma."

"I mean, we are what we are. Everything else is what we see. *We* see. Not what they see."

"You mean I don't exist. I'm just a figment of your imagination."

"And I'm just a figment of yours."

Cindy gave a little shiver, and held her close. "That's philosophy. I'm not into that. What about his old man? In Canada." Another letter had arrived that day.

"He gives me the creeps," Joanna said.

Gradually the cell became filled with a growing sense of excitement, of anticipation, and of fear. Joanna didn't want to think about it. Apparently she had been here for two years. Two years! It seemed like two minutes, sometimes. Save when she looked at the children.

"She's menstruating," Mrs Partridge said in a stage whisper that might have been heard outside the walls. Joanna reached across the table to squeeze her daughter's hands.

"It's no big thing, really," Helen said.

Then, on the day of Cindy's parole hearing, it was a case of being alone, waiting. And then exploding. "Yes!" Cindy shouted, returning after the interview. "They're going for it." She hadn't been inside three years!

"Listen," she said, holding Joanna's hands. "I'm here because I kept cool. That's what you have to do. Keep cool, and do what the Boss tells you, and it'll happen."

Three out of five equals twelve out of twenty, Joanna thought. And Cindy didn't have a single black mark against her. Not a day in solitary. "Listen," Cindy said. "When I'm out, anything I can do, you name it. You want me to go see your kids, just say so." Joanna bit her lip. Cindy sighed. "Still a cut above the rest of us, eh? You don't want me showing up and upsetting what's left of their lives. I can't blame you. Well, the best of luck."

Joanna found herself in the Office. "I hope," Mrs Anstey said, "that you have learned something, Joanna, from Cindy. There was a young woman, from entirely the wrong side of the tracks, who got herself into a very similar situation."

"Except that she got five years, and I got twenty," Joanna pointed out.

Mrs Anstey regarded her for some moments. "She didn't actually kill anyone, and she pleaded guilty," she said at last. "That always helps. She also behaved herself when she was in here. That was greatly to her advantage."

"You mean she submitted to rape and mistreatment," Joanna said.

Mrs Anstey sighed. "You simply have to get over these antagonisms if you are going to prosper here, Joanna."

"Is it possible, to prosper here?" Joanna asked.

"If you wish to do so, certainly. I have left you very much to yourself over the past couple of years, Joanna. This was because I felt you would need a longer period than was usual to settle in here. And I think I was correct in that judgement. I told Cindy to look after you, and I think she has done a very good job. But that has been a probationary period, so to speak. Now Cindy is gone, you have to consider the next few years. First, we have to consider your new cellmate."

"I'd rather be left alone," Joanna said.

"I'm sure. But that is simply not possible. Then we need to consider your job. Do you enjoy working in the garden?"

Joanna shrugged. "Not really."

"What would you prefer to do?"

Joanna frowned at her, while nervous bells began to ring in her ears; this woman was actually being kind to her? "I'd like to work in the library."

"Of course. An ideal job for someone of your intellectual abilities." Mrs Anstey flicked some papers on her desk. "Unfortunately, all the library jobs are held. For the next couple of years, at least. We shall have to find you something else to do, that you might find amenable, until one of those jobs becomes vacant." Another flick of the papers. "I think I have it. My personal secretary leaves next month. Would you like her job?"

Joanna raised her head. "Doing what?"

"Principally filing and attending to my diary. It is a job that requires a good deal of initiative, and some intellectual capability. It also carries a great number of privileges. One which I am sure you would appreciate is a cell of your own."

"I don't think you have finished," Joanna said.

"We would have to work fairly closely together," Mrs Anstey said.

"I thought that might be the case," Joanna agreed.

"Would you enjoy that?" Mrs Anstey's cheeks were pink.

"No," Joanna said.

"Oh, come now, Joanna, don't you think I know everything that goes on in my jail? You and Cindy were lovers. Don't you think I know that?"

"Yes," Joanna said. "I think we did become lovers. I was, am, still very fond of her."

"And who do you think told her to become your lover? How do you think she got out of here so quickly?"

Joanna stared at her. "I didn't know that. I'm very sorry."

"Why should you be sorry?"

"Because I thought I had at last found a genuine human being."

"They don't exist, not in prison," Mrs Anstey told her. "In here you do what you are told, or you are punished. Cindy did what she was told, and she made you happy, for a while. Did she not?"

"Yes," Joanna said. "She made me happy, for a while."

"That's all that matters, in prison. Now, I am proposing to make you happy for as long as I can. Which will be as short a time as I can, if you follow me. There is no prospect of your appearing before a parole board for eight years after your sentence was confirmed, that is another five years from now. However, my recommendations carry a great deal of weight. I can save you perhaps a year, by having your hearing brought forward in front of others. And I can make those five or, hopefully, four years, very easy for you. Would you not like that?"

"Yes," Joanna said. "I would like that."

"Good. Well, then, as soon as Marian gets her parole, which should be in about a month, I will have you regraded as my secretary, and you will move into Marian's cell."

"And you will come and sleep with me every night," Joanna said.

Mrs Anstey raised her eyebrows. "Why, no, my dear. You will come and sleep with me, whenever I wish you to." She smiled. "My bed is far more comfortable than any prison bunk."

"I will see you damned first," Joanna said.

Mrs Anstey leaned back in her chair. "I'm not sure I understand you. You and Cindy . . ."

"Cindy and I had something going," Joanna said. "We liked each other, and maybe we did get to love each other. We *loved*. I don't suppose you can understand that. We loved. I'm not a whore, about to jump from one bed into another for the sake of a kiss and a cuddle and a hand between the legs. Not even to get a year off my sentence."

Mrs Anstey glared at her. "You are a stupid woman, Joanna Orton. And an arrogant bitch. I would have thought you'd have learned to come to terms with life by now."

"Not your terms, ma'am."

They held each other's gaze for several seconds, then Mrs Anstey suddenly swept her hand across her desk, scattering papers, pens, paperclips, files, in every direction. At the same time she leapt to her feet, leaned across the desk, seized Joanna by the bodice and the headscarf, and jerked her forward. Taken by surprise, Joanna thudded into the desk with a force that winded her. Her knees gave way and she fell down the outside of the desk, jarring her chin.

Mrs Anstey had released her, and now fell backwards, with a deliberate force that sent her chair also tumbling over. Then she regained her feet, pressing her bell. Joanna held on to the desk and pulled herself up, gasping, stroking her chin where it was sore from the blow. And behind her the door burst open and several guards ran in, headed by Angie. "She attacked me," Mrs Anstey shouted. "The bitch attacked me."

Joanna gasped, and turned to face them, to have her arms seized and pulled behind her back, and handcuffs affixed to her wrists. She panted with desperate anger, and kicked at her, had her legs swept from beneath her so that she struck the floor with a thump, and was again winded. "Don't break anything,"

Mrs Anstey warned, getting up and pushing hair from her eyes. "I don't want anything to show."

Angie grinned. "Bruises won't show more than a week. Eh, Joanna?"

Joanna managed to sit up painfully, and Angie put her foot between her breasts and pushed her flat again. "Not in here," Mrs Anstey said. "Is there anyone in solitary?"

"Not at the moment, ma'am."

"Well, that's where she's going anyway. Take her along there."

Joanna got her breath back, and now she screamed, as loudly as she could. "Can't have that," Angie said, kneeling beside her head, rolling up a handkerchief and stuffing it into her mouth. My God, Joanna thought. This can't be happening. Not to me! "Up," Angie said, holding her shoulders and dragging her to her feet, now assisted by two of the other women. "You know what I think, ma'am," Angie said. "A good old-fashioned thrashing. That's what she needs."

"No," Mrs Anstey said. "She'll have to be examined by Dr Prinney, soon enough. There can't be any marks. Put her in a straitjacket. She's hysterical. We have to let the fit pass. Right?"

"Right, ma'am." Angie grinned, and jerked her head. Joanna was dragged out of the office by the four women. She tried to kick again and again had her legs swept from under her, so that she was frog-marched the next few feet. "You going to walk?" Angie asked. "Because we might just drop you."

She was holding Joanna's right thigh, under her dress, fingers tightening and relaxing, moving to and fro. That was almost worse than the prospect of being dropped, face down, on to the stone floor; but her hands were still handcuffed behind her back, and she knew she would bruise her face terribly. "Scream, and I'll shove this stick right up your ass," Angie told her. "Now, you walking?"

She pulled the handkerchief from Joanna's mouth.

"I'll walk," Joanna panted.

"Now you're showing a little sense," Angie said.

"Hm," Dr Prinney commented. "Hm."

He was a small, precise man in his forties, who, if he enjoyed having charge of the bodies of more than a hundred women, some of whom were quite attractive, and one, at least, now stretched out before him, was quite beautiful, never revealed the slightest emotion.

"You really are quite fit, Orton."

"Do you know what they did to me?"

"I have received a report. You were in a straitjacket for two days. I'm afraid that was inevitable, after you went berserk and attacked the Governor."

"I did not attack the Governor," Joanna insisted. "She attacked me."

"I would keep your voice down, if I were you," Prinney said. "I'm afraid I find such wild accusations quite impossible to believe. You say you were beaten? That is absurd, in an English prison. There is not a mark on your body."

"They were careful not to leave marks."

"Orton," Prinney said severely, "I am not going to keep you in this hospital, because there is nothing at all wrong with you, physically. You could do with a little more weight, but that is up to you; the food is available, all you have to do is eat it. Now, you are leaving here within the hour. If you keep your mouth shut and behave yourself, you will go back to your cell and the company of your, ah, fellow convicts. If you persist in throwing out wild and unsubstantiated accusations, I am going to have to send you to the psychiatric ward, and you may not find that as pleasant. It's entirely up to you."

"And I suppose all of this is going to go on my record? Even if it is a pack of lies."

"I'm afraid it is already on your record, Orton."

So, once again she had to surrender, to suppress the boiling anger that kept threatening to overwhelm her, to drive her into some fresh act of violent defiance, which would put back her release. Survival was the name of the game. No matter what was done to her, or what she had to accept. Actually, this second explosion made her life far more acceptable than before. Mrs Anstey had apparently got the message, and Joanna had a sneaking feeling that Dr Prinney might also have had a word with her. After all, Joanna Orton had once been an important and respected figure; while she was in prison it might be possible to suggest to her that no one was going to believe anything she said anyway, and that she would be making life much worse for herself. But once she got out . . .

The plot, on the part of the guards and the Governor, became to ignore her and let her get on with it. Because, hopefully, once she got out she would be a forgotten, irrelevant figure. While in the eyes of the inmates, she was even more the heroine, to be revered rather than ignored. She might deny that it ever happened, but it was accepted that she had attacked the Boss. After having attacked Mary Eldridge! She had become a legend in her own lifetime, in prison no less than she had once been in the business world.

Her new cellmate, Belinda, was a handsome if raw-boned young woman in for manslaughter. She found the prospect of several years behind bars just as unacceptable as had Joanna, and needed a good deal of comforting and reassurance. Within a few months she was Joanna's abject slave, and as she was large, and had been convicted for kicking a rival in love to death after having knocked her down, she equally was someone the other inmates preferred to please than to pester. While she wanted only to please Joanna, not only because of her reputation, but because she recognised the intellectual superiority of her cellmate.

But for Joanna the hell into which she had stumbled grew ever more inescapable as the seventies reached their end. According to William, Petherick was keeping his head above water, although with inflation well into double figures, and the country beleaguered by strikes as the steadily weakening Labour administration failed to get to grips with any of the real problems, survival in business was just as grim a task as survival in prison. When in 1979 the Conservatives won back power after six years, everyone was looking for an upturn in business affairs, but for the moment things only seemed to get worse. Not, Joanna thought bitterly, than any of it mattered to her!

William himself was apparently doing quite well at his new job, and he seemed content enough in his marriage, although as Norma had never become a mother Joanna had to suppose that his problem was a residue of that bullet that had so nearly killed him all those years ago. But Billy had lost his job again, and William said that he and Tilly were having a difficult time.

He had no news of Peter Young, but when she asked if John Giffard would visit her, he pulled a face. "Giffard is dead."

"Eh?" Joanna could not believe her ears.

"He had a heart attack."

"Oh, poor John!" She had never been quite sure how old he was, but as he had been Howard's lawyer before she had even come on the scene he had to be at least twenty years older than herself. Still, a heart attack . . . "Would you like me to get one of his partners?"

Joanna considered. She had been so sure that Giffard would believe what she had to tell him, that he might be able to get back at Mrs Anstey in some way, but she knew none of his partners, except for one. "There was a woman," she said. "Jeanette Corder. Perhaps I could see her."

"I'll arrange it," William promised.

Her own investments were a source of concern. What little capital William had been able to rescue for her from the wreck of Caribee Shipping barely provided the income for the upkeep of Mrs Partridge and the children. The following week they should have visited her. But Mrs Partridge came alone. "What's happened?" Joanna's voice was sharp.

"Well, madam, I thought I should come alone this week, because you'll have to instruct me."

"Go on."

"It's Helen. She's been seeing a man."

"Just what do you mean?"

Mrs Partridge sighed. "I think she's having an affair."

"She's only sixteen!" Joanna bit her lip. She had been only sixteen when she had first attracted the attention of Howard Edge. Of course, she had waited another two years before surrendering, but morals at the beginning of the sixties were a little different to morals at the end of the seventies. And without a mother . . .

Mrs Partridge was sighing again, No doubt she was remembering that teenage girl Howard had brought home on that never-to-be-forgotten night. "How do you know this?" Joanna asked, trying to keep her voice down as she knew that the women at the other tables were trying to listen.

"Staying out late, telephone calls, things about her clothes . . . I don't know if I can cope, Madam."

"You have to cope," Joanna said fiercely. "Please, Mrs Partridge. If you gave up . . . I'd give up too."

"You are coming home, soon, Mrs Orton?"

"Soon," Joanna said. It had to be soon. "But please send her to see me, next week. It would be best if she came alone."

She had, in fact, noticed a certain furtiveness creeping into Helen's personality over the past year. She had reckoned this was to be expected, as the girl had grown into a teenager having to live with the concept that her mother was a condemned murderess; it had not occurred to her that there might have been an outside cause. Although possibly the two were connected.

Now, as she sat across the table from her daughter, she wondered why it hadn't happened sooner. Helen was almost a carbon copy of herself, her beauty perhaps enhanced by the slight sharpness of feature she had inherited from Howard. While at sixteen her figure was perfection. "Why do they all look at me like that?" she asked. "One would think they were men."

"Half of them wish they were," Joanna pointed out. "There's not much else to do in a place like this. Don't tell me you've never had a girlfriend."

Helen flushed. "I prefer men."

"Doesn't everyone, when they're available? When you say men, I assume you mean boys."

"Well . . ." Helen's flush deepened. "Boys are such creeps."

"True. Would you like to tell me about him?"

"Mrs Partridge has been at you."

"She's concerned, yes. I don't find that unreasonable. She feels responsible for you. She *is* responsible for you."

"Just so long as she doesn't interfere."

"Whether she interferes or not depends on what I tell her to do. So why don't you tell me, first?"

Helen leaned across the table, grasping her mother's hands. "His name is Harry and he's an absolutely dreamboat."

"I'm sure he is. What does he do?"

"Well . . ." the flush was back. "Actually, he's not doing anything right now. But he's all right. He's old enough to be unemployed, and collect the dole."

"That being?"

"Twenty-four."

Joanna actually felt a sense of relief. She had immediately supposed he would be an ageing lecher – rather like Howard, in fact. But Howard had not been on the dole. "And you're madly in love," she suggested.

Helen pulled her hands away. "We're very fond of each other."

"How fond?"

"Oh, Mummy! We use a condom, if that's what's bothering you."

To Joanna's distress, she had clearly upset the girl, because Helen did not visit the following week. Or the week after. But then, neither did Raisul. Mrs Partridge came as usual.

"It's very difficult for him," she explained. "There's been some trouble at school."

"What kind of trouble?"

"Well, madam, boys will be boys. And Raisul is obviously not English, even if he speaks like an Englishman. He has a temper."

"Will you please tell me what has happened?"

Mrs Partridge sighed. "They started taunting him about coming here, visiting his murdering mother, and he attacked them."

"He attacked them?"

"He seems to have gone berserk. I had to go and talk with the headmaster. He was suspended, you see. But I managed to sort that out. Only . . . he told me . . ." she gazed at Joanna with enormous eyes.

"Go on."

"Raisul told me that he didn't want to come here any more. Not right now. I didn't feel I could force him."

"Of course you must not force him," Joanna said. She had shed all her tears.

"Kids," Belinda commented. "They're more trouble than they're worth."

"Do you have any?" Joanna couldn't believe she did; she was only twenty-two.

"Sure, I had one," Belinda said. "I gave it away."

"You what?"

"I wrapped him up nice and snug and left him on a doorstep."

"My God!"

"Oh, he was found, and looked after, and adopted. I think he's doing fine."

"And you have no regrets?"

"In here? Wouldn't you be better off without any?"

Joanna wondered if she was right. But gradually it seemed she was being more and more isolated from the world. Her world.

But her world no longer existed.

* * *

Jeanette Corder came, as requested. "I gather you're having a difficult time," she remarked.

"Not any more. I'm a senior citizen. But . . ." she told her the solicitor about the straitjacket, the assaults.

"Sounds beastly," Jeanette commented.

"Can't we do something about it?"

"Can you prove your allegations?"

"We've all experienced it, in some degree or other."

"You mean your fellow prisoners would give supporting evidence?"

Joanna considered. While they were mostly afraid of her, very few of them had ever shown any sign of liking her. Even Cindy had found her a convenience. Jeanette was studying her expression. "If you were to bring accusations like that into the open, and you failed to have them confirmed or accepted, it would set back your chance of a parole by a good distance."

"Have I any chance of a parole?"

"Of course. As you say, that rumpus was a long time ago. You've been here four years. You're halfway there."

"Have you any idea what it is like to contemplate spending another four years in this place, losing touch with my family, my own children, for God's sake, watching my business collapse . . ."

"Your business collapsed four years ago, Mrs Orton. I know the situation with the children is difficult, but your aim in life should be to get out of here just as quickly as you can, so you can get back to them."

"And, of course," Joanna said. "I am a convicted murderess, so I shouldn't really complain."

"I'm afraid that sums it up," Jeanette said.

Once again, the idea of suicide became attractive. And this time it would not, apparently, have a great impact upon Helen and Raisul – they wanted nothing more to do with her. She did not suppose there was a single solitary soul in all the world who would give a damn. She would be buried in the prison cemetery, and forgotten. All those great days in the past, the adventures and the romances, the thrill of being written about in the newspapers and interviewed by the media, the crises that she had always successfully negotiated, would all be history. But they were already history.

"Mail," Belinda said.

"Throw it in the can," Joanna recommended.

"It's from Canada. You know anyone in Canada?"

"It's from the creep who was Sean Connor's father. Or so he says. He's been writing me for years."

"Shit! What does he say? That you should've been torn apart with red hot pincers?"

Joanna actually smiled. "No, funnily enough. He says that he forgives me, understand me, sympathises with me. Seems Sean always was a bad egg. So his dad sent him off. Oh, he always supported him, bought him expensive cars, but they were effectively estranged. And he knew just how much of a satyr Sean was. I didn't."

"Sounds like he's pretty well-heeled," Belinda remarked.

"I suppose he must be. I've never really thought about it."

"But you don't want to read his letter."

"I'm not in the mood. Bin it."

"Ah . . . would you mind if I read it?" Belinda asked. "Nobody ever writes me."

Joanna rolled on her stomach. "Go ahead, if it turns you on."

Belinda climbed into the upper bunk, and slit the envelope. Then she lay down to read it, slowly, Joanna knew, because she was no great reader. "Sounds a real nice guy," she remarked. "Complains a bit that you've never replied to any of his letters."

"Chance would be a fine thing."

"Yeah. And . . . holy Jesus Christ!"

"Eh?" Joanna rolled on to her back again, stared at the heaving mattress above her.

"You won't believe this."

"I don't see how I can, if you won't tell me what it is. He's being abusive, I suppose."

"No," Belinda said, and started to laugh.

"I am going to break your neck," Joanna threatened. "Give me that letter."

Belinda hung it over the edge of the bunk. "You'd better read it. He wants you to marry him."

# Chapter Ten

# The Bride

Joanna found it difficult to believe what she was reading.

'*Although you have never replied to any of my letters,*' wrote Michael Johannsson, '*I feel a definite affinity between us that has nothing to do with my son. I have not been able to say exactly what my feelings are, previous to now, because my wife was still living. Although we have been estranged for many years, we were never actually divorced, nor did I consider this to be appropriate over the last three years, aware as I was that she was dying of cancer. That is behind me now, and I am only aware that I owe you more than I can possibly convey, perhaps an entire lifetime. I have, as you know, followed both your case and your situation with great interest, and I am aware that there remains four years before you can be released from prison, but that is no reason why we should not marry now.*

*I understand that it would be an enormous step for you, to agree to marry a man you have never seen, and who is the father of a man who so outraged you. However, I believe there are certain mitigating factors which may make me acceptable to you. You will forgive me, I am sure, for raising matters that must still be painful for you, but I know how much you have suffered, both financially and socially, by your imprisonment. May I take the liberty of saying that I am an extremely wealthy man, and that I intend to do everything in my power to restore you to that position you once enjoyed and so richly deserve. In token of the above, should you agree to my proposal, I would be prepared immediately to take all the financial burden of your children off your hands, relocate them to more salubrious surroundings, if that is what you wish, and generally in every way alleviate their position. Again, if that is your wish. As for the future . . .'*

Joanna laid down the letter. She had thought she had shed all her tears. This poor, lonely old man!

"You are going to say yes?" Belinda begged.

"Of course I can't accept."

"Why not? If he's as rich as he claims, you have it made. So do your kids."

"The idea is obscene."

"Because you had his son? So what's a bit of incest between friends? It wasn't as if you married the guy."

"I'd be selling myself," Joanna said.

"Shit, darling, don't we all? Would you have married your first husband, that shipowner, if he'd been a busker playing outside the Odeon? Would you have married that Arab guy if he hadn't been a prince?"

The temptation was enormous. *I will restore you to the wealth and position you once enjoyed, and deserve.* How she wanted that. How she wanted to revenge herself on all those people who had abandoned her to a lifetime in this cell. How she wanted to emerge from ashes of her life, like a phoenix, and cock her finger at them all. Did he understand that? Could he possibly guess it? And would he accept it?

What did she have to do to achieve her objective? Say yes, to a man she had never seen. He had not even sent her a photograph. Perhaps he was too grotesque to risk it! And then, eventually, go to bed with him. He would be getting the best of the bargain. Even in four years time she would only just be forty, and if there were silver threads amongst the gold, a bottle would very quickly take care of those. As for the rest . . . her body was as strong and as desirable as it had ever been. There was the problem. Her body. It had become an intensely private matter to her, to be yielded on very rare occasions, when the sexuality in her nature took control. But those moments were becoming more and more rare. Now she would be required to uncover herself, in every possible way, all over again. Perhaps he was too old for sex!

She showed the letter to the Reverend Ingle the following Sunday. "Remarkable," he commented. "You say this man has been writing to you for years?"

"Since I was convicted," she said. "And I think he was trying to get in touch with me before that."

"And you have never replied?"

"He's the father of the man I am supposed to have killed, Reverend."

Ingle stroked his chin. "And now you want to marry him."

"No. He wants to marry me."

"Hm. I think you want to think very carefully about this, Orton. You described his son in court as a satyr, if I remember correctly."

"He behaved like one, certainly."

"And this man is his father." Joanna bit her lip. "He may have some thoughts of revenge," Ingle suggested. "This business of taking over the care and upbringing of your children. I don't like the sound of that. Suppose he's a paedophile?" Joanna's head began to spin. "And then, he claims to be a wealthy man. What proof has he given you of this?"

"Shit," she muttered.

"Of course I understand how important it is for you to have something to look forward to, and there can be no doubt that *were* you to marry the father of the man you killed, it would weigh very heavily with the parole board. But you need to be very sure that you are not exchanging one hell for another."

"And you won't advise me."

"I have advised you, Orton. But the decision must be yours."

Once upon a time, Joanna reflected, she would not have needed, or heeded, advice. She would have sized up a situation and made her decision. Had being sent to prison, being in prison, so reduced her personality? She asked William to come and see her, showed him the letter. "Wow!" he commented.

"Can you find out something about him for me?"

"I'll try. If he's a really wealthy man something should be available."

Meanwhile she replied to Johannsson's last letter.

> '*Forgive me for never having written to you before,*' she wrote, '*but I found it difficult to accept that you actually wished to be friends with the woman who was responsible for your son's death. And now, to wish to marry me . . . I am enormously flattered, of course, but again, if you'll forgive me, while you appear to know everything about me, I know nothing about you, except what you have chosen to tell me. I do not even know what you look like!*
>
> *Nor do I know any of your plans, supposing we did marry. Would we live in Canada, or in England? Would you wish to have children? There are so many questions to be considered.*'

She waited with some anxiety for a reply, because she knew that her mind was slowly making itself up. Worse than the thought of the four years left to her had always been the thought that she would emerge to nothing, no money, no career, and now, it seemed more and more with every week that her children did not come to see her, no family either. Michael Johannsson promised a new life – if anything he claimed was true.

* * *

"Here we go," Belinda said. "It's another biggee."

Joanna's hands were trembling as she slit the envelope, which contained several separate pieces of paper and a photograph. Michael Johannsson was standing beside an expensive car; she thought it might be a Cadillac. He looked as if he was several inches over six feet tall, with a build to match. His face was large, and strong, his hair white and receding. He was casually dressed, but the clothes were clearly expensive. "Let's see," Belinda asked.

Joanna handed her the photograph without a word, picked up the balance sheet, which covered the last year of the Johannsson Mining Corporation, revealing assets of twelve-point-four million dollars, a turnover of eight million, and a profit of three-point-two million. This, too, she handed to Belinda. "Jesus," Belinda muttered. "Can I be your maid?"

This time the letter itself was short.

*'We shall live wherever you wish, and we shall start a family whenever, or if ever, you wish. Unless I hear from you in the negative within the next month, I shall start things moving. I have a nodding acquaintance with the Home Secretary, so we shouldn't have too many problems.'*

She had to do nothing but sit back and wait. "Oh, please let me be your maid," Belinda begged.

William came to see her the following week. "He seems to be genuine," he said.

"I know." Joanna gave him the balance sheet.

"Wow," he commented.

"What position does he hold?"

"President."

"And his equity?"

"Eighty-five per cent."

It was her turn to mutter, "Wow. What's the current rate of exchange?"

"Low. Roaming around one-fifty."

That meant Michael Johannsson's company was worth about eight million pounds, of which six-point-eight belonged to him. She had once been just about as wealthy as that. Once! "So you're going to go ahead?"

Suppose he's a satyr, like his son, or a paedophile, Reverend Ingle had suggested. But she could insist that Mrs Partridge remained in charge. As for his bed manners . . . she thought she could suffer anything to get her hands on six million pounds. There was that old mercenary streak, what the tabloids had called her ruthless determination, surfacing again. And how good it was to feel it, when she thought it had been crushed out of her for ever! "Tell me about Petherick."

"As I have told you before, times are hard. But getting better. Or at least, people are coming to terms with a high rate of inflation. Every government says it means to tackle it, but as long as the governments all have commitments to the welfare state which far outrun their income, it doesn't look likely to go away."

"About Petherick. Is he MD?"

"Actually, no. Your old friend Andy Gosling is now MD."

Joanna frowned. "I thought he sold out to Petherick?"

"That was the original deal. But when things were very bad, Andy bought back a controlling interest. Petherick has sold his entire stock. Rumour has it that Andy really stretched himself to make it. But now he and his friends own the company."

"You never told me."

"I didn't want to upset you. You were having a pretty hard time, remember."

"Andy Gosling," she said, thoughtfully.

"With that fellow, Holroyd. You know, the chap who bought Dick's shares."

"Let me get this straight," Joanna said. "Holroyd works for Andy?"

"He does now. There's a suspicion he always did. It's not

something one can say openly, of course, because of the risk of slander or libel. But it was all fairly pat. As you may remember, Townsend's involved as well. He's the second biggest shareholder, but that fellow Amalia has a sizeable holding as well."

"I remember them all," Joanna said.

It was William's turn to frown. "You're not going after them?"

"I am going to turn them inside out," Joanna said. "But that's between you and me."

He was looking very uneasy. "It'll cost you."

"I'm going to have it."

"You mean this chap Johannsson has it. Will he go along with a hostile takeover which could cost a million or two?"

"He's said he will. I'll just straighten that out."

Joanna was summoned to the Office. "Is this some kind of a joke, Orton?"

Joanna raised her eyebrows. "What, ma'am?"

"I have a communication here from the Home Office, informing me that you are to be married, here in Liddleton, on Saturday next."

"Oh, that," Joanna said, as casually as she could.

"Why was I not informed of this development, before?"

"I did not think you would be interested, ma'am." Mrs Anstey glared at her. "My fiancé told me he would make all the arrangements. As he seems to have done."

"This man . . . this Johannsson – what do you know of him?"

Joanna smiled at her. "I know that he is very rich, and that he is a personal friend of the Home Secretary."

Mrs Anstey's jaw dropped. But she quickly recovered. "And does *he* know that you have at least another four years to spend in here?"

"Yes, ma'am, he does. He knows all about me. You see, he's the father of the man I killed."

*Coup de grace*! Mrs Anstey was left speechless. While

Joanna and Belinda hugged each other. "I'm to have a night with him," Joanna said. "Would you believe that I'm scared stiff?"

"I wouldn't believe it," Belinda said. "Not you, Joanna. Please can I be your maid?"

"Come and see me when you get out," Joanna promised.

Because she *was* nervous. Indeed she was terrified, more afraid than at any previous time in her life. Her relationships with Howard Edge and Prince Hasim had just happened, overtaking her before she had been properly aware of them. Taking over the management of Caribee Shipping had been a similarly instant event, a matter for quick decisions, supported by the devil-may-care attitude of knowing that she had nothing to lose. Well, she told herself, did she have anything to lose this time? The difference was that she was thirty-seven instead of twenty, and that she had suffered every indignity a woman could. But that had to have made her tougher, stronger, more than ever ruthlessly determined to regain the top. Surely.

But to share . . . had she ever shared, with anyone? She had never shared with Howard, because she had been his mistress for most of their relationship, and he had been a secretive man, tending to keep his plans as well as his fears and fancies to himself. She had felt they were going to share, after their marriage, but that had lasted less than a fortnight. She had never shared with Prince Hasim, because to him she had always been a magnificent toy, a thing of enormous value, to be handled with the utmost gentle care, but nonetheless never to be considered as an equal.

She had never shared with Dick, because the reverse had been the care with him, only he had never even been a magnificent toy. Sometimes she felt she had come close to sharing with Cindy, or even Belinda. But she knew these were temporary situations, born of a mutual misery, a mutual need to have another's arms to hold one tight, when the misery threatened to overwhelm. Such relations would not stand the cold light of day. And now . . . Michael Johannsson.

A big man, in every way. She had never had relations with a *big* man.

"You may use the interview room," Angie told Joanna, escorting her along the catwalk. The entire block was singing and cheering, while Joanna's knees seemed to have turned to jelly.

Then they were in a more solid corridor, and she was being shown into the room where last she had met John Giffard. "I'll be right outside," Angie told her.

Joanna took a deep breath, and the door clanged behind her. "Would you believe," Michael Johannsson said, "that this is the first time I have ever been inside a prison?" He was exactly as he had appeared in the photograph, a huge bear of a man.

Joanna licked her lips. "It's not all it's cracked up to be."

She waited, unable to move, uncertain what was required of her. "Pretty grim, huh?" His accent was only slightly nasal.

"Pretty."

There were two chairs at the table. He pulled one out for her. She moved towards him, and sat down. Still he had not touched her. He sat in the other chair, facing her. "I've never been in a situation like this before, either," he confessed.

"Me neither. I was sorry to hear about your wife."

He shrugged. "As I said, we lived apart for the past ten years."

"Yes."

They gazed at each other. "About your son . . ."

"No," he said. "Never again. Promise me."

"Oh! Right." She felt an enormous sense of relief. But that didn't mean Sean wouldn't lie in bed between them.

"I bought you this." He felt in his pocket and produced the ring box. "I've been told it's not a good idea for you to wear it in prison, but I'd like you to look at it."

Her hands trembled as she opened the box and gazed at the sapphire set in diamonds. It must be just about as valuable as my ruby, she thought. That was locked away in her safe deposit box. "It's magnificent."

"It's yours. Waiting for you, I guess. As am I." Once again they stared at each other. "There's so much that needs saying," Michael Johannsson said. "And I'm not sure now is the time or place. I want you to know that I meant every word I have ever said, and that once you get out of here I am going to make you the happiest woman in the world."

"As I shall try to be everything you expect of me."

He grinned. "Kind of formal. But I guess we both know what we mean. Would we be breaking any rules if I were to kiss you?"

"I suppose we would. But I don't think it would matter."

"What about you?"

"I would like that," Joanna said.

"You will be married in the prison chapel," Mrs Anstey told her. "You may have one attendant." She paused.

"Belinda, please, ma'am." Mrs Anstey nodded; she had expected that. "And my children," Joanna said.

Mrs Anstey raised her eyebrows. "I will see if permission can be obtained."

"And my brother and his wife."

"My dear Orton, this is a prison."

"I have made the request, ma'am."

"And I will forward it. After the ceremony, you will be allowed one night with your husband. The Home Secretary has very generously allowed this to be spent outside the prison, at an hotel. You are being granted parole for that one night, and your husband has guaranteed that you will be returned here the next morning. I assume you have enough sense to go along with this."

"Yes," Joanna said.

"Well . . ." Mrs Anstey's smile was cold. "I will wish you joy of it."

"Will you be attending the ceremony, ma'am?"

"Why, do you know, I think I might."

Someone else to get even with, Joanna thought, when I am finally out of here.

Mrs Partridge was allowed to bring down a choice of Joanna's clothes – she had rescued them from Caribee House before the company had reclaimed it – and Joanna chose a simple white suit. As she had lost weight it required altering, but was promised for the day. "How are the children taking the idea?" she asked.

Mrs Partridge flushed. "Helen doesn't approve."

"Has she met Mr Johannsson?"

"He came to call. And he's taking a new apartment for us."

"But you're staying on?" Joanna was anxious.

"I'll be there just as long as you want me, madam."

"Dear Mrs Partridge." Joanna squeezed her hand. "Why doesn't Helen approve? Was it something about him she didn't like?"

"Well, madam . . ." Mrs Partridge went into one of her flushing routines. "I don't think there is anything about the gentleman himself she didn't like. It's the idea. She's at that age, you see. Romance, love, belief in love, is everything. She doesn't believe you love Mr Johannsson, or can possibly love him. Ever."

I am selling myself, for freedom and power, Joanna thought. Something out of Faust. But she did not think Michael Johannsson was Mephistopheles. "I think he'll have to grow on her, as he'll have to grow on me. What about Raisul?"

"He doesn't say much. He's a deep one."

"And you? What do you think about Mr Johannsson?"

"It's not for me to say, madam."

"I'm asking you to."

"He's seems a very nice gentleman, madam."

Joanna knew that was all she was going to get out of her.

The wedding suit duly arrived on the day before the ceremony, and the entire block attended the fitting, which was made in the recreation area. Mary collapsed into tears.

"You're going to be so happy," she sobbed. "I know it."

The following day the whole prison seemed to be humming. This was an event that transcended the grim reality of their lives, a sort of fairytale taking place in their very midst. Belinda had also been allowed to wear her own clothes for the occasion, and Angie dressed Joanna's hair. It was the first time in five years she had had a shampoo and set, and it felt so good. "Used to be a hairdresser, a long time ago," Angie said.

She had even managed to find a bouquet of flowers. Once again they were clapped and cheered all the way out of the block, and straight into the chapel, where Reverend Ingle was waiting for them, together with William and Norma, looking apprehensive, Mrs Partridge, looking even more apprehensive . . . and Raisul. "Oh, madam," Mrs Partridge said, hugging her. "She wouldn't come. She just wouldn't come. And I couldn't force her."

"Of course you couldn't," Joanna said.

"I'll sort it out," Michael said. Joanna looked up at him, the solid bulk of him, so massive, so reassuring. He could sort anything out, she was sure. And he had a lot to do.

She hardly heard the ceremony, hardly felt the kisses and the congratulations, even from Mrs Anstey. She stared at the two rings, because Michael had insisted upon slipping on the engagement ring first. "Just for tonight," he said.

Then she was sitting in the back of a car and the gates were swinging open. The last time those gates had opened for her had been the day she had gone to her appeal hearing. When they had closed on her return she had supposed that was the end of her life. When they closed on her return this time, it would be merely another chapter, opening, towards the future. But before then . . . she glanced at Michael, found him staring at her. "It would be banal to ask if you are happy," he said. "But are you content? Be truthful."

"I think I am as content as a woman in my position has any

right to expect," Joanna said. "I'm sorry about Helen. You understand that it's been fairly traumatic for her."

"I understand. Have you any objection if I see what I can do?"

She continued to gaze at him for several seconds. He could be a paedophile, Ingle had said. But she couldn't believe it of this man, save that she was conditioned to be suspicious of all men. "I'd be grateful," she said.

"Kid gloves, I promise," he said.

"Yes, please." She forced a smile. "I'm afraid she has a lot of her mother in her."

"I figured that the first time I met her," he said.

They drove in silence, while Joanna looked out of the window at the countryside. It was all but dark, but she savoured every tree, every winking light in a house window. Yet was totally aware of the man sitting beside her, who had not yet touched her, who had only, in fact, touched her twice in his life. Am I going to scream? she wondered. The last man who had touched her, sexually, had been this man's son, and that had been five years ago. They turned through wrought-iron gates and down a tree-lined drive. "It's not the Savoy," Michael said. "But it's quiet. And they don't have a clue who we are. So, no honeymoon special. We're just passing through. Right?"

"Yes," she said. Yet it was all she could do to stop herself shaking when they reached reception. Michael, who seemed to have thought of everything, had provided two heavy suitcases, although she didn't even have a change of clothes, to her knowledge. She stood to one side, trying to ignore the glances of the other guests in the lobby – their interest had only to be because she was a good-looking woman, she kept telling herself – and then they were in the lift and mounting upwards. The bellhop took them along to their room, drew the curtains back from the picture window to show the floodlighting in the hotel park, placed their suitcases on the stand, accepted Michael's tip, and withdrew.

Joanna stood at the window, looking out, listening to what

was happening behind her. The door closed. "I thought we'd eat in the room," Michael said. "We have so little time."

She turned. "Of course."

"Would you like to look at the menu?"

"You order."

He did so, then opened the minibar and uncorked a bottle of champagne, filled two glasses. "Here's to us."

She drank, gazing at him. He kissed her, very lightly. "What would you like more than anything else in the world, at this moment?"

"A hot bath."

"Voila!" He gestured at the bathroom, then went into it and turned on the taps.

"Should I have said something different?" she asked.

"Not in the least."

She took off her coat and hung it up, then unzipped her dress. He sat on the bed. "Do you mind if I watch?"

"You're my husband." She hung the dress up next to the coat, stepped out of her shoes, sat down to roll down her stockings.

"I suppose you know that you are an incredibly attractive woman," he remarked.

"It's got me into a fair amount of trouble." She realised her hands were trembling as she dropped the second stocking on the floor, and reached behind herself to unfasten her bra. It was a very long time since she had done that in the presence of a man. Indeed, as in her heyday she had never worn such things, she could not remember the last time she had done so. And this man was still a stranger. She dropped that too on the floor.

"That bath must be just about ready," he said, and went into the bathroom to turn off the taps. He was such a gentleman!

She stepped out of her knickers, went to the bathroom door, encountered him coming out. They stared at each other. "I'm flesh and blood," she said.

"So am I," he said, and took her in his arms.

She soaked, slowly and luxuriously, while she listened to their dinner being served. When she got out of the bath, Michael was there with a white robe to wrap her in. She had washed her hair, and it lay damply on her shoulders. He had also undressed and wore a dressing gown. They sat opposite each other to eat, and drink champagne. "Can you stand the thought of sex?" he asked.

"I'm your wife."

He grinned. "Doesn't mean all that much nowadays. I want you to want it."

"I do," she said. "But . . . you'll have to be gentle. It's been a long time."

"I'll be gentle."

He lifted her in his arms to carry her to the bed, carefully removed the bathrobe, kissed her mouth, her lips, her eyes, her cheeks, her chin. When his mouth moved lower she closed her eyes. He was taking possession of her, in his own way, and she wanted to be possessed. Even when he rolled her on her stomach to her back and her buttocks, while she instinctively tensed as memory flooded back, she slowly relaxed as she realised that this man was a gentle man.

When he entered her, she felt like a virgin again. Now his movements grew more violent, but they were always controlled, always careful to avoid pain. She did not climax, but she had not expected to, after so long. It was sufficient to have him covering her, his passion spent, his sweat mingling with hers.

He raised his head to look at her, and she kissed him. "We have all the time in the world, my darling," she said. "All the rest of our lives."

"To hear you say that . . . hey, I never gave you your wedding present."

"Do I get one?"

He rolled off the bed, went to his suitcase. "You get fifty thousand," he said.

# Chapter Eleven

# Family Matters

Joanna sat up, heart pounding, as he brought the share certificates back to her. "Oh, my," she said. "Oh, my. But how?"

"I, or rather, my brokers, made the lady an offer she couldn't resist."

"Alicia? But . . . she said she always wanted to maintain a stake in the company."

"In Caribee Shipping. That no longer exists. Nor will it ever again, unless someone takes control of Petherick Shipping and restores the name." Joanna clasped both hands to her neck. "Her shares in Caribee were exchanged for shares in Petherick," Michael explained. "But of course whereas Caribee had a million, Petherick has four, so fifty thousand shares does not represent a very big part of the company. And the price has remained low, because of all the inflationary pressures we've been suffering. So, as I said, the lady couldn't refuse an offer of virtually twice their current value."

"I never thought Alicia would sell out to me, under any circumstances," Joanna said.

"I doubt she would, and she didn't. In any event, I don't think it would be a good idea were anyone in the City to discover that you are back in business. Nor did I think it a good idea for me to be involved, as the story of this marriage is going to be public all over Britain tomorrow. The shares have been bought by a holding company, J & J Ltd., which I have set up on your behalf."

"J & J?" she said.

"Joanna and Johannsson."

"Oh, Michael," she said. "I think I'm going to cry."

"My agents will keep their eyes and ears open, and buy whatever snippets they can, until you're ready to go to work," Michael said.

She lay with her head on his shoulder, while outside the darkness began to fade. Neither had slept; there had been no time for sleep. And they had had sex twice more. She had not expected that in a man of fifty-six. He had been insatiable. But then, so had she. She felt she was in a dream. "Will you really back me to regain control of the company?" she asked.

"That was the deal."

She raised her head. "Do you think that matters, now?"

"Yes, I do. I intend to make you the happiest woman in the world."

"Suppose I told you that I already am the happiest woman in the world?"

He kissed her. "You'd be lying. And even if you were, I'm going to make you happier yet." They had not once mentioned Sean's name.

The cheering and the hand-clapping, the stamping of feet and the banging of utensils, echoed through the prison for a good hour after the gates had again closed behind Joanna. Mrs Anstey's mouth was twisted. "I can see you've had a good night, Orton," she said. "Or, I suppose, I have to start calling you Johannsson. Joanna Johannsson. What a mouthful. I hope you are not expecting any special treatment."

"No, ma'am," Joanna said as primly as possible. She was back in her prison uniform, and yesterday and last night might never have been. But it had been, and her new engagement ring was on its way to her safety deposit box to join her old engagement ring – together with fifty thousand shares in Petherick Shipping. She was on her way, with less than four years to go.

Considerably on her way, although she didn't then know it. "You must tell us all about it," the women said during recreation.

Joanna was happy to do that, omitting all the really important matters such as the shares and the promise of the future, concentrating on the food she had eaten, the room in which she had spent the night – which was what they really wanted to hear about in any event. "You must be the happiest woman in the world," Belinda said, when they were alone in their cell.

"That's what Michael said," Joanna mused. "And I believed it, then. Now . . ."

"So what's another four years? You have so much waiting for you."

So much, Joanna thought. Helen! Four years might just complete an irreconcilable break, unless Michael could work something. Four years.

"This is incredible," Mrs Anstey said, slapping the report on her desk. "You are allowed out, for one night, and you're pregnant? At your age?"

"With respect, ma'am," Joanna said. "I am thirty-seven. That is not too old to have a child."

Mrs Anstey snorted; presumably she had never had children. None of the inmates were even sure that she had ever actually been married. "This will have to go to the parole board, and probably the Home Office as well," she said disdainfully. "I suppose you think it will help you get out of here sooner."

"Yes, I do," Joanna said.

Mrs Anstey glared at her.

"Must be some guy," Belinda had said enviously. "Nervous?"

"Scared stiff," Joanna confessed. But she gave no sign of it as she sat in a straight chair before the board.

"This is about the most unusual case I have ever come across," said the chairperson, a rather large woman, who was flanked by another woman and by a man who looked almost as scared as Joanna felt – but she suspected he was scared of the chairperson. "I can't see any point in asking you any questions," the chairperson said, "as we know where you are going and what you will be doing when you leave here. Nor does there appear to be any point in considering your record of misbehaviour while in here; indeed, we have been specifically instructed not to do so. You have friends in high places, Mrs Johannsson. Just remember that even such friends will not be able to help you if you get into trouble again. Dismissed."

Belinda was waiting to hug her and kiss her. "Can I be your maid?"

"Just as soon as you get out," Joanna assured her.

Michael himself came to collect her. "Who says miracles never happen?"

Joanna hugged him and kissed him, then leaned back in the front seat of the Mercedes; he was driving himself.

I am free, she thought. Free, free, free. Minutes later they were on the M4. "Where are we going?" she asked.

"I have a flat in London. I've arranged a little party there."

She sat up again. "Oh, lord!"

"Don't you like the idea?"

"Well . . . these clothes don't fit very well any more, and I haven't had my hair done, and—"

"Just relax," he suggested. "It's you that's important."

"Who's going to be there?"

"Raisul and Mrs Partridge will be there, and your brother and his wife . . ."

"And Matilda?"

"Ah, no. She declined. Sorry about that."

"And Helen?"

"She declined as well."

"I've a lot to do," Joanna said, half to herself. She was looking at houses. They were entering London's suburbs She didn't really want to meet anyone, until she had got her bearings.

"Did I do the right thing?" Michael asked, anxiously, glancing at her expression.

"Of course you did. They're my family."

"My family too, now," he reminded her.

She squeezed his hand.

They left the motorway and were in Chelsea. They turned off the main road and into a quiet square. "Shit!" Michael commented.

Joanna had been leaning back again. Now she sat up, and saw the crowd of photographers and reporters outside one of the houses. "Now who the fuck would have done that?" Michael asked. He was clearly very angry.

"Mrs Anstey, I would say. I'm not her favourite person. Michael . . ."

"I know." He turned left and drove out of the square, rejoined the main road. "We'll go to an hotel."

"But the party?"

"We'll have it there."

It was not a howling success. Quite apart from having the venue so suddenly shifted, there was so much between them all, to be said, alleviated, at some time in the future, but not all at once. At the wedding there had been no time for anything more than perfunctory greetings and congratulations, with William no doubt remembering how bitter she had been when last they had met. Now she smiled at them all, but the bitterness remained. "What do you want to do now?" Michael asked when the guests had departed. "I mean, tomorrow, or whatever. Bearing in mind that you don't *have* to do anything."

"I know," she said. "Believe me, one half of me just wants to get into bed beneath scented sheets and lie there for ever and ever. But I've already lost five years out of my life. Then the other half of me wants to take off to some deserted island and just lie in the sun for a month."

"That's entirely practical."

"It isn't really. What about the baby?"

"A month in the sun will probably do him good. Or her."

"And Helen?"

"As she's been behaving oddly for a long time now, I can't see that another month is doing to do harm."

"Did you see her?"

"No. I got her address from Mrs Partridge, and called and asked her to lunch, but she hung up on me. I didn't figure I had the right to go round and slap her bottom, so I left it there."

There was so much to be done, but the baby came first. Although she desperately wanted to have Michael's child, for the first time Joanna regretted being pregnant at such a time. Even when Howard had died and left her carrying Helen, the pregnancy had worked to her advantage. Now it was only a handicap. But, she reminded herself, had she not been pregnant, she would still be in jail.

"What about Raisul?" Michael asked, when they were able to get into the flat, in the small hours of the next day, when the papparazzi had gone home to bed. Joanna had spent two hours at her hairdressers, and felt a new woman. "Do you wish him to move in with us?" It was a two-bedroom apartment.

Another problem. Raisul had seemed to be delighted to see her again, but there had been no spontaneous warmth in his hug. She was virtually a stranger to him, and he, taller than she, broad-shouldered, every inch the young man rather than the little boy she remembered, was most certainly a stranger to her. If they were to live together again beneath the same roof, it was going to have to be a large roof.

There was also the matter of Michael himself. He was her saviour in every possible way, but they remained largely strangers, only slowly feeling their way towards that mutual understanding, and acceptance, that is essential where two people are to live together in harmony. He was going out of his way to be nice to her, to satisfy her every whim, but there were certain whims she could not convey to him without risking causing offence – and that she dared not risk. Her principal problem was coming to grips with the total lack of privacy in which she found herself. She had always been an intensely private person. During the year she had been Howard Edge's mistress, she had always had a room to herself. What might have happened after their marriage she did not know, because Howard had died on their honeymoon.

Prince Hasim had also maintained a separate bedroom, because that was how Arab princes lived. Nor had he encroached on her life at all. That she wanted to continue running her shipping line had amused him. That she had had a house in the country amused him even more. But all he had ever wanted from her was her body when he felt the urge, and her company in society. Dick had always been very much the junior partner, and she had continued to sleep alone, except when *she* had the urge. Even in prison, although she had had to share a cell, both Cindy and Belinda had quickly gathered that she wanted her privacy, and as they had both been afraid of her, they had accepted the situation.

Such a point of view was totally foreign to Michael's way of life, and she could tell that he had never even considered it a possibility for a married couple. Equally, his concept of the best way for them to form a couple was to share every moment, awake or asleep. This was something she had to go along with. But to have others in the house would surely complicate matters, especially where one of the others would be her son, and the other . . . "And Mrs Partridge?"

"Hm. I can see we will have to buy a house."

"Who's occupying Caribee House at the moment?"

He raised his eyebrows, then grinned. "I can find out. Do you really think they'd sell?"

"Depends who it is," Joanna said. "And what state his finances are in."

Michael still had Helen's phone number, but Joanna decided against telephoning, and got her address from Mrs Partridge. Mrs Partridge and Raisul had been removed to a more up-market apartment, and the old lady was looking quite prosperous. But she was as worried and anxious as ever. "You realise she's living with this man of hers, madam?" she said.

"I do. I'm not going to come over the heavy-handed mother,

Mrs Partridge. But I do want her to do something with her life."

"I don't think she'll go back to school."

"I left school when I was sixteen," Joanna pointed out. "She can go to a secretarial college. That's what I did." And who knows, she thought: she might meet another Howard Edge.

Michael wanted to accompany her, but she decided against it. "This is mother and daughter talk," she said.

"Remember, she's not yet an adult in the eyes of the law," he said. "If you don't like the set-up, you can make her come home."

Joanna smiled. "Invoke the law and drag her home with a couple of bobbies. I've had just about all the law I can stand, Michael. This has to be done with TLC."

She took a taxi to the address, disturbingly, a street in Brixton. The moment she stepped down from her taxi she regretted having worn her mink. But she had faced tougher opposition than these jeering youths, so she merely looked at them before entering the house; there was no bell and the street door was open. Mrs Partridge said that as far as she knew Helen had a job, so Joanna had waited until half-past six. The apartment was a walk-up, three flights, and she was quite out of breath by the time she reached the landing. She didn't care much for the cleanliness of the stairs, or the rather sour smell with which she was surrounded.

She rang the bell, and again, before the door was opened by an unshaven young man wearing a vest and pants, who goggled at her mink in consternation. "You must be Harry," Joanna suggested. "Is Helen in?"

"Shit!" he commented, as the penny dropped. "No, she ain't."

"But you are expecting her, I suppose?"

"Yeah."

"Then do you mind if I come in and wait? I'm her mother."

"Yeah," he said again, hesitated, then stepped back.

Joanna stepped inside, and was even more assailed by

the sour smell. But the whole room was sour, with various discarded articles of clothing draped over the chairs and the overstuffed settee. Only the tape deck in the corner looked either new or cared for. There was a door leading to a bedroom at the rear of the room; as it was open, she could tell it was hardly more tidy in there. "Helen ain't the neatest person in the world," Harry explained, scooping some clothes off of a chair.

"And it's not part of your business to help her," Joanna commented.

"I'm the man of the house," he agreed. "Why don't you sit down, Mrs Orton."

"The name is now Johannsson," Joanna pointed out, and took off her mink before sitting in the vacant chair; the mink she draped across the other chair, mainly occupied by clothes.

"Yeah. I forgot. Drink? There's beer."

"I don't suppose you have a cup of tea?"

"I don't drink tea. Maybe Helen will make you one, when she gets in."

"I'll look forward to that." She was trying to determine whether this was his natural appearance and behaviour, or whether he was being deliberately antagonistic to a woman he had to feel had come to disrupt his living arrangements. She hoped it was the latter. "What sort of work do you do?" she asked.

"Work? How'm I to get work?"

"You mean Helen supports you."

"Only in a manner of speaking. I get the dole."

"Of course. But I am sure you hope to do better."

"I'm happy." He opened a beer for himself, cleared some more clothes off the settee with a sweep of his arm, slumped on to the cushions, legs thrown wide. "What's it feel like, to be out?"

"It feels very pleasant," Joanna said.

"But you're on parole, right? You step out of line, and it's back inside. Right?"

"That depends what you mean by stepping out of line,"

Joanna said carefully, wondering if he was going to assault her.

But at that moment a key turned in the lock, and Helen came in, puffing, her arms filled with bags of groceries. "Sorry I'm late, love. There was this man . . ." she paused, her mouth open.

"She wants a word," Harry said. He didn't get up, either to greet Helen or to relieve her of any of the bags.

Helen crossed the room and dumped the lot on the table, stayed there for a moment, facing the wall, obviously getting her emotions and her thoughts under control. Joanna observed that she looked quite well, had her figure under control, her hair neat and clean, but her clothes were shabby, her shoes down at the heel, and the cloth coat had had some loose threads. Now she turned. "Well, it's good to see you, Mother. After so long."

Joanna had got up, and was standing, waiting for her to come to her. Helen did move towards her, halfway across the room, then checked, glancing at Harry. "I see you two have met."

"Yes," Joanna said.

"Well . . . I wish you'd called to say you were coming."

"So you could have been out?"

"No, I would have tidied the place up."

"Do you think we could have a little time together?" Joanna asked. "Alone?"

Helen hesitated, then looked at Harry again. "Would you mind?"

"I'm not being put out of my home by an ex-con," Dave declared.

Helen bit her lip, while Joanna felt as if she had been slapped in the face. "You can go down to the boozer for half an hour," Helen said.

"What with?"

She opened her handbag and took out a five-pound note. "Use this."

"No," Joanna said. "I'll leave. Perhaps you'd telephone me,

Helen, and we'll meet up." She stumbled down the stairs and into the street; she felt physically sick.

Joanna did not dare tell Michael the truth about her meeting with Helen; she felt he would be so angry he might assault Harry. She had to stick to half truths, tell him that she and Helen were going to have a meal together, as they'd found talking difficult in the flat. Michael was, in any event, preoccupied, and pleased with himself. "I've found out about Caribee House," he announced. "It belongs to Petherick, of course, but it's for sale. Seems large country houses aren't viable in the days of looming recession and rising interest rates."

"Gosh," she said, and looked at him.

He grinned. "Would you really like it? Seems it's gone down a bit. It hasn't been occupied over the last few years. We'd have to spend some money renovating it. But I have an idea you'd enjoy that."

"Oh, Michael," she said. "Would you really buy it?"

He winked. "If it's in as bad condition as they say, we'll get it cheap. We've a viewing tomorrow."

Joanna was so excited she hardly slept. And again she felt physically sick as the Mercedes turned into that so familiar drive. But maybe it was just the baby.

A young man was waiting for them with the keys. "I feel I should tell you, Mr Johannsson, Mrs Johannsson, that this house used to belong to that Mrs Orton, you may remember, the woman who murdered her boyfriend, way back."

Joanna looked at Michael, and they both smiled; he didn't have a clue. "We're not superstitious," Michael assured him.

The salesman unlocked the door and they stepped into that so familiar hall. Everything was very much as she had left it, save for the dust and the cobwebs. "When Mrs Orton was sent down," the young man explained, "her children lived here for a while, with their nanny, but then the company was wound up, and the new owners took it over."

"What happened to the children?" Joanna asked.

"Haven't a clue," the young man said. "Then the new owners lived here for a while, not as a home, but as a weekend cottage, really."

"When you say the new owners, who exactly do you mean?" Joanna asked.

The young man opened his file, hunted through the various documents there. "Chap called Gosling. But he wasn't married, and I suppose he found it a bit large for him. He stopped using it at all about four years ago, and since then it's stood empty."

"Let's go upstairs," Joanna said.

She led them up, and from bedroom to bedroom. "My word," remarked the young man. "One would almost suppose you had been here before, Mrs Johannsson."

"I'm clairvoyant," Joanna told him.

"I am so excited," she told Michael, as they drove home.

"No ghosts?"

"Oh . . . oh, my God! What about you?"

"Not for me. But we'll completely redecorate that drawing room. It's a big house. You will be able to have Raisul and Mrs Partridge move back in. Think they'll like that?"

"I should think they'll adore that. Are you going to tell Gosling who we are?"

He shook his head. "Not until we're in a position to topple him off his perch. The house will be bought by J&J. What about Helen? There's room for her too."

"That's up to her," Joanna said. "There isn't room for that slob she's living with."

They met for lunch at a bistro in Soho. "He's not bad, really," Helen said. "It's just that he regards himself as unfortunate."

"Because he can't get, or hold, a job? Has he tried hard enough?"

"He gets angry with people, and answers back, and then gets fired."

"Why do you stay with him?"

Helen flushed. "We get on."

"You mean he's good in bed. Men who are good in bed aren't altogether unique, you know."

"You don't understand," Helen said. "I can't live lies. I like to talk, and I like to tell the truth."

"Ah," Joanna said. "And the moment, in your spells of candour, you tell your date that your mother is in jail, for murder, they sort of sidle off."

"Well . . . perhaps it's not quite as simple as that."

"Whereas Harry didn't sidle off. He waited to insult me."

Helen bit her lip. "He always says what comes naturally."

"But I am no longer in gaol. I am now again a wealthy woman, or at least I'm married to a very wealthy man who happens to be indulging me. Suppose I told you that we are buying back Caribee House? Would you move back in?" Joanna asked.

"Back there? How can you? It's where . . ." guiltily she glanced at the nearest tables. "You'll have nightmares!"

"I think I've learned to cope with nightmares," Joanna said. "Will you?"

Helen ate, slowly. "I must do my own thing, Mummy. I simply have to."

"And your own thing is working as a shop assistant and living with a layabout."

Helen flushed, but this was at least partly anger. "That is my own thing, at the moment, yes."

"What happens when you get pregnant?"

"I get pregnant. But it won't happen. I'm on the pill."

"Clever you. Helen . . ." Joanna leaned across the table and held her daughter's hand. "If you won't come back home, will you work for me?"

Helen frowned. "For you? What as?"

"As soon as I'm back in business, I'll give you as job."

"You're going back into business? Who'd employ a—" she bit her lip.

"Ex-con?" Joanna gave a grim smile. "Probably no one. But I don't intended to be employed. I intend to do the employing."

"You reckon?" Helen drank her coffee. "Thanks for the meal, Mummy. I don't want us to quarrel, really. But . . ."

"You need to do your own thing. You haven't answered my question. Will you come and work for me? It's not going to take too long for me to set things up. As soon as my baby's born."

Helen's jaw dropped. "You're pregnant?"

Joanna grinned. "Unlike you modern women, I have never taken the pill. Yes, I'm pregnant."

"But you hardly know the man!"

"Well, now, I have actually known him, in a Biblical sense, for four months."

"You mean you got pregnant on your wedding night? What a hoot!"

"Absolutely. But you are going to have a little baby brother, or sister, in five months' time. Now answer my question?"

"Tell you what," Helen said, "ask me again, when you're back in business." Her tone said, if it ever happens.

Joanna reckoned she had made as much progress in that direction as she could, short of making Helen a ward of court, and she did not want that kind of publicity right now. She wanted time to stand still until she had her baby. It was amusing to remember that she had been in this position once before – when she had been carrying Helen! Then all her dreams, plans, fears and hopes had had to be put on hold, until her delivery. Then she had desperately wanted a boy, because a boy had been necessary, by the terms of Howard's will. Well, she had survived having a girl. Now it didn't matter.

For the time being she could occupy herself with redecorating Caribee House. She so wanted to have the baby in that house, where both Helen and Raisul had been born. But five months . . . It seemed an eternally long time, as the new Conservative Government set about putting the nation's finances in order, which inevitably brought on a recession, with unemployment threatening to go through the roof. This meant that it was easier to get the various contracts on the house fulfilled; Joanna went down almost every day, even when her belly was swollen. It was a dream to keep her going, until she was ready for . . . she wasn't quite sure for what. "Do you think I am a mean and vicious woman?" she asked Michael.

"You mean because you wish to get even with those wretches who sold your company from under you? No, I don't think that is at all mean and vicious. Providing you don't let it take over your life."

"Um," she said. Because in many ways it had already taken over her life. Buying Caribee House was less gaining a victory over Andy Gosling than slapping Alicia in the face. The remarkable thing was that no one had yet worked out who J&J was. And she didn't want them to until she was ready.

She gave birth at the beginning of June, 1981. Caribee House was only just ready, and her doctor was astounded when she insisted upon having the baby at home, in such ill-prepared conditions. But he, like so many people in the past, was getting the message that when Joanna Johannsson made a decision, it would be implemented. He moved in a staff of nurses and they coped very well. The baby was a boy, who she named Howard. Michael did not object.

Then she could sit back and relax. Mrs Partridge and Raisul duly moved in, but the rest of the servants were new. However, Charlie was out of gaol and she contacted him to let him know that his old job was waiting for him; he was back behind the wheel of her Mercedes a week later.

William and Norma, and their children were, of course, totally supportive. She did not know what they made of her, or said of her, in the privacy of their own home, but they came down to Caribee House to watch the last redecorations set into place, and complimented her on her taste. William did mention, when they were alone together, "Quite an achievement, Sis, getting the old place back together."

"I'm pleased," Joanna said.

"So . . . what next?"

"The company."

He pulled his nose. "Have you any idea what that is going to cost?"

"Some."

"But you're going to do it anyway?"

"In time. But now, you see, I have all the time in the world."

He went away a sorely worried man, although as with Helen, Joanna promised him a job once she had regained the company.

And it was happening. "Here's an item of news that may interest you," Michael said at dinner. "There's talk in the city that entrepreneur James Holroyd is in financial difficulties." Joanna put down her wine glass. He grinned at her. "I've told your man Prim to make him an offer for his portfolio. In the name of J&J. And providing he still has any Petherick stock. We may have to accumulate some worthless paper, but as long as there's good stuff as well . . ."

"Oh, Michael," she said. "I don't deserve you, really I don't."

"Well," he said, "there's more than one opinion about that." A fortnight later the deal was completed. "You now hold, anonymously, twelve percent of Petherick Shipping," Michael said. "Mind you, Gosling, or his accountants or stockbrokers or whatever, are going to start to think some time soon."

"Start to worry, you mean," she said happily.

But in fact she reckoned Andy, like all of London, was getting geared up for the royal wedding in a month's time. So was she. But she was jerked out of her contentment on the evening of fourth July when the phone rang. She picked it up and gave the number, as was usual.

"Mummy!" Helen screamed. "Help me! Mummy! They're breaking down the door! Help me!"

# Chapter Twelve

# The Phoenix

"Helen!" Joanna shouted. "Call the police!"

"They're all around," Helen screamed. "But they can't stop the mob. Mummy!"

"I'll be there as soon as I can," Joanna promised, and slammed down the phone. "Charlie!" she bawled, as she ran down the stairs.

"What's happened, Mother?" Raisul stood in the door of his bedroom, where he had been doing his homework.

"There's some kind of riot in Brixton," Joanna said. "Helen's in trouble. Charlie! Get out the car."

"I'll come with you," Raisul said. Joanna looked at him in surprise; he had never offered to go anywhere with her since her return from prison. He flushed. "Well," he said, "if Helen needs help . . ."

"Mrs Partridge!" Joanna shouted. "I have to go out. Keep an eye on the baby, will you?" She grabbed her mink and pulled it over her shirt and jeans as she ran down to the front hall. Charlie was holding the door for her. Just like old times, she thought; just like old times. Only now she had Raisul, helping her into the car. "Find out what's happening," she told Charlie, as the Mercedes roared down the road.

He switched on the radio. ". . . huge gangs of black youths," said the announcer. "Police are trying to contain them, but the situation is completely out of hand. As I watch, a police van has been overturned and set on fire. Thank heavens there doesn't seem to have been anyone inside. Listen to the shattering of glass; there is wholesale looting going on. It will be a miracle if no one is killed tonight."

"God, God, God," Joanna said. "Charlie . . ."

"We'll get there, Mrs Johannsson. You got any idea where Mr Johannsson is?"

"He was at his club. I should've called him."

"I reckon he must know there's a riot," Charlie said.

"But not that Helen may be involved," Joanna said. Raisul squeezed her hand, and impulsively she threw her arm round his shoulder, hugging him close.

Now they were in the city, and forced to drive slower. Charlie knew all the best routes, yet it was still an hour after they had left the house before they got close to Brixton, and now progress was slowed even more by the traffic jams, as people either tried to get towards the riot or away from it. "This isn't doing any good," Joanna said. "Let us out."

"You going in there on foot?" Charlie demanded.

"Park the car and follow," Joanna said. "You know the address."

She got out, Raisul at her side. They certainly made much quicker time on foot, jostled from time to time by the gathering crowd, some of whom were quick to notice and take offence at Joanna's mink, but with Raisul at her side, taller than most of them and heavily built, no one actually interfered with her. Now the noise from in front of them was immense, and at the end of the street they were stopped by several policemen, who wore riot gear. "Where do you think you're going, lady?" one asked.

Joanna checked the street sign; Helen's flat was one block away. "My daughter is down there," she said.

"Well, she shouldn't be," said another policeman.

"She lives there," Joanna snapped. "I have to get her out."

"Listen," said the first policeman, "you go down there, wearing that coat, and you'll be lynched."

"Then here." Joanna took off the mink and crammed it into his arms. "You keep it." He was too surprised to react, and she darted past him, Raisul behind her. Both policemen shouted after them, but they could hardly hear them because of the racket around them.

To their right, several cars were on fire, with people dancing round them. At the end of the next street there was a solid phalanx of policemen, advancing behind riot shields. To their left where there were several shops, a mass of people were looting the various smashed windows, and some of the buildings were on fire. But in front of them there were more fires. Where Helen lived! "Hurry," Joanna said, and they ran across the street to the far pavement. No one paid them any attention; there were people running to and fro all around them, screaming and shouting. Nor did Joanna's yellow hair seem to antagonise people; wearing jeans and a jumper she could have been a rioter herself.

Joanna turned down the next street, and checked. Two of the houses were on fire, and one of them was the apartment building. There was a fire engine, but it was temporarily inactive as it was being bombarded with stones and other missiles from further down the street. Panting, Joanna and Raisul got into its shelter, and found themselves beside a helmeted officer. "Animals," he said. "Goddamned animals."

"That house," Joanna panted.

"If we could get some water on it . . ."

"I think my daughter may be in there."

He gave her a devastated look. "You know that?"

"She was there an hour ago. She telephoned me."

"Well, if she has any sense she'll have got out."

"Maybe she couldn't. I have to get inside."

The man tilted his helmet to scratch his head. But as with so many men, and women, he was feeling the force of Joanna's personality. "Hey," he bawled at his men, who were all sheltering from the missiles. "Let's get some water on that house."

The engine was started up. The hose was already connected to the nearby hydrant, and now a jet burst upon the street door. It was the ground floor flat that was actually burning, set alight by a molotov cocktail hurled through the window. Joanna was more worried about the smoke that was billowing up the stairwell. "The ladder," she shouted. "We have to use the ladder. The third floor."

More orders, and the turntable swung round to place the ladder against one of the the third floor windows. The mob hooted their derision, and more missiles were thrown, but now a line of policemen arrived behind them, and they began to break up. One of the firemen clambered up. Joanna followed. "Hey!" bawled the officer. "You can't do that! Come back down here!!"

Joanna ignored him and kept on climbing. "You'll fall!" the officer shouted in desperation. "Dick, go get that crazy woman."

"Take care, Mum!" Raisul shouted.

The fire officer glared at him. "That your mother? She ought to be locked up!"

"Been there, done that," Raisul told him.

The lead fireman, concentrating and unaware of the chaos behind him, reached the window and peered in. The sash was down but not locked, and he threw it up easily enough. "Anyone in there?" he shouted.

"Help me, please!"

"Helen!" Joanna shouted.

The fireman looked down. "What the fuck . . . ?"

"Listen," Joanna snapped. "Get in there and get my daughter."

He gulped, and climbed through the window. Joanna climbed behind him, while the man sent to fetch her down paused in the opening, having made an ineffectual grab at her. "Jesus, this floor is hot," the first fireman said. "It'll go any moment." He pointed at wisps of smoke seeping under the door. "I don't see anybody."

"Help me, please!" Helen screamed.

Joanna pushed the fireman aside and ran across the floor, feeling the heat rising about her. She threw open the bedroom door, blinked in the gloom, saw a bare foot sticking out from beneath the bed. She dropped to her hands and knees, peered into the gloom; the fireman joined her and used his flashlight, and they both looked at the naked girl, huddled against the far wall. "Come on," Joanna said. "You're safe now." She grasped Helen's ankle and dragged the girl towards her.

Helen whimpered with pain and misery. The fireman hastily got up, shone his torch round the room, and located a bathrobe hanging from the hook on the door. He handed this to Joanna, and Joanna wrapped Helen in the robe as she drew her out. "Oh, Mummy," Helen moaned. "Oh, Mummy."

"We have to get out of here," the fireman said.

Smoke was now definitely filtering into the room, making breathing difficult, and the heat was increasing. Joanna held Helen close as they stumbled across the bedroom and into the lounge. Dick was still sitting astride the windowsill. "This building is about to go," he said.

Joanna handed him Helen, and he retreated on to the ladder, now bathed in the glare of a searchlight. The crowd actually applauded.

"She's in a bad state," said Dr Hobart. "She really should stay in hospital for a few days, for observation."

"I want her home," Joanna said.

"I'm not sure she wants that."

"She's not eighteen," Joanna said. "I'll decide what she wants." He surrendered, and Helen was transferred to the Mercedes. Joanna sat beside her. "There's no necessity to talk if you don't want to," she said. "But I have to ask – what happened to Harry?"

"The bastard ran out," Helen said in a low voice. "There was this banging on the door, and we knew there were several men there. That's when I telephoned you. I'm sorry. I panicked. I didn't know what to do. We tried nine-nine-nine, and they said they'd get to us as soon as they could, but that they were having problems."

"Darling," Joanna said. "Who else were you going to try, save your mother?"

"They didn't manage to break in for another fifteen minutes," Helen said, in a low monotone. "But then the door gave. When they came in, Harry, who'd been making all sorts of aggressive noises and had armed himself with a poker, charged them, broke through them, and ran down the stairs."

"He could have been going for help," Joanna suggested, much as she disliked the man.

"He never came back," Helen said. "So there I was . . . with these four guys."

Joanna gave her a hug.

"How was it with you?" Helen asked.

"With me?"

"When you were raped."

"I was never actually raped," Joanna said.

"I know. You killed the bastard who tried it. Oh, Mother – there were four of them." Raisul and Charlie, in the front, sat rigid.

"We understand, darling," Joanna said. "You have nothing to reproach yourself with. And it is so good to have you coming home." She held the girl close. "So good."

It was four in the morning before they reached Caribee House, and Michael was waiting for them. "I have been so *worried*," he said.

"I know," Joanna said. "But what was I to do? I had to go after her."

"Of course you did. Is she all right?"

"She has been beaten and raped," Joanna said. "No woman is ever all right, after something like that. But she's my daughter. Yes, she's going to be all right, as you put it."

His shoulders sagged. "I should've been here."

"I'm glad you weren't."

"And the bastards who did it?"

Joanna sighed. "I don't suppose they'll ever be caught. There was so much going on."

"I never thought I'd hear you say something like that."

She raised her head. "Maybe even I'm coming to realise there are some things you just have to let go. Let's go see the baby."

He caught her arm. "But there are some things you don't mean to let go, right?" She checked, looking down at him. He grinned. "One of the reasons I was delayed in town this evening; friend Amalia is in trouble." Joanna came back down the stairs. "I didn't want to tell you till I was sure. But he's overstretched in every direction. Principally to his bookmaker. I had my people have a chat with that worthy, and persuaded him to call."

"You didn't use heavy stuff?"

"Not in the sense you mean. We simply offered to match Amalia's debts, two to one, if he was called in."

"Oh, Michael . . . but the cost . . ."

"Not so much as you might think. There are differing values of wealth. Amalia is on the bottom rung. So what's a man to do? Start looking at his portfolio. And Petherick shares are around the bottom of *that* rung, at the moment."

"You mean he's sold up?"

"J&J are now in possession of thirty-one per cent of Petherick shares."

"Michael!" she screamed, and hugged him. "But Andy . . . ?"

"Oh, sure. He and Townsend still have fifty-one. But I'll bet you they're not the only ones up late tonight."

Joanna supposed she should be the most miserable mother in the world, because of what had happened to Helen. Instead she was the happiest woman in the world. As Michael had promised she would be. But the happiness was not merely because she felt, she knew, she was going to win in her battle for total rehabilitation. It was compounded because, no matter what had happened, she had reassembled her immediate family.

Now she wanted to go the whole way.

William and Norma were really not a problem. They both came down to Caribee House the next day. Helen remained in bed, and they did not see her. But there was enough to talk about. The tabloids had, of course, gone wild with the story of how Joanna – EX-CONVICT . . . CONVICTED MURDERESS . . . CITY WHIZZKID AGAIN ON THE LOOSE . . . ANXIOUS MUM CLIMBS LADDER TO RESCUE DAUGHTER – had behaved.

She was even visited by her probation officer, who warned her that she had, technically, broken the law. "You mean you're going to send me back to prison?" Joanna asked, softly, "For rescuing my daughter?" The woman had flushed with embarrassment, and soon left.

William, while delighted, was as usual cautious. "Seems they can't keep you out of the news," he remarked, as they sat together on the sofa.

"One would think they'd concentrate on the riot," she remarked.

"Not quite as exciting, perhaps. Have you heard from Gosling?"

"Why, no. Should I have?"

"Well, maybe he didn't know where you were, before. But he'll know now. Did you know that Petherick Shipping is in trouble?" Joanna raised her eyebrows. "Oh, of course they're suffering like everyone else from high interest rates and what have you. But they're also in real trouble. There's rumour in the City of a hostile takeover bid."

"Good heavens," Joanna said. "I wonder who that can be."

They gazed at each other, then both burst out laughing at the same time. Then William grew serious. "J&J," he said thoughtfully. "Andy's not a fool, you know, sis."

"I'm sure he's not."

"And as long as he and Townsend are sitting on fifty-one per cent . . ."

"There's work to be done. I agree. But we will do it. Every chain is only as strong as its weakest link."

"Meaning Townsend?"

"He has his fingers in a lot of pies. Some of them are going to get burned."

William looked across the room to where Michael was chatting with Norma and Raisul. "And he's going to back you all the way."

"It's what he wants to do. Now tell me about Tilly."

William sighed. "Not so good. Billy has been made redundant again. I believe they'll have to sell their house. She's talking about emigrating to Australia."

"Does Australia want people like them?"

"We'll have to see. Sis . . ."

"Yes," Joanna said. "I suppose I'll have to pick up the pieces. And Billy knows the ropes. Tell him I want to see him."

"And Tilly?"

"Her too, if she wants to come."

"Townsend," Michael said, sitting up in bed, surrounded by sheets of prints-out. "Thomas O'Reilly Townsend. Tot."

Joanna peered over his shoulder. "Where on earth did you get all that?"

"I have people working on him. And Gosling. Gosling's finances seem in pretty good shape, with one proviso. He seems to have sunk everything he has into Petherick Shipping. He owns thirty-five per cent of the shares, and with Townsend's backing he therefore controls the company. He doesn't seem to have much outside that, but he has no big outside debts, either. No, Tot is the man we have to work on. Sweep him away, and Gosling is on a hiding to nothing."

"And?"

"He has some debts. We're working on them, but I don't think they're sufficient to make him sell up. Anyway, he wouldn't dare without Andy's agreement, and that won't be forthcoming for the reasons I've just given. Andy *has* to keep control of Petherick, or he's on his uppers. What we have to do is make Townsend more frightened of us, even if he doesn't know who we are, than he is of Andy."

Joanna hugged herself. "Sounds illegal."

"We're not going to break any laws. At least, none that can be traced back to us. You prepared to be patient?"

"You bet."

He kissed her. "Then we'll just let them sweat a while. Finding out who we are."

Patience. It was a great temptation to go down to the City and look at Caribee Building, now renamed Petherick Building. But it had to be resisted. It was a curious summer. The Brixton riots might have ended, but there were riots in several other cities in the country, as heat and unemployment took hold, and yet at the same time the entire country was winding itself up for the royal wedding that promised so much.

William duly brought Billy to see Joanna; Tilly still preferred to stay away. Then he left them alone, Joanna having intimated that what she had to say to Billy was confidential. "She's proud," Billy said. He looked a wreck of the good-looking, confident man she had once known; she reckoned he might have a drink problem.

"What's she got to be proud about?" she asked. "I'm the one who's done all the suffering."

"It was not leaving her in charge of the children," Billy said. "That really hurt."

And didn't do the children a lot of good either, Joanna thought. "Now I hear you're emigrating."

"Well, we'd like to. If all the papers come through."

"What do you expect to find in Australia that you haven't been able to find here?"

"Work, for one thing."

"You can have a job, if you're prepared to work."

He frowned at her, suspiciously. "Working for you?"

"That's right. I reckon you know I expect utter loyalty, and utter commitment, too."

He licked his lips. "Doing what? You back in business?"

"I intend to be. Do you want the job?"

"As long as it's legal."

"You keep it legal. Your brief is Tom Townsend. I want his shares. I want to find something that will make him sell. This must be done in absolute secrecy. You find me something."

"And when I do?"

"When you do, I'll have control of Petherick Shipping, and you'll have a permanent job there."

"I'll see what I can do."

"You'll have to do better than that. You have six months, at a thousand pounds a month."

"A thousand? Did you say a thousand?"

"Yes. Six months. If you don't come up with something by then, you're out. And Billy, if anyone, *anyone*, finds out what you're up to, you're out on the spot."

Billy gulped. "Does that include Tilly?"

"Tilly is at the top of the list," Joanna told him.

"There's a woman to see you," Mrs Partridge said.

Joanna was in the study, where she spent a lot of time. She seldom left Caribee House now, leaving the business details of J&J to Michael, who enjoyed going up to London. She only wanted to go to London if she could go to Caribee Building. Besides, she wanted to be near to Helen, who was only slowly recovering from her traumatic experience. She wanted to be around if that creep Harry ever attempted to show up. But he hadn't so far. Now she could tell from Mrs Partridge's tone that she did not approve of the caller. "Did she give a name?" Joanna asked.

"Yes, madam: Belinda Grant."

"Belinda!" Joanna cried, and ran into the hall. "Oh, Belinda . . ." they embraced. "But I didn't expect you out so soon."

"Good behaviour," Belinda said. "Did I do right in coming?"

"Of course you did. I promised you a job. You have it." They hugged again, while Mrs Partridge surveyed them somewhat grimly. "This is Belinda," Joanna explained. "She's going to be my maid."

Which was easier said than done. Belinda knew nothing about being a lady's maid. But Joanna was happy to teach her. Not only because of her promise, and because Belinda was eager to learn, but because Belinda had other talents to go with her five-foot-eleven-inch height; she was as strong as any man and quite as happy as any man to engage in a punch-up. Joanna's instincts told her that a bodyguard, such as she had had when she and Matilda had been on the same wavelength, might come in very handy over the next few months.

Michael was amused, if just a little cautious. He had, of course, met Belinda at the wedding, and remembered that she and Joanna had been very close. "Did you ever sleep together?" he asked. "I don't mean in the sense that you shared a cell."

"Would it make you mad if I said yes?"

"Not in the slightest."

"You'd be titillated," she teased. "Because like all men you have a weakness for lesbians. Taken together, as it were." Then she was serious. "Yes, we slept together, sometimes. But it wasn't like you think. Oh, sure, there was sex. We're both virile human beings. But it was a necessity, from loneliness, despair, if you like. In prison, if you can't reach out and touch somebody, mentally, you go round the bend."

"I do understand that," he said. "You can take her to bed any time you wish."

"You don't understand," she said. "I'm not lonely any more. I have you, I have my children, I have my home, and I have all the future in the world."

"And what does she have?" he asked, quietly. Perhaps he did understand, after all.

Joanna decided against going up to town to watch the wedding.

So the whole family gathered round the big downstairs television, drinking champagne and eating turkey sandwiches.

"The wedding of the century," Belinda said. "I think I'm going to cry."

It was a week later, when Joanna was on her weekly visit to her hairdresser in the village, that she encountered Alicia. She had just come outside, and was waiting for Belinda. Belinda accompanied her everywhere, but had gone off to do some shopping while her mistress was being attended to, and as usual was late coming back. Something else Joanna could appreciate; like her, Belinda was only savouring the inexpressible feeling of being free after being locked up for several years.

So she was content to wait, and watch the passers-by. She instinctively took a step backwards when the little car pulled in to the pavement in front of her. "So it's true," Alicia said, rolling down her window.

For a moment Joanna did not recognise her. Eight years ago Alicia had been trimly attractive; this woman was overweight and had shadows under her eyes. "Alicia!" she cried. "How nice to see you. My, you're looking well." Alicia snorted, switched off her engine and got out. "What brings you to this neck of the woods?" Joanna asked.

"I was hearing a rumour, that it was you who had bought Caribee House," Alicia said. "I wanted to know if it was true. And it is, apparently."

Joanna frowned. "Just where did you hear this rumour?"

"Well, it wasn't a rumour. I put two and two together, when I read in the paper how the ex-convict Joanna Johannsson had raced from her home in Berkshire to the rescue of her daughter. There is only one place in Berkshire that you'd want to live."

"Of course," Joanna said. "And how is your friend, Stephen?"

"I have no idea," Alicia said.

"And no replacement?"

"So you're riding high, wide and handsome again," Alicia remarked. "Look, people are beginning to notice us. Why don't we go some place and have a coffee?"

"I'd love to. I'm just waiting on a friend."

She looked along the street to where Belinda was striding towards them; Belinda always strode. "Good lord!" Alicia commented. "Where did you find her?"

"She was my cellmate," Joanna explained. "We'd both killed a man, but her lawyer was cleverer than mine, and she got away with manslaughter. Now she's my bodyguard."

Alicia gulped. "Well, maybe we'll leave the coffee." She got back into her car. "Bodyguard? Anyone would think you were going back into business." Then she frowned. "Shit!" she said. "You *are* going back into business. J&J. What a fool I've been. You bought my shares!"

"J&J bought your shares," Joanna said, carefully.

"And you control J&J. You bitch!"

"Have we got trouble?" Belinda asked pleasantly, having come close enough to overhear the last remark.

"I think Mrs Edge is just leaving," Joanna said.

"The famous Alicia," Belinda commented. "I've heard of you, famous Alicia." Alicia engaged gear with a tremendous scraping, and drove off.

"Actually," Joanna said, "we may have trouble." Because if Alicia could add two and two and get four, so could Andy Gosling.

The following week, Billy came down to see her. "Don't tell me you've come up with something already?" Joanna asked, receiving him in the study. Michael, as usual, had gone up to town.

"Could be." Billy was looking much better. He had bought himself a new suit, and there was a spring in his step.

"So?"

"How high will you go for Townsend's shares?"

"Explain."

"Well, I did to him what they once did to you. I telephoned him and offered to buy his holding."

"What did you offer?"

"They're currently trading at three hundred and fifteen pence. I offered to buy him out at four hundred. Was that all right?"

"Six hundred thousand? That's two-point-four million! I'd have to clear that with Michael. What was his reaction?"

"Said he'd think about it. Which is why I reckon I might have to go higher. But he's interested."

Joanna stroked her chin. If Townsend was interested, he'd hardly go bleating to Andy, because Andy would put the stopper on any suggestion of a sell-out. But two-point-four million . . . she squared her shoulders. Once she had taken that kind of money in her stride. And it would give her control. "Let me talk with Michael and come back to you. Did you make a date for speaking with Townsend again?"

"We're to meet the day after tomorrow."

"You mean he knows who you are?"

"No way. I'm Mr Smith."

Joanna frowned. "And you never met when I was running Caribee?"

"No, we didn't. You wouldn't ever give me a seat on the board, remember?"

"As things have turned out, that was a lucky escape for all of us, wasn't it? I'll give you Michael's confirmation, or not, tomorrow."

"And if it's not?"

"You just don't keep the appointment."

"Right."

She telephoned Michael, and as she didn't want to discuss it over the phone, he came down for lunch. "Then it's in the bag," he said.

"You mean you'll authorise the expenditure? Suppose he holds out for more?"

"If he goes for it, we've got him. Is Montgomery any good as a negotiator?"

"He was, once. A long time ago."

"Well, he can go up to five. Only if he has to."

"Michael, that's three million pounds."

"I said I'd spend whatever it took to give you back your company, Jo."

"Oh, Michael . . . I don't know what to say."

"Then don't say anything. Anyway, my darling, it's a good investment. I reckon that with you back in charge, those shares will soon be back to something like eight. I'll just about double my money."

She telephoned Billy. "So, it's all up to you."

"Jesus," he said. "Five hundred . . ."

"Only if you have to," she reminded him.

"Yeah. Oh, yeah. I'll screw the bastard, Jo. That's a promise."

"Just get the shares, Billy. What time is your meeting?"

"Nine o'clock tonight. In a pub just off the Portobello Road. The Bell & Jewel."

Joanna wrinkled her nose. "Whose idea was that?"

"His."

"Well, go easy. When will you call me?"

"Hopefully tonight. Up to midnight all right?"

"You call me any time you like, Billy. I won't mind being woken up to hear that news."

"Excited?" Michael asked at dinner.

"I'm surprised I can eat," Joanna said.

"What's up?" Raisul asked.

"A big deal," Michael told him.

"The biggest deal of my life," Joanna said.

"You mean you could get the company back?"

"That's it."

"Oh, Mother . . ." Helen burst into tears, as she was liable to do any any moment. "I am so happy for you."

"For us all, darling," Joanna said. "And we have Michael to thank for it."

Michael grinned. "He hasn't gone for it yet."

On Michael's recommendation she took a sleeping pill. "No use just lying there, wondering what's happening," he said.

"I'll wake you up when he calls." But when Joanna awoke it was broad daylight and Mrs Partridge was bringing in her breakfast. She sat up, pushed hair from her face. "Where is Mr Johannsson?"

"He's breakfasting downstairs, madam, with the children."

"Will you tell him I'm up?" She drank juice and coffee, and Michel came in. "Nothing?"

"I'm afraid not. But don't be downhearted. There are a million and one reasons why he should not have called during the night."

"Hm." Yet she was tense, switched on the television to look at the breakfast news. This was mostly concerned with the contest for the deputy-leadership of the Labour Party, in which Denis Healey had just beaten Anthony Wedgwood-Benn. Joanna was only interested in politics in so far as it influenced share prices and interest rates, and as Labour was out of power they could not affect those issues. She was about to switch off when the newsreader said, "Police are appealing for witnesses after the fatal shooting of two men last night in a street in north London. The men have not yet been identified, but it is known they had been drinking together in the Bell & Jewel public house. They left together, and got into a Ford Cortina which may have belonged to one of the men. Before they could drive off, however, someone stepped up to the car and shot them both through the head. Both men died instantly . . ."

Joanna clasped both hands to her throat, while Michael, who had been in the bathroom, hurried back in. "You don't think . . . ?"

"Has to be," Joanna said. "Oh, my God!"

"Listen, there are a thousand and one thugs in London," Michael said. "That sounds like a gangland assassination to me."

"If you mean it was a hit," Joanna said, "I agree with you." She got out of bed, went to the bathroom herself.

Michael followed. "Gosling? Would he go that far?"

"As you said the other day, Michael, if he loses control of

Petherick, he's on his uppers. That can make a man quite desperate."

"Jesus! What are we going to do?"

"Find out, firstly, if it was Billy and Townsend who were killed, and secondly . . ." she hesitated.

"Go on."

"Who Townsend has willed his shares to."

Michael gulped. "Some people would say you have ice water in your veins."

"Some people already have. I hope you know better. But the fact is, if there is some clause that says those shares go to Andy . . ."

"I'll see what I can discover. And Billy?"

"I know," Joanna said. "I want Gosling for murder, as well."

"That could be hard to prove."

"If he did it, or ordered it done, we have to be able to prove it, Michael. And there is no one else in the world would want both Billy and Townsend dead, at this particular moment. Can I leave that with you? I have to do something about Matilda."

"Listen," Belinda said. "I'd like to help."

"How, exactly?" Joanna asked.

"Well, I have friends who might know something." She grinned. "Be able to do something. Please let me help, Joanna. I owe you so much."

"Don't be a goose," Joanna said.

"It's true. You've made my life over. And now the thought of that thug ruining yours . . . I want to help you. I have to help you."

Joanna hugged her. "You're an absolute sweetie. But this isn't your problem. Don't worry. We'll sort it out."

Belinda looked sceptical.

William was on the line almost before she had finished speaking. "Have you seen the news? The bodies have been identified."

"I saw the news," Joanna said.

"Jo, was Billy doing something for you?"

"He was working for me, yes. Have you seen Tilly?"

"No. But . . ."

"Give me her address."

"I'd better come with you."

"No," Joanna said. "This I have to do for myself."

It was a tiny, untidy flat. The door was opened by Tilly's eldest, Miriam – she was named after her grandmother – a girl of fifteen, who stared at her famous aunt with wide eyes. "May I come in?" Joanna asked. The girl bit her lip. She had been crying, that was obvious. "I'd like to see your mother," Joanna said.

The girl stepped aside. "She's in the bedroom."

George, two years younger than his sister, peered at her from a littered lounge. Joanna smiled at him, and opened the bedroom door. Matilda was sprawled across the bed, only half dressed, staring at the television set. A tumbler of gin stood on the table; it was a quarter to eleven in the morning. "Go away," she said. "I told you to go away."

"If you're referring to the children, I think that might be a good idea," Joanna said. "Would you like me to take them home with me? They could stay there until things settle down."

Matilda rolled on her back. "What do *you* want?"

"To say how sorry I am."

Matilda sat up. "Billy was working for you! He wouldn't tell me. But now I'm sure."

Joanna sighed, and sat beside her on the bed. "Yes, he was working for me."

"And people who work for you wind up dead, right?" Joanna really didn't have a reply to that. "Even William should have been dead," Matilda said. "It's a miracle he survived that bullet."

"I know," Joanna said.

"But you don't care."

"I do care," Joanna said. "I can't give you back Billy. But

I can take you home, and your children, and look after you. We're family, remember?"

William and Norma came out to dinner, the first time in a very long time the entire family had sat down to dinner together; even Helen came down. But Belinda was missing. "She went out," Mrs Partridge explained. "Just left. Said she had someone to see."

Michael looked quizzical. "Just how much do you know about that young woman's background?" he asked.

"Actually, very little," Joanna confessed. "Save that she is a self-confessed killer."

"Good Lord," Norma commented.

"In her own milieu," Joanna said. "Which was petty crime."

"Or not so petty," Michael said. "I've been doing some investigating. That chap she is supposed to have cut down in a lovers' tiff was a well-known mobster."

Joanna frowned. "Meaning what?"

"My investigator thinks it was a contract. And that her lawyers, and a good number of her witnesses, were employed by the mob, which is why she got a reduced sentence for manslaughter rather than murder."

"Holy shit!" William commented.

"But . . . she's absolutely faithful to me," Joanna said. "I'd swear that on the Bible."

"And I'd believe you," Michael said. They gazed at each other, then Joanna got up and left the table to go into the study. Michael followed her. "What are you going to do? I thought you hated the guy? That you wanted only to bring him down?"

"I do. But I'm not having another death on my conscience," Joanna said, already dialling. "Hello," she said. "Is Mr Gosling at home. Tell him Joanna Johannsson is calling, and that I need to speak with him, most urgently. The butler," she whispered at Michael, standing anxiously by.

"Joanna!" Andy sounded as confident as ever. "Long time no speak? How was Liddleton?"

"The experience of a lifetime. Andy, I have got to see you, now."

"Do you, now. Is it to do with buying, or selling, shares? I know all the tricks that you have been up to, Joanna. Did you seriously take me for a fool?"

"I never took you for a murderer, Andy."

There was a moment's silence. Then he said. "You have just uttered the most complete slander."

"And I am sure you are recording this conversation," Joanna said. "Now let me say again, Andy, either you come down here, or I shall come to you. But it has to be now."

"And I say, forget it." He hung up.

"We'll go up to town anyway," Joanna said.

Michael nodded, and called for Charlie.

The phone rang. "Maybe he's changed his mind," Joanna said, and picked it up. "For you."

Michael took it, listened, frowned, and then grinned. "That's great. Keep close."

"Townsend?' Joanna asked.

"One of my people, yes. Townsend's will was read this afternoon. Seems he had a live-in friend."

"Male or female?"

"Male. To whom he left everything. The word from my agent is that the shares could be up for grabs."

"And they'll be grabbed by Andy, if we don't do something."

"If your suspicions are correct, Jo," Michael said, "we might be a whole lot better off not doing anything."

"It's a temptation," Joanna said. "But would you believe that I have never, in all my life, deliberately been involved in anyone's death? I don't want to start now, not even with a slug like Andy Gosling."

"I hoped you'd say that," Michael agreed.

Charlie raced through the London suburbs to reach Andy's Kensington flat; it reminded Joanna of her equally mad drive to rescue Helen. And this time? To rescue the man she most loathed in all the world? Or the woman who had become her most faithful servant? Charlie found parking about a hundred yards from the flat, and all three of them leapt out and ran along the pavement. It was a third-floor flat, and lights glowed in the windows; it was now quite dark.

Joanna pressed the street bell, and again, but there was no reply. "Shit!" she muttered.

"I can open the street door, madam," Charlie said.

She looked at Michael. "Maybe we'll all be able to share a cell," he remarked.

"Do it."

Charlie broke the glass with his elbow. It made a sharp noise, but there was no one on the street. Carefully he reached through and released the latch. "No burglar alarm?" Michael wondered.

"We're not as sophisticated in London as you people are on the other side of the Atlantic," Joanna said.

The door swung in, and they hurried up the stairs. There was no answer when they knocked on the flat door, either. Joanna looked at Charlie. "If you have a credit card, madam . . . ?"

Michael produced one, and a moment later they were in the flat, looking around them in horror. The lights were still on, and just inside the doorway a man lay on his back stabbed through the heart. He was no one Joanna had ever seen before. But on the far side of the room Andy Gosling lay, also on his back, and he too had been stabbed, several times. "Don't touch anything," Michael advised.

The three of them stood together in the centre of the room. "What do we do?" Joanna asked.

"Get the hell out of here, and back out to Caribee House," he advised.

"What do we do when she comes home?" Joanna asked, as Charlie drove through the night.

"I don't think she's going to do that," Michael said.

"But . . . that poor girl. She did it for me."

"As she killed before, for her previous employers."

Joanna shuddered.

"It's a tangled world," remarked Inspector Lawton. "I understand, Mrs Johannsson, that Mr Gosling was a business partner of yours."

"A long time ago," Joanna said. "He took over the company when I was sent to prison."

"But you have been trying to get it back."

"I have. I think I have done so. Or am about to do so."

"With Mr Gosling's consent?"

"No," Joanna said. "It was to be a hostile takeover."

"Which will be assisted by Mr Gosling's death."

"Are you accusing me of something, Inspector?"

"No, no, Mrs Johannsson. It's just all, well, very coincidental. No doubt it will all be cleared up when we arrest whoever committed the murders."

"I'm sure it will," Joanna said. "I assume you have leads."

The inspector closed his notebook with a snap. "We have some evidence that Mr Gosling entertained a young woman in his flat shortly before he was killed. That is to say, we have a witness who says he saw a young woman entering the flat, and another witness who says she saw a young lady leaving the flat about half an hour later."

"Then you have a description?" Joanna's heart was pounding quite painfully.

"Nothing of any value. Tall, well-built, dark-haired . . ." he regarded Joanna speculatively, considering the short, slender, yellow-haired figure in front of him. "Unfortunately, the woman appears to have disappeared into thin air." He stood up. "I'm sorry to have troubled you, Mrs Johannsson. Loose ends, you know."

"That poor girl," Joanna said, when Michael had seen the inspector out.

"Why poor? She's doing what she does best."

"And when she returns here, asking for help?"

"I told you, she's not going to do that. She reckons she's paid her debt to you. To society, if you like. She'll have gone back to her own kind."

"And that's a load off your mind."

"Yes," he said seriously. "It is. She, and Andy, were your last links to your past. Now there's only the future to look forward to. Why don't we join the family for dinner? They're all here. Your old friend Peter Young is here as well. You'll want to talk to him about restructuring the company." He winked. "And changing the name back to Caribee Shipping. It's all yours, my darling."

She looked up at him. "Yes," she said. "Thanks to you, Michael. I shall never be able to thank you."

"Thank me by being you."

"Yes, but I'm not me anymore. I feel sort of . . . well, it's difficult to explain."

He waited.

"So many people have passed by, and on, and I'm still here. What's more, I'm back on top, and they . . . what I'm trying to say is, I'm not the woman who used to square her shoulders and stick out her chin and say to herself, get out of my way, world, I'm coming through. I'm too aware of how near I came to disaster, so often, and of how many people I hurt while careering along. I don't even hate Mrs Anstey or Angie anymore, would you believe it? Maybe I've grown up."

He took her into his arms. "And that is the greatest thank you of all," he said as he kissed her.

per debt to you. To society, if you like. She'll have gone back to her own kind."

"And that's a load off your mind."

"Yes," he said earnestly. "It is. She and Mark have been kind ness itself [illegible]. Now there's only the matter of [illegible] [illegible]

[illegible]

She looked up at him. "Yes," she said. [illegible] [illegible] [illegible]

"Thank you [illegible]."

[illegible] difficult to explain.

[illegible]

[illegible]